*A man w*
*Tough, han*

# ON
# KIND

**Two international bestselling authors deliver two dramatic, emotional stories featuring their trademark gorgeous heroes.**

*We're proud to present*

MILLS & BOON

# Spotlight

*a chance to buy collections of bestselling novels by favourite authors every month – they're back by popular demand!*

*August 2008*

**Romancing the Crown: Max & Elena**

*Featuring*

*The Disenchanted Duke* by Marie Ferrarella
*Secret-Agent Sheikh* by Linda Winstead Jones

**One of a Kind**

*Featuring*

*Lionhearted* by Diana Palmer
*Letters to Kelly* by Suzanne Brockmann

*September 2008*

**Romancing the Crown: Leila & Gage**

*Featuring*

*Virgin Seduction* by Kathleen Creighton
*Royal Spy* by Valerie Parv

**Their Baby Girl…?**

*Featuring*

*The Baby Mission* by Marie Ferrarella
*Her Baby Secret* by Victoria Pade

# ONE OF A KIND

Lionhearted
DIANA PALMER

Letters to Kelly
SUZANNE BROCKMANN

MILLS & BOON
*Pure reading pleasure*

*All the characters in this book have no existence outside the imagination of the author, and have no relation whatsoever to anyone bearing the same name or names. They are not even distantly inspired by any individual known or unknown to the author, and all the incidents are pure invention.*



*This collection is first published in Great Britain 2008.*
*Harlequin Mills & Boon Limited,*
*Eton House, 18-24 Paradise Road, Richmond, Surrey TW9 1SR*



*ISBN: 978 0 263 86107 5*

*064-0808*

*Printed and bound in Spain*
*by Litografia Rosés S.A., Barcelona*

# Lionhearted

## DIANA PALMER

# *100 Reasons to Celebrate*

We invite you to join us in celebrating Mills & Boon's centenary. Gerald Mills and Charles Boon founded Mills & Boon Limited in 1908 and opened offices in London's Covent Garden. Since then, Mills & Boon has become a hallmark for romantic fiction, recognised around the world.

We're proud of our 100 years of publishing excellence, which wouldn't have been achieved without the loyalty and enthusiasm of our authors and readers.

*Thank you!*

Each month throughout the year there will be something new and exciting to mark the centenary, so watch for your favourite authors, captivating new stories, special limited edition collections...and more!

Dear Reader,

With this book, the Hart brothers of Jacobsville are all happily married and building families. For me, it's very sad to see the last Hart bachelor tie the knot, because their biscuit mania gave me some wonderful story lines. However, as with all things, we have to move on.

I have hinted in past books about the impish Janie Brewster, and she caught the wedding bouquets at both Micah Steele's and Rey Hart's weddings – so I thought that would give you the idea that she was fated to marry rather soon. What I didn't realise was how wild a story she and Leo would have when they started getting serious. I think I spent most of the book laughing while it unfolded daily on my computer screen. My husband is now convinced that I'm nuts, having had his Western movies on TV almost constantly interrupted by maniacal laughter from the direction of my office! Talk about the patience of Job! After having put up with me and my profession for over a quarter of a century, he's no stranger to my quirks. I could never have gone so far without him – and without all of you. When I count all my blessings, I don't sleep. It's a long list.

I hope you like Leo's story. He has a really rocky road to the altar, and Janie shows him that she's no shrinking daisy! Another interesting little sidebar that popped up was Cash Grier. I didn't actually plan to put him in this book, but he was suddenly there and refused to leave. You don't argue with a guy like this, so I let him do pretty much what he wanted.

Thank you, as always, for years of loyalty and kindness and prayers. You know already that I am your biggest fan.

Love,

*Diana Palmer*

To the FAO Schwarz gang on Peachtree Road,
Atlanta, and at the Internet Customer
Service Department.

Thanks!

# *Prologue*

Leo Hart felt alone in the world. The last of his bachelor brothers, Rey, had gotten married and moved out of the house almost a year ago. That left Leo, alone, with an arthritic housekeeper who came in two days a week and threatened to retire every day. If she did, Leo would be left without a biscuit to his name, or even a hope of getting another one unless he went to a restaurant every morning for breakfast. Considering his work schedule, that was impractical.

He leaned back in the swivel chair at his desk in the office he now shared with no one. He was happy for his brothers. Most of them had families now, except newly married Rey. Simon and Tira had two little boys. Cag and Tess had a boy. Corrigan and Dorie had a boy and a baby girl. When he looked back, Leo realized that women had been a missing commodity in his life of late. It was late September. Roundup was just over, and there had been so much going on at the ranch, with business, that he'd hardly had time for a night out. He was feeling it.

Even as he considered his loneliness, the phone rang.

"Why don't you come over for supper?" Rey asked when he picked up the receiver.

"Listen," Leo drawled, grinning, "you don't invite your brother over to dinner on your honeymoon."

"We got married after Christmas last year," Rey pointed out.

"Like I said, you're still on your honeymoon," came the amused reply. "Thanks. But I've got too much to do."

"Work doesn't make up for a love life."

"You'd know," Leo chuckled.

"Okay. But the invitation's open, whenever you want to accept it."

"Thanks. I mean it."

"Sure."

The line went dead. Leo put the receiver down and stretched hugely, bunching the hard muscles in his upper arms. He was the boss as much as his brothers on their five ranch properties, but he did a lot of the daily physical labor that went with cattle raising, and his tall, powerful body was evidence of it. He wondered sometimes if he didn't work that hard to keep deep-buried needs at bay. In his younger days, women had flocked around him, and he hadn't been slow to accept sensual invitations. But he was in his thirties now, and casual interludes were no longer satisfying.

He'd planned to have a quiet weekend at home, but Marilee Morgan, a close friend of Janie Brewster's, had cajoled him into taking her up to Houston for dinner and to see a ballet she had tickets for. He was partial to ballet, and Marilee explained that she couldn't drive herself because her car was in the shop. She was easy on the eyes, and she was sophisticated. Not that Leo was tempted to let himself be finagled into any sort of intimacy with her. He didn't want her carrying tales of his private life to Janie, who had an obvious and uncomfortable crush on him.

He knew that Marilee would never have asked him to

take her any place in Jacobsville, Texas, because it was a small town and news of the date would inevitably get back to Janie. It might help show the girl that Leo was a free agent, but it wouldn't help his friendship with Fred Brewster to know that Leo was playing fast and loose with Janie's best friend. Some best friend, he thought privately.

But taking Marilee out would have one really good consequence—it would get him out of a dinner date at the Brewsters' house. He and Fred Brewster were friends and business associates, and he enjoyed the time he spent with the older man. Well, except for two members of his family, he amended darkly. He didn't like Fred's sister, Lydia. She was a busybody who had highfalutin ideas. Fortunately, she was hardly ever around and she didn't live with Fred. He had mixed feelings about Fred's daughter Janie, who was twenty-one and bristling with psychology advice after her graduation from a junior college in that subject. She'd made Cag furious with her analyses of his food preferences, and Leo was becoming adept at avoiding invitations that would put him in her line of fire.

Not that she was bad looking. She had long, thick light brown hair and a neat little figure. But she also had a crush on Leo, which was very visible. He considered her totally unacceptable as a playmate for a man his age, and he knocked back her attempts at flirting with lazy skill. He'd known her since she was ten and wearing braces on her teeth. It was hard to get that image out of his mind.

Besides, she couldn't cook. Her rubber chicken dinners were infamous locally, and her biscuits could be classified as lethal weapons.

Thinking about those biscuits made him pick up the phone and dial Marilee.

She was curt when she picked up the phone, but the minute he spoke, her voice softened.

"Well, hello, Leo," she said huskily.

"What time do you want me to pick you up Saturday night?"

There was a faint hesitation. "You won't, uh, mention this to Janie?"

"I have as little contact with Janie as I can. You know that," he said impatiently.

"Just checking," she teased, but she sounded worried. "I'll be ready to leave about six."

"Suppose I pick you up at five and we'll have supper in Houston before the ballet?"

"Wonderful! I'll look forward to it. See you then."

"See you."

He hung up, but picked up the receiver again and dialed the Brewsters' number.

As luck would have it, Janie answered.

"Hi, Janie," he said pleasantly.

"Hi, Leo," she replied breathlessly. "Want to talk to Dad?"

"You'll do," he replied. "I have to cancel for dinner Saturday. I've got a date."

There was the faintest pause. It was almost imperceptible. "I see."

"Sorry, but it's a long-standing one," he lied. "I can't get out of it. I forgot when I accepted your dad's invitation. Can you give him my apologies?"

"Of course," she told him. "Have a good time."

She sounded strange. He hesitated. "Something wrong?" he asked.

"Nothing at all! Nice talking to you, Leo. Bye."

Janie Brewster hung up and closed her eyes, sick with disappointment. She'd planned a perfect menu. She'd practiced all week on a special chicken dish that was tender and succulent. She'd practiced an exquisite crème brûlée as well, which was Leo's favorite dessert. She could even use the little tool to caramelize the sugar topping, which had taken a while to perfect. All that work, and for nothing.

She'd have been willing to bet that Leo hadn't had a date for that night already. He'd made one deliberately, to get out of the engagement.

She sat down beside the hall table, her apron almost stiff with flour, her face white with dustings of it, her hair disheveled. She was anything but the picture of a perfect date. And wasn't it just her luck? For the past year, she'd mounted a real campaign to get Leo to notice her. She'd flirted with him shamelessly at Micah Steele's wedding to Callie Kirby, until a stabbing scowl had turned her shy. It had angered him that she'd caught the bouquet Callie had thrown. It had embarrassed her that he glared so angrily at her. Months later, she'd tried, shyly, every wile she had on him, with no success. She couldn't cook and she was not much more than a fashion plate, according to her best friend, Marilee, who was trying to help her catch Leo. Marilee had plenty of advice, things Leo had mentioned that he didn't like about Janie, and Janie was trying her best to improve in the areas he'd mentioned. She was even out on the ranch for the first time in her life, trying to get used to horses and cattle and dust and dirt. But if she couldn't get Leo to the house to show him her new skills, she didn't have a lot of hope.

''Who was that on the phone?'' Hettie, their housekeeper, called from the staircase. ''Was it Mr. Fred?''

''No. It was Leo. He can't come Saturday night. He's got a date.''

''Oh.'' Hettie smiled sympathetically. ''There will be other dinners, darlin'.''

''Of course there will,'' Janie said and smiled back. She got out of the chair. ''Well, I'll just make it for you and me and Dad,'' she said, with disappointment plain in her voice.

''It isn't as if Leo has any obligation to spend his weekends with us, just because he does a lot of business with

Mr. Fred,'' Hettie reminded her gently. ''He's a good man. A little old for you, though,'' she added hesitantly.

Janie didn't answer her. She just smiled and walked back into the kitchen.

Leo showered, shaved, dressed to the hilt and got into the new black Lincoln sports car he'd just bought. Next year's model, and fast as lightning. He was due for a night on the town. And missing Janie's famous rubber chicken wasn't going to disappoint him one bit.

His conscience did nag him, though, oddly. Maybe it was just hearing Janie's friend, Marilee, harp on the girl all the time. In the past week, she'd started telling him some disturbing things that Janie had said about him. He was going to have to be more careful around Janie. He didn't want her to get the wrong idea. He had no interest in her at all. She was just a kid.

He glanced in the lighted mirror over the steering wheel before he left the sprawling Hart Ranch. He had thick blond-streaked brown hair, a broad forehead, a slightly crooked nose and high cheekbones. But his teeth were good and strong, and he had a square jaw and a nice wide mouth. He wasn't all that handsome, but compared to most of his brothers, he was a hunk. He chuckled at that rare conceit and closed the mirror. He was rich enough that his looks didn't matter.

He didn't fool himself that Marilee would have found him all that attractive without his bankroll. But she was pretty and he didn't mind taking her to Houston and showing her off, like the fishing trophies he displayed on the walls of his study. A man had to have his little vanities, he told himself. But he thought about Janie's disappointment when he didn't show up for supper, her pain if she ever found out her best friend was stabbing her in the back, and he hated the guilt he felt.

He put on his seat belt, put the car in gear, and took off

down the long driveway. He didn't have any reason to feel guilty, he told himself firmly. He was a bachelor, and he'd never done one single thing to give Janie Brewster the impression that he wanted to be the man in her life. Besides, he'd been on his own too long. A cultural evening in Houston was just the thing to cure the blues.

# *Chapter One*

Leo Hart was half out of humor. It had been a long week as it was, and now he was faced with trying to comfort his neighbor, Fred Brewster, who'd just lost the prize young Salers bull that Leo had wanted to buy. The bull was the offspring of a grand champion whose purchase had figured largely in Leo's improved cross-breeding program. He felt as sad as Fred seemed to.

''He was fine yesterday,'' Fred said heavily, wiping sweat off his narrow brow as the two men surveyed the bull in the pasture. The huge creature was lying dead on its side, not a mark on it. ''I'm not the only rancher who's ever lost a prize bull, but these are damned suspicious circumstances.''

''They are,'' Leo agreed grimly, his dark eyes surveying the bull. ''It's just a thought, but you haven't had a problem with an employee, have you? Christabel Gaines said they just had a bull die of unknown causes. This happened after they fired a man named Jack Clark a couple of weeks ago. He's working for Duke Wright now, driving a cattle truck.''

''Judd Dunn said it wasn't unknown causes that killed

the bull, it was bloat. Judd's a Texas Ranger,'' Fred reminded him. ''If there was sabotage on the ranch he co-owns with Christabel, I think he'd know it. No, Christabel had that young bull in a pasture with a lot of clover and she hadn't primed him on hay or tannin-containing forage beforehand. She won't use antibiotics, either, which would have helped prevent trouble. Even so, you can treat bloat if you catch it in time. It was bad luck that they didn't check that pasture, but Christabel's shorthanded and she's back at the vocational school full-time, too. Not much time to check on livestock.''

''They had four other bulls that were still alive,'' Leo pointed out, scowling.

Fred shrugged. ''Maybe they didn't like clover, or weren't in the same pasture.'' He shook his head. ''I'm fairly sure their bull died of bloat. That's what Judd thinks, anyway. He says Christabel's unsettled by having those movie people coming next month to work out a shooting schedule on the ranch and she's the only one who thinks there was foul play.'' Fred rubbed a hand through his silver hair. ''But to answer your question—yes, I did wonder about a disgruntled ex-employee, but I haven't fired anybody in over two years. So you can count out vengeance. And it wasn't bloat. My stock gets antibiotics.''

''Don't say that out loud,'' Leo chuckled. ''If the Tremaynes hear you, there'll be a fight.''

''It's my ranch. I run it my way.'' Fred looked sadly toward the bull again. He was having financial woes the likes of which he'd never faced. He was too proud to tell Leo the extent of it. ''This bull is a hell of a loss right now, too, with my breeding program under way. He wasn't insured, so I can't afford to replace him. Well, not just yet,'' he amended, because he didn't want Leo to think he was nearly broke.

''That's one problem we can solve,'' Leo replied. ''I've got that beautiful Salers bull I bought two years ago, but it's time I replaced him. I'd have loved to have had yours, but while I'm looking for a replacement, you can borrow mine for your breeding season."

"Leo, I can't let you do that," Fred began, overwhelmed by the offer. He knew very well what that bull's services cost.

Leo held up a big hand and grinned. "Sure you can. I've got an angle. I get first pick of your young bulls next spring."

"You devil, you," Fred said, chuckling. "All right, all right. On that condition, I'll take him and be much obliged. But I'd feel better if there was a man sitting up with him at night to guard him."

Leo stretched sore muscles, pushing his Stetson back over his blond-streaked brown hair. It was late September, but still very hot in Jacobsville, which was in southeastern Texas. He'd been helping move bulls all morning, and he was tired. "We can take care of security for him," Leo said easily. "I've got two cowboys banged up in accidents who can't work cattle. They're still on my payroll, so they can sit over here and guard my bull while they recuperate."

"And we'll feed them," Fred said.

Leo chuckled. "Now that's what I call a real nice solution. One of them," he confided, "eats for three men."

"I won't mind." His eyes went back to the still bull one more time. "He was the best bull, Leo. I had so many hopes for him."

"I know. But there are other champion-sired Salers bulls," Leo said.

"Sure. But not one like that one," he gestured toward the animal. "He had such beautiful conformation—" He broke off as a movement to one side caught his attention. He turned, leaned forward and then gaped at his approaching daughter. "Janie?" he asked, as if he wasn't sure of her identity.

Janie Brewster had light brown hair and green eyes.

She'd tried going blond once, but these days her hair was its natural color. Straight, thick and sleek, it hung to her waist. She had a nice figure, a little on the slender side, and pretty little pert breasts. She even had nice legs. But anyone looking at her right now could be forgiven for mistaking her for a young bull rider.

She was covered with mud from head to toe. Even her hair was caked with it. She had a saddle over one thin shoulder, leaning forward to take its weight. The separation between her boots and jeans was imperceptible. Her blouse and arms were likewise. Only her eyes were visible, her eyebrows streaked where the mud had been haphazardly wiped away.

''Hi, Daddy,'' she muttered as she walked past them with a forced smile. ''Hi, Leo. Nice day.''

Leo's dark eyes were wide-open, like Fred's. He couldn't even manage words. He nodded, and kept gaping at the mud doll walking past.

''What have you been doing?'' Fred shouted after his only child.

''Just riding around,'' she said gaily.

''Riding around,'' Fred murmured to himself as she trailed mud onto the porch and stopped there, calling for their housekeeper. ''I can't remember the last time I saw her on a horse,'' he added.

''Neither can I,'' Leo was forced to admit.

Fred shook his head. ''She has these spells lately,'' he said absently. ''First it was baling hay. She went out with four of the hands and came home covered in dust and thorns. Then she took up dipping cattle.'' He cleared his throat. ''Better to forget that altogether. Now it's riding. I don't know what the hell's got into her. She was all geared up to transfer to a four-year college and get on with her psychology degree. Then all of a sudden, she announces that she's going to learn ranching.'' He threw up his hands. ''I'll never understand children. Will you?'' he asked Leo.

Leo chuckled. "Don't ask me. Fatherhood is one role in life I have no desire to play. Listen, about my bull," he continued. "I'll have him trucked right over, and the men will come with him. If you have any more problems, you just let me know."

Fred was relieved. The Harts owned five ranches. Nobody had more clout than they did, politically and financially. The loan of that bull would help him recoup his losses and get back on his feet. Leo was a gentleman. "I'm damned grateful, Leo. We've been having hard times lately."

Leo only smiled. He knew that the Brewsters were having a bad time financially. He and Fred had swapped and traded bulls for years—although less expensive ones than Fred's dead Salers bull—and they frequently did business together. He was glad he could help.

He did wonder about Janie's odd behavior. She'd spent weeks trying to vamp him with low-cut blouses and dresses. She was always around when he came to see Fred on business, waiting in the living room in a seductive pose. Not that Janie even knew how to be seductive, he told himself amusedly. She was twenty-one, but hardly in the class with her friend Marilee Morgan, who was only four years older than Janie but could give Mata Hari lessons in seduction.

He wondered if Marilee had been coaching her in tomboyish antics. That would be amusing, because lately Marilee had been using Janie's tactics on him. The former tomboy-turned-debutante had even finagled him into taking her out to eat in Houston. He wondered if Janie knew. Sometimes friends could become your worst enemy, he thought. Luckily Janie only had a crush on him, which would wear itself out all the faster once she knew he had gone out with her best friend. Janie was far too young for him, and not only in age. The sooner she realized it, the better. Besides, he didn't like her new competitive spirit. Why was she trying to compete with her father in ranch management all of a sudden? Was it a liberation thing? She'd never shown any such inclination before, and her new appearance was appalling. The one thing Leo had admired about her was the elegance and sophistication with which she dressed. Janie in muddy jeans was a complete turnoff.

He left Fred at the pasture and drove back to the ranch, his mind already on ways and means to find out what had caused that healthy bull's sudden demise.

Janie was listening to their housekeeper's tirade through the bathroom door.

"I'll clean it all up, Hettie," she promised. "It's just dirt. It will come out."

"It's red mud! It will never come out!" Hettie was grumbling. "You'll be red from head to toe forever! People will mistake you for that nineteenth-century Kiowa, Satanta, who painted everything he owned red, even his horse!"

Janie laughed as she stripped off the rest of her clothes and stepped into the shower. Besides being a keen student of Western history, Hettie was all fire and wind, and she'd blow out soon. She was such a sweetheart. Janie's mother had died years ago, leaving behind Janie and her father and Hettie—and Aunt Lydia who lived in Jacobsville. Fortunately, Aunt Lydia only visited infrequently. She was so very house-proud, so clothes conscious, so debutante! She was just like Janie's late mother, in fact, who had raised Janie to be a little flower blossom in a world of independent, strong women. She spared a thought for her mother's horror if she could have lived long enough to see what her daughter had worn at college. There, where she could be herself, Janie didn't wear designer dresses and hang out with the right social group. Janie studied anthropology, as well as the psychology her aunt Lydia had insisted on—and felt free to insist, since she helped pay Janie's tuition.

But Janie spent most of her weekends and afternoons buried in mud, learning how to dig out fragile pieces of ancient pottery and projectile points.

But she'd gone on with the pretense when she was home—when Aunt Lydia was visiting, of course—proving her worth at psychology. Sadly, it had gone awry when she psychoanalyzed Leo's brother Callaghan last year over the asparagus. She'd gone to her room howling with laughter after Aunt Lydia had hung on every word approvingly. She was sorry she'd embarrassed Cag, but the impulse had been irresistible. Her aunt was *so* gullible. She'd felt guilty afterward, though, for not telling Aunt Lydia her true interests.

She finished her shower, dried off, and changed into new clothes so that she could start cleaning up the floors where she'd tracked mud. Despite her complaints, Hettie would help. She didn't really mind housework. Neither did Janie, although her late mother would be horrified if she could see her only child on the floor with a scrub brush alongside Hettie's ample figure.

Janie helped with everything, except cooking. Her expertise in the kitchen was, to put it mildly, nonexistent. But, she thought, brightening, that was the next thing on her list of projects. She was undergoing a major self-improvement. First she was going to learn ranching—even if it killed her—and then she was going to learn to cook.

She wished this transformation had been her idea, but actually, it had been Marilee's. The other girl had told her, in confidence, that she'd been talking to Leo and Leo had told her flatly that the reason he didn't notice Janie was that she didn't know anything about ranching. She was too well-dressed, too chic, too sophisticated. And the worst thing was that she didn't know anything about cooking, either, Marilee claimed. So if Janie wanted to land that big, hunky fish, she was going to have to make some major changes.

It sounded like a good plan, and Marilee had been her friend since grammar school, when the Morgan family had moved next door. So Janie accepted Marilee's advice with great pleasure, knowing that her best friend would never steer her wrong. She was going to stay home—not go back to college—and she was going to show Leo Hart that she could be the sort of woman who appealed to him. She'd work so hard at it, she'd have to succeed!

Not that her attempts at riding a horse were anything to write home about, she had to admit as she mopped her way down the long wooden floor of the hall. But she was a rancher's daughter. She'd get better with practice.

She did keep trying. A week later, she was making biscuits in the kitchen—or trying to learn how—when she dropped the paper flour bag hard on the counter and was dusted from head to toe with the white substance.

It would have to be just that minute that her father came in the back door with Leo in tow.

"Janie?" her father exclaimed, wide-eyed.

"Hi, Dad!" she said with a big grin. "Hi, Leo."

"What in blazes are you doing?" her father demanded.

"Putting the flour in a canister," she lied, still smiling.

"Where's Hettie?" he asked.

Their housekeeper was hiding in the bedroom, supposedly making beds, and trying not to howl at Janie's pitiful efforts. "Cleaning, I believe," she said.

"Aunt Lydia not around?"

"Playing bridge with the Harrisons," she said.

"Bridge!" her father scoffed. "If it isn't bridge, it's golf. If it isn't golf, it's tennis… Is she coming over today to go over those stocks with me or not?" he persisted, because they jointly owned some of his late wife's shares and couldn't sell them without Lydia's permission. If he could ever find the blasted woman!

''She said she wasn't coming over until Saturday, Dad,'' Janie reminded him.

He let out an angry sigh. ''Well, come on, Leo, I'll show you the ones I want to sell and let you advise me. They're in my desk...damn bridge! I can't do a thing until Lydia makes up her mind.''

Leo gave Janie a curious glance but he kept walking and didn't say another word to her. Minutes later, he left—out the front door, not the back.

Janie's self-improvement campaign continued into the following week with calf roping, which old John was teaching her out in the corral. Since she could now loop the rope around a practice wooden cow with horns, she was progressing to livestock.

She followed John's careful instruction and tossed her loop over the head of the calf, but she'd forgotten to dig her heels in. The calf hadn't. He jerked her off her feet and proceeded to run around the ring like a wild thing, trying to get away from the human slithering after him at a breakneck pace.

Of course, Leo would drive up next to the corral in time to see John catch and throw the calf, leaving Janie covered in mud. She looked like a road disaster.

This time Leo didn't speak. He was too busy laughing. Janie couldn't speak, either, her mouth was full of mud. She gave both men a glare and stomped off toward the back door of the house, trailing mud and unspeakable stuff, fuming the whole while.

A bath and change of clothes improved her looks and her smell. She was resigned to finding Leo gone when she got out, so she didn't bother to dress up or put on makeup. She wandered out to the kitchen in jeans and a loose long-sleeved denim shirt, with her hair in a lopsided ponytail and her feet bare.

''You'll step on something sharp and cripple yourself,''

Hettie warned, turning from the counter where she was making rolls, her ample arms up the elbows in flour.

"I have tough feet," Janie protested with a warm smile. She went up and hugged Hettie hard from behind, loving the familiar smells of freshly washed cotton and flour that seemed to cling to her. Hettie had been around since Janie was six. She couldn't imagine life without the gray-haired, blue-eyed treasure with her constantly disheveled hair and worried expression. "Oh, Hettie, what would we do without you?" she asked on a sigh, and closed her eyes.

"Get away, you pest," Hettie muttered, "I know what you're up to…Janie Brewster, I'll whack you!"

But Janie was already out of reach, dangling Hettie's apron from one hand, her green eyes dancing with mischief.

"You put that back on me or you'll get no rolls tonight!" Hettie raged at her.

"All right, all right, I was only kidding," Janie chuckled. She replaced the apron around Hettie's girth and was fastening it when she heard the door open behind her.

"You stop teaching her these tricks!" Hettie growled at the newcomer.

"Who, me?" Leo exclaimed with total innocence.

Janie's hands fumbled with the apron. Her heart ran wild. He hadn't left. She'd thought he was gone, and she hadn't bothered with her appearance. He was still here, and she looked like last year's roast!

"You'll drop that apron, Janie," Leo scolded playfully.

Janie glanced at him as she retied the apron. "You can talk," she chided. "I hear your housekeepers keep quitting because you untie aprons constantly! One kept a broom handle!"

"She broke it on my hard head," he said smugly. "What are you making, Hettie?"

"Rolls," she said. She glanced warily at Leo. "I can't make biscuits. Sorry."

He gave her a hard glare. "Just because I did something a little offbeat..."

"Carried that little chef right out of his restaurant, with him kicking and screaming all the way, I heard," Hettie mused, eyes twinkling.

"He said he could bake biscuits. I was only taking him home with me to let him prove it," Leo said belligerently.

"That's not what he thought," Hettie chuckled. "I hear he dropped the charges...?"

"Nervous little guy," Leo said, shaking his head. "He'd never have worked out, anyway." He gave her a long look. "You sure you can't bake a biscuit? Have you ever tried?"

"No, and I won't. I like working here," she said firmly.

He sighed. "Just checking." He peered over her shoulder fondly. "Rolls, huh? I can't remember when I've had a homemade roll."

"Tell Fred to invite you to supper," Hettie suggested.

He glanced at Janie. "Why can't she do it?"

Janie was tongue-tied. She couldn't think at all.

The lack of response from her dumbfounded Leo. To have Janie hesitate about inviting him for a meal was shocking. Leo scowled and just stared at her openly, which only made her more nervous and uncertain. She knew she looked terrible. Leo wanted a woman who could do ranch work and cook, but surely he wanted one who looked pretty, too. Right now, Janie could have qualified for the Frump of the Year award.

She bit her lower lip, hard, and looked as if she were about to cry.

"Hey," he said softly, in a tone he'd never used with her before, "what's wrong?"

"Have to let this rise," Hettie was murmuring after she'd covered the dough and washed her hands, oblivious to what was happening behind her. "Meanwhile I'm going to put another load of clothes in the washer, darlin'," she called to Janie over her shoulder.

The door into the dining room closed, but they didn't notice.

Leo moved closer to Janie, and suddenly his big, lean hands were on her thin shoulders, resting heavily over the soft denim. They were warm and very strong.

Her breath caught in the back of her throat while she looked up into black eyes that weren't teasing or playful. They were intent, narrow, faintly glittering. There was no expression on his handsome face at all. He looked into her eyes as if he'd never seen them, or her, before—and she looked terrible!

"Come on," he coaxed. "Tell me what's wrong. If it's something I can fix, I will."

Her lips trembled. Surely, she could make up something, quick, before he moved away!

"I got hurt," she whispered in a shameful lie. "When the calf dragged me around the corral."

"Did you?" He was only half listening. His eyes were on her mouth. It was the prettiest little mouth, like a pink bow, full and soft, just barely parted over perfect, white teeth. He wondered if she'd been kissed, and how often. She never seemed to date, or at least, he didn't know about her boyfriends. He shouldn't be curious, either, but Marilee had hinted that Janie had more boyfriends than other local girls, that she was a real rounder.

Janie was melting. Her knees were weak. Any minute, she was going to be a little puddle of love looking up at his knees.

He felt her quiver under his hands, and his scowl grew darker. If she was as sophisticated as Marilee said she was, why was she trembling now? An experienced woman would be winding her arms around his neck already, offering her mouth, curving her body into his…

His fingers tightened involuntarily on her soft arms. "Come here," he said huskily, and tugged her right up against his tall, muscular body. Of all the Harts, he was the tallest, and the most powerfully built. Janie's breasts pressed into his diaphragm. She felt him tauten at the contact, felt his curiosity as he looked down into her wide, soft, dazed eyes. Her hands lightly touched his shirtfront, but hesitantly, as if it embarrassed her to touch him at all.

He let out a soft breath. His head was spinning with forbidden longings. Janie was barely twenty-one. She was the daughter of a man he did business with. She was off-limits. So why was he looking at her mouth and feeling his body swell sensuously at just the brush of her small breasts against him?

''Don't pick at my shirt,'' he said quietly. His voice was unusually deep and soft, its tone unfamiliar. ''Flatten your hands on my chest.''

She did that, slowly, as if she were just learning how to walk. Her hands were cold and nervous, but they warmed on his body. She stood very still, hoping against hope that he wasn't going to regain the senses she was certain he'd momentarily lost. She didn't even want to breathe, to do anything that would distract him. He seemed to be in a trance, and she was feeling dreams come true in the most unexpected and delightful way.

He smiled quizzically. ''Don't you know how?''

Her lips were dry. She moistened them with just the tip of her tongue. He seemed to find that little movement fascinating. He watched her mouth almost hungrily. ''How... to...do what?'' she choked.

His hand went to her cheek and his thumb suddenly ran roughly over her lips, parting them in a whip of urgent, shocking emotion. ''How to do this,'' he murmured as his head bent.

She saw the faint smile on his hard mouth as his lips parted. They brushed against hers in tiny little whispers of contact that weren't nearly enough to feed the hunger he was coaxing out of her.

Her nails curled into his shirt and he tensed. She felt

thick hair over the warm, hard muscles of his chest. Closer, she felt the hard, heavy thunder of his pulse there, under her searching hands.

''Nice,'' he whispered. His voice was taut now, like his body against her.

She felt his big hands slide down her waist to her hips while he was playing with her mouth in the most arousing way. She couldn't breathe. Did he know? Could he tell that she was shaking with desire?

Her lips parted more with every sensuous brush of his mouth against them. At the same time, his hands moved to her narrow hips and teased against her lower spine. She'd never felt such strange sensations. She felt her body swell, as if it had been stung all over by bees, but the sensation produced pleasure instead of pain.

He nibbled at her upper lip, feeling it quiver tentatively as his tongue slid under it and began to explore. One lean hand slid around to the base of her hips and slowly gathered them into his, in a lazy movement that made her suddenly aware of the changing contours of his body.

She gasped and pulled against his hand.

He lifted his head and searched her wide, shocked green eyes. ''Plenty of boyfriends, hmm?'' he murmured sarcastically, almost to himself.

''Boy…friends?'' Her voice sounded as if she were being strangled.

His hand moved back to her waist, the other one moved to her round chin and his thumb tugged gently at her lower lip. ''Leave it like this,'' he whispered. His mouth hovered over hers just as it parted, and she found herself going on tiptoe, leaning toward him, almost begging for his mouth to come down and cover hers.

But he was still nibbling at her upper lip, gently toying with it, until he tilted her chin and his teeth tugged softly at the lower lip. His mouth brushed roughly over hers, teaching it to follow, to plead, then to demand something more urgent, more thorough than this slow torment.

Her nails bit into his chest and she moaned.

As if he'd been waiting patiently for that tiny little sound, his arms swallowed her up whole and his eyes, when they met hers, glittered like candlelight from deep in a cave.

His hand was in her ponytail, ripping away the rubber band so that he could catch strands of it in his strong fingers and angle her face just where he wanted it.

"Maybe you are old enough..." he breathed just before his mouth plunged deeply into hers.

She tautened all over with heated pleasure. Her body arched against him, no longer protesting the sudden hardness of him against her. She reached up to hold him, to keep that tormenting, hungry mouth against her lips. It was every dream she'd ever dreamed, coming true. She could hardly believe it was happening here, in broad daylight, in the kitchen where she'd been trying so hard to learn to make things that would please him. But he seemed to be pleased, just the same. He groaned against her lips, and his arms were bruising now, as if he wasn't quite in control. That was exciting. She threw caution to the winds and opened her mouth deliberately under the crush of his, inviting him in.

She felt his tongue go deep into the soft darkness, and she shivered as his mouth devoured hers.

Only the sound of a door slamming penetrated the thick sensual fog that held them both in thrall.

Leo lifted his head, slowly, and looked down into a face he didn't recognize. Janie's green eyes were like wet emeralds in her flushed face. Her lips were swollen, soft, sensual. Her body was clinging to his. He had her off the floor in his hungry embrace, and his body was throbbing with desire.

He knew that she could feel him, that she knew he was aroused. It was a secret thing, that only the two of them knew. It had to stay that way. He had to stop. This was wrong…!

He let go of her slowly, easing her back, while he sucked in a long, hard breath and shivered with a hunger he couldn't satisfy. He became aware of the rough grip he had on her upper arms and he relaxed it at once. He'd never meant to hurt her.

He fought for control, reciting multiplication tables silently in his mind until he felt his body unclench and relax.

It troubled him that he'd lost control so abruptly, and with a woman he should never have touched. He hadn't meant to touch her in the first place. He couldn't understand why he'd gone headfirst at her like that. He was usually cool with women, especially with Janie.

The way she was looking at him was disturbing. He was going to have a lot of explaining to do, and he didn't know how to begin. Janie was years too young for him, only his body didn't think so. Now he had to make his mind get himself out of this predicament.

"That shouldn't have happened," he said through his teeth.

She was hanging on every word, deaf to meanings, deaf to denials. Her body throbbed. "It's like the flu," she said, dazed, staring up at him. "It makes you…ache."

He shook her gently. "You're too young to have aches," he said flatly. "And I'm old enough to know better than to do something this stupid. Are you listening to me? This shouldn't have happened. I'm sorry."

Belatedly, she realized that he was backtracking. Of course he hadn't meant to kiss her. He'd made his opinion of her clear for years, and even if he liked kissing her, it didn't mean that he was ready to rush out and buy a ring. Quite the opposite.

She stepped away from him, her face still flushed, her eyes full of dreams she had to hide from him.

"I…I'm sorry, too," she stammered.

''Hell,'' he growled, ramming his hands into his pockets. ''It was my fault. I started it.''

She moved one shoulder. ''No harm done.'' She cleared her throat and fought for inspiration. It came unexpectedly. Her eyes began to twinkle wickedly. ''I have to take lessons when they're offered.''

His eyebrows shot up. Had he heard her say that, or was he delusional?

''I'm not the prom queen,'' she pointed out. ''Men aren't thick on the ground around here, except old bachelors who chew tobacco and don't bathe.''

''I call that prejudice,'' he said, relaxing into humor.

''I'll bet you don't hang out with women who smell like dirty horses,'' she said.

He pursed his lips. Like hers, they were faintly swollen. ''I don't know about that. The last time I saw you, I recall, you were neck-deep in mud and sh—''

''You can stop right there!'' she interrupted, flushing.

His dark eyes studied her long hair, liking its thick waves and its light brown color. ''Pity your name isn't Jeanie,'' he murmured. ''Stephen Foster wrote a song about her hair.''

She smiled. He liked her hair, at least. Maybe he liked her a little, too.

She was pretty when she smiled like that, he thought, observing her. ''Do I get invited to supper?'' he drawled, lost in that soft, hungry look she was giving him. ''If you say yes, I might consider giving you a few more lessons. Beginner class only, of course,'' he added with a grin.

# *Chapter Two*

Janie was sure she hadn't heard him say that, but he was still smiling. She smiled back. She felt pretty. No makeup, no shoes, disheveled—and Leo had kissed her anyway. She beamed. At least, she beamed until she remembered the Hart bread mania. Any of them would do anything for a biscuit. Did that extend to homemade rolls?

"You're looking suspicious," he pointed out.

"A man who would kidnap a poor little pastry chef might do anything for a homemade roll," she reminded him.

He sighed. "Hettie makes wonderful rolls," he had to admit.

"Oh, you!" She hit him gently and then laughed. He was impossible. "Okay, you can come to supper."

He beamed. "You're a nice girl."

Nice. Well, at least he liked her. It was a start. It didn't occur to her, then, that a man who was seriously interested in her wouldn't think of her as just "nice."

Hettie came back into the room, still oblivious to the undercurrents, and got out a plastic bowl. She filled it with

English peas from the crisper. ''All right, my girl, sit down here and shell these. You staying?'' she asked Leo.

''She said I could,'' he told Hettie.

''Then you can go away while we get it cooked.''

''I'll visit my bull. Fred's got him in the pasture.''

Leo didn't say another word. But the look he gave Janie before he left the kitchen was positively wicked.

But if she thought the little interlude had made any permanent difference in her relationship with Leo, Janie was doomed to disappointment. He came to supper, but he spent the whole time talking genetic breeding with Fred, and although he was polite to Janie, she might as well have been on the moon.

He didn't stay long after supper, either, making his excuses and praising Hettie for her wonderful cooking. He smiled at Janie, but not the way he had when they were alone in the kitchen. It was as if he'd put the kisses out of his mind forever, and expected her to act as if he'd never touched her. It was disheartening. It was heartbreaking. It was just like old times, except that now Leo had kissed her and she wanted him to do it again. Judging by his attitude over supper, she had a better chance of landing a movie role.

She spent the next few weeks remembering Leo's hungry kisses and aching for more of them. When she wasn't daydreaming, she was practicing biscuit-making. Hettie muttered about the amount of flour she was going through.

''Janie, you're going to bankrupt us in the kitchen!'' the older woman moaned when Janie's fifth batch of biscuits came out looking like skeet pigeons. ''That's your second bag of flour today!''

Janie was glowering at her latest effort on the baking sheet. ''Something's wrong, and I can't decide what. I mean, I put in salt and baking powder, just like the recipe said...''

Hettie picked up the empty flour bag and read the label. Her eyes twinkled. "Janie, darlin', you bought self-rising flour."

"Yes. So?" she asked obliviously.

"If it's self-rising, it already has the salt and baking powder in it, doesn't it?"

Janie burst out laughing. "So that's what I'm doing wrong! Hand me another bag of flour, could you?"

"This is the last one," Hettie said mournfully.

"No problem. I'll just drive to the store and get some more. Need anything?"

"Milk and eggs," Hettie said at once.

"We've got four chickens," Janie exclaimed, turning, "and you have to buy eggs?"

"The chickens are molting."

Janie smiled. "And when they molt, they don't lay. Sorry. I forgot. I'll be back in a jiffy," she added, peeling off her apron.

She paused just long enough to brush her hair out, leaving it long, and put on a little makeup. She thrust her arms into her nice fringed leather jacket, because it was seasonably cool outside as well as raining, and popped into her red sports car. You never could tell when you might run into Leo, because he frequently dashed into the supermarket for frozen biscuits and butter when he was between cooks.

Sure enough, as she started for the checkout counter with her milk, eggs and flour, she spotted Leo, head and shoulders above most of the men present. He was wearing that long brown Australian drover's coat he favored in wet weather, and he was smiling in a funny sort of way.

That was when Janie noticed his companion. He was bending down toward a pretty little brunette who was chattering away at his side. Janie frowned, because that dark wavy hair was familiar. And then she realized who it was. Leo was talking to Marilee Morgan!

She relaxed. Marilee was her friend. Surely, she was talking her up to Leo. She almost rushed forward to say hello, but what if she interrupted at a crucial moment? There was, after all, the annual Jacobsville Cattleman's Ball in two weeks, the Saturday before Thanksgiving. It was very likely that Marilee was dropping hints right and left that Janie would love Leo to escort her.

She chuckled to herself. She was lucky to have a friend like Marilee.

If Janie had known what Marilee was actually saying to Leo, she might have changed her mind about the other woman's friendship and a lot of other things.

"It was so nice of you to drive me to the store, Leo," Marilee was cooing at Leo as they walked out. "My wrist is really sore from that fall I took."

"No problem," he murmured with a smile.

"The Cattleman's Ball is week after next," Marilee added coyly. "I would really love to go, but nobody's asked me. I won't be able to drive by then, either, I'm sure. It was a bad sprain. They take almost as long as a broken bone to heal." She glanced up at him, weighing her chances. "Of course, Janie's told everybody that you're taking her. She said you're over there all the time now, that it's just a matter of time before you buy her a ring. Everybody knows."

He scowled fiercely. He'd only kissed Janie, he hadn't proposed marriage, for God's sake! Surely the girl wasn't going to get possessive because of a kiss? He hated gossip, especially about himself. Well, Janie could forget any invitations of that sort. He didn't like aggressive women who told lies around town. Not one bit!

"You can go with me," he told Marilee nonchalantly. "Despite what Janie told you, I am no woman's property, and I'm damned sure not booked for the dance!"

Marilee beamed. "Thanks, Leo!"

He shrugged. She was pretty and he liked her company. She wasn't one of those women who felt the need to constantly compete with men. He'd made his opinion about that pretty clear to Marilee in recent weeks. It occurred to him that Janie was suddenly trying to do just that, what with calf roping and ranch work and hard riding. Odd, when she'd never shown any such inclination before. But her self-assured talk about being his date for the ball set him off and stopped his mind from further reasoning about her sudden change of attitude.

He smiled down at Marilee. "Thanks for telling me about the gossip," he added. "Best way to curb it is to disprove it publicly."

"Of course it is. You mustn't blame Janie too much," she added with just the right amount of affection. "She's very young. Compared to me, I mean. If we hadn't been neighbors, we probably wouldn't be friends at all. She seems so…well, so juvenile at times, doesn't she?"

Leo frowned. He'd forgotten that Marilee was older than Janie. He thought back to those hard, hungry kisses he'd shared with Janie and could have cursed himself for his weakness. She was immature. She was building a whole affair on a kiss or two. Then he remembered something unexpectedly.

He glanced down at Marilee. "You said she had more boyfriends than anybody else in town."

Marilee cleared her throat. "Well, yes, *boy*friends. Not men friends, though," she added, covering her bases. It was hard to make Janie look juvenile if she was also a heartbreaking rounder.

Leo felt placated, God knew why. "There's a difference."

Marilee agreed. A tiny voice in her mind chided her for being so mean to her best friend, but Leo was a real hunk, and she was as infatuated with him as Janie was. All was fair in love and war, didn't they say? Besides, it was highly unlikely that Leo would ever ask Janie out—but, just in case, Marilee had planted a nice little suspicion in his mind to prevent that. She smiled as she walked beside him to his truck, dreaming of the first of many dances and being in Leo's arms. One day, she thought ecstatically, he might even want to marry her!

Janie went through two more bags of flour with attempts at biscuits that became better with each failed try. Finally, after several days' work, she had produced an edible batch that impressed even Hettie.

In between cooking, she was getting much better on horseback. Now, mounted on her black-and-white quarter horse, Blackie, she could cut out a calf and drive it into the makeshift corral used for doctoring sick animals. She could throw a calf, too, with something like professionalism, despite sore muscles and frequent bruises. She could rope, after a fashion, and she was riding better all the time. At least the chafing of her thighs against the saddle had stopped, and the muscles had acclimatized to the new stress being placed on them.

Saturday night loomed. It was only four days until the Cattleman's Ball, and she had a beautiful spaghetti-strapped lacy oyster-white dress to wear. It came to her ankles and was low-cut in front, leaving the creamy skin of her shoulders bare. There was a side-slit that went up her thigh, exposing her beautiful long legs. She paired the dress with white spiked high heels sporting ankle straps which she thought were extremely sexy, and she had a black velvet coat with a white silk lining to defend against the cold evening air. Now all she lacked was a date.

She'd expected Leo to ask her to the ball after those hungry kisses, despite his coolness later that day. But he hadn't been near the ranch since he'd had supper with her and her father. What made it even more peculiar was that he'd talked with her father out on the ranch several times.

He just didn't come to the house. Janie assumed that he was regretting those hard kisses, and was afraid that she was taking him too seriously. He was avoiding her. He couldn't have made it plainer.

That made it a pretty good bet that he wasn't planning to take her to any Cattleman's Ball. She phoned Marilee in desperation.

The other woman sounded uneasy when she heard Janie's voice, and she was quick to ask why Janie had phoned.

"I saw you with Leo in the grocery store week before last," Janie began, "and I didn't interfere, because I was sure you were trying to talk him into taking me to the ball. But he didn't want to, did he?" she added sadly.

There was a sound like someone swallowing, on the other end of the phone. "Well, actually, no. I'm sorry." Marilee sounded as if she were strangling on the words.

"Don't feel bad," Janie said gently. "It's not your fault. You're my best friend in the whole world. I know you tried."

"Janie..."

"I had this beautiful white dress that I bought specially," Janie added on a sigh. "Well, that's that. Are you going?"

There was a tense pause. "Yes."

"Good! Anybody I know?"

"N...no," Marilee stammered.

"You have fun," Janie said.

"You...uh...aren't going, are you?" Marilee added.

Her friend certainly was acting funny, Janie thought. "No, I don't have a date," Janie chuckled. "There'll be other dances, I guess. Maybe Leo will ask me another time." After he's got over being afraid of me, she added silently. "If you see him," she said quickly, "you might mention that I can now cut out cattle and throw a calf. And I can make a biscuit that doesn't go through the floor when dropped!"

She was laughing, but Marilee didn't.

"I have to get to the hairdresser, Janie," Marilee said. "I'm really sorry...about the ball."

"Not your fault," Janie repeated. "Just have enough fun for both of us, okay?"

"Okay. See you."

The line went dead and Janie frowned. Something must be very wrong with Marilee. She wished she'd been more persistent and asked what was the matter. Well, she'd go over to Marilee's house after the dance to pump her for all the latest gossip, and then she could find out what was troubling her friend.

She put the ball to the back of her mind, despite the disappointment, and went out to greet her father as he rode in from the pasture with two of his men.

He swung out of the saddle at the barn and grinned at her. "Just the girl I wanted to see," he said at once. He pulled out his wallet. "I've got to have some more work gloves, just tore the last pair I had apart on barbed wire. How about going by the hardware store and get me another pair of those suede-palmed ones, extra large?"

"My pleasure," Janie said at once. Leo often went to the hardware store, and she might accidentally run into him there. "Be back in a jiffy!"

"Don't speed!" her father called to her.

She only chuckled, diving into her sports car. She remembered belatedly that she didn't have either purse or car keys, or her face fixed, and jumped right back out again to rectify those omissions.

Ten minutes later, she was parking her car in front of the Jacobsville Hardware Store. With a wildly beating heart, she noticed one of the black double-cabbed Hart Ranch trucks parked nearby. Leo! She was certain it was Leo!

With her heart pounding, she checked her makeup in the rearview mirror and tugged her hair gently away from her cheeks. She'd left it down today deliberately, remembering that Leo had something of a weakness for long hair. It was thick and clean, shining like a soft brown curtain. She was wearing a long beige skirt with riding boots, and a gold satin blouse. She looked pretty good, even if she did say so herself! Now if Leo would just notice her…

She walked into the hardware store with her breath catching in her throat as she anticipated Leo's big smile at her approach. He was the handsomest of the Hart brothers, and really, the most personable. He was kindness itself. She remembered his soft voice in her kitchen, asking what was wrong. Oh, to have that soft voice in her ear forever!

There was nobody at the counter. That wasn't unusual, the clerks were probably waiting on customers. She walked back to where the gloves were kept and suddenly heard Leo's deep voice on the other side of the high aisle, unseen.

"Don't forget to add that roll of hog wire to the order," he was telling one of the clerks.

"I won't forget," Joe Howland's pleasant voice replied. "Are you going to the Cattleman's Ball?" Joe added just as Janie was about to raise her voice and call to Leo over the aisle.

"I guess I am," Leo replied. "I didn't plan to, but a pretty friend needed a ride and I'm obliging."

Janie's heart skipped and fell flat. Leo already had a date? Who? She moved around the aisle and in sight of Leo and Joe. Leo had his back to her, but Joe noticed her and smiled.

"That friend wouldn't be Janie Brewster, by any chance?" Joe teased loudly.

The question made Leo unreasonably angry. "Listen, just because she caught the bouquet at Micah Steele's wedding is no reason to start linking her with me," he said shortly. "She may have a good family background, she may be easy on the eyes, she may even learn to cook someday—miracles still happen. But no matter what she does, or how well, she is never going to appeal to me as a woman!'' he added. ''Having her spreading ludicrous gossip about our relationship all over town isn't making her any more attractive to me, either. It's a dead turnoff!''

Janie felt a shock like an electric jolt go through her. She couldn't even move for the pain.

Joe, horrified, opened his mouth to speak.

Leo made a rough gesture with one lean hand, burning with pent-up anger. ''She looks like the rough side of a corncob lately, anyway,'' Leo continued, warming to his subject. ''The only thing she ever had going for her were her looks, and she's spent the last few weeks covered in mud or dust or bread flour. She's out all hours proving she can compete with any man on the place and she can't stop bragging about what a great catch she's made with me. She's already told half the town that I'm a kiss short of buying her an engagement ring. That is, when she isn't putting it around that I'm taking her to the Cattleman's Ball, when I haven't even damned well asked her! Well, she's got her eye on the wrong man. I don't want some half-baked kid with a figure like a boy and an ego the size of my boots! I wouldn't have Janie Brewster for a wife if she came complete with a stable of purebred Salers bulls, and that's saying something. She makes me sick to my stomach!''

Joe had gone pale and he was grimacing. Curious, Leo turned…and there was Janie Brewster, staring at him down the aisle with a face as tragic as if he'd just taken a whittling knife to her heart.

''Janie,'' he said slowly.

She took a deep, steadying breath and managed to drag her eyes away from his face. ''Hi, Joe,'' she said with a wan little smile. Her voice sounded choked. She couldn't possibly look for gloves, she had to get away! ''Just wanted to check and see if you'd gotten in that tack Dad ordered last week,'' she improvised.

''Not just yet, Janie,'' Joe told her in a gentle tone. ''I'm real sorry.''

''No problem. No problem at all. Thanks, Joe. Hello, Mr. Hart,'' she said, without really meeting Leo's eyes, and she even managed a smile through her tattered dignity. ''Nice day out, isn't it? Looks like we might even get that rain we need so badly. See you.''

She went out the door with her head high, as proudly as a conquering army, leaving Leo sick to his stomach for real.

''Why the hell didn't you say something?'' Leo asked Joe furiously.

''Didn't know how,'' Joe replied miserably.

''How long had she been standing there?'' Leo persisted.

''The whole time, Leo,'' came the dreaded reply. ''She heard every word.''

As if to punctuate the statement, from outside came the sudden raucous squeal of tires on pavement as Janie took off toward the highway in a burst of speed. She was driving her little sports car, and Leo's heart stopped as he realized how upset she was.

He jerked his cell phone out of his pocket and dialed the police department. ''Is that Grier?'' he said at once when the call was answered, recognizing Jacobsville's new assistant police chief's deep voice. ''Listen, Janie Brewster just lit out of town like a scalded cat in her sports car. She's upset and it's my fault, but she could kill herself. Have you got somebody out on the Victoria road who could pull her over and give her a warning? Yeah. Thanks, Grier. I owe you one.''

He hung up, cursing harshly under his breath. ''She'll be spitting fire if anybody tells her I sent the police after her, but I can't let her get hurt.''

''Thought she looked just a mite too calm when she walked out the door,'' Joe admitted. He glanced at Leo and grimaced. ''No secret around town that she's been sweet on you for the past year or so.''

''If she was, I've just cured her,'' Leo said, and felt his heart sink. ''Call me when that order comes in, will you?''

''Sure thing.''

Leo climbed into his truck and just sat there for a minute, getting his bearings. He could only imagine how Janie felt right now. What he'd said was cruel. He'd let his other irritations burst out as if Janie were to blame for them all. What Marilee had been telling him about Janie had finally bubbled over, that was all. She'd never done anything to hurt him before. Her only crime, if there was one, was thinking the moon rose and set on Leo Hart and taking too much for granted on the basis of one long kiss.

He laughed hollowly. Chances were good that she wouldn't be thinking it after this. Part of him couldn't help blaming her, because she'd gone around bragging about how he was going to marry her, and how lucky he was to have a girl like her in his life. Not to mention telling everybody he was taking her to the Cattleman's Ball.

But Janie had never been one to brag about her accomplishments, or chase men. The only time she'd tried to vamp Leo, in fact, had been in her own home, when her father was present. She'd never come on to him when they were alone, or away from her home. She'd been old-fashioned in her attitudes, probably due to the strict way she'd been raised. So why should she suddenly depart from a lifetime's habits and start spreading gossip about Leo all over Jacobsville? He remembered at least once when she'd stopped another woman from talking about a girl in trouble, adding that she hated gossip because it was like spreading poison.

He wiped his sweaty brow with the sleeve of his shirt and put his hat on the seat beside him. He hated what he'd said. Maybe he didn't want Janie to get any ideas about him in a serious way, but there would have been kinder methods of accomplishing it. He didn't think he was ever going to forget the look on her face when she heard what he was saying to Joe. It would haunt him forever.

Meanwhile, Janie was setting new speed records out on the Victoria Road. She'd already missed the turnoff that led back toward Jacobsville and her father's ranch. She was seething, hurting, miserable and confused. How could Leo think such things about her? She'd never told anybody how she felt about him, except Marilee, and she hadn't been spreading gossip. She hated gossip. Why did he know so little about her, when they'd known each other for years? What hurt the most was that he obviously believed those lies about her.

She wondered who could have told him such a thing. Her thoughts went at once to Marilee, but she chided herself for thinking ill of her only friend, her best friend. Certainly it had to be an enemy who'd been filling Leo's head full of lies. But…she didn't have any enemies that she knew of.

Tears were blurring her eyes. She knew she was going too fast. She should slow down before she wrecked the car or ran it into a fence. She was just thinking about that when she heard sirens and saw blue lights in her rearview mirror.

Great, she thought. Just what I need. I'm going to be arrested and I'll spend the night in the local jail….

She stopped and rolled down her window, trying unobtrusively to wipe away the tears while waiting for the uniformed officer to bend down and speak to her.

He came as a surprise. It wasn't a patrolman she knew, and she knew most of them by sight at least. This one had black eyes and thick black hair, which he wore in a ponytail. He had a no-nonsense look about him, and he was wearing a badge that denoted him as the assistant chief.

"Miss Brewster?" he asked quietly.

"Y…yes."

"I'm Cash Grier," he introduced himself. "I'm the new assistant police chief here."

"Nice to meet you," she said with a watery smile. "Sorry it has to be under these circumstances." She held out both wrists with a sigh. "Want to handcuff me?"

He pursed his lips and his black eyes twinkled unexpectedly. He didn't look like a man who knew what humor was. "Isn't that a little kinky for a conversation? What sort of men *are* you used to?"

She hesitated for just a second before she burst out laughing. He wasn't at all the man he appeared to be. She put her hands down.

"I was speeding," she reminded him.

"Yes, you were. But since you don't have a rap sheet, you can have a warning, just this once," he added firmly. "The speed limit is posted. It's fifty on all county roads."

She peered up at him. "This is a *county* road?" she emphasized, which meant that he was out of his enforcement area.

Nodding, he grinned. "And you're right, I don't have any jurisdiction out here, so that's why you're getting a warning and a smile." The smile faded. "In town, you'll get a ticket and a heavy scowl. Remember that."

"I will. Honest." She wiped at her eyes again. "I got a little upset, but I shouldn't have taken it out on the road. I'm sorry. I won't do it again."

"See that you don't." His dark eyes narrowed as if in memory. "Accidents are messy. Very messy."

"Thanks for being so nice."

He shrugged. "Everybody slips once in a while."

"That's exactly what I did..."

"I didn't mean you," he interrupted. His lean face took on a faintly dangerous cast. "I'm not nice. Not ever."

She was intimidated by that expression. "Oh."

He wagged a finger at her nose. "Don't speed."

She put a hand over her heart. "Never again. I promise."

He nodded, walked elegantly to his squad car and drove toward town. Janie sat quietly for a minute, getting herself back together. Then she started the car and went home, making up an apology for her father about his gloves without telling him the real reason she'd come home without them. He said he'd get a new pair the next day himself, no problem.

Janie cried herself to sleep in a miserable cocoon of shattered dreams.

As luck would have it, Harley Fowler, Cy Parks's foreman, came by in one of the ranch pickup trucks the very next morning and pulled up to the back door when he saw Janie walk out dressed for riding and wearing a broad-brimmed hat. Harley's boss Cy did business with Fred Brewster, and Harley was a frequent visitor to the ranch. He and Janie were friendly. They teased and played like two kids when they were together.

"I've been looking for you," Harley said with a grin as he paused just in front of her. "The Cattleman's Ball is Saturday night and I want to go, but I don't have a date. I know it's late to be asking, but how about going with me? Unless you've got a date or you're going with your dad…?" he added.

She grinned back. "I haven't got a date, and Dad's away on business and has to miss the ball this year. But I do have a pretty new dress that I'm dying to wear! I'd love to go with you, Harley!"

"Really?" His lean face lit up. He knew Janie was sweet on Leo Hart, but it was rumored that he was avoiding her like measles these days. Harley wasn't in love with Janie, but he genuinely liked her.

"Really," Janie replied. "What time will you pick me up?"

"About six-thirty," he said. "It doesn't start until seven, but I like to be on time."

"That makes two of us. I'll be ready. Thanks, Harley!"

"Thank you!" he said. "See you Saturday."

He was off in a cloud of dust, waving his hand out the window as he pulled out of the yard. Janie sighed with relief. She wanted nothing more in the world than to go to that dance and show Leo Hart how wrong he was about her chasing him. Harley was young and nice looking. She liked him. She would go and have a good time. Leo would be able to see for himself that he was off the endangered list, and he could make a safe bet that Janie would never go near him again without a weapon! As she considered it, she smiled coldly. Revenge was petty, but after the hurt she'd endured at Leo's hands, she felt entitled to a little of it. He was never going to forget this party. Never, as long as he lived.

# *Chapter Three*

The annual Jacobsville Cattleman's Ball was one of the newer social events of the year. It took place the Saturday before Thanksgiving like clockwork. Every cattleman for miles around made it a point to attend, even if he avoided all other social events for the year. The Ballenger brothers, Calhoun and Justin, had just added another facility to their growing feedlot enterprise, and they looked prosperous with their wives in gala attire beside them. The Tremayne brothers, Connal, Evan, Harden, and Donald, and their wives were also in attendance, as were the Hart boys; well, Corrigan, Callaghan, Rey and Leo at least, and their wives. Simon and Tira didn't attend many local events except the brothers' annual Christmas party on the ranch.

Also at the ball were Micah Steele, Eb Scott, J. D. Langley, Emmett Deverell, Luke Craig, Guy Fenton, Ted Regan, Jobe Dodd, Tom Walker and their wives. The guest list read like a who's who of Jacobsville, and there were so many people that the organizers had rented the community center for it. There was a live country-western band, a buffet table that could have fed a platoon of starving men, and enough liquor to drown a herd of horses.

Leo had a highball. Since he hadn't done much drinking in recent years, his four brothers were giving him strange looks. He didn't notice. He was feeling so miserable that even a hangover would have been an improvement.

Beside him, Marilee was staring around the room with wide, wary eyes.

"Looking for somebody?" Leo asked absently.

"Yes," she replied. "Janie said she wasn't coming, but that isn't what your sister-in-law Tess just told me."

"What did she say?"

Marilee looked worried. "Harley Fowler told her he was bringing Janie."

"Harley?" Leo scowled. Harley Fowler was a courageous young man who'd actually backed up the town's infamous mercenaries—Eb Scott, Cy Parks and Micah Steele—when they helped law enforcement face down a gang of drug dealers the year before. Harley's name hadn't been coupled with any of the local belles, and he was only a working-class cowboy. Janie's father might be financially pressed at the moment, but his was a founding family of Jacobsville, and the family had plenty of prestige. Fred and his sister-in-law Lydia would be picky about who Janie married. Not, he thought firmly, that Janie was going to be marrying Harley....

"Harley's nice," Marilee murmured. "He's Cy Parks's head foreman now, and everybody says he's got what it takes to run a business of his own." What Marilee didn't add was that Harley had asked her out several times before his raid on the drug lord with the local mercenaries, and she'd turned him down flat. She'd thought he bragged and strutted a little too much, that he was too immature for her. She'd even told him so. It had made her a bitter enemy of his.

Now she was rather sorry that she hadn't given him a

chance. He really was different these days, much more mature and very attractive. Not that Leo wasn't a dish. But she felt so guilty about Janie that she couldn't even enjoy his company, much less the party. If Janie showed up and saw her with Leo, she was going to know everything. It wasn't conducive to a happy evening at all.

"What's wrong?" Leo asked when he saw her expression.

"Janie's never going to get over it if she shows up and sees me with you," she replied honestly. "I didn't think how it would look..."

"I don't belong to anybody," Leo said angrily. "It's just as well to let Janie know that. So what if she does show up? Who cares?"

"I do," Marilee sighed.

Just as she spoke, Janie came in the door with a tall, good-looking, dark-haired man in a dark suit with a ruffled white shirt and black bow tie. Janie had just taken off her black velvet coat and hung it on the rack near the door. Under it, she was wearing a sexy white silk gown that fell softly down her slender figure to her shapely ankles. The spaghetti strips left her soft shoulders almost completely bare, and dipped low enough to draw any man's eyes. She was wearing her thick, light brown hair down. It reached almost to her waist in back in a beautiful, glossy display. She wore just enough makeup to enhance her face, and she was clinging to Harley's arm with obvious pleasure as they greeted the Ballengers and their wives.

Leo had forgotten how pretty Janie could look when she worked at it. Lately, he'd only seen her covered in mud and flour. Tonight, her figure drew eyes in that dress. He remembered the feel of her in his arms, the eager innocence of her mouth under his, and he suddenly felt uneasy at the way she was clinging to Harley's arm.

If he was uncomfortable, Marilee was even more so. She stood beside Leo and looked as if she hated herself. He took another long sip of his drink before he guided her toward Harley and Janie.

"No sense hiding, is there?" he asked belligerently.

Marilee sighed miserably. "No sense at all, I guess."

They moved forward together. Janie noticed them and her eyes widened and darkened with pain for an instant. Leo's harsh monologue at the hardware store had been enough to wound her, but now she was seeing that she'd been shafted by her best friend, as well. Marilee said Janie didn't know her date, but all along, apparently, she'd planned to come with Leo. No wonder she'd been so curious about whether or not Janie was going to show up.

Everything suddenly made perfect sense. Marilee had filled Leo up with lies about Janie gossiping about him, so that she could get him herself. Janie felt like an utter fool. Her chin lifted, but she didn't smile. Her green eyes were like emerald shards as they met Marilee's.

"H...hi, Janie," Marilee stammered, forcing a smile. "You said you weren't coming tonight."

"I wasn't," Janie replied curtly. "But Harley was at a loose end and didn't have a date, so he asked me." She looked up at the tall, lean man beside her, who was some years younger than Leo, and she smiled at him with genuine affection even through her misery. "I haven't danced in years."

"You'll dance tonight, darlin'," Harley drawled, smiling warmly as he gripped her long fingers in his. He looked elegant in his dinner jacket, and there was a faint arrogance in his manner now that hadn't been apparent before. He glanced at Marilee and there was barely veiled contempt in the look.

Marilee swallowed hard and avoided his piercing gaze.

"I didn't know you could dance, Harley," Marilee murmured, embarrassed.

He actually ignored her, his narrow gaze going to Leo. "Nice turnout, isn't it?" he asked the older man.

''Nice,'' Leo said, but he didn't smile. ''I haven't seen your boss tonight.''

''The baby had a cold,'' Harley said. ''He and Lisa don't leave him when he's sick.'' He looked down at Janie deliberately. ''Considering how happy the two of them are, I guess marriage isn't such a bad vocation after all,'' he mused.

''For some, maybe,'' Leo said coldly. He was openly glaring at Harley.

''Let's get on the dance floor,'' Harley told Janie with a grin. ''I'm anxious to try out that waltz pattern I've been learning.''

''You'll excuse us, I'm sure,'' Janie told the woman who was supposed to be her best friend. Her eyes were icy as she realized how she'd been betrayed by Marilee's supposed ''help'' with Leo.

Marilee grimaced. ''Oh, Janie,'' she groaned. ''Let me explain....''

But Janie wasn't staying to listen to any halfhearted explanations. ''Nice to see you, Marilee. You, too, Mr. Hart,'' she added with coldly formal emphasis, not quite meeting Leo's eyes. But she noted the quick firming of his chiseled lips with some satisfaction at the way she'd addressed him.

''Why do you call him Mr. Hart?'' Harley asked as they moved away.

''He's much older than we are, Harley,'' she replied, just loudly enough for Leo to hear her and stiffen with irritation. ''Almost another generation.''

''I guess he is.''

Leo took a big swallow of his drink and glared after them.

''She'll never speak to me again,'' Marilee said in a subdued tone.

He glared at her. ''I'm not her personal property,'' he said flatly. ''I never was. It isn't your fault that she's been gossiping and spreading lies all over town.''

Marilee winced.

He turned his attention back to Janie, who was headed onto the dance floor with damned Harley. ''I don't want her. What the hell do I care if she likes Harley?''

The music changed to a quick, throbbing Latin beat. Matt Caldwell and his wife, Leslie, were out on the dance floor already, making everybody else look like rank beginners. Everybody clapped to the rhythm until the very end, when the couple left the dance floor. Leo thought nobody could top that display until Harley walked to the bandleader, and the band suddenly broke into a Strauss waltz. That was when Harley and Janie took the floor. Then, even Matt and Leslie stood watching with admiration.

Leo stared at the couple as if he didn't recognize them. Involuntarily, he moved closer to the dance floor to watch. He'd never seen two people move like that to music besides Matt and Leslie.

The rhythm was sweet, and the music had a sweeping beauty that Janie mirrored with such grace that it was like watching ballet. Harley turned and Janie followed every nuance of movement, her steps matching his exactly. Her eyes were laughing, like her pretty mouth, as they whirled around the dance floor in perfect unison.

Harley was laughing, too, enjoying her skill as much as she enjoyed his. They looked breathless, happy—young.

Leo finished his drink, wishing he'd added more whiskey and less soda. His dark eyes narrowed as they followed the couple around the dance floor as they kept time to the music.

''Aren't they wonderful?'' Marilee asked wistfully. ''I don't guess you dance?''

He did. But he wasn't getting on that floor and making a fool of himself with Marilee, who had two left feet and the sense of rhythm of a possum.

''I don't dance much,'' Leo replied tersely.

She sighed. ''It's just as well, I suppose. That would be a hard act to follow.''

''Yes.''

The music wound to a peak and suddenly ended, with Janie draped down Harley's side like a bolt of satin. His mouth was almost touching hers, and Leo had to fight not to go onto the floor and throw a punch at the younger man.

He blinked, surprised by his unexpected reaction. Janie was nothing to him. Why should he care what she did? Hadn't she bragged to everyone that he was taking her to this very dance? Hadn't she made it sound as if they were involved?

Janie and Harley left the dance floor to furious, genuine applause. Even Matt Caldwell and Leslie congratulated them on the exquisite piece of dancing. Apparently, Harley had been taking lessons, but Janie seemed to be a natural.

But the evening was still young, as the Latin music started up again and another unexpected couple took the floor. It was Cash Grier, the new assistant police chief, with young Christabel Gaines in his arms. Only a few people knew that Christabel had been married to Texas Ranger Judd Dunn since she was sixteen—a marriage on paper, only, to keep herself and her invalid mother from losing their family ranch. But she was twenty-one now, and the marriage must have been annulled, because there she was with Cash Grier, like a blond flame in his arms as he spun her around to the throbbing rhythm and she matched her steps to his expert ones.

Unexpectedly, as the crowd clapped and kept time for them, handsome dark-eyed Judd Dunn himself turned up in evening dress with a spectacular redhead on his arm. Men's heads turned. The woman was a supermodel, internationally famous, who was involved at a film shoot out at Judd and Christabel's ranch. Gossip flew. Judd watched Christabel with Grier and glowered. The redhead said something to him, but he didn't appear to be listening. He watched the two dancers with a rigid posture and an expression more appropriate for a duel than a dance. Christabel ignored him.

''Who is that man with Christabel Gaines?'' Marilee asked Leo.

''Cash Grier. He used to be a Texas Ranger some years ago. They say he was in government service as well.''

Leo recalled that Grier had been working in San Antonio with the district attorney's office before he took the position of assistant police chief in Jacobsville. There was a lot of talk about Grier's mysterious past. The man was an enigma, and people walked wide around him in Jacobsville.

''He's dishy, isn't he? He dances a *paso doble* even better than Matt, imagine that!'' Marilee said aloud. ''Of course, Harley does a magnificent waltz. Who would ever have thought he'd turn out to be such a sexy, mature man...''

Leo turned on his heel and left Marilee standing by herself, stunned. He walked back to the drinks table with eyes that didn't really see. The dance floor had filled up again, this time with a slow dance. Harley was holding Janie far too close, and she was letting him. Leo remembered what he'd said about her in the hardware store, and her wounded expression, and he filled another glass with whiskey. This time he didn't add soda. He shouldn't have felt bad, of course. Janie shouldn't have been so possessive. She shouldn't have gossiped about him...

''Hi, Leo,'' his sister-in-law Tess, said with a smile as she joined him, reaching for a clear soft drink.

''No booze, huh?'' he asked with a grin, noting her choice.

''I don't want to set a bad example for my son,'' she teased, because she and Cag had a little boy now. ''Actually, I can't hold liquor. But don't tell anybody,'' she added. ''I'm the wife of a tough ex-Special Forces guy. I'm supposed to be a real hell-raiser.''

He smiled genuinely. ''You are,'' he teased. ''A lesser

woman could never have managed my big brother and an albino python all at once.''

''Herman the python's living with his own mate these days,'' she reminded him with a grin, ''and just between us, I don't really miss him!'' She glanced toward her husband and sighed. ''I'm one lucky woman.''

''He's one lucky man.'' He took a sip of his drink and she frowned.

''Didn't you bring Marilee?'' she asked.

He nodded. ''Her wrist was still bothering her too much to drive, so I let her come with me. I've been chauffeuring her around ever since she sprained it.''

Boy, men were dense, Tess was thinking. As if a woman couldn't drive with only one hand. She glanced past him at Marilee, who was standing by herself watching as a new rhythm began and Janie moved onto the floor with Harley Fowler. ''I thought she was Janie's best friend,'' she mentioned absently. ''You can never tell about people.''

''What do you mean?''

She shrugged. ''I overheard her telling someone that Janie had been spreading gossip about you and her all over town.'' She shook her head. ''That's not true. Janie's so shy, it's hard for her to even talk to most men. I've never heard her gossip about anyone, even people she dislikes. I can't imagine why Marilee would tell lies about her.''

''Janie told everybody I was bringing her to the ball,'' he insisted with a scowl.

''Marilee told people that Janie said that,'' Tess corrected. ''You really don't know, do you? Marilee's crazy about you. She had to cut Janie out of the picture before she could get close to you. I guess she found the perfect way to do it.''

Leo started to speak, but he hesitated. That couldn't be true.

Tess read his disbelief and just smiled. ''You don't believe me, do you? It doesn't matter. You'll find out the truth sooner or later, whether you want to or not. I've got to find Cag. See you later!''

Leo watched her walk away with conflicting emotions. He didn't want to believe—he *wouldn't* believe—that he'd been played for a sucker. He'd seen Janie trying to become a cattleman with his own eyes, trying to compete with him. He knew that she wanted him because she'd tried continually to tempt him when he went to visit her father. She flirted shamelessly with him. She'd melted in his arms, melted under the heat of his kisses. She hadn't made a single protest at the intimate way he'd held her. She felt possessive of him, and he couldn't really blame her, because it was his own lapse of self-control that had given her the idea that he wanted her. Maybe he did, physically, but Janie was a novice and he didn't seduce innocents. Her father was a business associate. It certainly wouldn't be good business to cut his own throat with Fred by making a casual lover of Janie.

He finished the whiskey and put the glass down. He felt light-headed. That was what came of drinking when he hadn't done it in a long time. This was stupid. He had to stop behaving like an idiot just because Fred Brewster's little girl had cut him dead in the receiving line and treated him like an old man. He forced himself to walk normally, but he almost tripped over Cag on the way.

His brother caught him by the shoulders. ''Whoa, there,'' he said with a grin. ''You're wobbling.''

Leo pulled himself up. ''That whiskey must be 200 proof,'' he said defensively.

''No. You're just not used to it. Leave your car here when it's time to go,'' he added firmly. ''Tess and I will drop Marilee off and take you home. You're in no fit state to drive.''

Leo sighed heavily. ''I guess not. Stupid thing to do.''

''What, drinking or helping Marilee stab Janie in the back?''

Leo's eyes narrowed on his older brother's lean, hard face. "Does Tess tell you everything?"

He shrugged. "We're married."

"If I ever get married," Leo told him, "my wife isn't going to tell anybody anything. She's going to keep her mouth shut."

"Not much danger of your getting married, with that attitude," Cag mused.

Leo squared his shoulders. "Marilee looks really great tonight," he pointed out.

"She looks pretty sick to me," Cag countered, eyeing the object of their conversation, who was standing alone against the opposite wall, trying to look invisible. "She should, too, after spreading that gossip around town about Janie chasing you."

"Janie did that, not Marilee," Leo said belligerently. "She didn't have any reason to make it sound like we were engaged, just because I kissed her."

Cag's eyebrows lifted. "You kissed her?"

"It wasn't much of a kiss," Leo muttered gruffly. "She's so green, it's pathetic!"

"She won't stay that way long around Harley," Cag chuckled. "He's no playboy, but women love him since he helped our local mercs take on that drug lord Manuel Lopez and won. I imagine he'll educate Janie."

Leo's dark eyes narrowed angrily. He hated the thought of Harley kissing her. He really should do something about that. He blinked, trying to focus his mind on the problem.

"Don't trip over the punch bowl," Cag cautioned dryly. "And for God's sake, don't try to dance. The gossips would have a field day for sure!"

"I could dance if I wanted to," Leo informed him.

Cag leaned down close to his brother's ear. "Don't 'want to.' Trust me." He turned and went back to Tess, smiling as he led her onto the dance floor.

Leo joined Marilee against the wall.

She glanced at him and grimaced. "I've just become the Bubonic Plague," she said with a miserable sigh. "Joe Howland from the hardware store is here with his wife," she added uncomfortably. "He's telling people what you said to Janie and that I was responsible for her getting the rough side of your tongue."

He glanced down at her. "How is it your fault?"

She looked at her shoes instead of at him. She felt guilty and hurt and ashamed. "I sort of told Janie that you said you'd like her better if she could ride and rope and make biscuits, and stop dressing up all the time."

He stiffened. He felt the jolt all the way to his toes. "You told her that?"

"I did." She folded her arms over her breasts and stared toward Janie, who was dancing with Harley and apparently having a great time. "There's more," she added, steeling herself to admit it. "It wasn't exactly true that she was telling people you were taking her to this dance."

"Marilee, for God's sake! Why did you lie?" he demanded.

"She's just a kid, Leo," she murmured uneasily. "She doesn't know beans about men or real life, she's been protected and pampered, she's got money, she's pretty...." She moved restlessly. "I like you a lot. I'm older, more mature. I thought, if she was just out of the picture for a little bit, you...you might start to like me."

Now he understood the look on Janie's face when he'd made those accusations. Tess was right. Marilee had lied. She'd stabbed her best friend in the back, and he'd helped her do it. He felt terrible.

"You don't have to tell me what a rat I am," she continued, without looking up at him. "I must have been crazy to think Janie wouldn't eventually find out that I was lying about her." She managed to meet his angry eyes. "She never gossiped about you, Leo. She wanted you to take her to this party so much that it was all she talked about for weeks. But she never told anybody you were going to. She thought I was helping her by hinting that she'd like you to ask her.'' She laughed coldly. ''She was the best friend I ever had, and I've stabbed her in the back. She'll never speak to me again after tonight, and I deserve whatever I get. For what it's worth, I'm really sorry.''

Leo was still trying to adjust to the truth. He could talk himself blue in the face, but Janie would never listen to him now. He was going to be about as welcome as a fly at her house from now on, especially if Fred found out what Leo had said to and about her. It would damage their friendship. It had already killed whatever feeling Janie had for him. He knew that without the wounded, angry glances she sent his way from time to time.

''You said you didn't want her chasing you,'' Marilee reminded him weakly, trying to find one good thing to say.

''No danger of that from now on, is there?'' he agreed, biting off the words.

''None at all. So a little good came out of it.''

He looked down at her with barely contained anger. ''How could you do that to her?''

''I don't even know.'' She sighed raggedly. ''I must have been temporarily out of my mind.'' She moved away from the wall. ''I wonder if you'd mind driving me home? I…I really don't want to stay any longer.''

''I can't drive. Cag's taking us home.''

''You can't drive? Why?'' she exclaimed.

''I think the polite way of saying it is that I'm stinking drunk,'' he said with glittery eyes blazing down at her.

She grimaced. No need to ask why he'd gotten that way. ''Sorry,'' she said inadequately.

''You're sorry. I'm sorry. It doesn't change anything.'' He looked toward Janie, conscious of new and painful regrets. It all made sense now, her self-improvement campaign. She'd been dragged through mud, thrown from horses, bruised and battered in a valiant effort to become what she thought Leo wanted her to be.

He winced. ‘‘She could have killed herself,’’ he said huskily. ‘‘She hadn’t been on a horse in ages or worked around cattle.’’ He looked down at Marilee with a black scowl. ‘‘Didn’t you realize that?’’

‘‘I wasn’t thinking at the time,’’ Marilee replied. ‘‘I’ve always worked around the ranch, because I had to. I never thought of Janie being in any danger. But I guess she was, at that. At least she didn’t get hurt.’’

‘‘That’s what you think,’’ Leo muttered, remembering how she’d looked at the hardware store.

Marilee shrugged and suddenly burst into tears. She dashed toward the ladies’ room to hide them.

At the same time, Harley left Janie at the buffet table and went toward the rest rooms himself.

Leo didn’t even think. He walked straight up to Janie and caught her by the hand, pulling her along with him.

‘‘What do you think you’re doing?’’ she raged. ‘‘Let go of me!’’

He ignored her. He led her right out the side door and onto the stone patio surrounded by towering plants that, in spring, were glorious in blossom. He pulled the glass door closed behind him and moved Janie off behind one of the plants.

‘‘I want to talk to you,’’ he began, trying to get his muddled mind to work.

She pulled against his hands. ‘‘I don’t want to talk to you!’’ she snapped. ‘‘You go right back in there to your date, Leo Hart! You brought Marilee, not me!’’

‘‘I want to tell you…’’ he tried again.

She aimed a kick at his shin that almost connected.

He sidestepped, overbalancing her so that she fell heavily against him. She felt good in his arms, warm, delicate and sweetly scented. His breath caught at the feel of her soft skin under his hands where the dress was low-cut in back.

"Harley will...be missing me!" she choked.

"Damn Harley," he murmured huskily and the words went into her mouth as he bent and took it hungrily.

His arms swallowed her, warm under the dark evening suit, where her hands rested just at his rib cage. His mouth was ardent, insistent, on her parted lips.

He forced them apart, nipping the upper one with his teeth while his hands explored the softness of her skin. He was getting drunk on her perfume. He felt himself going taut as he registered the hunger he was feeling to get her even closer. It wasn't enough....

His hands went to her hips and jerked them hard into the thrust of his big body, so that she could feel how aroused he was.

She stiffened and then tried to twist away, frantic at the weakness he was making her feel. He couldn't do this. She couldn't let him do it. He was only making a point, showing her that she couldn't resist him. He didn't even like her anymore. He'd brought her best friend to the most talked-about event in town!

"You...let me go!" she sobbed, tearing her mouth from his. "I hate you, Leo Hart!"

He was barely able to breathe, much less think, but he wasn't letting go. His eyes glittered down at her. "You don't hate me," he denied. "You want me. You tremble every time I get within a foot of you. It's so noticeable a blind man couldn't mistake it." He pulled her close, watching her face as her thighs touched his. "A woman's passion arouses a man's," he whispered roughly. "You made me want you."

"You said I made you sick," she replied, her voice choking on the word.

"You do." His lips touched her ear. "When a man is this aroused, and can't satisfy the hunger, it makes him sick," he said huskily, with faint insolence. He dragged her hips against his roughly. "Feel that? You've got me so hot

I can't even think...!'' Leo broke off abruptly as Janie stomped on his foot.

''Does that help?'' she asked while he was hobbling on the foot her spiked heel hadn't gone into.

She moved back from him, shaking with desire and anger, while he cursed roundly and without inhibition.

''That's what you get for making nasty remarks to women!'' she said furiously. ''You don't want me! You said so! You want Marilee. That's why you're taking her around with you. Remember me? I'm that gossiping pest who runs after you everywhere. Except that I'll never do it again, you can bet your life on that! I wouldn't have you on ice cream!''

He stood uneasily on both feet, glaring at her. ''Sure you would,'' he said with a venomous smile. His eyes glittered like a diamondback uncoiling. ''Just now, I could have had you in the rosebushes. You'd have done anything I wanted.''

He was right. That was what hurt the most. She pushed back her disheveled hair with a trembling hand. ''Not anymore,'' she said, feeling sick. ''Not when I know what you really think of me.''

''Harley brought you,'' he said coldly. ''He's a boy playing at being a man.''

''He's closer to my age than you are, Mr. Hart!'' she shot back.

His face hardened and he took a quick step toward her.

''That's what you've said from the start,'' she reminded him, near tears. ''I'm just a kid, you said. I'm just a kid with a crush, just your business associate's pesky daughter.''

He'd said that. He must have been out of his mind. Looking at her now, with that painful maturity in her face, he couldn't believe he'd said any such thing. She was all woman. And she was with Harley. Damn Harley!

''Don't worry, I won't tell Dad that you tried to seduce

me on the patio with your new girlfriend standing right inside the room,'' she assured him. ''But if you ever touch me again, I'll cripple you, so help me God!''

She whirled and jerked open the patio door, slamming it behind her as she moved through the crowd toward the buffet table.

Leo stood alone in the cold darkness with a sore foot, wondering why he hadn't kept his mouth shut. If a bad situation could get worse, it just had.

# *Chapter Four*

Janie and Harley were back on the dance floor by the time Leo made his way inside, favoring his sore foot.

Marilee was standing at the buffet table, looking as miserable as he felt.

"Harley just gave me hell," she murmured tightly as he joined her. "He said I was lower than a snake's belly, and it would serve me right if Janie never spoke to me again." She looked up at him with red-rimmed eyes. "Do you think your brother would mind dropping us off now? He could come right back..."

"I'll ask him," Leo said, sounding absolutely fed up.

He found Cag talking to Corrigan and Rey at the buffet table. Their wives were in another circle, talking to each other.

"Could you run Marilee home now and drop me off on the way back?" he asked Cag in a subdued tone.

Corrigan gaped at him. "You've never left a dance until the band packed up."

Leo sighed. "There's a first time for everything."

The women joined them. Cag tugged Tess close. ''I have to run Leo and Marilee home.''

Tess's eyebrows went up. ''Now? Why so early?''

Leo glared. His brothers cleared their throats.

''Never mind,'' Cag said quickly. ''I won't be a minute...''

''Rey and I would be glad to do it...'' Meredith volunteered, with a nod from her husband.

''No need,'' Dorie said with a smile, cuddling close to her husband. ''Corrigan can run Leo and Marilee home and come right back. Can't you, sweetheart?'' she added.

''Sure I can,'' he agreed, lost in her pretty eyes.

''But you two don't usually leave until the band does, either,'' Leo pointed out. ''You'll miss most of the rest of the dance if you drive us.''

Corrigan pursed his lips. ''Oh, we've done our dancing for the night. Haven't we, sweetheart?'' he prompted.

Dorie's eyes twinkled. She nodded. ''Indeed we have! I'll just catch up on talk until he comes back. We can have the last dance together. Don't give it a thought, Leo.''

Leo was feeling the liquor more with every passing minute, but he was feeling all sorts of undercurrents. The women looked positively gleeful. His brothers were exchanging strange looks.

Corrigan looked past Leo to Cag and Rey. ''You can all come by our house after the dance,'' he promised.

''What for?'' Leo wanted to know, frowning suspiciously.

Corrigan hesitated and Cag scowled.

Rey cleared his throat. ''Bull problems,'' he said finally, with a straight face. ''Corrigan's advising me.''

''He's advising me, too,'' Cag said with a grin. ''He's advising both of us.''

All three of them looked guilty as hell. ''I know more about bulls than Corrigan does,'' Leo pointed out. ''Why don't you ask me?''

''Because you're in a hurry to go home,'' Corrigan improvised. ''Let's go.''

Leo went to get Marilee. She said a subdued, hurried goodbye to Cag and Rey and then their wives. Leo waited patiently, vaguely aware that Cag and Rey were standing apart, talking in hushed whispers. They were both staring at Leo.

As Marilee joined him, Leo began to get the idea. Corrigan had sacrificed dancing so that he could pump Leo for gossip and report back to the others. They knew he was drinking, which he never did, and they'd probably seen him hobble back into the room. Then he'd wanted to leave early. It didn't take a mind reader to put all that together. Something had happened, and his brothers—not to mention their wives—couldn't wait to find out what. He glared at Corrigan, but his brother only grinned.

''Let's go, Marilee,'' Leo said, catching her by the arm.

She gave one last, hopeful glance at Janie, but was pointedly ignored. She followed along with Leo until the music muted to a whisper behind them.

When Marilee had been dropped off, and they were alone in the car, Corrigan glanced toward his brother with mischievous silvery eyes and pursed his lips.

''You're limping.''

Leo huffed. ''You try walking normally when some crazy woman's tried to put her heel through your damned boot!''

''Marilee stepped on you?'' Corrigan said much too carelessly.

''Janie stepped on me, on purpose!''

''What were you doing to her at the time?''

Leo actually flushed. It was visible in the streetlight they stopped under waiting for a red light to change on the highway.

''Well!'' Corrigan exclaimed with a knowing expression.

''She started it,'' he defended himself angrily. ''All these months, she's been dressing to the hilt and waylaying me every time I went to see her father. She damned near seduced me on the cooking table in her kitchen last month, and then she goes and gets on her high horse because I said a few little things I shouldn't have when she was eavesdropping!''

''You said a lot of little things,'' his brother corrected. ''And from what I hear, she left town in a dangerous rush and had to be slowed down by our new assistant chief. In fact, you called and asked him to do it. Good thinking.''

''Who told you that?'' Leo demanded.

Corrigan grinned. ''Our new assistant chief.''

''Grier can keep his nose out of my business or I'll punch it for him!''

''He's got problems of his own, or didn't you notice him step outside with Judd Dunn just before we left?'' Corrigan whistled softly. ''Christabel may think she's her own woman, but Judd doesn't act like any disinterested husband I ever saw.''

''He's got a world famous model on his arm,'' Leo pointed out.

''It didn't make a speck of difference once he saw Christabel on that dance floor with Grier. He was ready to make a scene right there.'' He glanced at Leo. ''And *he* wasn't drinking,'' he emphasized.

''I am not jealous of Janie Brewster,'' Leo told him firmly.

''Tell that to Harley. He had to be persuaded not to go after you when Janie came back inside in tears,'' Corrigan added, letting slip what he'd overheard.

That made it worse. ''Harley can mind his own damned business, too!''

''He is. He likes Janie.''

''Janie's not going to fall for some wet-behind-the-ears would-be world-saver,'' Leo raged.

"He's kind to her. He teases her and picks at her. He treats her like a princess." He gave his brother a wry glance. "I'll bet he wouldn't try to seduce her in the rose-bushes."

"I didn't! Anyway, there weren't any damned rose-bushes out there."

"How do you know that?"

Leo sighed heavily. "Because if there had been, I'd be wearing them."

Corrigan chuckled. Having had his own problems with the course of true love, he could sympathize with his brother. Sadly, Leo had never been in love. He'd had crushes, he'd had brief liaisons, but there had never been a woman who could stand him on his ear. Corrigan was as fascinated as their brothers with the sudden turn of events. Leo had tolerated Janie Brewster, been amused by her, but he'd never been involved enough to start a fight with her, much less sink two large whiskeys when he hardly even touched beer.

"She's got a temper, fancy that?" Corrigan drawled.

Leo sighed. "Marilee was telling lies," he murmured. "She said Janie had started all sorts of gossip about us. I'd kissed her, and liked it, and I was feeling trapped. I thought the kiss gave her ideas. And all the time… Damn!" he ground out. "Tess knew. She told me that Marilee had made up the stories, and I wouldn't listen."

"Tess is sharp as a tack," his older brother remarked.

"I'm as dull as a used nail," Leo replied. "I don't even know when a woman is chasing me. I thought Janie was. And all the time, it was her best friend Marilee." He shook his head. "Janie said I was the most conceited man she ever met. Maybe I am." He glanced out the window at the silhouettes of buildings they passed in the dark. "She likes Harley. That would have been funny a few months ago, but he keeps impressive company these days."

"Harley's matured. Janie has, too. I thought she handled

herself with dignity tonight, when she saw you with Marilee.'' He chuckled. ''Tira would have emptied the punch bowl over her head,'' he mused, remembering his redheaded sister-in-law's temper.

''Simon would have been outraged,'' he added. ''He hates scenes. You're a lot like him,'' he said unexpectedly, glancing at the younger man. ''You can cut up, but you're as somber as a judge when you're not around us. Especially since we've all married.''

''I'm lonely,'' Leo said simply. ''I've had the house to myself since Rey married Meredith and moved out, almost a year ago. Mrs. Lewis retired. I've got no biscuits, no company…''

''You've got Marilee,'' he was reminded.

''Marilee sprained her wrist. She's needed me to drive her places,'' Leo said drowsily.

''Marilee could drive with one hand. I drove with a broken arm once.''

Leo didn't respond. They were driving up to the main ranch house, into the driveway that made a semicircle around the front steps. The security lights were on, so was the porch light. But even with lights on in the front rooms of the sprawling brick house, it looked empty.

''You could come and stay with any of us, whenever you wanted to,'' Corrigan reminded him. ''We only live a few miles apart.''

''You've all got families. Children. Well, except Meredith and Rey.''

''They're not in a hurry. Rey's the youngest. The rest of us are feeling our ages a bit more.''

''Hell,'' Leo growled, ''you're only two years older than me.''

''You're thirty-five,'' he was reminded. ''I'll be thirty-eight in a couple of months.''

''You don't look it.''

''Dorie and the babies keep me young,'' Corrigan admitted with a warm smile. ‘‘Marriage isn’t as bad as you think it is. You have someone to cook for you, a companion to share your sorrows when the world hits you in the head, and your triumphs when you punch back. Not to mention having a warm bed at night.’’

Leo opened the door but hesitated. ‘‘I don’t want to get married.’’

Corrigan’s pale eyes narrowed. ‘‘Dorie was just a little younger than Janie when I said the same thing to her. I mistook her for an experienced woman, made a very heavy pass, and then said some insulting things to her when she pulled back at the last minute. I sent her running for the nearest bus, and my pride stopped me from carrying her right back off it again. She went away. It was eight long years before she came home, before I was able to start over with her.’’ His face hardened. ‘‘You know what those years were like for me.’’

Leo did. It was painful even to recall them. ‘‘You never told me why she left.’’

Corrigan rested his arm over the steering wheel. ‘‘She left because I behaved like an idiot.’’ He glanced at his brother. ‘‘I don’t give a damn what Marilee’s told you about Janie, she isn’t any more experienced than Dorie was. Don’t follow in my footsteps.’’

Leo wouldn’t meet the older man’s eyes. ‘‘Janie’s a kid.’’

‘‘She’ll grow up. She’s making a nice start, already.’’

Leo brushed back his thick, unruly hair. ‘‘I was way out of line with her tonight. She said she never wanted to see me again.’’

‘‘Give her time.’’

‘‘I don’t care if she doesn’t want to see me,’’ Leo said belligerently. ‘‘What the hell do I want with a mud-covered little tomboy, anyway? She can’t even cook!’’

‘‘Neither can Tira,’’ Corrigan pointed out. ‘‘But she’s a

knockout in an evening gown. So is our Janie, even if she isn't as pretty as Marilee."

Leo shrugged. "Marilee's lost a good friend."

"She has. Janie won't ever trust her again, even if she can forgive her someday."

Leo glanced back at his older brother. "Isn't it amazing how easy it is to screw up your whole life in a few unguarded minutes?"

"That's life, *compadre.* I've got to go. You going to be okay?"

Leo nodded. "Thanks for the ride." He glowered at Corrigan. "I guess you're in a hurry to get back, right?"

Corrigan's eyes twinkled. "I don't want to miss the last dance!"

Or the chance to tell his brothers everything that had happened. But, what the hell, they were family.

"Drive safely," Leo told Corrigan as he closed the car door.

"I always do." Corrigan threw up his hand and drove away.

Leo disarmed the alarm system and unlocked the front door, pausing to relock it and rearm the system. He'd been the victim of a mugging last October in Houston, and it had been Rey's new wife, Meredith, who had saved him from no worse than a concussion. But now he knew what it was to be a victim of violent crime, and he was much more cautious than he'd ever been before.

He tossed his keys on his chest of drawers and took off his jacket and shoes. Before he could manage the rest, he passed out on his own bed.

Janie Brewster was very quiet on the way home. Harley understood why. He and Janie weren't an item, but he hated seeing a woman cry. He'd wanted, very badly, to punch Leo Hart for that.

"You should have let me hit him, Janie," he remarked thoughtfully.

She gave him a sad little smile. "There's been enough gossip already, although I appreciate the thought."

"He was drinking pretty heavily," Harley added. "I noticed that one of his brothers took him and Marilee home early. Nice of him to find a designated driver, in that condition. He looked as if he was barely able to walk without staggering."

Janie had seen them leave, with mixed emotions. She turned her small evening bag in her lap. "I didn't know he drank hard liquor at all."

"He doesn't," Harley replied. "Eb Scott said that he'd never known Leo to take anything harder than a beer in company." He glanced at her. "That must have been some mixer you had with him."

"He'd been drinking before we argued," she replied. She looked out the darkened window. "Odd that Marilee left with him."

"You didn't see the women snub her, I guess," he murmured. "Served her right, I thought." His eyes narrowed angrily as he made the turn that led to her father's ranch. "It's low to stab a friend in the back like that. Whatever her feelings for Hart, she should have put your feelings first."

"I thought you liked her, Harley."

He stiffened. "I asked her out once, and she laughed."

"What?"

He stared straight ahead at the road, the center of which was lit by the powerful headlights of the truck he was driving. "She thought it was hilarious that I had the nerve to ask her to go on a date. She said I was too immature."

Ouch, she thought. A man like Harley would have too much pride to ever go near a woman who'd dented his ego that badly.

He let out a breath. "The hell of it is, she was right,"

he conceded with a wry smile. ''I had my head in the clouds, bragging about my mercenary training. Then I went up against Lopez with Eb and Cy and Micah.'' He grimaced. ''I didn't have a clue.''

''We heard that it was a firefight.''

He nodded. His eyes were haunted. ''My only experience of combat was movies and television.'' His lean hands gripped the wheel hard. ''The real thing is less...comfortable. And that's all I'll say.''

''Thank you for taking me to the ball,'' she said, changing the subject because he'd looked so tormented.

His face relaxing, he glanced at her. ''It was my pleasure. I'm not ready to settle down, but I like you. Anytime you're at a loose end, we can see a movie or get a burger.''

She chuckled. ''I feel the same way. Thanks.''

He pursed his lips and gave her a teasing glance. ''We could even go dancing.''

''I liked waltzing.''

''I want to learn those Latin dances, like Caldwell and Grier.'' He whistled. ''Imagine Grier doing Latin dances! Even Caldwell stood back and stared.''

''Mr. Grier is a conundrum,'' she murmured. ''Not the man he seems, on the surface.''

''How would you know?'' he asked.

She cleared her throat. ''He stopped me for speeding out on the Victoria road.''

''Good for him. You drive too fast.''

''Don't you start!''

He frowned. ''What was he doing out there? He doesn't have jurisdiction outside Jacobsville.''

''I don't know. But he's very pleasant.''

He hesitated. ''There's some, shall we say, unsavory gossip about him around town,'' he told her.

''Unsavory, how?'' she asked, curious.

''It's probably just talk.''

''Harley!''

He slowed for a turn. ''They say he was a government assassin at one point in his life.''

She whistled softly. ''You're kidding!''

He glanced at her. ''When I was in the Rangers, I flew overseas with a guy who was dressed all in black, armed to the teeth. He didn't say a word to the rest of us. I learned later that he was brought over for a very select assignment with the British commandos.''

''What has that got to do with Grier?''

''That's just the thing. I think it *was* Grier.''

She felt cold chills running up her arms.

''It was several years ago,'' he reiterated, ''and I didn't get a close look, but sometimes you can tell a man just by the way he walks, the way he carries himself.''

''You shouldn't tell anybody,'' she murmured, uneasy, because she liked Grier.

''I never would,'' Harley assured her. ''I told my boss, but nobody else. Grier isn't the sort of man you'd ever gossip about, even if half the things they tell are true.''

''There's more?'' she exclaimed.

He chuckled. ''He was in the Middle East helping pinpoint the laser-guided bombs, he broke up a spy ring in Manhattan as a company agent, he fought with the freedom fighters in Afghanistan, he foiled an assassination attempt against one of our own leaders under the nose of the agency assigned to protect them...you name it, he's done it. Including a stint with the Texas Rangers and a long career in law enforcement between overseas work.''

''A very interesting man,'' she mused.

''And intimidating to our local law enforcement guys. Interesting that Judd Dunn isn't afraid of him.''

''He's protective of Christabel,'' Janie told him. ''She's sweet. She was in my high school graduating class.''

''Judd's too old for her,'' Harley drawled. ''He's about Leo Hart's age, isn't he, and she's just a few months older than you.''

He was insinuating that Leo was too old for her. He was probably right, but it hurt to hear someone say it. Nor was she going to admit something else she knew about Christabel, that Judd had married the girl when she was just sixteen so that she wouldn't lose her home. Christabel was twenty-one and Judd had become her worst enemy.

"Sorry," Harley said when he noticed her brooding expression.

"About what?" she asked, diverted.

"I guess you think I meant Leo Hart's too old for you."

"He is," she said flatly.

He looked as if he meant to say more, but the sad expression on her face stopped him. He pulled into her driveway and didn't say another word until he stopped the truck at her front door.

"I know how you feel about the guy, Janie," he said then. "But you can want something too much. Hart isn't a marrying man, even if his brothers were. He's a bad risk."

She turned to face him, her eyes wide and eloquent. "I've told myself that a hundred times. Maybe it will sink in."

He grimaced. He traced a pattern on her cheek with a lean forefinger. "For what it's worth, I'm no stranger to unreturned feelings." He grimaced. "Maybe some of us just don't have the knack for romance."

"Speak for yourself," she said haughtily. "I have the makings of a Don Juanette, as Leo Hart is about to discover!"

He tapped her cheek gently. "Stop that. Running wild won't change anything, except to make you more miserable than you are."

She drew in a long breath. "You're right, of course. Oh, Harley, why can't we make people love us back?"

"Wish I knew," he said. He leaned forward and kissed her lightly on the lips. "I had fun. I'm sorry you didn't."

She smiled. "I did have fun. At least I didn't end up at the ball by myself, or with Dad, to face Leo and Marilee."

He nodded, understanding. "Where is your dad?"

"Denver," she replied on a sigh. "He's trying to interest a combine in investing in the ranch, but you can't tell anybody."

He scowled. "I didn't realize things were that bad."

She nodded. "They're pretty bad. Losing his prize bull was a huge financial blow. If Leo hadn't loaned him that breeding bull, I don't know what we'd have done. At least he likes Dad," she added softly.

It was Harley's opinion that he liked Fred Brewster's daughter, too, or he wouldn't have been putting away whiskey like that tonight. But he didn't say it.

"Can I help?" he asked instead.

She smiled at him. "You're so sweet, Harley. Thanks. But there's not much we can do without a huge grubstake. So," she added heavily, "I'm going to give up school and get a job."

"Janie!"

"College is expensive," she said simply. "Dad can't really afford it right now, and I'm not going to ask him to try. There's a job going at Shea's..."

"You can't work at Shea's!" Harley exclaimed. "Janie, it's a roadhouse! They serve liquor, and most nights there's a fight."

"They serve pizza and sandwiches, as well, and that's what the job entails," she replied. "I can handle it."

It disturbed Harley to think of an innocent, sweet girl like Janie in that environment. "There are openings at fast-food joints in town," he said.

"You don't get good tips at fast-food joints. Stop while you're ahead, Harley, you won't change my mind," she said gently.

"If you take the job, I'll stop in and check on you from time to time," he promised.

"You're a sweetheart, Harley," she said, and meant it. She kissed him on the cheek, smiled, and got out of the cab. "Thanks for taking me to the ball!"

"No sweat, Cinderella," he said with a grin. "I enjoyed it, too. Good night!"

"Good night," she called back.

She went inside slowly, locking the door behind her. Her steps dragging, she felt ten years older. It had been a real bust of an evening all around. She thought about Leo Hart and she hoped he had the king of hangovers the next morning!

The next day, Janie approached the manager of Shea's, a nice, personable man named Jed Duncan, about the job.

He read over her résumé while she sat in a leather chair across from his desk and bit her fingernails.

"Two years of college," he mused. "Impressive." His dark eyes met hers over the pages. "And you want to work in a bar?"

"Let me level with you," she said earnestly. "We're in financial trouble. My father can't afford to send me back to school, and I won't stand by and let him sink without trying to help. This job doesn't pay much, but the tips are great, from what Debbie Connor told me."

Debbie was her predecessor, and had told her about the job in the first place. Be honest with Jed, she'd advised, and lay it on the line about money. So Janie did.

He nodded slowly, studying her. "The tips are great," he agreed. "But the customers can get rowdy. Forgive me for being blunt, Miss Brewster, but you've had a sheltered upbringing. I have to keep a bouncer here now, ever since Calhoun Ballenger had it out with a customer over his ward—now his wife—and busted up the place. Not that Calhoun wasn't in the right," he added quickly. "But it became obvious that hot tempers and liquor don't mix, and you can't run a roadhouse on good intentions."

She swallowed. ''I can get used to anything, Mr. Duncan. I would really like this job.''

''Can you cook?''

She grinned. ''Two months ago, I couldn't. But I can now. I can even make biscuits!''

He chuckled. ''Okay, then, you should be able to make a pizza. We'll agree that you can work for two weeks and we'll see how it goes. You'll waitress and do some cooking. If you can cope, I'll let you stay. If not, or if you don't like the work, we'll call it quits. That suit you?''

She nodded. ''It suits me very well. Thank you!''

''Does your father know about this?'' he added.

She flushed. ''He will, when he gets home from Denver. I don't hide things from him.''

''It's not likely that you'll be able to hide this job from him,'' he mused with a chuckle. ''A lot of our patrons do business with him. I wouldn't like to make more enemies than I already have.''

''He won't mind,'' she assured him with a smile. She crossed her fingers silently.

''Then come along and I'll acquaint you with the job,'' Jed said, moving around the desk. ''Welcome aboard, Miss Brewster.''

She smiled. ''Thanks!''

## *Chapter Five*

Fred Brewster came home from Denver discouraged. ''I couldn't get anybody interested,'' he told Janie as he flopped down in his favorite easy chair in the living room. ''Everybody's got money problems, and the market is down. It's a bad time to fish for partners.''

Janie sat down on the sofa across from him. ''I got a job.''

He just stared at her for a minute, as if he didn't hear her. ''You what?''

''I got a job,'' she said, and smiled at him. ''I'll make good money in tips. I start tonight.''

''Where?'' he asked.

''A restaurant,'' she lied. ''You can even come and eat there, and I'll serve you. You won't have to tip me, either!''

''Janie,'' he groaned. ''I wanted you to go back and finish your degree.''

She leaned forward. ''Dad, let's be honest. You can't afford college right now, and if I went, it would have to be on work-study. Let me do this,'' she implored. ''I'm young and strong and I don't mind working. You'll pull out of this, Dad, I know you will!'' she added gently. ''Everybody has bad times. This is ours.''

He scowled. ''It hurts my pride...''

She knelt at his feet and leaned her arms over his thin, bony knees. ''You're my dad,'' she said. ''I love you. Your problems are my problems. You'll come up with an angle that will get us out of this. I don't have a single doubt.''

Those beautiful eyes that were so like his late wife's weakened his resolve. He smiled and touched her hair gently. ''You're like your mother.''

''Thanks!''

He chuckled. ''Okay. Do your waitress bit for a few weeks and I'll double my efforts on getting us out of hock. But no late hours,'' he emphasized. ''I want you home by midnight, period.''

That might be a problem. But why bother him with complications right now?

''We'll see how it goes,'' she said easily, getting to her feet. She planted a kiss on his forehead. ''I'd better get you some lunch!''

She dashed into the kitchen before he could ask any more questions about her new employment.

But she wasn't so lucky with Hettie. ''I don't like the idea of you working in a bar,'' she told Janie firmly.

*''Shhhh!''* Janie cautioned, glancing toward the open kitchen door. ''Don't let Dad hear you!''

Hettie grimaced. ''Child, you'll end up in a brawl, sure as God made little green apples!''

''I will not. I'm going to waitress and make pizzas and sandwiches, not get in fights.''

Hettie wasn't convinced. ''Put men and liquor together, and you get a fight every time.''

''Mr. Duncan has a bouncer,'' she confided. ''I'll be fine.''

''Mr. Hart won't like it,'' she replied.

''Nothing I do is any of Leo Hart's business anymore,''

Janie said with a glare. ''After the things he's said about me, his opinion wouldn't get him a cup of coffee around here!''

''What sort of things?'' Hettie wanted to know.

She rubbed her hands over the sudden chill of her arms. ''That I'm a lying, gossiping, man-chaser who can't leave him alone,'' she said miserably. ''He was talking about me to Joe Howland in the hardware store last week. I heard every horrible word.''

Hettie winced. She knew how Janie felt about the last of the unmarried Hart brothers. ''Oh, baby. I'm so sorry!''

''Marilee lied,'' she added sadly. ''My best friend! She was telling me what to do to make Leo notice me, and all the time she was finding ways to cut me out of his life. She was actually at the ball with Leo. He took her...'' She swallowed hard and turned to the task at hand. Brooding was not going to help her situation. ''Want a sandwich, Hettie?''

''No, darlin', I'm fine,'' the older woman told her. She hugged Janie warmly. ''Life's tangles work themselves out if you just give them enough time,'' she said, and went away to let that bit of homespun philosophy sink in.

Janie was unconvinced. Her tangles were bad ones. Maybe her new job would keep Leo out of her thoughts. At least she'd never have to worry about running into him at Shea's, she told herself. After Saturday night, he was probably off hard liquor for life.

By Saturday night, Janie had four days of work under her belt and she was getting used to the routine. Shea's opened at lunchtime and closed at eleven. Shea's served pizza and sandwiches and chips, as well as any sort of liquor a customer could ask for. Janie often had to serve drinks in between cooking chores. She got to recognize some of the customers on sight, but she didn't make a habit of speaking to them. She didn't want any trouble.

Her father had, inevitably, found out about her nocturnal activities. Saturday morning, he'd been raging at her for lying to him.

"I do work in a restaurant," she'd defended herself. "It's just sort of in a bar."

"You work in a bar, period!" he returned, furious. "I want you to quit, right now!"

It was now or never, she told herself, as she faced him bravely. "No," she replied quietly. "I'm not giving notice. Mr. Duncan said I could work two weeks and see if I could handle it, and that's just what I'm going to do. And don't you dare talk to him behind my back, Dad," she told him.

He looked tormented. "Girl, this isn't necessary!"

"It is, and not only because we need the money," she'd replied. "I need to feel independent."

He hadn't considered that angle. She was determined, and Duncan did have a good bouncer, a huge man called, predictably, Tiny. "We'll see," he'd said finally.

Janie had won her first adult argument with her parent. She felt good about it.

Harley showed up two of her five nights on the job, just to check things out. He was back again tonight. She grinned at him as she served him pizza and beer.

"How's it going?" he asked.

She looked around at the bare wood floors, the no-frills surroundings, the simple wooden tables and chairs and the long counter at which most of the customers—male customers—sat. There were two game machines and a jukebox. There were ceiling fans to circulate the heat, and to cool the place in summer. There was a huge dance floor, where people could dance to live music on Friday and Saturday night. The band was playing now, lazy Western tunes, and a couple was circling the dance floor alone.

"I really like it here," she told Harley with a smile. "I feel as if I'm standing on my own two feet for the first time in my life.'' She leaned closer. ''And the tips are really nice!''

He chuckled. ''Okay. No more arguments from me.'' He glanced toward Tiny, a huge man with tattoos on both arms and a bald head, who'd taken an immediate liking to Janie. He was reassuringly close whenever she spoke to customers or served food and drinks.

''Isn't he a doll?'' Janie asked, smiling toward Tiny, who smiled back a little hesitantly, as if he were afraid his face might crack.

''That's not a question you should ask a man, Janie,'' he teased.

Grinning, she flipped her bar cloth at him, and went back to work.

Leo went looking for Fred Brewster after lunch on Monday. He'd been out of town at a convention, and he'd lost touch with his friend.

Fred was in his study, balancing figures that didn't want to be balanced. He looked up as Hettie showed Leo in.

''Hello, stranger,'' Fred said with a grin. ''Sit down. Want some coffee? Hettie, how about...!''

''No need to shout, Mr. Fred, it's already dripping,'' she interrupted him with a chuckle. ''I'll bring it in when it's done.''

''Cake, too!'' he called.

There was a grumble.

''She thinks I eat too many sweets,'' Fred told Leo. ''Maybe I do. How was the convention?''

''It was pretty good,'' Leo told him. ''There's a lot of talk about beef exports to Japan and improved labeling of beef to show country of origin. Some discussion of artificial additives,'' he confided with a chuckle. ''You can guess where that came from.''

''J. D. Langley and the Tremayne brothers.''

''Got it in one guess.'' Leo tossed his white Stetson into

a nearby chair and sat down in the one beside it. He ran a hand through his thick gold-streaked brown hair and his dark eyes pinned Fred. ''But aside from the convention, I've heard some rumors that bother me,'' he said, feeling his way.

''Oh?'' Fred put aside his keyboard mouse and sat back. He'd heard about Janie's job, he thought, groaning inwardly. He drew in a long breath. ''What rumors?'' he asked innocently.

Leo leaned forward, his crossed arms on his knees. ''That you're looking for partners here.''

''Oh. That.'' Fred cleared his throat and looked past Leo. ''Just a few little setbacks...''

''Why didn't you come to me?'' Leo persisted, scowling. ''I'd loan you anything you needed on the strength of your signature. You know that.''

Fred swallowed. ''I do...know that. But I wouldn't dare. Under the circumstances.'' He avoided Leo's piercing stare.

''What circumstances?'' Leo asked with resignation, when he realized that he was going to have to pry every scrap of information out of his friend.

''Janie.''

Leo's breath expelled in a rush. He'd wondered if Fred knew about the friction between the two of them. It was apparent that he did. ''I see.''

Fred glanced at him and winced. ''She won't hear your name mentioned,'' he said apologetically. ''I couldn't go to you behind her back, and she'd find out anyway, sooner or later. Jacobsville is a small town.''

''She wouldn't be likely to find out when she's away at college,'' Leo assured him. ''She has gone back, hasn't she?''

There was going to be an explosion. Fred knew it without saying a word. ''Uh, Leo, she hasn't gone back, exactly.''

His eyebrows lifted. ''She's not here. I asked Hettie. She flushed and almost dragged me in here without saying anything except Janie wasn't around. I assumed she'd gone back to school."

"No. She's, uh, got a job, Leo. A good job," he added, trying to reassure himself. "She likes it very much."

"Doing what, for God's sake?" Leo demanded. "She has no skills to speak of!"

"She's cooking. At a restaurant."

Leo felt his forehead. "No fever," he murmured to himself. It was a well-known fact that Janie could burn water in a pan. He pinned Fred with his eyes. "Would you like to repeat that?"

"She's cooking. She can cook," he added belligerently at Leo's frank astonishment. "Hettie spent two months with her in the kitchen. She can even make..." he started to say "biscuits" and thought better of it "...pizza."

Leo whistled softly. "Fred, I didn't know things were that bad. I'm sorry."

"The bull dying was nobody's fault," Fred said heavily. "But I used money I hoped to recoup to buy him, and there was no insurance. Very few small ranchers could take a loss like that and remain standing. He was a champion's offspring."

"I know that. I'd help, if you'd let me," Leo said earnestly.

"I appreciate it. But I can't."

There was a long, pregnant pause. "Janie told you about what happened at the ball, I suppose," Leo added curtly.

"No. She hasn't said a single word about that," Fred replied. He frowned. "Why?" He understood, belatedly, Leo's concerned stare. "She did tell me about what happened in the hardware store," he added slowly. "There's more?"

Leo glanced away. "There was some unpleasantness at the ball, as well. We had a major fight." He studied his big hands. "I've made some serious mistakes lately. I believed some gossip about Janie that I should never have credited. I know better now, but it's too late. She won't let me close enough to apologize.''

That was news. ''When did you see her?'' Fred asked, playing for time.

''In town at the bank Friday,'' he said. ''She snubbed me.'' He smiled faintly. It had actually hurt when she'd given him a harsh glare, followed by complete oblivion to his presence. ''First time that's happened to me in my life.''

''Janie isn't usually rude,'' Fred tried to justify her behavior. ''Maybe it's just the new job…''

''It's what I said to her, Fred,'' the younger man replied heavily. ''I really hurt her. Looking back, I don't know why I ever believed what I was told.''

Fred was reading between the lines. ''Marilee can be very convincing, Janie said. And she had a case on you.''

''It wasn't mutual,'' Leo said surprisingly. ''I didn't realize what was going on. Then she told me all these things Janie was telling people…'' He stopped and cursed harshly. ''I thought I could see through lies. I guess I'm more naive than I thought I was.''

''Any man can be taken in,'' Fred reassured him. ''It was just bad luck. Janie never said a word about you in public. She's shy, although you might not realize it. She'd never throw herself at a man. Well, not for real,'' he amended with a faint smile. ''She did dress up and flirt with you. She told Hettie it was the hardest thing she'd ever done in her life, and she agonized over it for days afterward. Not the mark of a sophisticated woman, is it?''

Leo understood then how far he'd fallen. No wonder she'd been so upset when she overheard him running down her aggressive behavior. ''No,'' he replied. ''I wish I'd seen through it.'' He smiled wryly. ''I don't like aggressive, sophisticated women,'' he confessed. ''Call it a fatal flaw. I liked Janie the way she was.''

''Harmless?'' Fred mused.

Leo flushed. ''I wouldn't say that.''

''Wouldn't you?'' Fred leaned back in his chair, smiling at the younger man's confusion. ''I've sheltered Janie too much. I wanted her to have a smooth, easy path through life. But I did her no favors. She's not a dress-up doll, Leo, she's a woman. She needs to learn independence, self-sufficiency. She has a temper, and she's learning to use that, too. Last week, she stood up to me for the first time and told me what she was going to do.'' He chuckled. ''I must confess, it was pretty shocking to realize that my daughter was a woman.''

''She's going around with Harley,'' Leo said curtly.

''Why shouldn't she? Harley's a good man—young, but steady and dependable. He, uh, did go up against armed men and held his own, you know.''

Leo did know. It made him furious to know. He didn't hang out with professional soldiers. He'd been in the service, and briefly in combat, but he'd never fought drug dealers and been written up in newspapers as a local hero.

Fred deduced all that from the look on Leo's lean face. ''It's not like you think,'' he added. ''She and Harley are friends. Just friends.''

''Do I care?'' came the impassioned reply. He grabbed up his Stetson and got to his feet. He hesitated, turning back to Fred. ''I won't insist, but Janie would never have to know if I took an interest in the ranch,'' he added firmly.

Fred was tempted. He sighed and stood up, too. ''I've worked double shifts for years, trying to keep it solvent. I've survived bad markets, drought, unseasonable cold. But this is the worst it's ever been. I could lose the property so easily.''

''Then don't take the risk,'' Leo insisted. ''I can loan you what it takes to get you back in the black. And I promise you, Janie will never know. It will be between the two of us. Don't lose the ranch out of pride, Fred. It's been in your family for generations.''

Fred grimaced. ''Leo…''

The younger man leaned both hands on the desk and impaled Fred with dark eyes. "Let me help!"

Fred studied the determination, the genuine concern in that piercing stare. "It would have to be a secret," he said, weakening.

Leo's eyes softened. "It will be. You have my word. Blake Kemp's our family attorney. I'll make an appointment. We can sit down with him and work out the details."

Fred had to bite down hard on his lower lip to keep the brightness in his eyes in check. "You can't possibly know how much..." He choked.

Leo held up a hand, embarrassed by his friend's emotion. "I'm filthy rich," he said curtly. "What good is money if you can't use it to help out friends? You'd do the same for me in a heartbeat if our positions were reversed."

Fred swallowed noticeably. "That goes without saying." He drew in a shaky breath. "Thanks," he bit off.

"You're welcome." Leo slanted his hat across his eyes. "I'll phone you. By the way, which restaurant is Janie working at?" he added. "I might stop by for lunch one day."

"That wouldn't be a good idea just yet," Fred said, feeling guilty because Leo still didn't know what was going on.

Leo considered that. "You could be right," he had to agree. "I'll let it ride for a few days, then. Until she cools down a little, at least." He grinned. "She's got a hell of a temper, Fred. Who'd have guessed?"

Fred chuckled. "She's full of surprises lately."

"That she is. I'll be in touch."

Leo was gone and Fred let the emotion out. He hadn't realized how much his family ranch meant to him until he was faced with the horrible prospect of losing it. Now, it would pass to Janie and her family, her children. God bless Leo Hart for being a friend when he needed one so desperately. He grabbed at a tissue and wiped his eyes. Life was good. Life was very good!

Fred was still up when Janie got home from work. She was tired. It had been a long night. She stopped in the kitchen to say good-night to Hettie before she joined her father in his study.

"Hettie said Leo came by," she said without her usual greeting. She looked worried. "Why?"

"He wanted to check on his bull," he lied without meeting her eyes.

She hesitated. "Did he…ask about me?"

"Yes," he said. "I told him you had a job working in a restaurant."

She stared at her feet. "Did you tell him which one?"

He looked anxious. "No."

She met his eyes. "You don't have to worry, Dad. It's none of Leo Hart's business where I work, or whatever else I do."

"You're still angry," he noted. "I understand. But he wants to make peace."

She swallowed, hearing all over again his voice taunting her, baiting her. She clenched both hands at her sides. "He wants to bury the hatchet? Good. I know exactly where to bury it."

"Now, daughter, he's not a bad man."

"Of course he's not. He just doesn't like me," she bit off. "You can't blame him, not when he's got Marilee."

He winced. "I didn't think. You lost your only friend."

"Some friend," she scoffed. "She's gone to spend the holidays in Colorado," she added smugly. "A rushed trip, I heard."

"I imagine she's too ashamed to walk down the main street right now," her father replied. "People have been talking about her, and that's no lie. But she's not really a bad woman, Janie. She just made a mistake. People do."

"You don't," she said unexpectedly, and smiled at him. "You're the only person in the world who wouldn't stab me in the back."

He flushed. Guilt overwhelmed him. What would she say when she knew that he was going to let Leo Hart buy into the ranch, and behind her back? It was for a good cause, so that she could eventually inherit her birthright, but he felt suddenly like a traitor. He could only imagine how she'd look at him if she ever found out....

"Why are you brooding?" she teased. "You need to put away those books and go to bed."

He stared at the columns that wouldn't balance and thought about having enough money to fix fences, repair the barn, buy extra feed for the winter, buy replacement heifers, afford medicine for his sick cattle and veterinarian's fees. The temptation was just too much for him. He couldn't let the ranch go to strangers.

"Do you ever think about down the road," Fred murmured, "when your children grow up and take over the ranch?"

She blinked. "Well, yes, sometimes," she confessed. "It's a wonderful legacy," she added with a soft smile. "We go back such a long way in Jacobsville. It was one of your great-uncles who was the first foreman of the Jacobs ranch properties when the founder of our town came here and bought cattle, after the Civil War. This ranch was really an offshoot of that one," she added. "There's so much history here!"

Fred swallowed. "Too much to let the ranch go down the tube, or end up in the hands of strangers, like the Jacobs place did." He shook his head. "That was sad, to see Shelby and Ty thrown off their own property. That ranch had been in their family over a hundred years."

"It wasn't much of a ranch anymore," she reminded him. "More of a horse farm. But I understand what you mean. I'm glad we'll have the ranch to hand down to our descendants.'' She gave him a long look. ''You aren't thinking of giving it up without a fight?''

''Heavens, no!''

She relaxed. ''Sorry. But the way you were talking...''

''I'd do almost anything to keep it in the family,'' Fred assured her. ''You, uh, wouldn't have a problem with me taking on a partner or an investor?''

''Of course not,'' she assured him. ''So you found someone in Colorado after all?'' she added excitedly. ''Somebody who's willing to back us?''

''Yes,'' he lied, ''but I didn't hear until today.''

''That's just great!'' she exclaimed.

He gave her a narrow look. ''I'm glad you think so. Then you can give up that job and go back to college...''

''No.''

His eyebrows went up. ''But, Janie...''

''Dad, even with an investor, we still have the day-to-day operation of the ranch to maintain,'' she reminded him gently. ''How about groceries? Utilities? How about cattle feed and horse feed and salt blocks and fencing?''

He sighed. ''You're right, of course. I'll need the investment for the big things.''

''I like my job,'' she added. ''I really do.''

''It's a bad place on the weekends,'' he worried.

''Tiny likes me,'' she assured him. ''And Harley comes in at least two or three times a week, mostly on Fridays and Saturdays, to make sure I'm doing all right. I feel as safe at Shea's as I do right here with you.''

''It's not that I mind you working,'' he said, trying to explain.

''I know that. You're just worried that I might get in over my head. Tiny doesn't let anybody have too much to drink before he makes them leave. Mr. Duncan is emphatic about not having drunks on the place.''

Fred sighed. ''I know when I'm licked. I may show up for pizza one Saturday night, though.''

She grinned. ''You'd be welcome! I could show you off to my customers.''

''Leo wanted to know where you were working,'' he said abruptly. ''He wanted to come by and see you.''

Her face tautened. ''I don't want to see him.''

''So I heard. He was, uh, pretty vocal about the way you snubbed him.''

She tossed back her hair. ''He deserved it. I'm nobody's doormat. He isn't going to walk all over me and get away with it!''

''He won't like you working at Shea's, no matter what you think.''

''Why do you care?'' she asked suspiciously.

He couldn't tell her that Leo might renege on the loan if he knew Fred was letting her work in such a dive. He felt guilty as sin for not coming clean. But he was so afraid of losing the ranch. It was Janie's inheritance. He had to do everything he could to keep it solvent.

''He's my friend,'' he said finally.

''I used to think he was mine, too,'' she replied. ''But friends don't talk about each other the way he was talking about me. As if I'd ever gossip about him!''

''I think he knows that now, Janie.''

She forced the anger to the back of her mind. ''I guess if he knew what I was doing, he'd faint. He doesn't think I can cook at all.''

''I did tell him you had a cooking job,'' he confided.

Her eyes lit up. ''You did? What did he say?''

''He was…surprised.''

''He was astonished,'' she translated.

''It bothered him that you snubbed him. He said he felt really bad about the things he said, that you overheard. He, uh, told me about the fight you had at the ball, too.''

Her face colored. ''What did he tell you?''

''That you'd had a bad argument. Seemed to tickle him that you had a temper,'' he added with a chuckle.

"He'll find out I have a temper if he comes near me again." She turned. "I'm going to bed, Dad. You sleep good."

"You, too, sweetheart. Good night."

He watched her walk away with a silent sigh of relief. So far, he thought, so good.

# *Chapter Six*

The following Wednesday, Leo met with Blake Kemp and Fred Brewster in Kemp's office, to draw up the instrument of partnership.

''I'll never be able to thank you enough for this, Leo,'' Fred said as they finished a rough draft of the agreement.

''You'd have done it for me,'' Leo said simply. ''How long will it take until those papers are ready to sign?'' he asked Kemp.

''We'll have them by Monday,'' Kemp assured him.

''I'll make an appointment with your receptionist on the way out,'' Leo said, rising. ''Thanks, Blake.''

The attorney shook his outstretched hand, and then Fred's. ''All in a day's work. I wish most of my business was concluded this easily, and amiably,'' he added wryly.

Leo checked his watch. ''Why don't we go out to Shea's and have a beer and some pizza, Fred?'' he asked the other man, who, curiously, seemed paler.

Fred was scrambling for a reason that Leo couldn't go to Shea's. ''Well, because, uh, because Hettie made chili!'' he remembered suddenly. ''So why don't you come home and eat with me? We've got Mexican corn bread to go with it!''

Leo hesitated. ''That does sound pretty good,'' he had to admit. Then he remembered. Janie would be there. He was uncomfortable with the idea of rushing in on her unexpectedly, especially in light of recent circumstances. He was still a little embarrassed about his own behavior. He searched for a reason to refuse, and found one. ''Oh, for Pete's sake, I almost forgot!'' he added, slapping his forehead. ''I'm supposed to have supper with Cag and Tess tonight. We're going in together on two new Santa Gertrudis bulls. How could I have forgotten…got to run, Fred, or I'll never make it on time!''

''Sure, of course,'' Fred said, and looked relieved. ''Have a good time!''

Leo chuckled. ''I get to play with my nephew. That's fun, all right. I like kids.''

''You never seemed the type,'' Fred had to admit.

''I'm not talking about having any of my own right away,'' Leo assured him. ''I don't want to get married. But I like all my nephews, not to mention my niece.''

Fred only smiled.

''Thanks for the offer of supper, anyway,'' he told the older man with a smile. ''Sorry I can't come.''

Fred relaxed. ''That's okay, Leo. More for me,'' he teased. ''Well, I'll go home and have my chili. Thanks again. If I can ever do anything for you, anything at all, you only have to ask.''

Leo smiled. ''I know that, Fred. See you.''

They parted in the parking lot. Leo got in his double-cabbed pickup and gunned the engine.

Fred got into his own truck and relaxed. At least, he thought, he didn't have to face Leo's indignation today. With luck, Leo might never realize what was going on.

Leo, honest to the core, phoned Cag and caged an invitation to supper to discuss the two new bulls the brothers were buying. But he had some time before he was due at his brother's house. He brooded over Fred's dead bull, and Christabel's, and he began to wonder. He had a bull from that same lot, a new lineage of Salers bulls that came from a Victoria breeder. Two related bulls dying in a month's time seemed just a bit too much for coincidence. He picked up the phone and called information.

Cag and Tess were still like newlyweds, Leo noted as he carried their toddler around the living room after supper, grinning from ear to ear as the little boy, barely a year old, smiled up at him and tried to grab his nose. They sat close together on the sofa and seemed to radiate love. They were watching him with equal interest.

"You do that like a natural," Cag teased.

Leo shifted the little boy. "Lots of practice," he chuckled. "Simon's two boys, then Corrigan's boy and their new girl, and now your son." He lifted an eyebrow. "Rey and Meredith are finally expecting, too, I hear."

"They are," Cag said with a sigh. He eyed his brother mischievously. "When are you planning to throw in the towel and join up?"

"Me? Never," Leo said confidently. "I've got a big house to myself, all the women I can attract, no responsibilities and plenty of little kids to spoil as they grow." He gave them an innocent glance. "Why should I want to tie myself down?"

"Just a thought," Cag replied. "You'll soon get tired of going all the way to town every morning for a fresh biscuit." Cag handed the baby back to Tess.

"I'm thinking of taking a cooking course," Leo remarked.

Cag roared.

"I could cook if I wanted to!" Leo said indignantly.

Tess didn't speak, but her eyes did.

Leo stuffed his hands in his pockets. "Well, I don't really want to,'' he conceded. ''And it is a long way to town. But I can manage.'' He sprawled in an easy chair. ''There's something I want to talk to you about—besides our new bulls.''

''What?'' Cag asked, sensing concern.

''Fred's big Salers bull that died mysteriously,'' Leo said. ''Christabel and Judd Dunn lost one, too, a young bull.''

''Judd says it died of bloat.''

''I saw the carcass, he didn't. He thinks Christabel made it up, God knows why. He wouldn't even come down from Victoria to take a look at it. It wasn't bloat. But she didn't call a vet out, and they didn't find any marks on Fred's bull.'' He sighed. ''Cag, I've done a little checking. The bulls are related. The young herd sire of these bulls died recently as well, and the only champion Salers bull left that's still walking is our two-year-old bull that I loaned to Fred, although it's not related to the dead ones.''

Cag sat up straight, scowling. ''You're kidding.''

Leo shook his head. ''It's suspicious, isn't it?''

''You might talk to Jack Handley in Victoria, the rancher we bought our bull from.''

''I did.'' He leaned forward intently. ''Handley said he fired two men earlier this year for stealing from him. They're brothers, John and Jack Clark. One of them is a thief, the other has a reputation for vengeance that boggles the mind. When one former employer fired Jack Clark, he lost his prize bull and all four young bulls he'd got from it. No apparent cause of death. Handley checked and found a pattern of theft and retribution with those brothers going back two years. At least four employers reported similar problems with theft and firing. There's a pattern of bull deaths, too. The brothers were suspects in a recent case in Victoria, but there was never enough evidence to convict anyone. Until now, I don't imagine anyone's connected the dots.''

"How the hell do they keep getting away with it?" Cag wanted to know.

"There's no proof. And they're brawlers," Leo said. "They intimidate people."

"They wouldn't intimidate us," Cag remarked.

"They wouldn't. But do you see the common thread here? Handley crossed the brothers. He had a new, expensive Salers bull that he bred to some heifers, and he sold all the young bulls this year, except for his seed bull. His seed bull, and all its offspring, which isn't many, have died. Christabel Gaines's young bull was one of Handley's, like Fred's. And Jack Clark was fired by Judd Dunn for stealing, too."

Cag was scowling. "Where are the brothers now?"

"I asked Handley. He says John Clark is working on a ranch near Victoria. We know that Jack, the one with a reputation for getting even, is right here in Jacobsville, driving a cattle truck for Duke Wright," Leo said. "I called Wright and told him what I know. He's going to keep an eye on the man. I called Judd Dunn, too, but he was too preoccupied to listen. He's smitten with that redheaded supermodel who's in the movie they're making on Christabel's ranch—Tippy Moore, the 'Georgia Firefly.'"

"He'll land hard, if I make my guess," Cag said. "She's playing. He isn't."

"He's married, too," Leo said curtly. "Something he doesn't seem to remember."

"He only married Christabel because she was going to lose the ranch after her father beat her nearly to death in a drunken rage. Her mother was an invalid. No way could the two of them have kept it solvent," Cag added. "That's not a real marriage. I'm sure he's already looked into annulling it when she turns twenty-one."

"She was twenty-one this month," Leo said. "Poor kid. She's got a real case on him, and she's fairly plain except for those soulful brown eyes and a nice figure. She couldn't compete with the Georgia Firefly.''

''So ask yourself what does a supermodel worth millions want with a little bitty Texas Ranger?'' Cag grinned.

Tess gave him a speaking look. ''As a happily married woman, I can tell you that if I wasn't hung up on you, Judd Dunn would make my mouth water.''

Cag whistled.

Leo shrugged. ''Whatever. But I think we should keep a close eye on our Salers bull, as well as Wright's new cattle-truck driver. Handley says Clark likes to drink, so it wouldn't hurt to keep an eye out at Shea's, as well.''

Cag frowned thoughtfully. ''You might have a word with Janie...''

''Janie?''

''Janie Brewster,'' his brother said impatiently. ''Tell her what the man looks like and have her watch him if he ever shows up out there.''

Leo stared at his brother. ''Will you make sense? Why would Janie be at Shea's roadhouse in the first place?''

Realization dawned. Cag looked stunned, and then uncomfortable.

Tess grimaced. ''He doesn't know. I guess you'd better tell him.''

''Tell me what?'' Leo grumbled.

''Well, it's like this,'' Cag said. ''Janie's been working at Shea's for a couple of weeks...''

''She's working in a bar?'' Leo exploded violently.

Cag winced. ''Now, Leo, she's a grown woman,'' he began calmly.

''She's barely twenty-one!'' he continued, unabashed. ''She's got no business working around drunks! What the hell is Fred thinking, to let her get a job in a place like that?''

Cag sighed. ''Talk is that Fred's in the hole and can

hardly make ends meet,'' he told Leo. ''I guess Janie insisted on helping out.''

Leo got to his feet and grabbed up his white Stetson, his lips in a thin line, his dark eyes sparking.

''Don't go over there and start trouble,'' Cag warned. ''Don't embarrass the girl with her boss!''

Leo didn't answer him. He kept walking. His footsteps, quick and hard, described the temper he was in. He even slammed the door on the way out, without realizing he had.

Cag looked at Tess worriedly as Leo's car careened down the driveway. ''Should I warn her?'' he asked Tess.

She nodded. ''At least she'll be prepared.''

Cag thought privately that it was unlikely that anybody could prepare for Leo in a temper, but he picked up the phone just the same.

Shea's wasn't crowded when Leo jerked to a stop in the parking lot. He walked into the roadhouse with blood in his eye. Three men at a table near the door stopped talking when they saw him enter. Apparently they thought he looked dangerous.

Janie was thinking the same thing. She'd assured Cag that she wasn't afraid of Leo, but it was a little different when the man was walking toward her with his eyes narrow and his lips compressed like that.

He stopped at the counter. He noted her long apron, her hands with a dusting of flour, a pencil behind her ear. She looked busy. There were three cowboys at the counter drinking beers and apparently waiting for pizzas. A teenage boy was pulling a pizza on a long paddle out of a big oven behind her.

''Get your things,'' he told Janie in a tone he hadn't used with her since she was ten and had gotten into a truck with a cowboy who offered her a trip to the visiting carnival. He'd busted up that cowboy pretty bad, and for reasons

Janie only learned later. She'd had a very close call. Leo had saved her. But she didn't need saving right now.

She lifted her chin and glared at him. The night of the ball came back to her vividly. "How's your foot?" she asked with sarcasm.

"My foot is fine. Get your things," he repeated curtly.

"I work here."

"Not anymore."

She crossed her arms. "You planning to carry me out kicking and screaming? Because that's the only way I'm leaving."

"Suits me." He started around the counter.

She picked up a pitcher of beer and dumped the contents on him. "Now you listen to me…Leo!"

The beer didn't even slow him down. He had her up in his arms and he turned, carrying her toward the door. She was kicking and screaming for all she was worth.

That attracted Tiny, the bouncer. He was usually on the job by six, but he'd arrived late today. To give him credit, the minute he saw Janie, he turned and went toward the big man bullying her.

He stepped in front of Leo. "Put her down, Leo," he drawled.

"You tell him, Tiny!" Janie sputtered.

"I'm taking her home where she'll be safe," Leo replied. He knew Tiny. The man was sweet-natured, but about a beer short of a six-pack on intelligence. He was also as big as a house. It didn't hurt to be polite. "She shouldn't be working in a bar."

"It isn't a bar," Tiny said reasonably. "It's a roadhouse. It's a nice roadhouse. Mr. Duncan don't allow no drunks. You put Miss Janie down, Leo, or I'll have to hit you."

"He'll do it," Janie warned. "I've seen him do it. He's hit men even bigger than you. Haven't you, Tiny?" she encouraged.

"I sure have, Miss Janie."

Leo wasn't backing down. He glared at Tiny. "I said," he replied, his voice dangerously soft, "I'm taking her home."

"I don't think she wants to go, Mr. Hart," came a new source of interference from the doorway behind him.

He swung around with Janie in his big arms. It was Harley Fowler, leaning against the doorjamb, looking intimidating. It would have been a joke a year ago. The new Harley made it look good.

"You tell him, Harley!" Janie said enthusiastically.

"You keep still," Leo told her angrily. "You've got no business working in a rough joint like this!"

"You have no right to tell me where I can work," Janie shot right back, red-faced and furious. "Won't Marilee mind that you're here pestering me?" she added viciously.

His cheeks went red. "I haven't seen Marilee in two weeks. I don't give a damn if I never see her again, either."

That was news. Janie looked as interested as Harley seemed to.

Tiny was still hovering. "I said, put her down," he persisted.

"Do you really think you can take on Tiny and me both?" Harley asked softly.

Leo was getting mad. His face tautened. "I don't know about Tiny," he said honestly, putting Janie back on her feet without taking his eyes off Harley. "But you're a piece of cake, son."

As he said it, he stepped forward and threw a quick punch that Harley wasn't expecting. With his mouth open, Harley tumbled backward over a table. Leo glared at Janie.

"You want this job, keep it," he said, ice-cold except for the glitter in those dark eyes. "But if you get slugged during a brawl or hassled by amorous drunks, don't come crying to me!"

"As…as if I ever…would!" she stammered, shocked by his behavior.

He turned around and stalked out the door without giving Harley a single glance.

Janie rushed to Harley and helped him back to his feet. "Oh, Harley, are you hurt?" she asked miserably.

He rubbed his jaw. "Only my pride, darlin'," he murmured with a rough chuckle. "Damn, that man can throw a punch! I wasn't really expecting him to do it." His eyes twinkled. "I guess you're a little more important to him than any of us realized."

She flushed. "He's just trying to run my life."

Tiny came over and inspected Harley's jaw. "Gonna have a bruise, Mr. Fowler," he said politely.

Harley grinned. He was a good sport, and he knew a jealous man when he saw one. Leo had wanted to deck him at the ball over Janie, but he'd restrained himself. Now, maybe, he felt vindicated. But Harley wished there had been a gentler way of doing it. His jaw was really sore.

"The beast," Janie muttered. "Come on, Harley, I'll clean you up in the bathroom before it gets crowded. Okay, guys, fun's over. Drink your beer and eat your pizzas."

"Yes, mother," one of the men drawled.

She gave him a wicked grin and led Harley to the back. She was not going to admit the thrill it had given her that Leo was worried about her job, or that people thought he was jealous of Harley. But she felt it all the way to her bones.

Leo was lucky not to get arrested for speeding on his way to Fred's house. He had the sports car flat-out on the four lane that turned onto the Victoria road, and he burned rubber when he left the tarmac and turned into Fred's graveled driveway.

Fred heard him coming and knew without a doubt what was wrong.

He stood on the porch with his hands in his jean pockets as he studied the darkening sky behind Leo, who was already out of the car and headed for the porch. His Stetson was pulled down right over his eyes, cocked as they said in cowboy vernacular, and Fred had never seen Leo look so much like a Hart. The brothers had a reputation for being tough customers. Leo looked it right now.

"I want her out of that damned bar," Leo told Fred flatly, without even a conventional greeting. "You can consider it a term of the loan, if you like, but you get her home."

Fred grimaced. "I did try to talk her out of it, when I found out where she was working," he said in his own defense. "Leo, she stood right up to me and said she was old enough to make her own decisions. What do I say to that? She's twenty-one and she told me she wasn't giving up her job."

Leo cursed furiously.

"What happened to your shirt?" Fred asked suddenly. He leaned closer and made a face. "Man, you reek of beer!"

"Of course I do! Your daughter baptized me in front of a crowd of cowboys with a whole pitcher of the damned stuff!" Leo said indignantly.

Fred's eyes opened wide. "Janie? My Janie?"

Leo looked disgusted. "She flung the pitcher at me. And then she set the bouncer on me and appealed to Harley Fowler for aid."

"Why did she need aid?" Fred asked hesitantly.

"Oh, she was kicking and screaming, and they thought she was in trouble, I guess."

"Kicking...?"

Leo's lips compressed. "All right, if you have to know, I tried to carry her out of the bar and bring her home. She resisted."

Fred whistled. "I'd say she resisted." He was trying very hard not to laugh. He looked at Leo's clenched fists. One, the right one, was bleeding. "Hit somebody, did you?"

''Harley,'' he returned uncomfortably. ''Well, he shouldn't have interfered! He doesn't own Janie, she's not his private stock. If he were any sort of a man, he'd have insisted that she go home right then. Instead, he stands there calmly ordering me to put her down. Ordering me. Hell! He's lucky it was only one punch!''

''Oh, boy,'' Fred said, burying his face in his hand. Gossip was going to run for a month on this mixer.

''It wasn't my fault,'' Leo argued, waving his hands. ''I went in there to save her from being insulted and harassed by drunk men, and look at the thanks I get? Drenched in beer, threatened by ogres, giggled at...''

''Who giggled?''

Leo shifted. ''This little brunette who was sitting with one of the Tremayne brothers' cowboys.''

Fred cleared his throat. He didn't dare laugh. ''I guess it was a sight to see.''

Grimacing, Leo flexed his hand. ''Damned near broke my fingers on Harley's jaw. He needs to learn to keep his mouth shut. Just because he's not afraid of drug lords, he shouldn't think he can take me on and win.''

''I'm sure he knows that now, Leo.''

Leo took a deep breath. ''You tell her I said she's going to give up that job, one way or the other!''

''I'll tell her.'' It won't matter though, he thought privately. Janie was more than likely to dig her heels in big time after Leo's visit to Shea's.

Leo gave him a long, hard stare. ''I'm not mean with money, I don't begrudge you that loan. But I'm not kidding around with you, Fred. Janie's got no business in Shea's, even with a bouncer on duty. It's a rough place. I've been there on nights when the bouncer didn't have time for a cup of coffee, and there's been at least one shooting. It's dangerous. Even more dangerous right now.''

Something in the younger man's tone made Fred uneasy. ''Why?''

"Fred, you don't breathe a word of this, even to Janie, understand?"

Fred nodded, curious.

Leo told him what he'd learned from Handley about the Clark brothers, and the loss of the related Salers bulls.

Fred's jaw flew open. "You think my bull was killed deliberately?"

"Yes, I do," Leo admitted solemnly. "I'm sorry to tell you that, because I can't prove it and neither can you. Clark is shrewd. He's never been caught in the act. If you can't prove it, you can't prosecute."

Fred let out an angry breath. "Of all the damned mean, low things to do!"

"I agree, and it's why I'm putting two men over here to watch my bull," he added firmly. "No sorry cattle-killer is going to murder my bull and get away with it. I'm having video cameras installed, too. If he comes near that bull, I'll have his hide in jail!"

Fred chuckled. "Don't I wish he'd try," he said thoughtfully.

"So do I, but I don't hold out a lot of hope," Leo returned. He moved his shoulders restlessly. The muscles were stretched, probably from Janie's violent squirming. He remembered without wanting to the feel of her soft breasts pressed hard against his chest, and he ached.

"Uh, about Janie," Fred continued worriedly.

Leo stared at him without speaking.

"Okay," the older man said wearily. "I'll try to talk some sense into her." He pursed his lips and peered up at Leo. "Of course, she could be a lot of help where she is right now," he murmured thoughtfully. "With the Clark man roaming around loose, that is. She could keep an eye on him if he comes into Shea's. If he's a drinking man, that's the only joint around that sells liquor by the drink."

"She doesn't know what he looks like," Leo said.

"Can't you find out and tell her?"

Leo sighed. ''I don't like her being in the line of fire.''

''Neither do I.'' Fred gave the other man a curious scrutiny. ''You and Harley and I could arrange to drop in from time to time, just to keep an eye on her.''

''She'll have to ask Harley. I won't.''

''You're thinking about it, aren't you?'' Fred persisted.

Leo was. His eyes narrowed. ''My brothers could drop in occasionally, and so could our ranch hands. The Tremaynes would help us out. I know Harden. I'll talk to him. And most of our cowhands go into Shea's on the weekend. I'll talk to our cattle foreman.''

''I know Cy Parks and Eb Scott,'' Fred told him. ''They'd help, too.''

Leo perked up. With so many willing spies, Janie would be looked after constantly, and she'd never know it. He smiled.

''It's a good idea, isn't it?''

Leo glared at him. ''You just don't want to have to make Janie quit that job. You're scared of her, aren't you? What's the matter, think she'd try to drown you in cheap beer, too?''

Fred burst out laughing. ''You have to admit, it's a shock to think of Janie throwing beer at anybody.''

''I guess it is, at that,'' Leo seconded, remembering how shy Janie had been. It was only after Marilee had caused so much trouble with her lies that Leo had considered Janie's lack of aggression.

In the past, that was, he amended, because he'd never seen such aggression as he'd encountered in little Janie Brewster just an hour ago.

He shook his head. ''It was all I could do not to get thrown on the floor. She's a handful when she's mad. I don't think I've ever seen her lose her temper before.''

''There's a lot about her you don't know,'' Fred said enigmatically.

''Okay, she can stay,'' Leo said at once. ''But I'll find

out what Clark looks like. I'll get a picture if I can manage it. Maybe Grier at the police station would have an idea. He's sweet on Christabel Gaines, and she lost a bull to this dude, so he might be willing to assist.''

''Don't get Judd Dunn mad,'' Fred warned.

Leo shrugged. ''He's too stuck on his pretty model to care much about Christabel right now, or Grier, either. I don't want any more bulls killed, and I want that man out of the way before he really hurts somebody.''

''Have you talked to his boss?''

''Duke Wright didn't have a clue that his new truck driver was such an unsavory character,'' Leo said, ''and he was keen to fire him on the spot. I persuaded him not to. He needs to be where we can watch him. If he puts a foot wrong, we can put him away. I love animals,'' Leo said in an uncharacteristically tender mood. ''Especially bulls. The kind we keep are gentle creatures. They follow us around like big dogs and eat out of our hands.'' His face hardened visibly. ''A man who could cold-bloodedly kill an animal like that could kill a man just as easily. I want Clark out of here. Whatever it takes. But Janie's going to be watched, all the time she's working,'' Leo added firmly. ''Nobody's going to hurt her.''

Fred looked at the other man, sensing emotions under the surface that Leo might not even realize were there.

''Thanks, Leo,'' he said.

The younger man squared his shoulders and shrugged. ''I've got to go home and change my shirt.'' He looked down at himself and smiled ruefully. ''Damn. I may never drink another beer.''

''It tastes better than it wears,'' Fred said, deadpan.

Leo gave him a haughty look and went home.

# *Chapter Seven*

Leo stopped by Cash Grier's office at the police station in Jacobsville, catching the new assistant chief of police on his lunch hour.

"Come on in," Grier invited. He indicated his big desk, which contained a scattering of white boxes with metal handles. "Like Chinese food? That's moo goo gai pan, that's sweet-and-sour pork, and that's fried rice. Help yourself to a plate."

"Thanks, but I had barbecue at Barbara's Café," Leo replied, sitting down. He noted with little surprise that the man was adept with chopsticks. "I saw Toshiro Mifune catch flies with those things in one of the 'Samurai Trilogy' films," he commented.

Grier chuckled. "Don't believe everything you see, and only half of what you hear," he replied. He gave Leo a dark-eyed appraisal over his paper plate. "You're here about Clark, I guess."

Leo's eyebrows jumped.

"Oh, I'm psychic," Grier told him straight-faced. "I learned that when I was in the CIA knocking off enemy government agents from black helicopters with a sniper kit.''

Leo didn't say a word.

Grier just shook his head. ''You wouldn't believe the stuff I've done, to hear people talk.''

''You're mysterious,'' Leo commented. ''You keep to yourself.''

Grier shrugged. ''I have to. I don't want people to notice the aliens spying on me.'' He leaned forward confidentially. ''You see them, too, don't you?'' he asked in a hushed tone.

Leo began to get it. He started laughing and was secretly relieved when Grier joined him. The other man leaned back in his chair, with his booted feet propped on his desk. He was as fit as Leo, probably in even better condition, if the muscles outlined under that uniform shirt were any indication. Grier was said to move like lightning, although Leo had never seen him fight. The man was an enigma, with his black hair in a rawhide ponytail and his scarred face giving away nothing—unless he wanted it to.

''That's more like it,'' Grier said as he finished his lunch. ''I thought I'd move to a small town and fit in.'' He smiled wryly. ''But people are all the same. Only the scenery changes.''

''It was the same for Cy Parks when he first moved here,'' Leo commented.

Grier gave him a narrow look. ''Are you asking a question?''

''Making a comment,'' Leo told him. ''One of our local guys was in the military during a conflict a few years back, in a special forces unit,'' he added deliberately, recounting something Cy Parks had told him about Harley Fowler. ''He saw you on a plane, out of uniform and armed to the teeth.''

Grier began to nod. ''It's a small world, isn't it?'' he asked pleasantly. He put down his plate and the chopsticks with deliberate preciseness. ''I did a stint with military intelligence. And with a few...government agencies.'' He met Leo's curious eyes. ''How far has that gossip traveled?''

''It got to Cy Parks and stopped abruptly,'' Leo replied, recalling what Cy had said to Harley about loose lips. ''Jacobsville is a small town. We consider people who live here family, whether or not we're related to them. Gossip isn't encouraged.''

Grier was surprised. He actually smiled. ''If you asked Parks, or Steele, or Scott why they moved here,'' he said after a minute, ''I imagine you'd learn that what they wanted most was an end to sitting with their backs to the wall and sleeping armed.''

''Isn't that why you're here?'' Leo wanted to know.

Grier met his eyes levelly. ''I don't really know why I'm here, or if I can stay here,'' he said honestly. ''I think I might eventually fit in. I'm going to give it a good try for six months,'' he added, ''no matter how many rubbernecked yahoos stand outside my office trying to hear every damned word I say!'' he raised his voice.

There were sudden, sharp footfalls and the sound of scurrying.

Leo chuckled. Grier hadn't even looked at the door when he raised his voice. He shrugged and smiled sheepishly. ''I don't have eyes in the back of my head, but I love to keep people guessing about what I know.''

''I think that may be part of the problem,'' Leo advised.

''Well, it doesn't hurt to keep your senses honed. Now. What do you want to know about Clark?''

''I'd like some way to get a photo of him,'' Leo confessed. ''A friend of mine is working at Shea's. I'm going to ask her if she'll keep an eye on who he talks to, what he does, if he comes in there. She'll need to know what he looks like.''

Grier sobered at once. ''That's dangerous,'' he said.

"Clark's brother almost killed a man he suspected of spying on him, up in Victoria. He made some threats, too."

Leo frowned. "Why are guys like that on the streets?"

"You can't shoot people or even lock them up without due process here in the States," Grier said with a wistful smile. "Pity."

"Listen, do they give you real bullets to go with that gun?" Leo asked, indicating the .45 caliber automatic in a shoulder holster that the man was wearing.

"I haven't shot anybody in months," Grier assured him. "I was a cyber crime specialist in the D.A.'s office San Antonio. I didn't really beat up that guy I was accused of harassing, I just told him I'd keep flies off him if he didn't level with me about his boss's illegal money laundering. I had access to his computerized financial records," he added with a twinkle in his dark eyes.

"I heard about that," Leo chuckled. "Apparently you used some access codes that weren't in the book."

"They let me off with a warning. When they checked my ID, I still had my old 'company' card."

Leo just shook his head. He couldn't imagine Grier being in trouble for very long. He knew too much. "All that specialized background, and you're handing out speeding tickets in Jacobsville, Texas."

"Don't knock it. Nobody's shot at me since I've been here." He got up and opened his filing cabinet with a key. "I have to keep it locked," he explained. "I have copies of documents about alien technology in here." He glanced at Leo to see if he was buying it and grinned. "Did you read that book by the Air Force guy who discovered night vision at a flying saucer crash?" He turned back to the files. "Hell, I should write a book. With what I know, governments might topple." He hesitated, frowned, with a file folder in his hand. "Our government might topple!"

"Clark?" Leo prompted.

"Clark. Right." He took a paper from the file, replaced

it, closed the cabinet and locked it again. ''Here. You don't have a clue where this photo came from, and I never saw you.''

Leo was looking at a photograph of two men, obviously brothers, in, of all things, a newspaper clipping. Incredibly, they'd been honored with a good citizen award in another Texas town for getting a herd of escaped cattle out of the path of traffic and back into a fenced pasture with broken electric fencing.

''Neat trick,'' Grier said. ''They cut the wire to steal the cattle, and then were seen rounding them up. Everybody thought they were saving the cattle. They had a tractor trailer truck just down the road and told people they were truck drivers who saw the cattle out and stopped to help.'' He laughed wholeheartedly. ''Can you believe it?''

''Can you copy this for me?''

''That's a copy of the original. You can have it,'' Grier told him. ''I've got two more.''

''You were expecting trouble, I gather,'' Leo continued.

''Two expensive bulls in less than a month, both from the same herd sire, is a little too much coincidence even for me,'' Grier said as he sat back down. ''When I heard Clark was working for Duke Wright, I put two and two together.''

''There's no proof,'' Leo said.

''Not yet. We'll give him a little time and see if he'll oblige us by hanging himself.'' He laced his lean, strong hands together on the desk in front of him. ''But you warn your friend not to be obvious. These are dangerous men.''

''I'll tell her.''

''And stop knocking men over tables in Shea's. It's outside the city limits, so I can't arrest you. But I can have the sheriff pick you up for brawling,'' Grier said abruptly, and he was serious. ''You can't abduct women in plain sight of the public.''

''I wasn't abducting her, I was trying to save her!''

''From what?''

''Fistfights!''

Grier lost it. He got up from his desk. ''Get out,'' he invited through helpless laughter. ''I have real work to do here.''

''If Harley Fowler said I hit him without provocation, he's lying,'' Leo continued doggedly. ''He never should have ordered me to put her down, and leave my hands free to hit him!''

''You should just tell the woman how you feel,'' Grier advised. ''It's simpler.'' He glanced at Leo's swollen hand. ''And less painful.''

Leo didn't really know how he felt. That was the problem. He gave Grier a sardonic look and left.

He worried about letting Janie get involved, even from the sidelines, with Clark. Of course, the man might not even come near Shea's. He might buy a bottle and drink on the ranch, in the bunkhouse. But it wasn't a long shot to think he might frequent Shea's if he wanted company while he drank.

He disliked anything that might threaten Janie, and he didn't understand why he hated Harley all of a sudden. But she was in a great position to notice a man without being obvious, and for everyone's sake, Clark had to be watched. A man who would kill helpless animals was capable of worse.

He went looking for her Sunday afternoon, in a misting rain. She wasn't at home. Fred said that she was out, in the cold rain no less, wandering around the pecan trees in her raincoat. Brooding, was how Fred put it. Leo climbed back into his pickup and went after her.

Janie was oblivious to the sound of an approaching truck. She had her hands in her pockets, her eyes on the ground ahead of her, lost in thought.

It had been a revelation that Leo was concerned about

her working at Shea's, and it had secretly thrilled her that he tried to make her quit. But he'd washed his hands of her when she wouldn't leave willingly, and he'd hurt her feelings with his comment that she shouldn't complain if she got in trouble. She didn't know what to make of his odd behavior. He'd given her a hard time, thanks to Marilee. But she hadn't been chasing him lately, so she couldn't understand why he was so bossy about her life. And she did feel guilty that he'd slugged poor Harley, who was only trying to help her.

The truck was almost on top of her before she finally heard the engine and jumped to the side of the ranch trail.

Leo pulled up and leaned over to open the passenger door. "Get in before you drown out there," he said.

She hesitated. She wasn't sure if it was safe to get that close to him.

He grimaced. "I'm not armed and dangerous," he drawled. "I just want to talk."

She moved closer to the open door. "You're in a very strange mood lately," she commented. "Maybe the lack of biscuits in your life has affected your mind."

Both eyebrows went up under his hat.

She flushed, thinking she'd been too forward. But she got into the truck and closed the door, removing the hood of her raincoat from her long, damp hair.

"You'll catch cold," he murmured, turning up the heat.

"It's not that wet, and I've got a lined raincoat."

He drove down the road without speaking, made a turn, and ended up in a field on the Hart ranch, a place where they could be completely alone. He put the truck in park, cut off the engine, and leaned back against his door to study her from under the wide brim of his Stetson. "Your father says you won't give up the job."

"He's right," she replied, ready to do battle.

His fingers tapped rhythmically on the steering wheel. "I've been talking to Grier," he began.

''Now listen here, you can't have me arrested because I won't quit my job!'' she interrupted.

He held up a big, lean hand. ''Not about that,'' he corrected. ''We've got a man in town who may be involved in some cattle losses. I want you to look at this picture and tell me if you've ever seen him in Shea's.''

He took the newspaper clipping out of his shirt pocket, unfolded it, and handed it to her.

She took it gingerly and studied the two faces surrounded by columns of newsprint. ''I don't know the man on the left,'' she replied. ''But the one on the right comes in Saturday nights and drinks straight whiskey,'' she said uneasily. ''He's loud and foul-mouthed, and Tiny had to ask him to leave last night.''

Leo's face tightened. ''He's vindictive,'' he told her.

''I'll say he is,'' she agreed at once. ''When Tiny went out to get into his car, all his tires were slashed.''

That was disturbing. ''Did he report it to the sheriff?''

''He did,'' she replied. ''They're going to look into it, but I don't know how they'll prove anything.''

Leo traced an absent pattern on the seat behind her head. They were silent while the rain slowly increased, the sound of it loud on the hood and cab of the truck. ''The man we're watching is Jack Clark,'' he told her, ''the man you recognize in that photo.'' He took it back from her, refolded it, and replaced it in his pocket. ''If he comes back in, we'd like you to see who he talks to. Don't be obvious about it. Tell Tiny to let it slide about his tires, I'll see that they're replaced.''

''That's nice of you,'' she replied.

He shrugged. ''He's protective of you. I like that.''

His eyes were narrow and dark and very intent on her face. She felt nervous with him all at once and folded her hands in her lap to try and keep him from noticing. It was like another world, closed up with him in a truck in a rainstorm. It outmatched her most fervent dreams of close contact.

"What sort of cattle deaths do you suspect him of?" she asked curiously.

"Your father's bull, for one."

Her intake of breath was audible. "Why would he kill Dad's bull?" she wanted to know.

"It was one of the offspring of a bull he killed in Victoria. He worked for the owner, who fired him. Apparently his idea of proper revenge is far-reaching."

"He's nuts!" she exclaimed.

He nodded. "That's why you have to be careful if he comes back in. Don't antagonize him. Don't stare at him. Don't be obvious when you look at him." He sighed angrily. "I hate the whole idea of having you that close to a lunatic. I should have decked Tiny as well as Fowler and carried you out of there anyway."

His level, penetrating gaze made her heart race. "I'm not your responsibility," she challenged.

"Aren't you?" His dark eyes slid over her from head to toe. His head tilted back at a faintly arrogant angle.

She swallowed. He looked much more formidable now than he had at Shea's. "I should go," she began.

He leaned forward abruptly, caught her under the arms, and pulled her on top of him. He was sprawled over the front seat, with one long, powerful leg braced against the passenger floorboard and the other on the seat. Janie landed squarely between his denim-clad legs, pressed intimately to him.

"Leo!" she exclaimed, horribly embarrassed at the intimate proximity and trying to get up.

He looped an arm around her waist and held her there, studying her flushed face with almost clinical scrutiny. "If you keep moving like that, you're going to discover the major difference between men and women in a vivid way, any minute.''

She stilled at once. She knew what he meant. She'd felt that difference with appalling starkness at the ball. In fact, she was already feeling it again. She looked at him and her face colored violently.

''I told you,'' he replied, pursing his lips as he surveyed the damage. ''My, my, didn't we know that men are easily aroused when we're lying full length on top of them?'' he drawled. ''We do now, don't we?''

She hit his shoulder, trying to hold on to her dignity as well as her temper. ''You let go of me!''

''Spoilsport,'' he chided. He shifted her so that her head fell onto his shoulder and he could look down into her wide, startled eyes. ''Relax,'' he coaxed. ''What are you so afraid of?''

She swallowed. The closeness was like a drug. She felt swollen. Her legs trembled inside the powerful cage his legs made for them. Her breasts were hard against his chest, and they felt uncomfortably tight as well.

He looked down at them with keen insight, even moving her back slightly so that he could see the hard tips pressing against his shirt.

''You stop...looking at that!'' she exclaimed without thinking.

He lifted an eyebrow and his smile was worldly. ''A man likes to know that he's making an impression,'' he said outrageously.

She bit her lower lip, still blushing. ''You're making too much of an impression already,'' she choked.

He leaned close and brushed his mouth lazily over her parted lips. ''My body likes you,'' he whispered huskily.

"It's making very emphatic statements about what it wants to do."

"You need...to speak...firmly to it," she said. She was trying to sound adult and firm, but her voice shook. It was hard to think, with his mouth hovering like that.

"It doesn't listen to reason," he murmured. He nibbled tenderly at her upper lip, parting it insistently from its companion. His free hand came up to tease around the corners of her mouth and down her chin to the opening her v-necked blouse made inside her raincoat.

His mouth worked on her lips while his hands freed her from the raincoat and slowly, absently, from her blouse as well. She was hardly aware of it. His mouth was doing impossibly erotic things to her lips, and one of his lean, strong hands was inside her blouse, teasing around the lacy edges of her brassiere.

The whole time, one long, powerful leg was sliding against the inside of her thigh, in a way so arousing that she didn't care what he did to her, as long as he didn't try to get up.

Her hands had worked their way into his thick, soft hair, and she was lifting up, trying to get closer to those slow, maddening fingers that were brushing against the soft flesh inside her bra. She'd never dreamed that a man could arouse her so quickly with nothing more invasive than a light brushing stroke of his hand. But she was on fire with hunger, need, aching need, to have him thrust those fingers down inside her frilly bra and close on her breast. It was torture to have him tease her like this. He was watching her face, too, watching the hunger grow with a dark arrogance that was going to make her squirm later in memory.

Right now, of course, she didn't care how he looked at her. If he would just slide that hand...down a...couple of...inches!

She was squirming in another way now, twisting her body ardently, pushing up against his stroking fingers while his mouth nibbled and nipped at her parted lips and his warm breath went into her mouth.

The rain was falling harder. It banged on the hood, and on top of the cab, with tempestuous fury. Inside, Janie could hear the tormented sound of her own breathing, feel her heartbeat shaking her madly, while Leo's practiced caresses grew slower and lazier on her taut body.

"Will you...please...!" she sputtered, gripping his arms.

"Will I please, what?" he whispered into her mouth.

"T...t...touch me!" she cried.

He nipped her upper lip ardently. "Touch you where?" he tormented.

Tears of frustration stung her eyes as they opened, meeting his. "You...know...where!"

He lifted his head. His face was taut, his eyes dark and glittery. He watched her eyes as his hand slowly moved down to where she ached to have it. She ground her teeth together to keep from crying out when she felt that big, warm, strong hand curl around her breast.

She actually shuddered, hiding her face in his throat as the tiny culmination racked her slender body and made it helpless.

"You are," he breathed, "the most surprising little treasure..."

His mouth searched for hers and suddenly ravished it while his hand moved on her soft flesh, molding it, tracing it, exploring it, in a hot, explosive silence. He kissed her until her mouth felt bruised and then she felt his hand move again, lifting free of her blouse, around to her back, unhooking the bra.

She didn't mind. She lifted up to help him free the catch. She looked up at him with wild, unsatisfied longing, shivering with reaction to the force of the desire he was teaching her.

"It will change everything," he whispered as he began to move the fabric away from her body. "You know that."

"Yes." She shivered.

Both hands slid against her rib cage, carrying the fabric up with them until he uncovered her firm, tip-tilted little breasts. He looked at them with pure pleasure and delight. His thumbs edged out and traced the wide, soft nipples until they drew into hard, dusky peaks. His mouth ached to taste them.

She shifted urgently in his arms, feeling him turn toward her, feeling his leg insinuate itself even more intimately against her. He looked into her dazed eyes as his hand pressed hard against the lowest part of her spine and moved her right in against the fierce arousal she'd only sensed before.

She gasped, but he didn't relent. If anything, he brought her even closer, so that he was pressed intimately to her and the sensations exploded like sensual fire in her limbs.

"Leo!" she cried out, shivering.

"You turn me on so hard that I can't even think," he ground out as he bent to her open mouth. "I didn't mean for this to happen, Janie," he groaned into her mouth as he turned her under him on the seat and pressed his hips down roughly against hers. "Feel me," he whispered. "Feel me wanting you!"

She was lost, helpless, utterly without hope. She clung to him with no thought for her virtue or the future. She was drowning in the most delicious erotic pleasure she'd ever dreamed of experiencing. She could feel him, feel the rough, thrusting rhythm of his big body as he buffeted her against the seat. Something hit her arm. She was twisted in his embrace, and one leg was almost bent backward as he crushed her under him. Any minute, limbs were going to start breaking, she thought, and even that didn't matter. She wanted him…! She didn't realize she'd said it aloud until she heard his voice, deep and strained.

"I want you, too," he whispered back.

She felt his hand between them, working at her jeans. His hand was unfastening them. She felt it, warm and strong, against her belly. It was sliding down. She moved to make it easier for him, her mouth savage under the devouring pressure of his lips…

Leo heard the loud roar of an approaching engine in his last lucid second before he went in over his head. He froze against Janie's warm, welcoming body. His head lifted. He could barely breathe.

He looked down into her wide, misty eyes. It only then occurred to him that they were cramped together on the seat, his body completely covering hers, her bra and blouse crumpled at her collarbone, her jeans halfway down over her hips.

"What the hell are we doing?!" he burst out, shocked.

"You mean you don't know?" she gasped with unconscious humor.

He looked at the windows, so fogged up that nothing was visible outside them. He looked down at Janie, lying drowsy and submissive under the heavy crush of him.

He drew his hand away from her jeans and whipped onto his back so that he could help her sit up. He slid back into his own seat, watching her fumble her clothes back on while he listened, shell-shocked, to the loud tone of a horn from the other vehicle.

Janie was a mess. Her lips were swollen. Her cheeks were flushed. Her clothes were wrinkled beyond belief. Her hair stood out all around from the pressure of his hands in it.

He was rumpled, too, his hair as much as hers. His hat was on the floorboard somewhere, streaked with water from her raincoat and dirt from the floor mats. His shirt had obvious finger marks and lipstick stains on it.

He just stared at her for a long moment while the other vehicle came to a stop beside his truck. He couldn't see anything. All the windows were thickly fogged. Absently, he dug in the side pocket of the door for the red rag he always carried. He wiped the fog from the driver's window and scowled as he saw his brother Cag sitting in another ranch truck, with Tess beside him. They were trying not to stare and failing miserably!

## *Chapter Eight*

Belatedly, Leo rolled the window down and glared at his brother and sister-in-law. ''Well?'' he asked belligerently.

''We just wondered if you were all right,'' Cag said, clearing his throat and trying very hard not to look at Janie. ''The truck was sitting out here in the middle of nowhere, but we didn't see anybody inside.''

''That's right,'' Tess said at once. ''We didn't see anybody. At all. Or anything.''

''Not anything.'' Cag nodded vigorously.

''I was showing Janie a photo of the Clark man,'' Leo said curtly. He pulled it out of his pocket. It was crumpled and slightly torn. He glared at it, trying to straighten it. ''See?''

Cag cleared his throat and averted his eyes. ''You, uh, should have taken it out of your pocket before you showed it to her… I'm going!''

Cag powered his window up with a knowing grin and gunned the engine, taking off in a spray of mud. Leo let his own window back up with flattened lips.

Janie was turned away from him, her shoulders shaking.

Odd little noises that she was trying to smother kept slipping out. She was about to burst trying not to laugh.

He leaned back against the seat and threw the clipping at her.

''It's not my fault,'' she protested. ''I was sitting here minding my own business when you got amorous.''

He pursed his swollen lips and gave her a look that would have melted butter. ''Amorous. That's a good word for it.''

She was coming down from the heights and feeling self-conscious. She picked up the clipping and handed it back to him, belatedly noticing his white Stetson at her feet. She picked it up, too, and grimaced. ''Your poor hat.''

He took it from her and tossed it into the small back seat of the double cab. ''It will clean,'' he said impatiently.

She folded her hands in her lap, toying with the streaked raincoat that she'd propped over her legs.

''Marilee caused a lot of trouble between us,'' he said after a minute, surprising her into meeting his somber gaze. ''I'm sorry about that.''

''You mean I don't really make you sick?'' she asked in a thin voice.

He winced. ''I was furious about what I thought you'd done,'' he confessed. ''It was a lie, Janie, like all the other terrible things I said. I'm sorry for every one of them, if it does any good.''

She toyed with a button on her raincoat and stared out the window at the rain. It did help, but she couldn't stop wondering if he hadn't meant it. Maybe guilt brought the apology out of him, rather than any real remorse. She knew he didn't like hurting people.

A long sigh came from the other side of the pickup. ''I'll drive you back home,'' he said after a minute, and put the truck in gear. ''Fasten your seat belt, honey.''

The endearment made her feel warm all over, but she didn't let it show. She didn't really trust Leo Hart.

He turned back onto the main road. "Fred and I are going to mob you with company at Shea's," he said conversationally. "Between us, we know most of the ranchers around Jacobsville. You can ask Harley to keep dropping in from time to time, and Fred and I will talk to the others."

She gave him a quick glance. "Harley's jaw was really bruised."

His eyes darkened. "He had no business interfering. You don't belong to damned Harley!"

She didn't know what to say. That sounded very much like jealousy. It couldn't be, of course.

His dark eyes glanced off hers. "Do you sit around in parked trucks with him and let him take your blouse off?" he asked suddenly, furiously.

"I do *not!*" she exploded.

He calmed down at once. He shifted in the seat, still uncomfortable from the keen hunger she'd kindled in his powerful body. "Okay."

Her long fingers clenched on the fabric of the coat. "You have no right to be jealous of me!" she accused angrily.

"After what we just did?" he asked pleasantly. "In your dreams, Janie."

"I don't belong to you, either," she persisted.

"You almost did," he replied, chuckling softly. "You have no idea what a close call that was. Cag and Tess saved you."

"Excuse me?"

He gave her a rueful glance. "Janie, I had your jeans half off, or have you forgotten already?"

"Leo!"

"I'm not sure I could have stopped," he continued, slowing to make a turn. "And you were no damned help at all," he added with affectionate irony, "twisting your hips against me and begging me not to stop."

She gasped. Her face went scarlet. "Of all the blatant…!"

"That's how it was, all right," he agreed. "Blatant. For the record, when a man gets that hard, it's time to call a halt any way you can, before you get in over your head. I can tell you haven't had much practice at it, but now is a good time to listen to advice."

"I don't need advice!"

"Like hell you don't. Once I got my mouth on your soft belly, you'd never have been able to make me stop."

She stared at him with slowly dawning realization. She remembered the hot, exquisite pleasure of his mouth on her breasts. She could only imagine how it would feel to let him kiss her there, on her hips, on her long legs....

"You know far too much about women," she gritted.

"You know absolutely nothing about men," he countered. He smiled helplessly. "I love it. You were in over your head the minute I touched you with intent. You'd have let me do anything I wanted." He whistled softly. "You can't imagine how I felt, knowing that. You were the sweetest candy I've ever had."

He was confounding her. She didn't know what to make of the remarks. He'd been standoffish, insulting, offensive and furious with her. Now he'd done a complete about-face. He was acting more like a lover than a big brother.

His dark eyes cut around sideways and sized up her expression. "Do you think things can just go back to the way they were before?" he asked softly. "I remember telling you that it was going to change everything."

She swallowed. "I remember."

"It already has. I look at you and get aroused, all over again," he said bluntly. "It will only get worse."

Her face flamed. "I will not have an affair with you."

"Great. I'm glad to know you have that much self-control. You can teach it to me."

"I won't get in a truck with you again," she muttered.

"I'll bring the car next time," he said agreeably. "Of course, we'll have to open both doors. I'll never be able to stretch out in the front seat the way I did in the cab of this truck.''

Her fingers clenched on the raincoat. ''That won't happen again.''

''It will if I touch you.''

She glared at him. ''You listen here...!''

He pulled the truck onto a dirt road that led through one of Fred's pastures, threw it out of gear, switched off the engine and reached for Janie with an economy of motion that left her gasping.

He had her over his lap, and his mouth hit hers with the force of a gust of wind. He burrowed into her parted lips while one lean hand went to her spine, grinding her into the fierce arousal that just the touch of her had provoked.

''Feel that?'' he muttered against her lips. ''Now try to stop me.''

She went under in a daze of pleasure. She couldn't even pretend to protest, not even when his big hand found her breast and caressed it hungrily right through the cloth of her blouse.

Her arms went around his neck. She lifted closer, shivering, as she felt the aching hunger of his body echo in her own. She moaned helplessly.

''Of all the stupid things I've done lately...'' He groaned, too, his big arms wrapping her up tight as the kiss went on and on and on.

He moved out from under the steering wheel and shifted her until she was straddling his hips, her belly lying against his aroused body so blatantly that she should have been shocked. She wasn't. He felt familiar to her, beloved to her. She wanted him. Her body yielded submissively to the insistent pressure of both his hands on her hips, dragging them against his in a fever of desire.

The approaching roar of a truck engine for the second time in less than an hour brought his head up. He looked down into Janie's heated face, at the position they were in.

His dazed eyes went out the windshield in time to see Fred's old pickup coming down the long pasture road about a quarter mile ahead of them.

He let out a word Janie had only heard Tiny use during heated arguments with patrons, and abruptly put her back in her own seat, pausing to forcefully strap her into her seat belt.

She felt shaky all over. Her eyes met his and then went involuntarily to what she'd felt so starkly against her hungry body. She flushed.

"Next time you'll get a better look," he said harshly. "I wish I could explain to you how it feels."

She wrapped her arms around her body. "I know…how it feels," she whispered unsteadily. "I ache all over."

The bad temper left him at once. He scowled as he watched her, half-oblivious to Fred's rapid approach. He couldn't take his eyes off her. She was delicious.

She managed to meet his wide, shocked eyes. "I'm sorry."

"For what?" he asked huskily. "You went in headfirst, just like I did."

She searched his eyes hungrily. Her body was on fire for him. "If you used something…" she said absently.

He actually flushed. He got back under the steering wheel and avoided looking at her. He couldn't believe what she was saying.

Fred roared up beside them and pulled onto the hard ground to let his window down.

"Rain's stopped," he told Leo. "I thought I'd run over to Eb Scott's place and have a talk with him about getting his cowboys to frequent Shea's at night."

"Good idea," Leo said, still flushed and disheveled.

Fred wisely didn't look too closely at either of them, but he had a pretty good idea of what he'd interrupted. "I won't be long, sweetheart," he told Janie.

"Okay, Dad. Be careful," she said in a husky voice.

He nodded, grinned, and took off.

Leo started the engine. He was still trying to get his breath. He stared at the dirt path ahead instead of at Janie. "I could use something," he said after a minute. "But lovemaking is addictive, Janie. One time would be a beginning, not a cure, do you understand?"

She shook her head, embarrassed now that her blood was cooling.

He reached out and caught one of her cold hands in his, intertwining their fingers. "You can't imagine how flattered I am," he said quietly. "You're a virgin, and you'd give yourself to me…"

She swallowed hard. "Please. Don't."

His hand contracted. "I'll drive you home. If you weren't working next Saturday, we could take in a movie and have dinner somewhere."

Her heart jumped up into her throat. "M…me?"

He looked down at her with the beginnings of possession. "You could wear that lacy white thing you wore to the ball," he added softly. "I like your shoulders bare. You have beautiful skin." His eyes fell to her bodice and darkened. "Beautiful breasts, too, with nice nipples…"

"Leo Hart!" she exclaimed, horrified.

He leaned over and kissed her hungrily. "I'll let you look at me next time," he whispered passionately. "Then you won't be so embarrassed when we compare notes."

She thought of seeing him without clothes and her whole face colored.

"I know what I said, but…" she protested.

He stopped the truck, bent, and kissed her again with breathless tenderness. "You've known me half your life, Janie," he said, and he was serious. He searched her worried eyes. "Am I the kind of man who takes advantage of a green girl?"

She was worried, too. "No," she had to admit.

His breathing was uneven as he studied her flushed face.

"I never would," he agreed. "You were special to me even before I kissed you the first time, in your own kitchen." His head bent again. His mouth trailed across hers in soft, biting little kisses that made her moan. "But now, after the taste of you I've just had, I'm going to be your shadow. You don't even realize what's happened, do you?"

"You want me," she said huskily.

His teeth nibbled her upper lip. "It's a little more complicated than sex." He kissed her again, hard, and lifted his head with flattering reluctance. "Look up addiction in the dictionary," he mused. "It's an eye-opener."

"Addiction?"

His nose brushed hers. "Do you remember how you moaned when I put my hands inside your blouse?"

She swallowed. "Yes."

"Now think how it would feel if I'd put my mouth on your breast, right over the nipple."

She shivered.

He nodded slowly. "Next time," he promised, his voice taut and hungry. "You have that to look forward to. Meanwhile, you keep your eyes and ears open, and don't do anything at work that gives Clark a hint that you're watching him," he added firmly.

"I'll be careful," she promised unsteadily.

His eyes were possessive on her soft face. "If he touches you, I'll kill him."

It sounded like a joke. It wasn't. She'd never seen that look in a man's eyes before. In fact, the way he was watching her was a little scary.

His big hand slid under her nape and brought her mouth just under his. "You belong to me, Janie," he whispered as his head moved down. "Your first man is going to be me. Believe it!"

The kiss was as arousing as it was tender, but it didn't last long. He forced himself to let her go, to move away. He started the truck again, put it in gear, and went back down the farm road. But his hand reached for hers involuntarily, his fingers curling into hers, as if he couldn't bear to lose contact with her. She didn't know it, but he'd reached a decision in those few seconds. There was no going back now.

Jack Clark did show up in the bar, on the following Friday night.

Janie hadn't told any of the people she worked with about him, feeling that any mention of what she knew about him might jeopardize her safety.

But she did keep a close eye on him. The man was rangy and uncouth. He sat alone at a corner table, looking around as if he expected trouble and was impatient for it to arrive.

A cowboy from Cy Parks's spread, one of Harley Fowler's men, walked to the counter and sat down, ordering a beer and a pizza.

"Hey, Miss Janie," he said with a grin that showed a missing front tooth. "Harley said to tell you he'd be in soon to see you."

"That's sweet of him," she said with a grin. "I'll just put your order in, Ned."

She scribbled the order on a slip of green paper and put it up on the long string for Nick, the teenage cook, with a clothespin.

"Where's my damned whiskey?" Clark shouted. "I been sitting here five minutes waiting for it!"

Janie winced as Nick glanced at her and shrugged, indicating the pizza list he was far behind on. He'd taken the order and got busy all of a sudden. Tiny was nowhere in sight. He was probably out back having a cigarette. Nick was up to his elbows in dough and pizza sauce. Janie had to get Clark's order, there was nobody else to do it.

She got down a shot glass, poured whiskey into it, and put it on one of the small serving trays.

She took it to Clark's table and forced a smile to her

lips. "Here you are, sir," she said, placing the shot glass in front of him. "I'm sorry it took so long."

Clark glared up at her from watery blue eyes. "Don't let that happen again. I don't like to be kept waiting."

"Yes, sir," she agreed.

She turned away, but he caught her apron strings and jerked her back. She caught her breath as his hand slid to the ones tied at her waist.

"You're kind of cute. Why don't you sit on my lap and help me drink this?" he drawled.

He was already half-lit, she surmised. She would have refused him the whiskey, if Tiny had been close by, despite the trouble he'd already caused. But now she was caught and she didn't know how to get away. All her worst fears were coming to haunt her.

"I have to get that man's drink," she pointed to Harley's cowboy. "I'll come right back, okay?"

"That boy can get his drink."

"He's making pizza," she protested. "Please."

That was a mistake. He liked it when women begged. He smiled at her. It wasn't a pleasant smile. "I said, come here!"

He jerked her down on his thin, bony legs and she screamed.

In a flash, two cowboys were on their feet and heading toward Clark, both of them dangerous looking.

"Well, looky, looky, you've got guardian angels in cowboy boots!" Clark chuckled. He stood up, dragging Janie with him. "Stay back," he warned, catching her hair in its braid. "Or else." He slapped her, hard, across the face, making her cry out, and his hand went into his pocket and came out with a knife. He flicked it and a blade appeared. He caught her around the shoulders from behind and brandished the knife. "Stay back, boys," he said again. "Or I'll cut her!"

The knife pressed against her throat. She was shaking.

She remembered all the nice self-defense moves she'd ever learned in her life from watching television or listening to her father talk. Now, she knew how useless they were. Clark would cut her throat if those men tried to help her. She had visions of him dragging her outside and assaulting her. He could do anything. There was nobody around to stop him. These cowboys weren't going to rush him and risk her life. If only Leo were here!

She was vaguely aware of Nick sliding out of sight toward the telephones. If he could just call the sheriff, the police, anybody!

Her hands went to Clark's wrist, trying to get him to release the press of the blade.

''You're hurting,'' she choked.

''Really?'' He pressed harder.

Janie felt his arm cutting off the blood to her head. Then she remembered something she'd heard of a female victim doing during an attack. If she fainted, he might turn her loose.

''Can't…breathe…'' she gasped, and closed her eyes. He might drop her if she sagged, he might cut her throat. She could die. But they'd get him. That would almost be worth it….

She let her body sag just as she heard a shout from the doorway. She pretended to lose consciousness. In the next few hectic seconds, Clark threw her to the floor so hard that she hit right on her elbow and her head, and groaned aloud with the pain of impact.

At the same moment, Leo Hart and Harley Fowler exploded into the room from the front door and went right for Clark, knife and all. They'd been in the parking lot, talking about Janie's situation, and had come running when they heard the commotion.

Harley aimed a kick at the knife and knocked it out of Clark's hands, but Clark was good with his feet, too. He landed a roundhouse kick in Harley's stomach and put him over a table. Leo slugged him, but he twisted around, got Leo's arm behind him and sent him over a table, too.

The two cowboys held back, aware of Leo's size and Harley's capability, and the fact that Clark had easily put both of them down.

There was a sudden silence. Janie dragged herself into a sitting position in time to watch Cash Grier come through the doorway and approach Clark.

Clark dived for the knife, rolled, and got to his feet. He lunged at Grier with the blade. The assistant police chief waited patiently for the attack, and he smiled. It was the coldest, most dangerous smile Janie had ever seen in her life.

Clark lunged confidently. Grier moved so fast that he was like a blur.

Seconds later, the knife was in Grier's hand. He threw it, slamming it into the wall next to the counter so deep that it would take Tiny quite some time, after the brawl, to pull it out again. He turned back to Clark even as the knife hit, fell into a relaxed stance, and waited.

Clark rushed him, tipsy and furious at the way the older man had taken his knife away. Grier easily sidestepped the intended punch, did a spinning heel kick that would have made Chuck Norris proud, and proceeded to beat the living hell out of the man with lightning punches and kicks that quickly put him on the floor, breathless and drained of will. It was over in less than three minutes. Clark held his ribs and groaned. Grier stood over him, not even breathing hard, his hand going to the handcuffs on his belt. He didn't even look winded.

Leo had picked himself up and rushed to Janie, propping her against his chest while she nursed her elbow.

"Is it broken?" he asked worriedly.

She shook her head. "Just bruised. Is my mouth bleeding?" she asked, still dazed from the confrontation.

He nodded. His face was white. He cursed his own helplessness. Between them, he and Harley should have been able to wipe the floor with Clark. He pulled out a white linen handkerchief and mopped up the bleeding lip and the cut on her cheek from Clark's nails. A big, bad bruise was already coming out on the left side of her face.

By now, Grier had Clark against a wall with a minimum of fuss. He spread the man's legs with a quick movement of his booted feet and nimbly cuffed him.

"I'll need a willing volunteer to see the magistrate and file a complaint," Grier asked.

"Right here," Harley said, wiping his mouth with a handkerchief. "I expect Mr. Hart will do the same."

"You bet," Leo agreed. "But I've got to get Janie home first."

"No rush," Grier said, with Clark by the neck. "Harley, you know where magistrate Burr Wiley lives, don't you? I'm taking Clark by there now."

"Yes, sir, I do, I'll drive right over there and swear out a complaint so you can hold that…gentleman," Harley agreed, substituting for the word he really meant to use. "Janie, you going to be okay?" he added worriedly.

She was wobbly, but she got to her feet, with Leo's support. "Sure," she said. She managed a smile. "I'll be fine."

"I'll get you!" Clark raged at Janie and Leo. "I'll get both of you!"

"Not right away," Grier said comfortably. "I'll have the judge set bail as high as it's possible to put it, and we'll see how many assault charges we can press."

"Count on me for two of them!" Janie volunteered fearlessly, wincing as her jaw protested.

"But not tonight," Leo said, curling his arm around her. "Come on, honey," he said gently. "I'll take you home."

They followed Grier with his prisoner and Harley out the door and over to Leo's big double-cabbed pickup truck.

He put her inside gently and moved around to the

driver's seat. She noticed then, for the first time, that he was in working clothes.

''You must have come right from work,'' she commented.

''We were moving livestock to a new pasture,'' he replied. ''One of the bulls got out and we had to chase him through the brush. Doesn't it show?'' he added with a nod toward his scarred batwing chaps and his muddy boots. ''I meant to be here an hour ago. Harley and I arrived together. Just in the nick of time, too.''

''Two of Cy Parks's guys were at the counter,'' she said, ''but when Clark threatened to cut me, they were afraid to rush him.''

He caught her hand in his and held it tight, his eyes going to the blood on her face, her blouse, her forearm. She was going to have a bruise on her pretty face. The sight of those marks made him furious.

''I'll be all right, thanks to all of you,'' she managed to say.

''We weren't a hell of a lot of help,'' he said with a rueful smile. ''Even Harley didn't fare well. Clark must have a military background of some sort. But he was no match for Grier.'' He shook his head. ''It was like watching a martial arts movie. I never even saw Grier move.''

She studied him while he started the truck and put their seat belts on. ''Did he hurt you?''

''Hurt my pride,'' he replied, smiling gently. ''I've never been put across a table so fast.''

''At least you tried,'' she pointed out. ''Thank you.''

''I should never have let you stay in there,'' he said. ''It's my fault.''

''It was my choice.''

He kissed her eyelids shut. ''My poor baby,'' he said softly. ''I'm not taking you to your father in this condition,'' he added firmly, noting the blood on her blouse and face. ''I'll take you home with me and clean you up, first.

We'll phone him and tell him there was a little trouble and you'll be late."

"Okay," she said. "But he's no wimp."

"I know that." He put the truck in gear. "Humor me. I want to make sure you're all right."

"I'm fine," she argued, but then she smiled. "You can clean me up, anyway."

He pursed his lips and smiled wickedly. "Best offer I've had all night," he replied as he pulled out of the parking lot.

# *Chapter Nine*

The house was quiet, deserted. The only light was the one in the living room. Leo led Janie down the hall to his own big bedroom, closed the door firmly, and led her into his spacious blue-tiled bathroom.

The towels were luxurious, sea-blue and white-striped blue towels, facecloths and hand towels. There were soaps of all sorts, a huge heated towel rack, and a whirlpool bath.

He tugged her to the medicine cabinet and turned her so that he could see her face. "You've got a bad scratch here," he remarked. He tilted her chin up, and found another smaller cut on the side of her throat, thankfully not close enough to an artery to have done much damage.

His hands went to her blouse. She caught them.

"It's all right," he said gently.

She let go.

He unfastened the blouse and tossed it onto the floor, looking her over for other marks. He found a nasty bruise on her shoulder that was just coming out. He unfastened the bra and let it fall, too, ignoring her efforts to catch it.

There was a bruise right on her breast, where Clark had held her in front of him.

"The bastard," he exclaimed, furious, as he touched the bruise.

"He got a few bruises, too, from Grier," she said, trying to comfort him. He looked devastated.

"He'd have gotten more from me, if I hadn't walked right into that punch," he said with self-contempt. "I can't remember the last time I took a stupid hit like that."

She reached up and touched his lean face gently. "It's all right, Leo."

He looked down at her bare breasts and his eyes narrowed hotly. "I don't like that bruise."

"I got a worse one when my horse threw me last month," she told him. "It will heal."

"It's in a bad place."

She smiled. "So was the other one."

He unzipped her jeans and she panicked.

He didn't take any notice. He bent and removed her shoes and socks and then stripped the jeans off her. She was wearing little lacy white briefs and his hands lingered on them.

"Leo!" she screeched.

He grimaced. "I knew it was going to be a fight all the way, and you're in no condition for another one." He unbraided her hair and let it tangle down her shoulders. He turned and started the shower.

"I can do this!" she began.

His hands were already stripping off the briefs. He stopped with his hands on her waist and looked at her with barely contained passion. "I thought you'd be in a class of your own," he said huskily. "You're a knockout, baby." He lifted her and stood her up in the shower, putting a washcloth in her hand before he closed the sliding glass door. "I'll get your things in the wash."

She was too shell-shocked to ask if he knew how to use

a washing machine. *Well, you fool,* she told herself, *you stood there like a statue and let him take your clothes off and stare at you! What are you complaining about?*

She bathed and used the shampoo on the shelf in the shower stall, scrubbing until she felt less tainted by Clark's filthy touch.

She turned off the shower and climbed out, wrapping herself in one of the sea-blue towels. It was soft and huge, big enough for Leo, who was a giant of a man. It swallowed her up whole.

Before she could wonder what she was going to do about something to wear, he opened the door and walked right in with a black velvet robe.

"Here," he said, jerking the towel away from her and holding out the robe.

She scurried into it, red-faced and embarrassed.

He drew her back against him and she realized that she wasn't the only one who'd just had a shower. He was wearing a robe, too. But his was open, and the only thing under it was a pair of black silk boxer shorts that left his powerful legs bare. His chest was broad and covered with thick, curling hair. He turned her until she was facing him, and his eyes were slow and curious.

"You'll have bruises. Right now, I want to treat those cuts with antibiotic cream. Then we'll dry your hair and brush it out." He smiled. "It's long and thick and glossy. I love your hair."

She smiled shyly. "It takes a lot of drying."

"I'm not in a hurry. Neither are you. I phoned your dad and told him as little as I could get away with."

"Was he worried?"

He lifted an eyebrow as he dug in the cabinet for the antibiotic cream. "About your virtue, maybe," he teased. "He thinks I've got you here so I can make love to you."

She felt breathless. "Have you?" she asked daringly.

He turned back to her with the cream in one big hand.

His eyes went over her like hands. "If you want it, yes. But it's up to you."

That was a little surprising. She stood docilely while he applied the cream to her cuts and then put it away. He hooked a hair dryer to a plug on the wall and linked his fingers through her thick light brown hair while he blew it dry. There was something very intimate about standing so close to him while he dried her hair. She thought she'd never get over the delight of it, as long as she lived. Every time she washed her hair from now on, she'd feel Leo's big hands against her scalp. She smiled, her head back, her eyes closed blissfully.

"Don't go to sleep," he teased as he put the hair dryer down.

"I'm not."

She felt his lips in her hair at the same moment she felt his hands go down over her shoulders and into the gap left by the robe.

If she'd been able to protest, that would have been the time to do it. But she hesitated, entranced by the feel of his hands so blatantly invading the robe, smoothing down over her high, taut breasts as if he had every right to touch her intimately whenever he felt like it.

Seconds later, the robe was gone, she was turned against him, his robe was on the floor, and she was experiencing her first adult embrace without clothing.

She whimpered at the fierce pleasure of feeling his bare, hair-roughened chest against her naked breasts. Her nails bit into the huge muscles of his upper arms as she sucked in a harsh breath and tried to stay on her feet.

"You like that, do you?" he whispered at her lips. "I know something that's even more exciting."

He picked her up in his arms and started kissing her hungrily. She responded with no thought of denying him whatever he wanted.

He carried her to the bed, paused to whip the covers and

the pillows out of the way, and placed her at the center of it. His hands went to the waistband of his boxer shorts, but he hesitated, grinding his teeth together as he looked at her nudity with aching need.

He managed to control his first impulse, which was to strip and bury himself in her. He eased onto the bed beside her, his chest pressing her down into the mattress while his mouth opened on her soft lips and pressed them wide apart.

"I've ached for this," he ground out, moving his hands from her breasts down her hips to the soft inside of her thighs. "I've never wanted anything so much!"

She tried to speak, but one of his hands invaded her in the most intimate touch she'd ever experienced. Her eyes flew open and she gaped up at him.

"You're old enough, Janie," he whispered, moving his hand just enough to make her tense. "And I've waited as long as I can."

As he spoke, he touched her delicately and when she protested, he eased down to cover her mouth with his. His fingers traced her, probed, explored her until she began to whimper and move with him. It was incredible. She was lying here, naked, in his bed, letting him explore her body as if it belonged to him. And she was…enjoying it. Glorying in it. Her back arched and she moaned as he found a pressure and a rhythm that lifted her off the bed on a wave of pleasure.

One of his long, powerful legs hooked over one of hers. She felt him at her hip, aroused and not hiding it. Through the thin silk, she was as aware of him as if he'd been naked.

"Touch me," he groaned. "Don't make me do it all. Help me."

She didn't understand what he wanted. Her hands went to his chest and began to draw through the thick hair there.

"No, baby," he whispered into her mouth. He caught one of her hands and tugged it down to the shorts he was wearing. "Don't be afraid. It's all right."

He coaxed her hand onto that part of him that was blatantly male. She gasped. He lifted his head and looked into her eyes, but he wouldn't let her hand withdraw. He spread her fingers against him, grimacing as the waves of pleasure hit him and closed his eyes on a shudder.

His reaction fascinated her. She knew so little. "Does it...hurt?"

"What?" he asked huskily. "Your hand, or what it's doing?"

"Both. Either."

He pressed her hand closer, looking down. "Look," he whispered, coaxing her eyes to follow his. It was intimate. But not intimate enough for him.

"Don't panic, baby," he whispered, levering onto his back. He ripped off the shorts and tossed them onto the carpet. He rolled onto his side and caught one of her hands, insistent now, drawing it to him.

She made a sound as she looked, for the first time, at an aroused male without a thing to conceal him except her hand.

"Don't be embarrassed," he whispered roughly. "I wouldn't want any other woman to see me like this."

"You wouldn't?"

He shook his head. It was difficult not to lose control. But he eased her fingers back to him and held them there. "I'm vulnerable."

Her eyes brightened. "Oh." She hadn't considered that he was as helpless as she was to resist the pleasure of what they were doing.

His own hand went back to her body. He touched her, as she was touching him, and he smiled at her fascination.

She couldn't believe it was happening at all. She stared up at him with all her untried longings in her eyes, on her rapt face. She belonged to him. He belonged to her. It was incredible.

"Are you going to?" she whispered.

He kissed her eyelids lazily. ''Going to what?''

''Take me,'' she whispered back.

He chuckled, deep in his throat. ''What a primitive description. It's a mutual thing, you know. Wouldn't you take me, as well?''

Her eyes widened. ''I suppose I would,'' she conceded. She stiffened and shivered. ''Oh!''

His eyes darkened. There was no more humor on his face as his touch became slowly invasive. ''Will you let me satisfy you?'' he asked.

''I don't...understand.''

''I know. That's what makes it so delicious.'' He bent slowly, but not to her mouth. His lips hovered just above her wide nipple. ''This is the most beautiful thing I've ever done with a woman,'' he whispered. His lips parted. ''I want nothing, except to please you.''

His mouth went down over the taut nipple in a slow, exquisite motion that eventually all but swallowed her breast. She felt his tongue moving against the nipple, felt the faint suction of his mouth. All the while, his hand was becoming more insistent, and far more intimate, on her body. He felt her acceptance, even as she opened her legs for him and began to moan rhythmically with every movement of his hands.

''Yes,'' he whispered against her breast when he felt the pulsing of her body. ''Let me, baby.'' He lifted his head and looked down into her eyes as she moaned piteously.

She was pulsating. She felt her body clench. She was slowly drifting up into a glorious, rhythmic heat that filled her veins, her arteries, the very cells of her body with exquisite pleasure. She'd never dreamed there was such pleasure.

''Janie, touch me, here,'' he whispered unsteadily.

She felt his hand curling around her fingers, teaching her, insistent, his breath jerky and violent as he twisted against her.

"Baby," he choked, kissing her hungrily. "Baby, baby!"

He moved, his big body levering slowly between her long legs. He knelt over her, his eyes wild, his body shuddering, powerfully male, and she looked up at him with total submission, still shivering from the taste of pleasure he'd already given her. It would be explosive, ecstatic. She could barely breathe for the anticipation. She was lost. He was going to have her now. She loved him. She was going to give herself. There was nothing that could stop them, nothing in all the world!

"Mr. Hart! Oh, Mr. Hart! Are you in here?"

Leo stiffened, his body kneeling between her thighs, his powerful hands clenching on them. He looked blindly down into her wide, dazed eyes. He shuddered violently and his eyes closed on a harsh muffled curse.

He threw himself onto the bed beside her, on his belly. He couldn't stop shaking. He gasped at a jerky breath and clutched the sheet beside his head as he fought for control.

"Mr. Hart!" the voice came again.

He suddenly remembered that he hadn't locked the bedroom door, and the cowboy didn't know that he wasn't alone. Even as he thought it, he heard the doorknob turn. "Open that door...and you're fired!" he shouted hoarsely. Beside him, Janie actually gasped as she belatedly realized what was about to happen.

The doorknob was released at once. "Sorry, sir, but I need you to come out here and look at this bull. I think there's something wrong with him, Mr. Hart! We got him loaded into one of the trailers and put him in the barn, but..."

"Call the vet!" he shouted. "I'll be there directly!"

"Yes, sir!"

Footsteps went back down the carpeted hall. Leo lifted his head. Beside him, Janie looked as shattered as he felt. Tears were swimming in her eyes.

He groaned softly, and pulled her to him, gently. "It's all right," he whispered, kissing her eyelids shut. "Don't cry, baby. Nothing happened."

"Nothing!" she choked.

His hands smoothed down the long line of her back. "Almost nothing," he murmured dryly.

She was horrified, not only at her own behavior, but at what had almost happened. "If he hadn't called to you," she began in a high-pitched whisper.

His hands tangled in her long hair and he brought her mouth under his, tenderly. He nibbled her upper lip. "Yes, I know," he replied gently. "But he did." He pulled away from her and got to his feet, stretching hugely, facing her. He watched her try not to look at him with amused indulgence. But eventually, she couldn't resist it. Her eyes were huge, shocked...delighted.

"Now, when we compare notes, you'll have ammunition," he teased.

She flushed and averted her eyes, belatedly noticing that she wasn't wearing clothes, either. She tugged the sheet up over her breasts, but it was difficult to feel regrets when she looked at him.

He was smiling. His eyes were soft, tender. He looked down at what he could see of her body above the sheet with pride, loving the faint love marks on her breasts that his mouth had made.

"Greenhorn," he chided at her scarlet blush. "Well, you know a lot more about men now than you did this morning, don't you?"

She swallowed hard. Her eyes slid down him. She didn't look away, but she was very flushed, and not only because of what she was seeing. Her body throbbed in the most delicious way.

"I think I'd better take you home. Now," he added with a rueful chuckle. "From this point on, it only gets worse."

He was still passionately aroused. He wondered if she

realized what it meant. He chuckled at her lack of comprehension. ''I could have you three times and I'd still be like this,'' he said huskily. ''I'm not easily satisfied.''

She shivered as she looked at him, her body yielded, submissive.

''You want to, don't you?'' he asked quietly, reading her expression. ''So do I. More than you know. But we're not going that far together tonight. You've had enough trauma for a Friday night.''

He caught her hand and pulled her up, free of the sheet and open to his eyes as he lead her back into the bathroom. He turned on the shower and climbed in with her, bathing both of them quickly and efficiently, to her raging embarrassment.

He dried her and then himself before he put his shorts back on and left her to get her things. He'd washed them while she was in the shower the first time and put them in the dryer. They were clean and sweet-smelling, and the bloodstains were gone.

But when she went to take them from him, he shook his head. ''One of the perks,'' he said softly. ''I get to dress you.''

And he did, completely. Then he led her to the dresser, and ran his own brush through her long, soft hair, easing it back from her face. The look in his eyes was new, fascinating, incomprehensible. She looked back at him with awe.

''Now you know something about what sex feels like, even though you're still very much a virgin,'' he said matter-of-factly. ''And you won't be afraid of the real thing anymore, when it happens, will you?''

She shook her head, dazed.

He put the brush down and framed her face in his big, lean hands. He wasn't smiling. ''You belong to me now,'' he said huskily. ''I belong to you. Don't agonize over what you let me do to you tonight. It's as natural as breathing.

Don't lie awake feeling shame or embarrassment. You saw me as helpless as I saw you. There won't be any jokes about it, any gossiping about it. I'll never tell another living soul what you let me do.''

She relaxed. She hadn't really known what to expect. But he sounded more solemn than he'd ever been. He was looking at her with a strange expression.

''Are you sorry?'' she asked in a hushed whisper.

''No,'' he replied quietly. ''It was unavoidable. I was afraid for you tonight. I couldn't stop Clark. Neither could Harley. Until Grier walked in, I thought you'd had it. What happened in here was a symptom of the fear, that's all. I wanted to hold you, make you part of me.'' He drew in a shaky breath and actually shivered. ''I wanted to go right inside you, Janie,'' he whispered bluntly. ''But we'll save that pleasure for the right time and place. This isn't it.''

She colored and averted her eyes.

He turned her face back to his. ''Meanwhile,'' he said slowly, searching her eyes, ''we'll have no more secrets, of any kind, between us.''

She stood quietly against him, watching his face. ''Nobody's seen me without my clothes since I was a little kid,'' she whispered, as if it was a fearful secret.

''Not that many women have seen me without mine,'' he replied unexpectedly. He smiled tenderly.

Her eyebrows arched.

''Shocked?'' he mused, moving away to pull clothes out of his closet and socks out of his drawers. He sat down to pull on the socks, glancing at her wryly. ''I'm not a playboy. I'm not without experience, but there was always a limit I wouldn't cross with women I only knew slightly. It gives people power over you when they know intimate things about you.''

''Yes,'' she said, moving to sit beside him on the bed, with her hands folded in her lap. ''Thanks.''

''For what?''

She smiled. ‘‘For making it feel all right. That I…let you touch me that way, I mean.’’

He finished pulling on his socks and tilted her face up to his. He kissed her softly. ‘‘I won’t ever touch another woman like that,’’ he whispered into her mouth. ‘‘It would be like committing adultery, after what we did on this bed.’’

Her heart flew up into the clouds. Her wide, fascinated eyes searched his. ‘‘Really?’’

He chuckled. ‘‘Are you anxious to rush out and experiment with another man?’’

She shook her head.

‘‘Why?’’

She smiled shyly. ‘‘It would be like committing adultery,’’ she repeated what he’d said.

He stood up and looked down at her with possession. ‘‘It was a near thing,’’ he murmured. ‘‘I don’t know whether to punch that cowboy or give him a raise for interrupting us. I lost it, in those last few seconds. I couldn’t have stopped.’’

‘‘Neither could I.’’ She lifted her mouth for his soft kiss. She searched his eyes, remembering what he’d told her. ‘‘But the books say a man can only do it once,’’ she blurted out, ‘‘and then he has to rest.’’

He laughed softly. ‘‘I know. But a handful of men can go all night. I’m one of them.’’

‘‘Oh!’’

He pulled up his slacks and fastened them before he shouldered into a knit shirt. He turned back to her, smoothing his disheveled hair. ‘‘I was contemplating even much more explosive pleasures when someone started shouting my name.’’

This was interesting. ‘‘More explosive pleasures?’’ she prompted.

He drew her up against him and held her close. ‘‘What we did and what we didn’t do, is the difference between licking an ice-cream cone and eating a banana split,'' he teased. ''What you had was only a small taste of what we can have together.''

''Wow,'' she said softly.

''Wow,'' he echoed, bending to kiss her hungrily. He sighed into her mouth. ''I was almost willing to risk getting you pregnant, I was so far gone.'' He lifted his head and looked at her. ''How do you feel about kids, Janie?''

''I love children,'' she said honestly. ''How about you?''

''Me too. I'm beginning to rethink my position on having them.'' His lean hand touched her belly. ''You've got nice wide hips,'' he commented, testing them.

She felt odd. Her body seemed to contract. She searched his eyes because she didn't understand what was happening to her.

''You can tell Shea's you're through,'' he said abruptly. ''I'm not risking you again. If we can't keep Clark in jail for the foreseeable future, we have to make plans to keep you safe.''

Her lips parted. She'd all but forgotten her horrible experience. She touched her throat and felt again the prick of the knife. ''You said he was vindictive.''

''He'll have to get through me,'' he said. ''And with a gun, I'm every bit his equal,'' he added.

She reached up and touched his hard mouth. ''I don't want you to get hurt.''

''I don't want you to get hurt,'' he seconded. His face twisted. ''Baby, you are the very breath in my body,'' he whispered, and reached for her.

She felt boneless as he kissed her with such passion and fire that she trembled.

''I wish I didn't have to take you home,'' he groaned at her lips. ''I want to make love to you completely. I want to lie against you and over you, and inside you!''

She moaned at his mouth as it became deep and insistent, devouring her parted lips.

He was shivering. He had to drag his mouth away from hers. He looked shattered. He touched her long hair with a hand that had a faint tremor. ''Amazing,'' he whispered gruffly. ''That I couldn't see it, before it happened.''

''See what?'' she asked drowsily.

His eyes fell to her swollen, parted lips. ''Never mind,'' he whispered. He bent and kissed her with breathless tenderness. ''I'm taking you home. Then I'll see about my bull. Tomorrow morning, I'll come and get you and we'll see about swearing out more warrants against Clark.''

''You don't think Clark will get out on bond?'' she asked worriedly.

''Not if Grier can prevent it.'' He reached for his truck keys and took her by the arm. ''We'll go out the back,'' he said. ''I don't want anyone to know you were here with me tonight. It wouldn't look good, even under the circumstances.''

''Don't worry, nobody will know,'' she assured him.

The next morning, Fred Brewster came into the dining room looking like a thunderstorm.

''What were you doing in Leo Hart's bedroom last night when you were supposed to be working, Janie?'' he asked bluntly.

She gaped at him with her mouth open. He was furious.

''How in the world...?'' she exclaimed.

''One of the Harts' cowboys went to get him about a sick bull. He saw Leo sneaking you out the back door!'' He scowled and leaned closer. ''And what the hell happened to your face? Leo said you had a troublesome customer and he was bringing you home! What the hell's going on, Janie?''

She was scrambling for an answer that wouldn't get her in even more trouble when they heard a pickup truck roar up the driveway and stop at the back door. A minute later there was a hard rap, and the door opened by itself.

Leo came in, wearing dressy boots and slacks, a white shirt with a tie, and a sports coat. His white Stetson had been cleaned and looked as if it had never been introduced to a muddy truck mat. He took off the hat and tossed it onto the counter, moving past Fred to look at Janie's face.

''Damn!'' he muttered, turning her cheek so that the violet bruise was very noticeable. ''I didn't realize he hit you that hard, baby!''

''Hit her?!'' Fred burst out. ''Who hit her, and what was she doing in your bedroom last night?!''

Leo turned toward him, his face contemplative, his dark eyes quiet and somber. ''Did she tell you?'' he asked.

''I never!'' Janie burst out, flushing.

''One of your cowboys mentioned it to one of my cowboys,'' Fred began.

Leo's eyes flashed fire. ''He'll be drawing his pay at the end of the day. Nobody, but nobody, tells tales about Janie!''

Father and daughter exchanged puzzled glances.

''Why are you so shocked?'' he asked her, when he saw her face. ''Do you think I take women to my house, ever?''

She hadn't considered that. Her lips parted on a shocked breath.

He glanced at Fred, who was still unconvinced. ''All right, you might as well know it all. Jack Clark made a pass at her in Shea's and when she protested, he pulled a knife on her.'' He waited for that to sink in, and for Fred to sit down, hard, before he continued. ''Harley and I got there about the same time and heard yelling. We went inside to find Janie with a knife at her throat. We rushed Clark, but he put both of us over a table. Janie's co-worker had phoned the sheriff, but none of the deputies were within quick reach, so they radioed Grier and he took Clark down and put him in jail.'' He grimaced, looking at Janie's face. ''She was covered with blood and so upset that she could hardly stand. I couldn't bring myself to take her home in that condition, so I took her home with me and cleaned her up and calmed her down first.''

Fred caught Janie's hand in his and held it hard. ''Oh, daughter, I'm sorry!''

''It's okay. We were trying to spare you, that's all,'' she faltered.

Leo pulled a cell phone from his pocket, dialed a number, and got his foreman. ''You tell Carl Turley that he's fired. You get him the hell out of there before I get home, or he'll need first aid to get off the ranch. Yes. Yes.'' His face was frightening. ''It was true. Clark's in jail now, on assault charges. Of course nothing was going on, and you can repeat that, with my blessing! Just get Turley out of there! Right.''

He hung up and put the phone away. He was vibrating with suppressed fury, that one of his own men would gossip about him and Janie, under the circumstances. ''So much for gossip,'' he gritted.

''Thanks, Leo,'' Fred said tersely. ''And I'm sorry I jumped to the wrong conclusion. It's just that, normally, a man wouldn't take a woman home with him late at night unless he was…well…''

''…planning to seduce her?'' Leo said for him. He looked at Janie and his eyes darkened.

She flushed.

''Yes,'' Fred admitted uncomfortably.

Leo's dark eyes began to twinkle as they wandered over Janie like loving hands. ''Would this be a bad time to tell you that I have every intention of seducing her at some future time?''

# *Chapter Ten*

Fred looked as if he'd swallowed a chicken, whole. He flushed, trying to forget that Leo had loaned him the money to save his ranch, thinking only of his daughter's welfare. "Now, look here, Leo..." he began.

Leo chuckled. "I was teasing. She's perfectly safe with me, Fred," he replied. He caught Janie's hand and tugged her to her feet. "We have to go see the magistrate about warrants," he said, sobering. "I want him to see these bruises on her face," he added coldly. "I don't think we'll have any problem with assault charges."

Janie moved closer to Leo. He made her feel safe, protected. He bent toward her, his whole expression one of utter tenderness. Belatedly, Fred began to understand what he was seeing. Leo's face, to him, was an open book. He was shocked. At the same time, he realized that Janie didn't understand what was going on. Probably she thought he was being brotherly.

"Don't you want breakfast first?" Fred offered, trying to get his bearings again.

For the first time, Leo seemed to notice the table. His

hand, holding Janie's, contracted involuntarily. Bacon, scrambled eggs, and...biscuits? Biscuits! He scowled, letting go of Janie's fingers to approach the bread basket. He reached down, expecting a concretelike substance, remembering that he and Rey had secretly sailed some of Janie's earlier efforts at biscuit-making over the target range for each other and used them for skeet targets. But these weren't hard. They were flaky, delicate. He opened one. It was soft inside. It smelled delicious.

He was barely aware of sitting down, dragging Janie's plate under his hands. He buttered a biscuit and put strawberry jam on it. He bit into it and sighed with pure ecstasy.

"I forgot about the biscuits," Janie told her father worriedly.

Fred glanced at their guest and grimaced. "Maybe we should have saved it for a surprise."

Leo was sighing, his eyes closed as he chewed.

"We'll never get to the magistrate's now," Janie thought aloud.

"He'll run out of biscuits in about ten minutes, at that rate," Fred said with a grin.

"I'll get another plate. We can split the eggs and bacon," Janie told her father, inwardly beaming with pride at Leo's obvious enjoyment of her efforts. Now, finally, the difficulty of learning to cook seemed worth every minute.

Leo went right on chewing, oblivious to movement around him.

The last biscuit was gone with a wistful sigh when he became aware of his two companions again.

"Who made the biscuits?" Leo asked Janie.

She grimaced. "I did."

"But you can't cook, honey," he said gently, trying to soften the accusation.

"Marilee said you didn't like me because I couldn't make biscuits or cook anything edible," she confessed without looking at him. "So I learned how."

He caught her fingers tightly in his. "She lied. But those were wonderful biscuits," he said. "Flaky and soft inside, delicately browned. Absolutely delicious."

She smiled shyly. "I can make them anytime you like."

He was looking at her with pure possession. "Every morning," he coaxed. "I'll stop by for coffee. If Fred doesn't mind," he added belatedly.

Fred chuckled. "Fred doesn't mind," he murmured dryly.

Leo scowled. "You look like a cat with a mouse."

Fred shrugged. "Just a stray thought. Nothing to worry about."

Leo held the older man's reluctant gaze and understood the odd statement. He nodded slowly. He smiled sheepishly as he realized that Fred wasn't blind at all.

Fred got up. "Well, I've got cattle to move. How's your bull, by the way?" he added abruptly, worried.

"Colic," Leo said with a cool smile. "Easily treated and nothing to get upset over."

"I'm glad. I had visions of you losing yours to Clark as well."

"He isn't from the same herd as yours was, Fred," Leo told him. "But even so, I think we'll manage to keep Clark penned up for a while. Which reminds me," he added, glancing at Janie. "We'd better get going."

"Okay. I'll just get the breakfast things cleared away first."

Leo sat and watched her work with a smitten expression on his face. Fred didn't linger. He knew a hooked fish when he saw one.

They swore out warrants and presented them to the sheriff. Clark had already been transferred to the county lockup, after a trip to the hospital emergency room the night before, and Leo and Janie stopped in to see Grier at the police station.

Grier had just finished talking to the mayor, a pleasant older man named Tarleton Connor, newly elected to his position. Connor and Grier had a mutual cousin, as did Grier and Chet Blake, the police chief. Chet was out of town on police business, so Grier was nominally in charge of things.

''Have a seat,'' Grier invited, his eyes narrow and angry on Janie's bruised face. ''If it's any consolation, Miss Brewster, Clark's got bruised ribs and a black eye.''

She smiled. It was uncomfortable, because it irritated the bruise. ''Thanks, Mr. Grier,'' she said with genuine appreciation.

''That goes double for me,'' Leo told him. ''He put Harley and me over a table so fast it's embarrassing to admit it.''

''Why?'' Grier asked, sitting down behind his desk. ''The man was a martial artist,'' he elaborated. ''He had a studio up in Victoria for a while, until the authorities realized that he was teaching killing techniques to ex-cons.''

Leo's jaw fell.

Grier shrugged. ''He was the equivalent of a black belt, too. Harley's not bad, but he needs a lot more training from Eb Scott before he could take on Clark.'' He pursed his lips and his eyes twinkled as he studied Leo's expression. ''Feel better now?''

Leo chuckled. ''Yes. Thanks.''

Grier glanced at Janie's curious expression. ''Men don't like to be overpowered by other men. It's a guy thing,'' he explained.

''Anybody ever overpower you?'' Leo asked curiously.

''Judd Dunn almost did, once. But then, I taught him everything he knows.''

''You know a lot,'' Janie said. ''I never saw anybody move that fast.''

''I was taught by a guy up in Tarrant County,'' Grier

told her with a smile. "He's on television every week. Plays a Texas Ranger."

Janie gasped.

"Nice guy," Grier added. "And a hell of a martial artist."

Leo was watching him with a twinkle in his own eyes. "I did think the spinning heel kick looked familiar."

Grier smiled. He sat up. "About Clark," he added. "His brother came to see him at the county lockup this morning and got the bad news. With only one charge so far, Harley's, he's only got a misdemeanor..."

"We took out a warrant for aggravated assault and battery," Leo interrupted. "Janie had a knife at her throat just before you walked in."

"So I was told." Grier's dark eyes narrowed on Janie's throat. The nick was red and noticeable this morning. "An inch deeper and we'd be visiting you at the funeral home this morning."

"I know," Janie replied.

"You kept your head," he said with a smile. "It probably saved your life."

"Can you keep Clark in jail?" she asked worriedly.

"I'll ask Judge Barnett to set bail as high as he can. But Clark's brother isn't going to settle for a public defender. He said he'd get Jack the best attorney he could find, and he'd pay for it." He shrugged. "God knows what he'll pay for it with," he added coldly. "John Clark owes everybody, up to and including his boss. So does our local Clark brother."

"He may have to have a public defender."

"We'll see. But meanwhile, he's out of everybody's way, and he'll stay put."

"What about his brother?" Leo wanted to know. "Is Janie in any danger?"

Grier shook his head. "John Clark went back to Victoria after he saw his brother. I had him followed, by one of my off-duty guys, just to make sure he really left. But I'd keep my eyes open, if I were you, just the same. These boys are bad news.''

''We'll do that,'' Leo said.

He drove Janie back to his own ranch and took her around with him while he checked on the various projects he'd initiated. He pulled up at the barn and told her to stay in the truck.

She was curious until she remembered that he'd fired the man who'd interrupted them the night before. She was glad about the interruption, in retrospect, but uneasy about the gossip that man had started about her and Leo.

He was back in less than five minutes, his face hard, his eyes blazing. He got into the truck and glanced at her, forcibly wiping the anger out of his expression.

''He's gone,'' he told her gently. ''Quit without his check,'' he added with a rueful smile. ''I guess Charles told him what I said.'' He shrugged. ''He wasn't much of a cowboy, at that, if he couldn't tell colic from bloat.''

She reached out and put her nervous fingers over his big hand on the steering wheel. He flinched and she jerked her hand back.

''No!'' He caught her fingers in his and held them tight. ''I'm sorry,'' he said at once, scowling. ''You've never touched me voluntarily before. It surprised me. I like it,'' he added, smiling.

She was flushed and nervous. ''Oh. Okay.'' She smiled shyly.

He searched her eyes with his for so long that her heart began to race. His face tautened. ''This won't do,'' he said in a husky, deep tone. He started the truck with a violent motion and drove back the way they'd come, turning onto a rutted path that led into the woods and, far beyond, to a pasture. But he stopped the truck halfway to the pasture, threw it out of gear, and cut off the engine.

He had Janie out of her seat belt and into his big arms in seconds, and his hungry mouth was on her lips before she could react.

She didn't have any instincts for self-preservation left. She melted into his aroused body, not even protesting the intimate way he was pressing her hips against his. Her arms curled around his neck and she kissed him back with enthusiasm.

She felt his hands going under her blouse, against her breasts. That felt wonderful. It was perfectly all right, because she belonged to him.

He lifted his mouth from hers, breathing hard, and watched her eyes while his hands caressed her. She winced and he caught his breath.

"I'm sorry!" he said at once, soothing the bruise he'd forgotten about. "I didn't mean to hurt you," he whispered.

She reached up to kiss his eyelids shut, feeling the shock that ran through him at the soft caress. His hands moved to her waist and rested there while he held his breath, waiting. She felt the hunger in him, like a living thing. Delighted by his unexpected submission to her mouth, she kissed his face softly, tenderly, drawing her lips over his thick eyebrows, his eyelids, his cheeks and nose and chin. They moved to his strong throat and lingered in the pulsating hollow.

One lean hand went between them to the buttons of his cotton shirt. He unfastened them quickly, jerking the fabric out of her way, inviting her mouth inside.

Her hands spread on the thick mat of hair that covered the warm, strong muscles of his chest. Her mouth touched it, lightly, and then not lightly. She moved to where his heart beat roughly, and then over the flat male nipple that was a counterpart to her own. But the reaction she got when she put her mouth over it was shocking.

He groaned so harshly that she was sure she'd hurt him.

She drew back, surprising a look of anguish on his lean face.

"Leo?" she whispered uneasily.

"It arouses me," he ground out, then he shivered.

She didn't know what to do next. He looked as if he ached to have her repeat the caress, but his body was as taut as a rope against her.

"You'll have to tell me what to do," she faltered. "I don't want to make it worse."

"Whatever I do is going to shock you speechless," he choked out. "But, what the hell...!"

He dragged her face back to his nipple and pressed it there, hard. "You know what I want."

She did, at some level. Her mouth eased down against him with a soft, gentle suction that lifted him back against the seat with a harsh little cry of pleasure. His hands at the back of her head were rough and insistent. She gave in and did what he was silently asking her for. She felt him shudder and gasp, his body vibrating as if it was overwhelmed by pleasure. He bit off a harsh word and trembled violently for a few seconds before he turned her mouth away from him and pressed her unblemished cheek against his chest. His hands in her hair trembled as they caressed her scalp. His heartbeat was raging under her mouth.

He fought to breathe normally. "Wow," he whispered unsteadily.

Her fingers tangled in the thick hair under them. "Did you really like it?" she whispered back.

He actually laughed, a little unsteadily. "Didn't you feel what was happening to me?"

"You were shaking."

"Yes. I was, wasn't I? Just the way you were shaking last night when I touched you..."

Her cheek slid back onto his shoulder so that she could look up into his soft eyes. "I didn't know a man would be sensitive, there, like a woman is."

He bent and drew his lips over her eyelids. "I'm sensitive, all right." His lips moved over her mouth and pressed there hungrily. "It isn't enough, Janie. I've got to have you. All the way."

"Right now?" she stammered.

He lifted his head and looked down at her in his arms. He was solemn, unsmiling, as he met her wide eyes. His body was still vibrating with unsatisfied desire. Deliberately, he drew her hips closer against his and let her feel him there.

She didn't protest. If anything, her body melted even closer.

One lean hand went to her belly and rested there, between them, while he searched her eyes. "I want…to make you pregnant," he said in a rough whisper.

Her lips fell open. She stared at him, not knowing what to say.

He looked worried. "I've never wanted that with a woman," he continued, as if he was discussing the weather. His fingers moved lightly on her body. "Not with anyone."

He was saying something profound. She hadn't believed it at first, but the expression on his face was hard to explain away.

"My father would shoot you," she managed to say weakly.

"My brothers would shoot me, too," he agreed, nodding.

She was frowning. She didn't understand.

He bent and kissed her, with an odd tenderness. He laughed to himself. "Just my luck," he breathed against her lips, "to get mixed up with a virgin who can cook."

"We aren't mixed up," she began.

His hand contracted against the base of her spine, grinding her into him, and one eyebrow went up over a worldly smile as she blushed.

She cleared her throat. "We aren't very mixed up," she corrected.

He nibbled at her upper lip. ''I look at you and get turned on so hard I can hardly walk around without bending over double. I touch you and I hurt all over. I dream of you every single night of my life and wake up vibrating.'' He lifted his head and looked down into her misty eyes. He wasn't smiling. He wasn't kidding. ''Never like this, Janie. Either we have each other, or we stop it, right now.''

Her fingers touched his face lovingly. ''You can do whatever you like to me,'' she whispered unsteadily.

His jaw tautened. ''Anything?''

She nodded. She loved him with all her heart.

His eyes closed. His arms brought her gently against him, and his mouth buried itself in her throat, pressing there hot and hard for a few aching seconds. Then he dragged in a harsh breath and sat up, putting her back in her seat and fastening her seat belt.

He didn't look at her as he fastened his own belt and started the truck. She sat beside him as he pulled out onto the highway, a little surprised that he didn't turn into the road that led to his house. She'd expected him to take her there. She swallowed hard, remembering the way they'd pleasured each other on his big bed the night before, remembering the look of his powerful body without clothes. She flushed with anticipated delight. She was out of her mind. Her father was going to kill her. She looked at Leo with an ache that curled her toes up inside her shoes, and didn't care if he did. Some things were worth dying for.

Leo drove right into town and pulled into a parking spot in front of the drugstore. Right, she thought nervously, he was going inside to buy...protection...for what they were going to do. He wanted a child, though, he'd said. She flushed as he got out of the truck and came around to open her door.

He had to unfasten her seat belt first. She didn't even have the presence of mind to accomplish that.

He helped her out of the truck and looked down at her

with an expression she couldn't decipher. He touched her cheek gently, and then her hair, and her soft mouth. His eyes were full of turmoil.

He tugged her away from the truck and closed her door, leading her to the sidewalk with one small hand tightly held in his fingers.

She started toward the drugstore.

"Wrong way, sweetheart," he said tenderly, and led her right into a jewelry store.

The clerk was talking to another clerk, but he came forward, smiling, when they entered the shop.

"May I help you find something?" he asked Leo.

"Yes," Leo said somberly. "We want to look at wedding bands."

Janie felt all the blood draining out of her face. It felt numb. She hoped she wasn't going to pass out.

Leo's hand tightened around her fingers, and slowly linked them together as he positioned her in front of the case that held engagement rings and wedding rings.

The clerk took out the tray that Leo indicated. Leo looked down at Janie with quiet, tender eyes.

"You can have anything you want," he said huskily, and he wasn't talking solely of rings.

She met his searching gaze with tears glistening on her lashes. He bent and kissed the wetness away.

The clerk averted his eyes. It was like peering through a private window. He couldn't remember ever seeing such an expression on a man's face before.

"Look at the rings, Janie," Leo said gently.

She managed to focus on them belatedly. She didn't care about flashy things, like huge diamonds. She was a country girl, for all her sophistication. Her eyes kept coming back to a set of rings that had a grape leaf pattern. The wedding band was wide, yellow gold with a white gold rim, the pattern embossed on the gold surface. The matching engagement ring had a diamond, but not a flashy one, and it contained the same grape leaf pattern on its circumference.

"I like this one," she said finally, touching it.

There was a matching masculine-looking wedding band. She looked up at Leo.

He smiled. "Do you want me to wear one, too?" he teased.

Her eyes were breathless with love. She couldn't manage words. She only nodded.

He turned his attention back to the clerk. "We'll take all three," he said.

"They'll need to be sized. Let me get my measuring rod," the clerk said with a big grin. The rings were expensive, fourteen karat, and that diamond was the highest quality the store sold. The commission was going to be tasty.

"It isn't too expensive?" Janie worried.

Leo bent and kissed the tip of her nose. "They're going to last a long time," he told her. "They're not too expensive."

She couldn't believe what was happening. She wanted to tell him so, but the clerk came back and they were immediately involved in having their fingers sized and the paperwork filled out.

Leo produced a gold card and paid for them while Janie looked on, still shell-shocked.

Leo held her hand tight when they went back to the truck. "Next stop, city hall," he murmured dryly. "Rather, the fire station—they take the license applications when city hall is closed. I forgot it was Saturday." He lifted both eyebrows at her stunned expression. "Might as well get it all done in one day. Which reminds me." He pulled out his cell phone after he'd put her in the truck and phoned the office of the doctors Coltrain. While Janie listened, spellbound, he made an appointment for blood tests for that afternoon. The doctors Coltrain had a Saturday clinic.

He hung up and slipped the phone back into his pocket

with a grin. "Marriage license next, blood tests later, and about next Wednesday, we'll have a nice and quiet small wedding followed by," he added huskily, "one hell of a long passionate wedding night."

She caught her breath at the passion in his eyes. "Leo, are you sure?" she wanted to know.

He dragged her into his arms and kissed her so hungrily that a familiar couple walking past the truck actually stared amusedly at them for a few seconds before hurrying on past.

"I'm sorry, baby. I can't...wait...any longer," he ground out into her eager mouth. "It's marriage or I'm leaving the state!" He lifted his head, and his eyes were tortured. He could barely breathe. "Oh, God, I want you, Janie!"

She felt the tremor in his big body. She understood what he felt, because it was the same with her. She drew in a slow breath. It was desire. She thought, maybe, there was some affection as well, but he was dying to have her, and that was what prompted marriage plans. He'd said often enough that he was never going to get married.

He saw all those thoughts in her eyes, even through the most painful desire he'd ever known. "I'll make you glad you said yes," he told her gruffly. "I won't ever cheat on you, or hurt you. I'll take care of you all my life. All of yours."

It was enough, she thought, to take a chance on. "All right," she said tenderly. She reached up and touched his hard, swollen mouth. "I'll marry you."

It was profound, to hear her say it. He caught his breath at the raging arousal the words produced in his already-tortured body. He groaned as he pressed his mouth hard into the palm of her hand.

She wasn't confident enough to tease him about his desire for her. But it pleased her that he was, at least, fiercely hungry for her in that way, if no other.

He caught her close and fought for control. ''We'd better go and get a marriage license,'' he bit off. ''We've already given Evan and Anna Tremayne an eyeful.''

''What?'' she asked drowsily.

''They were walking past when I kissed you,'' he said with a rueful smile.

''They've been married for years,'' she pointed out.

He rubbed his nose against hers. ''Wait until we've been married for years,'' he whispered. ''We'll still be fogging up windows in parked trucks.''

''Think so?'' she asked, smiling.

''Wait and see.''

He let go of her, with obvious reluctance, and moved back under the steering wheel. ''Here we go.''

They applied for the marriage license, had the blood tests, and then went to round up their families to tell them the news.

Janie's aunt Lydia had gone to Europe over the holidays on an impromptu sightseeing trip, Fred Brewster told them when they gave him the news. ''She'll be livid if she misses the wedding,'' he said worriedly.

''She can be here for the first christening,'' Leo said with a grin at Janie's blush. ''You can bring Hettie with you, and come over to the ranch for supper tomorrow night,'' he added, amused at Fred's lack of surprise at the announcement. ''I've invited my brothers to supper and phoned Barbara to have it catered. I wanted to break the news to all of them at once.''

''Hettie won't be surprised,'' Fred told them, tongue-in-cheek. ''But she'll enjoy a night out. We'll be along about six.''

''Fine,'' Leo said, and didn't offer to leave Janie at home. He waited until she changed into a royal-blue pantsuit with a beige top, and carried her with him to the ranch.

He did chores and paperwork with Janie right beside him, although he didn't touch her.

"A man only has so much self-control," he told her with a wistful sigh. "So we'll keep our hands off each other, until the wedding. Fair enough?"

She grinned at him. "Fair enough!"

He took her home after they had supper at a local restaurant. "I'd love to have taken you up to Houston for a night on the town," he said when he walked her to her door. "But not with your face like that." He touched it somberly. "Here in Jacobsville, everybody already knows what happened out at Shea's last night. In Houston, people might think I did this, or allowed it to happen." He bent and kissed the painful bruise. "Nobody will ever hurt you again as long as I live," he swore huskily.

She closed her eyes, savoring the soft touch of his mouth. "Are you sure you want to marry me?" she asked.

"I'm sure. I'll be along about ten-thirty," he added.

She looked up at him, puzzled. "Ten-thirty?"

He nodded. "Church," he said with a wicked grin. "We have to set a good example for the kids."

She laughed, delighted. "Okay."

"See you in the morning, pretty girl," he said, and brushed his mouth lightly over hers before he bounded back down the steps to his car and drove off with a wave of his hand.

Fred was amazed that Leo did take her to church, and then came back to the house with her for a lunch of cold cuts. He and Fred talked cattle while Janie lounged at Leo's side, still astounded at the unexpected turn of events. Fred couldn't be happier about the upcoming nuptials. He was amused that Hettie had the weekend off and didn't know what had happened. She had a shock coming when she arrived later in the day.

Leo took Janie with him when he went home, approving

her choice of a silky beige dress and matching high heels, pearls in her ears and around her throat, and her hair long and luxurious down her back.

''Your brothers will be surprised,'' Janie said worriedly on the way there.

Leo lifted an eyebrow. ''After the Cattleman's Ball? Probably not,'' he said. Then he told her about Corrigan offering to drive him home so that he could pump him for information to report back to the others.

''You were very intoxicated,'' she recalled, embarrassed when she recalled the fierce argument they'd had.

''I'd just found out that Marilee had lied about you,'' he confided. ''And seeing you with damned Harley didn't help.''

''You were jealous,'' she realized.

''Murderously jealous,'' he confessed at once. ''That only got worse, when you took the job at Shea's.'' He glanced at her. ''I'm not having you work there any longer. I don't care what compromises I have to make to get you to agree.''

She smiled to herself. ''Oh, I don't mind quitting,'' she confessed. ''I'll have enough to do at the ranch, after we're married, getting settled in.''

''Let's try not to talk about that right now, okay?''

She stared at him, worriedly. ''Are you getting cold feet?'' she asked.

''I'll tell you what I'm getting,'' he said, turning dark eyes to hers. And he did tell her, bluntly, and starkly. He nodded curtly at her scarlet flush and directed his attention back at the road. ''Just for the record, the word 'marriage' reminds me of the words 'wedding night,' and I go nuts.''

She whistled softly.

''So let's think about food and coffee and my brothers and try not to start something noticeable,'' he added in a deep tone. ''Because all three of them are going to be looking for obvious signs and they'll laugh the place down if they see any.''

''We can recite multiplication tables together,'' she agreed.

He glanced at her with narrow eyes. ''Great idea,'' he replied sarcastically. ''That reminds me of rabbits, and guess what rabbits remind me of?''

''I know the Gettysburg Address by heart,'' she countered. ''I'll teach it to you.''

''That will put me to sleep.''

''I'll make biscuits for supper.''

He sat up straight. ''Biscuits? For supper? To go with Barbara's nice barbecue, potato salad and apple pie. Now that's an idea that just makes my mouth water! And here I am poking along!'' He pushed down on the accelerator. ''Honey, you just said the magic word!''

She chuckled to herself. Marriage, she thought, was going to be a real adventure.

# *Chapter Eleven*

Not only did Corrigan, Rey, and Cag show up for supper with their wives, Dorie, Meredith and Tess, but Simon and Tira came all the way from Austin on a chartered jet. Janie had just taken off her apron after producing a large pan of biscuits, adding them to the deliciously spread table that Barbara and her assistant had arranged before they left.

All four couples arrived together, the others having picked up Simon and Tira at the Jacobsville airport on the way.

Leo and Janie met them at the door. Leo looked unprepared.

''All of you?'' he exclaimed.

Simon shrugged. ''I didn't believe them,'' he said, pointing at the other three brothers. ''I had to come see for myself.''

''We didn't believe him, either,'' Rey agreed, pointing at Leo.

They all looked at Janie, who moved closer to Leo and blushed.

''If she's pregnant, you're dead,'' Cag told Leo pointedly

when he saw the look on Janie's face. He leaned closer before Leo could recover enough to protest. ''Have you been beating her?''

''She is most certainly not pregnant!'' Leo said, offended. ''And you four ought to know that I have never hit a woman in my life!''

''But he hit the guy who did this to me,'' Janie said with pride, smiling up at him as she curled her fingers into his big ones.

''Not very effectively, I'm afraid,'' Leo confessed.

''That's just because the guy had a black belt,'' Janie said, defending Leo. ''Nobody but our assistant police chief had the experience to bring him down.''

''Yes, I know Grier,'' Simon said solemnly. ''He's something of a legend in law enforcement circles, even in Austin.''

''He has alien artifacts in his filing cabinet, and he was a government assassin,'' Janie volunteered with a straight face.

Everybody stared at her.

''He was kidding!'' Leo chuckled.

She grinned at him. He wrinkled his nose at her. They exchanged looks that made the others suddenly observant. All at once, they became serious.

''We can do wedding invitations if we e-mail them tonight,'' Cag said offhand. He pulled a list from his pocket. ''This is a list of the people we need to invite.''

''I can get the symphony orchestra to play,'' Rey said, nodding. ''I've got their conductor's home phone number in my pocket computer.'' He pulled it out.

''We can buy the gown online and have it overnighted here from Neiman-Marcus in Dallas,'' Corrigan volunteered. ''All we need is her dress size. What are you, a size ten?''

Janie balked visibly, but nodded. ''Here comes her father,'' Dorie said enthusiastically, noting the new arrival.

''I'll e-mail the announcement to the newspaper,'' Tess said. ''They have a Tuesday edition, we can just make it. We'll need a photo.''

There was a flash. Tira changed the setting on her digital camera. ''How's this?'' She asked, showing it to Tess and Meredith.

''Great!'' Meredith said. ''We can use Leo's computer to download it and e-mail it straight to the paper, so they'll have it first thing tomorrow. We can e-mail it to the local television station as well. Come on!''

''Wait for me! I'll write the announcement,'' Dorie called to Corrigan, following along behind the women.

''Hey!'' Janie exclaimed.

''What?'' Tira asked, hesitating. ''Oh, yes, the reception. It can be held here. But the cake! We need a caterer!''

''Cag can call the caterer,'' Simon volunteered his brother.

''It's my wedding!'' Janie protested.

''Of course it is, dear,'' Tira said soothingly. ''Let's go, girls.''

The women vanished into Leo's study. The men went into a huddle. Janie's father and Hettie came in the open door, looking shell-shocked.

''Never mind them,'' Leo said, drawing Janie to meet her parent and her housekeeper. ''They're taking care of the arrangements,'' he added, waving his hand in the general direction of his brothers and sisters-in-law. ''Apparently, it's going to be a big wedding, with a formal gown and caterers and newspaper coverage.'' He grinned. ''You can come, of course.''

Janie hit him. ''We were going to have a nice, quiet little wedding!''

''You go tell them what you want, honey,'' he told Janie. ''Just don't expect them to listen.''

Hettie started giggling. Janie glared at her.

''You don't remember, do you?'' the housekeeper asked

Janie. ''Leo helped them do the same thing to Dorie, and Tira, and Tess, and even Meredith. It's payback time. They're getting even.''

''I'm afraid so,'' Leo told Janie with a smug grin. ''But look at the bright side, you can just sit back and relax and not have to worry about a single detail.''

''But, my dress...'' she protested.

He patted her on the shoulder. ''They have wonderful taste,'' he assured her.

Fred was grinning from ear to ear. He never would have believed one man could move so fast, but he'd seen the way Leo looked at Janie just the morning before. It was no surprise to him that a wedding was forthcoming. He knew a man who was head over heels when he saw one.

By the end of the evening, Janie had approved the wedding gown, provided the statistics and details of her family background and education, and climbed into the car with Leo to let him take her home.

''The rings will be ready Tuesday, they promised,'' he told her at her father's door. He smiled tenderly. ''You'll be a beautiful bride.''

''I can't believe it,'' she said softly, searching his lean face.

He drew her close. ''Wednesday night, you'll believe it,'' he said huskily, and bent to kiss her with obvious restraint. ''Now, good night!''

He walked to the car. She drifted inside, wrapped in dreams.

It was a honey of a society wedding. For something so hastily concocted, especially with Christmas approaching, it went off perfectly. Even the rings were ready on time, the dress arrived by special overnight delivery, the blood tests and marriage license were promptly produced, the minister engaged, press coverage assured, the caterer on time—nothing, absolutely nothing, went wrong.

Janie stood beside Leo at the Hart ranch at a makeshift arch latticed with pink and white roses while they spoke their vows. Janie had a veil, because Leo had insisted. And after the last words of the marriage ceremony were spoken, he lifted the veil from Janie's soft eyes and looked at her with smoldering possession. He bent and kissed her tenderly, his lips barely brushing hers. She had a yellowing bruise on one cheek and she was careful to keep that side away from the camera, but Leo didn't seem to notice the blemish.

''You are the most beautiful bride who ever spoke her vows,'' he whispered as he kissed her. ''And I will cherish you until they lay me down in the dark!''

She reached up and kissed him back, triggering a burst of enthusiastic ardor that he was only able to curb belatedly. He drew away from her, smiling sheepishly at their audience, caught her hand, and led her back to the house through a shower of rice.

The brothers were on the job even then. The press was delicately prompted to leave after the cake and punch were consumed, the symphony orchestra was coaxed to load their instruments. The guests were delicately led to the door and thanked. Then the brothers carried their wives away in a flurry of good wishes and, at last, the newlyweds were alone, in their own home.

Leo looked at Janie with eyes that made her heart race. ''Alone,'' he whispered, approaching her slowly, ''at last.''

He bent and lifted her, tenderly, and carried her down the hall to the bedroom. He locked the door. He took the phone off the hook. He closed the curtains. He came back to her, where she stood, a little apprehensive, just inside the closed door.

''I'm not going to hurt you,'' he said softly. ''You're a priceless treasure. I'm going to be slow, and tender, and

I'm going to give you all the time you need. Don't be afraid of me.''

''I'm not, really,'' she said huskily, watching him divest her of the veil and the hairpins that held her elaborate coiffure in place with sprigs of lily of the valley. ''But you want me so much,'' she tried to explain. ''What if I can't satisfy you?''

He laughed. ''You underestimate yourself.''

''Are you sure?''

He turned her around so that he could undo the delicate hooks and snaps of her gown. ''I'm sure.''

She let him strip her down to her lacy camisole, white stockings and lacy white garter belt, her eyes feeding on the delighted expression that claimed his lean face.

''Beautiful,'' he said huskily. ''I love you in white lace.''

''You're not bad in a morning coat,'' she teased, liking the vested gray ceremonial rig he was wearing.

''How am I without it?'' he teased.

''Let's find out.'' She unbuttoned his coat and then the vest under it. He obligingly stripped them off for her, along with his tie, and left the shirt buttons to her hands. ''You've got cuff links,'' she murmured, trying to release them.

''I'll do it.'' He moved to the chest of drawers and put his cuff links in a small box, along with his pocket change and keys. He paused to remove his shirt and slacks, shoes and socks before he came back to her, in silky gray boxer shorts like the ones he'd worn the night they were almost intimate.

''You are...magnificent,'' she whispered, running her hands over his chest.

''You have no idea how magnificent, yet.'' He unsnapped the shorts and let them fall, coaxing her eyes to him. He shivered at the expression on her face, because he was far more potent than he'd been the one time she'd looked at him like this.

While she was gaping, he unfastened the camisole with

a delicate flick of his fingers and unhooked the garter belt. He stripped the whole of it down her slender body and tipped her back onto the bed while he pulled the stockings off with the remainder of her clothing.

He pulled back the cover and tossed the pillows off to the side before he arranged her on the crisp white sheets and stood over her, vibrating with desire, his eyes eating her nude body, from her taut nipples to the visible trembling of her long, parted legs.

She watched him come down to her with faint apprehension that suddenly vanished when he pressed his open mouth down, hard, right on her soft belly.

He'd never touched her like that, and in the next few feverish minutes, she went from shock to greater shock as he displayed his knowledge of women.

"No, you can't, you can't!" she sobbed, but he was, he did, he had!

She arched up toward his mouth with tears of tortured ecstasy raining down her cheeks in a firestorm of sensation, sobbing as the pleasure stretched her tight as a rope under the warm, expert motions of his lips.

She gasped as the wave began to hit her. Her eyes opened, and his face was there, his body suddenly right over hers, his hips thrusting down. She felt him, and then looked and saw him, even as she felt the small stabbing pain of his invasion. The sight of what was happening numbed the pain, and then it was gone all together as he shifted roughly, dragging his hips against hers as he enforced his possession of her innocence.

Her nails bit into his long back as he moved on her, insisting, demanding. His face, above her, was strained, intent.

"Am I hurting you?" he ground out.

"N...no!" she gasped, lifting toward him, her eyes wide, shocked, fascinated.

He looked down, lifting himself so that he could watch

her body absorb him. "Look," he coaxed through his teeth. "Look, Janie. Look at us."

She glanced down and her breath caught at the intimate sight that met her eyes. She gasped.

"And we've barely begun," he breathed, shifting suddenly, fiercely, against her.

She sobbed, shivering.

He did it again, watching her face, assessing her reaction. "I can feel you, all around me, like a soft, warm glove," he whispered, his lips compressing as pleasure shot through him with every deepening motion of his hips. "Take me, baby. Take me inside you. Take all of me. Make me scream, baby," he murmured.

She was out of her mind with the pleasure he was giving her. She writhed under him, arching her hips, pushing against him, watching his face. She shifted and he groaned harshly. She laughed, through her own torment, and suddenly cried out as the pleasure became more and more unbearable. Her hands went between them, in a fever of desire.

"Yes," he moaned as he felt her trembling touch. "Yes. Oh…God…baby…do it, do it! Do it!"

She was going to die. She opened her eyes and looked at him, feeling her body pulse as he shortened and deepened his movements, watching her with his mouth compressed, his eyes feverish.

"Do it…harder," she choked.

He groaned in anguish and his hips ground into hers suddenly, his hands catching her wrists and slamming them over her head as he moved fiercely above her, his eyes holding hers prisoner as his body enforced its possession violently.

She felt her body strain to accommodate him and in the last few mad seconds, she wondered if she would be able to…

He blurred in her sight. She was shaking. Her whole

body rippled in a shuddering parody of convulsions, whipping against his while her mouth opened, gasping at air, and her voice uttered sounds she'd never heard from it in her entire life.

"Get it," he groaned. "Yes. Get it...!"

He cried out and then his body, too, began to shudder rhythmically. A sound like a harsh sob tore from his throat. He groaned endlessly as his body shivered into completion. Seconds, minutes, hours, an eternity of pleasure later, he collapsed on her.

They both shivered in the aftermath. She felt tears on her face, in her mouth. She couldn't breathe. Her body ached, even inside, and when she moved, she felt pleasure stab her in the most secret places, where she could still feel him.

She sobbed, her nails biting into the hands pinning her wrists.

He lifted his head. "Look at me," he whispered, and when she did, he began to move again.

She sobbed harder, her legs parting, her hips lifting for him, her whole body shivering in a maelstrom of unbelievable delight.

"I can go again, right now," he whispered huskily, holding her eyes. "Can you? Or will it hurt?"

"I can't...feel pain," she whimpered. Her eyes closed on a shiver and then opened again, right into his. "Oh, please," she whispered brokenly. "Please, please...!"

He began to move, very slowly. "I love watching you," he whispered breathlessly. "Your face is beautiful, like this. Your body..." He looked down at it, watching its sensuous movements in response to his own. "I could eat you with a spoon right now, Mrs. Hart," he added shakily. "You are every dream of perfection that I've ever had."

"And you...are mine," she whispered. She lifted up to him, initiating the rhythm, whimpering softly as the pleasure began to climb all over again. ''I love you...so much,'' she sobbed.

His body clenched. He groaned, arched, his face going into her throat as his body took over from his mind and buffeted her violently.

She went over the edge almost at once, holding on for dear life while he took what he wanted from her. It was feverish, ardent, overwhelming. She thought she might faint from the ecstasy when it throbbed into endless satiation. He went with her, every second of the way. She felt him when his body gave up the pleasure he sought, felt the rigor, heard the helpless throb of his voice at her ear when he shuddered and then relaxed completely.

She held him close, drinking in the intimate sound and feel and scent of his big body over hers in the damp bed. It had been a long, wild loving. She'd never imagined, even in their most passionate encounters, that lovemaking would be like this.

She told him so, in shy whispers.

He didn't answer her. He was still, and quiet, for such a long time that she became worried.

''Are you all right?'' she whispered at his ear. Over her, she could hear and feel the beat of his heart as it slowly calmed.

His head lifted, very slowly. He looked into her wide eyes. ''I lost consciousness for a few seconds,'' he said quietly. He touched her lower lip, swollen from the fierce pressure of his mouth just at the last. ''I thought...I might die, trying to get deep enough to satisfy us both.''

She flushed.

He put his finger over her lips. He wasn't smiling. He moved deliberately, letting her feel him. ''You aren't on the Pill,'' he said. ''And I was too hot to even think of any sort of birth control. Janie,'' he added, hesitantly, ''I think I made you pregnant.''

Her eyes searched his. ''You said you wanted to,'' she reminded him in a whisper.

''I do. But it should have been your choice, too,'' he continued, sounding worried.

She traced his long, elegant nose and smiled with delicious exhaustion. ''Did you hear me shouting, Leo, stop and run to the pharmacy to buy protection!''

He laughed despite the gravity of the situation. ''Was that about the time I was yelling, 'get it, baby'?''

She hit his chest, flushed, and then laughed.

''You did, too, didn't you?'' he asked with a smug grin. ''So did I. Repeatedly.'' He groaned as he moved slowly away from her and flopped onto his back, stretching his sore muscles. ''Damn, I'm sore! And I told you I could go all night, didn't I?''

She sat up, torn between shock and amusement as she met his playful eyes. ''Sore? Men get sore?''

''When they go at it like that, they do,'' he replied sardonically. ''What a wedding night,'' he said, whistling through his lips as he studied her nude body appreciatively. ''If they gave medals, you could have two.''

Her eyebrows arched. ''Really? I was...I was all right?''

He tugged her down to him. ''Women have egos, too, don't they?'' he asked tenderly. He pushed her damp hair away from her cheeks and mouth. ''You were delicious. I've never enjoyed a woman so much.''

''I didn't know anything at all.''

He brought her head down and kissed her eyelids. ''It isn't a matter of knowledge.''

She searched his eyes. ''You had enough of that for both of us,'' she murmured.

''Bodies in the dark,'' he said, making it sound unimportant. ''I wanted to have you in the light, Janie,'' he said solemnly. ''I wanted to look at you while I was taking you.''

''That's a sexist remark,'' she teased.

"You took me as well," he conceded. He touched her mouth with a long forefinger. "I've never seen anything so beautiful," he whispered, and sounded breathless. "Your face, your body..." His face clenched. "And the pleasure." His eyes closed and he shivered. "I've never known anything like it." His eyes opened again. "It was love," he whispered to her, scowling. "Making love. Really making love."

Her breath caught in her throat. She traced his sideburn to his ear. "Yes."

"Do you know what I'm trying to tell you?" he asked quietly.

She looked down into his eyes and saw it there. Her heart jumped into her throat. "You're telling me that you love me," she said.

He nodded. "I love you. I knew it when Clark assaulted you, and I went at him. It hurt my pride that I couldn't make him beg for forgiveness. I cleaned you up and dried your hair, and knew that I loved you, all at once. It was a very small step from there to a wedding ring." He brought hers to his lips and kissed it tenderly. "I couldn't bear the thought of losing you. Not after that."

She smiled dreamily. "I loved you two years ago, when you brought me a wilted old daisy you'd picked out in the meadow, and teased me about it being a bouquet. You didn't know it, but to me, it was."

"I've given you a hard time," he told her, with obvious regret. "I'm sorry."

She leaned down and kissed him tenderly. "You made up for it." She moved her breasts gently against his chest. "I really can go all night," she whispered. "When you've recovered, I'll show you."

He chuckled under the soft press of her mouth, and his big arms swallowed her. "When *you're* recovered, I'll let you. I love you, Mrs. Hart. I love you with all my heart."

"I love you with all mine." She kissed him again, and thought how dreams did, sometimes, actually come true.

A week later, they celebrated their first Christmas together at a family party, to which Janie's father, aunt Lydia and Hettie were also invited. After kissing her with exquisite tenderness beneath the mistletoe, Leo gave Janie an emerald necklace, to match her eyes he said, and she gave him an expensive pocket watch, with his name and hers engraved inside the case.

On New Year's Eve, the family gathered with other families at the Jacobsville Civic Center for the first annual celebration. A live band played favorites and couples danced on the polished wood floor. Calhoun Ballenger had mused aloud that since Jacobsville's economy was based on cattle and agriculture, they should drop a pair of horns instead of a ball to mark the new year. He was red-faced at the celebration, when the city fathers took him seriously and did that very thing.

While Leo and Janie stood close together on the patio of the second floor ballroom to watch the neon set of longhorns go down to the count, a surprising flurry of snow came tumbling from the sky to dust the heads of the crowd.

"It's snowing!" Janie exclaimed, holding out a hand to catch the fluffy precipitation. "But it never snows in Jacobsville! Well, almost never."

Leo caught her close as the horns went to the bottom of the courthouse tower across the street and bent to her mouth, smiling. "One more wish come true," he teased, because he knew how much she loved snow. "Happy New Year, my darling," he whispered.

"Happy New Year," she whispered back, and met his kiss with loving enthusiasm, to the amused glances of the other guests. They were, after all, newlyweds.

The new year came and soon brought with it unexpected

tragedy. John Clark went back to Victoria to get his jailed brother a famous attorney, but he didn't have any money. So he tried to rob a bank to get the money. He was caught in the act by a security guard and a Texas Ranger who was working on a case locally. Judd Dunn was one of the two men who exchanged shots with Clark in front of the Victoria Bank and Trust. Clark missed. Judd and the security guard didn't. Ballistics tests were required to pinpoint who fired the fatal bullet.

Jack Clark, still in jail in Victoria, was let out long enough to attend his brother's funeral in Victoria. He escaped from the kindly sheriff's deputy who was bringing him back in only handcuffs instead of handcuffs and leg chains. After all, Jack Clark had been so docile and polite, and even cried at his brother's grave. The deputy was rewarded for his compassion by being knocked over the head twice with the butt of his own .38 caliber service revolver and left for dead in a driving rain in the grass next to the Victoria road. Later that day, his squad car was found deserted a few miles outside Victoria.

It was the talk of the town for several days, and Leo and Janie stayed close to home, because they knew Clark had scores to settle all around Jacobsville. They were in their own little world, filled with love. They barely heard all the buzz and gossip. But what they did hear was about Tippy Moore and Cash Grier.

"Tippy's not Grier's sort," Janie murmured sleepily. They didn't do a lot of sleeping at night, even now. She cuddled up in her husband's lap and nuzzled close. "He needs someone who is gentle and sweet. Not a harpy."

He wrapped her up close and kissed the top of her head. "What would you know about harpies?" he teased. "You're the sweetest single human being I've ever known."

She smiled.

"Well, except for me, of course," he added.

''Leo Hart!'' she exclaimed, drawing back.

''You said I was sweet,'' he murmured, bending his head. ''You said it at least six times. You were clawing my back raw at the time, and swearing that you were never going to live through what I was doing to you...''

She tugged his head down and kissed him hungrily. ''You're sweet, all right,'' she whispered raggedly. ''Do it again...!''

He groaned. They were never going to make it to the bed. But the doors were locked...what the hell.

An hour later, he carried her down the hall to their bedroom and tucked her up next to him, exhausted and still smiling.

''At least,'' he said wearily, ''Hopefully Clark will go to prison for a long, long time when he's caught. He won't be in a position to threaten you again.''

''Or you.'' She curled closer. ''Did I tell you that Marilee phoned me yesterday?''

He stiffened. ''No.''

She smiled. ''It's okay. She only wanted to apologize. She's going to Europe to visit her grandmother in London. I told her to have a nice trip.''

''London's almost far enough away.''

She sighed, wrapping her arms around him. ''Be generous. She'll never know what it is to be as happy as we are.''

''Who will?'' he teased, but the look he gave her was serious. He touched her hair, watching her succumb to sleep.

He lay awake for a long time, his eyes intent on her slender, sleeping body. She made wonderful biscuits, she could shoot a shotgun, she made love like a fairy. He wondered what he'd ever done in his life to deserve her.

''Dreams,'' she whispered, shocking him.

''What, honey?''

She nuzzled her face into his throat and melted into him. ‘‘Dreams come true,’’ she whispered, falling asleep again.

He touched her lips with his and smoothed back her long hair. ‘‘Yes, my darling,’’ he whispered with a long, sweet smile. ‘‘Dreams come true.’’

* * * * *

# Letters to Kelly

# SUZANNE BROCKMANN

*SUZANNE BROCKMANN*

lives just west of Boston in a house always filled with her friends – actors, musicians, storytellers, artists and teachers. When not writing award-winning romances about US Navy SEALs, among others, she sings in an a cappella group called Serious Fun, manages the professional acting careers of her two children, volunteers at the Appalachian Benefit Coffeehouse and always answers letters from readers. Send her an SAE with return postage along with your letter to PO Box 5092, Wayland, MA 01778, USA.

To my wonderful mother, Lee Brockmann,
who's been waiting a long tme for this one.

# *Chapter 1*

Kelly O'Brien lugged her heavy canvas bag of books into the back door of the university newspaper office. The spring day was hot, and a trickle of sweat dripped uncomfortably down her back.

She heaved the book bag onto her desk with a crash, and pushed back the damp strands of long, dark hair that had escaped from her bun. With a sigh, she peeled off her jacket and undid the top buttons of her sleeveless blouse, shaking the neckline slightly to let fresh air circulate against her overheated body.

"Psst."

Kelly looked up to see Marcy Reynolds, the school newspaper's student photographer, hissing at her. Marcy's brown eyes were lit with excitement, her pixielike face alive with curiosity.

"There's some guy sitting in the front office, waiting for you," Marcy said, handing Kelly several pink phone message slips. "No. Correction—this is not just some guy. This is a Man, with a capital *M.* And quite possibly *the* most gorgeous man who has ever crossed the threshold of this humble establishment.''

Kelly smiled. ''Oh, come on—''

''I'm serious,'' the younger woman said. As she shook her head, her large hoop earrings bumped the sides of her face. ''We're talking major heart-attack material. *Very* tall, blond, green eyes—he's a dead ringer for Mel Gibson's cuter, younger brother. The man is a walking blue jeans ad, Kelly. His legs are about a mile long, and those buns...''

Kelly laughed in disbelief. ''He sounds too good to be true,'' she said.

''He looks like one of the heroes from those romance novels you're writing. He's been sitting there for forty-five minutes,'' Marcy complained, running her fingers through her short black hair, ''totally blowing my concentration.''

''Is he a student?''

''He's too old,'' Marcy said. ''I mean, unless he took some time off from school, but not only a few years, like you. Like serious time, maybe ten years. I'd say he's maybe thirty. He's got those sexy little crinkly laugh lines around his eyes. Check him out—he's a total babe.''

''Maybe he's a professor,'' Kelly said. ''Did he say what he wants?''

''*You're* what he wants.'' Marcy smirked. ''That's all he said. I told him I didn't know when you'd be back—that you could be gone for hours. But he just said he'd wait. He said something about waiting seven years, and that another few hours wouldn't kill him. Have you been keeping this man on the shelf for *seven years?*''

"Seven years ago I was only sixteen," Kelly said. She moved to the glass partition that separated the front office from the back. The blinds were down and shut, and she moved one aluminum slat a fraction of an inch and peeked out.

Her heart stopped.

T. Jackson Winchester the Second.

It couldn't be.

But it was.

He was the only person in the outer office and he sat by the door, one ankle resting on one knee, leaning casually back in his chair, as comfortable as if he were in his own living room. He wore a royal-blue polo shirt with both buttons open, revealing his sun-kissed neck and chest. His shirt was tucked into a pair of faded blue jeans that hugged his muscular thighs. On his feet he wore Docksiders but no socks. His ankles were strong and tan.

He was reading the latest copy of the school newspaper, and his eyes were down, hidden by long, dark lashes. Kelly didn't need to see his eyes to know they were a remarkable mix of colors, with a ring of yellow gold, like solar flares, that surrounded his pupils. The edges of his irises were brilliant green. And sandwiched between the green and the gold was the ocean. Like the ocean, his eyes changed. They could be stormy gray, or dark blue-black, or even a deep, mysterious shade of green. She could remember looking into his eyes, into a warm swirl of colored fire, his lips curving up into a smile as he bent to kiss her—

Kelly shook her head, pushing the thought away. She looked at him again, closely this time, searching for signs of age, signs of change.

He was wearing his golden hair longer than she'd

ever seen him wear it before, hanging down several inches over his collar, thick and wavy and blond and soft. His face had a few more lines, but if anything, he was even more handsome than ever.

He looked really good.

But he'd always looked good. He'd looked good when she'd first met him, and he'd been hung over at the time. She could still remember that morning as if it were yesterday, not eleven years ago....

Twelve-year-old Kelly had opened the door quietly, carefully, then slipped into the darkened guest bedroom. She had heard the clock ticking, and the sound of slow, steady breathing.

Her brother Kevin's mysterious college roommate was lying sprawled out on the bed, long legs escaping from beneath the covers that were twisted around him. One arm was flung above his head, the other lay across his bare chest.

His name was T. Jackson Winchester the Second. Kevin had called from school to tell her parents about the freshman dorm and about his roommate. Kelly had been particularly impressed by the length of his roommate's name. Kevin had told their father that T. Jackson was from Cape Cod, and he drove a Triumph Spitfire.

What did the T. stand for? Kelly had wondered. And what color was the Spitfire?

Red. She'd made a point of looking out onto the driveway first thing when she woke up. The Spitfire was shiny and red, with a black convertible top.

Kelly stepped closer to T. Jackson Winchester the Second, to get a better look at him in the dimness of the room, to see what a rich college roommate looked like.

He had an awful lot of muscles. Kevin was eighteen, and he had lots of muscles, too, but Kelly had never given his muscles a second glance. He was her brother, sometimes a pain in the neck, sometimes a creep, but mostly fun.

This guy, however, was not her brother.

She swallowed hard, looking down at his messy blond hair and his handsome face. He was definitely a ten. A living ten. Kelly had seen some tens before on television or in the movies. But before this, she'd never met one face-to-face.

His face was perfectly shaped with a long, straight nose and a strong jawline. His eyebrows were two slightly curved light brown lines above the thick eyelashes that lay against the smooth, tanned skin of his cheeks. His lips were neither too thin nor too thick, and nicely shaped. Even in sleep, they tended to curve upward, as if a smile was his natural expression.

Kelly leaned even closer, wondering what color his eyes were, then wondering with a flash of giddiness what color his underpants were. She clapped her hand over her mouth to keep a laugh from escaping and backed away from the bed.

She'd come into this room with a purpose, and although checking out T. Jackson Winchester the Second was interesting, that wasn't why she'd crept in. She moved quietly to the closet. The door was closed, and she silently slid it open, carefully stopping it before it bumped the frame.

Oh, man, her mother had moved her rock-collecting gear up onto the top shelf.

Kelly was tall for her age, but she still couldn't reach the backpack that sat on the top shelf in the closet. Not without climbing on a chair.

The only chair in the room was clear over on the other side, below the shaded window. Stealthily Kelly moved toward it. T. Jackson Winchester the Second had draped his jeans and shirt over the back of the chair last night before he climbed into bed.

Staggered into bed was more like it. Kelly wrinkled her nose as she smelled the odor of stale cigarette smoke and beer that seemed to cling to T. Jackson's clothes. He and Kevin had been to some kind of wild party last night. Some *illegal* wild party.

The drinking age in Massachusetts was twenty-one. She'd heard her father arguing with Kevin about that. Her brother insisted if he was old enough to register for the draft, then he was old enough to drink. Her father had countered by saying if he was old enough to drink, then he was also old enough to always pick a designated driver. Dad had added that if he ever caught Kevin drinking and driving, no matter *how* old he was, he'd be grounded for ten years.

From the looks of ol' T. Jackson Winchester the Second, Kevin had probably been last night's designated driver.

Kelly dropped the clothes onto the floor and wrestled the heavy chair toward the closet. But she didn't see the big high-top sneakers that were lying in the way, and she tripped, hitting the floor with a crash and a yelp as the chair fell on top of her.

Before she could move, the chair was pulled away. "Are you all right?" T. Jackson Winchester the Second said raspily, frowning down at her with concern.

Red.

He was wearing boxer shorts and they were red. As Kelly stared way, way up at him, she wondered whether it was a coincidence, or if he always matched his underwear to the color of the car he was driving.

"Did you hurt yourself, kid?" he asked, after clearing his throat noisily and swallowing hard as if his mouth was dry. He reached out a hand to help her to her feet.

His hand was big and warm, with long, strong fingers and carefully manicured nails. Kelly let go quickly, afraid to be caught clinging foolishly, grinning at him like an idiot.

"I'll live," she said. She was going to get some big bruise on her leg where the chair had hit her, but she wasn't about to tell T. Jackson Winchester the Second about it.

As she watched, he crossed to the bedside table and drained a glass of water that was sitting there.

"Ugh," she said, wrinkling her nose. "Isn't that warm?"

He glanced at her, putting the empty glass back down. "It's wet," he said. "That's all that matters." He ran his hands over his face and looked longingly at the bed. "What time is it?" he asked.

"About quarter to nine," she told him. "How tall *are* you exactly?"

He sat down on the bed, resting his forehead in his hands. "Exactly?" he asked, looking up at her through his fingers, a glint of amusement in his eyes. "Six foot four and one quarter inches."

"That's tall." Kelly nodded. "I'm Kelly O'Brien," she added.

T. Jackson Winchester the Second straightened up the best that he could and held out his hand. "Pleased to meet you, Kelly O'Brien," he said, somehow managing to smile. "I'm Jax, Kevin's roommate."

Kelly took his hand, shaking it firmly. "T. Jackson Winchester the Second," she said. "I know."

Green eyes. He had green eyes, rimmed with red. "Christmas in October," she said, and grinned.

Somehow he understood that she was talking about his eyes, and he smiled ruefully. "I look bad, huh?"

Kelly nodded. "You look like hell."

He laughed with a flash of straight, white teeth. Forget ten. He was clearly an eleven.

"Sorry I woke you up," she said. "I was trying to get my backpack down from the closet shelf."

"This isn't your room, is it?" he said, frowning slightly as he looked around at the impersonal guest room, at the blandly patterned bedspread, the flower print on the curtains, the beige carpeting.

"Nah," Kelly said. "I just use the closet because I'm overflowing my own. What does the T. stand for?"

He looked at her blankly. "The...what?"

"In your name," she said patiently. "You know. *T.* Jackson...? And you call yourself Jacks? Like the game? Or is it a plural, as if there's two of you?"

He laughed again, then winced as if his head hurt. "No, there's only one of me. It's spelled *J-A-X,*" he said. "It's a nickname."

"And the *T.?*"

"Tyrone," he said with a grimace.

"Ew."

"Yeah. That's why I keep it an initial."

"Tyrone," Kelly said slowly. "Ty. Well, it's not really *that* bad. But 'Jax' is pretty weird. Why don't you go for the entire initial thing? You know, call yourself T.J.?"

He stood slowly, steadying himself on one of the bedposts. "It's taken," he said. "My father is T.J."

"The First."

"You got it."

"Doesn't that actually make you *Junior?*" Kelly asked critically. "I mean, this 'the Second' stuff is kind of pompous, don't you think?"

Jax grinned, crossing toward the closet. "If you ask me, the whole Winchester existence is kind of pompous."

"I'll call you T.," she decided. "I like that better than Jax."

He turned toward her. "Look, if I get your backpack down for you, will you let me go back to sleep?"

She smiled. "Promise to take me for a ride later in your Spitfire and you've got a deal."

Jackson smiled back at her, his warm green eyes taking her in from the top of her boyishly short hair, to her faded turtleneck with the too-short sleeves and her skinny wrists sticking out, to her ragged jeans and right down to her worn-out cowboy boots. He stared at her for so long that Kelly wiped her nose, wondering if maybe it was running.

But his smile slowly faded, and he frowned down at himself, as if suddenly aware he was half-naked. "I probably shouldn't be standing here in my underwear, talking to you like this."

"I've seen Kevin in his underwear more times than I can count," Kelly scoffed. "It's no big deal."

"Yeah, but Kev's your brother," Jax said. "I'm not."

Looking at him, Kelly was glad that he wasn't. No one should have a brother who looked as good as T. Jackson Winchester the Second.

"Something tells me that your father wouldn't approve." Jax grinned. "And I don't want to be forced into any kind of a shotgun wedding, no matter how pretty you are."

Kelly felt herself blush. "Don't be a jerk," she warned him. "I know exactly what I look like." She was a skinny beanpole with a faintly feminine face. If she stretched her imagination, she could use the word *pretty* to describe her eyes. But only her eyes.

"Is this what you need?" Jax asked, pointing to a blue backpack in the closet.

She nodded.

He swung it down, but it was heavier than he thought, and he had to lunge to keep from dropping it. "God," he said, "what have you got in here? Rocks?"

Kelly smiled, taking the knapsack from him, her muscles straining as she slipped it over her shoulder. "Yeah. It's my rock collection."

Jax looked surprised, then he laughed. "You're into geology, huh?" he said. "Will you show me your collection later?"

"Yeah." Kelly nodded, smiling at him again. She turned to go, but looked back at him, her hand on the doorknob. "T. Jackson Winchester the Second," she said, "you're not a dweeb. I like you. My brother's lucky he got you for a roommate."

He'd laughed again as Kelly had gone out the door. "I like you, too, Kelly," she'd heard him say. "And *I'm* lucky that I got a roommate with a sister like you. See you later...."

Kelly now lowered the slat on the blinds, and looking down, realized that she had scrunched the phone message slips she'd been holding into a tight wad of paper.

"Do you know him?" Marcy's words finally penetrated.

"Yeah," Kelly said slowly.

"Who *is* he?"

Good question. Was he a childhood friend? A friend of the family? An almost-lover? Kelly went for the obvious. "He was my brother's college roommate," she said. She turned to Marcy suddenly. "Do me a favor and tell him that I just called and told you that I wasn't coming back in today."

Marcy was looking at her as if she had finally lost her mind. "And just which telephone line is it that you supposedly called on?" she said. "The one that rings silently?"

"Tell him—" Kelly was grabbing wildly now. "Tell him *you* called me."

Marcy folded her arms across her chest, the bangles and bracelets she wore on her wrists jangling. "I talked to the man for maybe five minutes when he first came in, but it was long enough for me to know he's no idiot," she said. "Now, if I go out there making excuses for you, girl, he's gonna realize that you took one look at him and ran away. And a man like that one—" she gestured toward the door to the outer office "—usually does only one thing when he's being run away from." She paused for emphasis. "He gives chase. So unless you want this guy following you all over town—and if you do, that's fine, because *I* sure wouldn't mind—you better take a nice deep breath, and go and talk to him."

Marcy was right. She was absolutely right.

Kelly walked to the door and, following her friend's advice, took a deep breath. She glanced back at Marcy for an extra dose of strength, then turned the doorknob.

# *Chapter 2*

Jax stared at the college newspaper without reading it. He tried thinking about the book he was writing, tried to plan the next scene, but he couldn't even keep his mind on that. He was nervous. What if Kelly didn't show up?

What if she did?

Relax, he ordered himself. It's just Kelly.

Just Kelly.

It had been seven years since the night of her junior prom.

God, his life could have been so different if he hadn't been so stupid. But he made a mistake, and here he was, seven years later, no closer to getting what he wanted.

Seven long, wasted years…

Jax wished he could go back in time, do it all over again. Well, not *all.* He'd skip the trip to Central America, thank you very much. Yeah, he'd pass on *that* ten-day news-gathering expedition that had turned into a twenty-month nightmare—

He took a deep breath. He had dreamed about Central America last night for the first time in a long time. He'd dreamed he was back in the prison and—

But he didn't want to think about *that,* either. He was better off just worrying about Kelly. Seven years was a long time. She must have changed. Lord knows he had.

But since yesterday, when Kevin had called and filled him in on the latest O'Brien family news, Jax felt twenty-two years old again. All of his optimism and hope flooded back, as if it had never faded and disappeared.

Kelly was back in Boston, Kevin had told him, finishing her college degree. She had gotten a divorce.

Even as Jax had talked to Kevin on the phone, even as he had made regretful noises over Kelly's failed marriage, he'd done a silent victory dance in his living room.

Kelly was single. She was single and she wasn't too young anymore. Jax smiled as he stared sightlessly down at the newspaper he was holding.

He could still see her, the way she had looked when he'd first met her. She'd been only twelve years old, no more than a child, but her dark blue eyes held the maturity and wisdom of a woman twice her age. With her dry wit, she was clearly intelligent, but it was her steady self-confidence that made him adore her—not to mention the promise of incredible beauty he could see in her face.

And as he found himself spending more and more time with the O'Briens, his feelings for Kelly grew as she did.

And though the O'Briens didn't have a fraction of the money that his parents had, in Jax's mind, the Winchesters were the losers.

Nolan and Lori O'Brien had been married twenty years when Jax had first met them, but they still loved each other, and maybe even more important, they still genuinely *liked* each other. And they truly loved their children. They couldn't give Kevin and Kelly expensive gifts, they couldn't even afford to send Kevin to Boston College without the help from his scholarship, but there was certainly no lack of love in that family.

And the O'Briens had opened their arms to Jax, encircling him with all the love and laughter and music that always seemed to shake the foundation of their little house.

Jax had even spent one entire summer living with them—along with Lori's recently divorced sister, Christa, and her three children. It had been a magnificent summer, the best he could remember. The house had been so crowded that he and Kevin had to sleep on bedrolls out on the screened-in porch. When it rained, they sought refuge on the floor in Kelly's room.

Kelly had been fourteen that summer, her long legs and arms beginning to change from skinny to willowy. She had grown her dark hair long, and she wore it in a single braid down her back.

She still called Jax "T." or sometimes even Tyrone. She was the only person in the universe he would let get away with that.

He hadn't gone out on a single date that entire summer, spending most of his evenings playing Risk or Monopoly with the ready crowd of O'Briens and relatives. But if anyone had accused him at that time of having anything other than a friendly, platonic love for Kelly, he would have furiously denied it. He was a twenty-year-old man, for crying out loud. Kelly was just a kid.

It wasn't until two years later, until the night of Kelly's junior prom—

"T. Jackson Winchester the Second." Kelly's husky voice interrupted his thoughts, and he looked up from the newspaper into a pair of familiar blue eyes.

Kelly.

Jax forced himself to move slowly. He slowly folded the newspaper and put it on the table beside him. He slowly got to his feet and smiled down at her.

God, she had become even more beautiful than she'd been the last time he'd seen her, four years ago at Kevin's wedding.

Her eyes were a deep, dark shade of blue and exquisitely shaped. Her skin was smooth and fair, contrasting with her rich brown hair and her long, dark eyelashes. Her face was elegantly heart-shaped, with a small, strong chin and a perfect nose. She was gorgeous. She'd always been remarkably pretty as a girl, but as a woman, she was breathtaking.

"Kelly." It came out little more than a whisper.

"How are you?" she asked. "What are you doing here?"

Jax cleared his throat and ran his hand through his hair. "I'm in town on business," he said. It wasn't entirely a lie. True, the business could just as easily have been done over the telephone, but... "I thought I'd come and ask you to have dinner with me. I didn't realize you were back in Boston until I spoke to Kevin yesterday."

As Kelly looked up into his eyes, she was struck by how little T. Jackson had changed. He was still the same poised, confident, charismatic and utterly charming man he'd always been. There was no situation he would be uncomfortable in, nothing that could rattle him—no, that wasn't entirely true. She *had* seen him severely shaken up, even out of control. But only once. It had been the night of her junior prom.

"So how about it?" Jax smiled as he returned her steady gaze. "Will you have dinner with me?"

It was Plan "A." He would take her to dinner tonight, and again tomorrow night, and by Wednesday she'd remember how good they were together. She'd realize that their friendship had survived all those years they'd spent apart. And then he'd kiss her goodnight, let her know he wanted them to be more than friends. By the end of the week, he'd ask her to marry him. It was fast, but it couldn't exactly be called a whirlwind courtship considering that he'd really started courting her back before he even realized it, back when she was only twelve years old.

It was a plan that would work. He knew it would work.

But he could see wariness in Kelly's eyes. "I don't think so," she said, shaking her head no.

She had turned him down. He hadn't figured *that* possibility when he was making his plan. This was one scenario he had never considered. Despite the heat of the day, Jax felt a sudden chill. Was he too late again? Was he destined to go through life with the woman he wanted always one step out of his reach?

"Are you seeing someone?" he asked.

Kelly looked away. "No."

Jax fought to hide his relief from showing on his face.

''It's just...not necessary for you to take me out to dinner,'' she said, pushing a wisp of hair from her face.

Jax laughed then. ''Says who?''

She sighed and crossed her arms in front of her. ''Look, I know Kevin called you because he's worried about me. I've been...a little down. Give me a break, I just got a divorce. I'm allowed to be depressed. I was brought up believing that marriage was permanent, but Brad and I didn't even manage to hold it together for three years.''

As Jax watched, she looked down at the floor. Her unhappiness was clearly evident in her eyes, in the tightness of her mouth. Good grief, another variable he hadn't considered. ''Do you still love him?'' he asked softly.

She glanced up at Jax, and her eyes were filled with tears. ''You know what the really stupid thing is, T.?''

He shook his head silently, wishing that he could take her in his arms. But he was held back by all those years of purposely not touching her. During the five years that he'd been in college, the five years that they'd been such good friends, he'd always been very careful not to touch her. Not casually, not at all. It was as if he subconsciously knew there could only be one kind of physical relationship between them, and that there would be nothing casual about it.

''I don't think I ever loved him,'' she said.

One of Kelly's tears ran down her cheek, and Jax couldn't stop from reaching out to brush it away. She took a step back, as if the contact had burned her.

''Don't.''

"Sorry," he said quickly. "I'm sorry."

Kelly wiped her face with the back of her hand, blinking away the rest of her tears. T. was looking at her with such anxiety in his eyes, it almost made her laugh. T. Jackson anxious? She wouldn't have believed it possible. She managed a shaky smile.

"You think I'm a real basket case, right?" she asked.

"I think you could use a friend," he said quietly.

"Yeah," she said, hugging her crossed arms close to her body, as if she were cold, as if it weren't more than eighty degrees in the newspaper office. "I could. But not you, Tyrone. Not this time."

"Why not?"

But it was as if she hadn't heard him. "Just tell Kevin I'm okay. I'm going to be fine. But I'll be fine a lot sooner without you hanging around, doing my brother a favor."

Jax choked on the air he was breathing. "I'm *not* here to do Kevin a favor," he said.

"Yeah, well, it wouldn't be the first time," Kelly said, "would it?"

Jax laughed, but then stopped as the meaning of what she was saying washed over him like a cold bucket of water. "Oh, God," he said. "You believed what Kevin said that morning after the prom?"

"Of course I believed him," Kelly said. "You didn't deny it." She turned toward the door to the back office. "I've got to go. Thanks for dropping by."

"Kelly, wait—"

But she was gone.

Jax stood there for a long time even though he knew she'd gone out the back door, even though he knew that she wasn't coming back.

So much for Plan "A."

* * *

Jax set his laptop computer on the dining table in his hotel suite, attached the power cord and plugged it into the wall. He hit the On switch and the computer wheezed to life.

He pulled his spiral notebook and his collection of computer disks out of his briefcase and found the one labeled Jared.

This book was an historical, with most of the action taking place during the Civil War era. He'd written a number of Civil War books before, so the research he'd had to do for this one had been minimal. This book was going to be fast and easy, especially since the story was one he was extremely familiar with.

He put the disk into the computer's drive and called up the job. After less than a week of work, he was already up to page 163, and he'd just finished writing the explosive, pivotal fight scene between Jared, the hero, and Edmund, the heroine's brother.

He quickly skimmed the last few pages that he'd written, but it was all still fresh in his memory, so he went right to work, starting the next scene.

> With bleakness in his eyes, Jared stared at the heavy wrought-iron gates that separated him from Sinclair Manor. The gates had been shut when night had fallen, just as they had been every night. In the morning the servants would come out, unlock them, and throw them open wide.
>
> As Jared stood in the darkness, his gaze moving up to the brightly lit house on the hill, he knew without a doubt that, day or night, he was

no longer welcome there. Those gates had been closed to him forever.

Jax stopped writing to take a sip from a can of soda. Now what? Now Jared had to get over that fence.

But Carrie was in there, and welcome or not, Jared meant to have her. With an effortless leap, he climbed up, up and over the sharp spikes that decked the top of the tall fence, letting himself drop lightly to the ground on the other side.

He'd made a promise to Carrie. It was a promise he intended to keep.

Keeping to the trees, moving quietly, the way he'd learned as a young boy in the wilds of Kentucky, he approached the manor house. He moved with purpose, his mouth set in a grim line of determination, making his dark good looks seem almost savage, making it seem as if more than just a quarter of the blood that ran through his veins was Indian.

His gaze quickly found Carrie's bedroom window—

"Whoa, wait a minute," Jax muttered as he stopped writing. "Where do you think *you're* going?"

In his mind he could see Jared turning to stare at him, arms crossed, eyebrow raised, impatience clearly written on the character's handsome face. "I'm going to see Carrie."

"Nuh-uh-uh," Jax chided gently. "According to my outline, you're supposed to meet her in the gazebo."

"Right," Jared said with exasperation. "Only, she doesn't show, her brother Edmund does, and he beats the crap out of me again, because I'm too noble to raise a hand against him on account of the fact that he used to be my best friend. In reality, I could whip him with one hand behind my back. I'm getting tired of this, and so will all your readers.'' He glanced up at Carrie's window again. ''It's time for some sex.''

Jax crossed his arms, leaning back with a sigh. His heroes were all alike. They all wanted immediate, instant gratification. They all loved the heroines desperately, and couldn't understand why Jax made them go through all sorts of contortions before being allowed to live happily ever after.

Of course, the *New York Times* bestseller list meant nothing to them.

''I love Carrie,'' Jared was arguing right now. ''And she loves me. I know it—she told me in that last scene you wrote. Face it, Jax, there's no way on earth I'd get on a boat for Europe and leave her behind. It's entirely out of character.''

''No, it's not,'' Jax said quietly. ''Not if you thought it was the best thing for Carrie.''

Jared sighed, shaking his head slowly. ''Carrie? Or Kelly? This is fiction, Jax. Don't get it confused with the things that went wrong in *your* life.''

''If things don't go wrong, there's no story,'' Jax pointed out. ''You want to climb up into Carrie's room and make love to her, right?''

Jared nodded.

''And you plan to sneak her out of the house, and take her with you to Europe.''

Jared nodded again, his eyes drawn once again to that dimly lit window on the second floor of the house.

''What are you going to do for money?'' Jax asked.

''Carrie is used to living a certain lifestyle. Have you thought about that?''

Jared shrugged. ''I know she loves me more than money,'' he said with an easy smile. ''As long as we're together, she'll be happy.''

''You're too perfect,'' Jax said in disgust. ''I've got to give you some insecurities, or some dark family secret.''

''Oh, please, not the dark family secret thing,'' Jared groaned. ''I'm already one-quarter Native American and dirt poor to boot. Isn't that scandalous enough?''

''Obviously not,'' Jax muttered. ''I'd like this book to have more than 175 pages, if you don't mind.''

''You want more pages?'' Jared asked, his face brightening. ''I've got a good idea. How about this—a hundred-page love scene? Just me and Carrie, and a hundred pages of bliss?''

Jax laughed out loud. ''My, oh my, a little horny today, aren't we?''

Jared's eyes were glued to Carrie's window. ''One hundred and sixty-three pages, and I've been trying to get my hands on Carrie since page one,'' he said. ''Two different times you bring me right to the brink of ecstasy, only to snatch her away from me at the last minute. I'm dying here, Jax. Give me a break.''

Jackson smiled suddenly. ''All right,'' he said. ''Go for it. Climb that trellis.''

> His hard gaze quickly found Carrie's bedroom window, and in a matter of moments, he was scaling the side of the house, climbing the trellis, unmindful of the thorns from the roses that scratched his hands.

Jared stopped climbing, and glared back at Jax. "You could have chosen ivy, but you had to use roses with thorns, didn't you? Man, you never give me a break."

"Roses are romantic," Jax said. "Besides, you're unmindful of them."

The window was open, and Jared quickly pushed it wider and slipped inside. He knew as soon as his feet touched her bedroom floor that something was wrong. With his heart pounding, Jared stared at the carefully stripped bed, at the empty vanity top, the barren bookshelf. Where were all of Carrie's things, all of her clutter? He strode to the wardrobe, swinging the doors open.

Empty.

All of her clothes were gone.

"Looking for something?" Edmund Sinclair's taunting voice made Jared whirl around. Carrie's brother was standing in the doorway, watching him, a sneer on his aristocratic face. "Or some*one?*"

"Where is she?" Jared's voice was harsh.

"She's gone," Edmund said. "My father thought it best if she went to visit some relatives for a while. Funny, I can't recall whether she went to Vermont or Connecticut. Or maybe it was Maine."

Jared spun to glare at Jax. "You son of a bitch," he spat. Two large strides brought him toward Edmund, and he hauled off and punched his former friend in the face. Without another word, Jared disappeared out the window.

Jax grinned and kept writing. Yeah, it was time for Edmund to get knocked down. He'd keep that in.

Jax parked his sports car on the street outside of Kelly's apartment. Looking up, he could see the lights on in her windows. He got out of the car, grabbing the handles of the bag that held the food he'd picked up at the Chinese restaurant down the street.

If Kelly wouldn't come to dinner, dinner would come to Kelly.

She lived on the second floor of a three-family house on a quiet residential street in the Boston suburbs. Jax climbed onto the front porch and pushed the middle of three doorbells.

The evening was warm, and Jax sat back on the porch railing, watching a couple kids ride their bicycles around and around in a driveway across the street. But then the porch light came on, the door creaked open and Kelly was standing behind the screen, looking out at him.

She was wearing cut-off jeans and a ratty T-shirt, and her hair was loose around her shoulders, cascading down her back in a long, dark sheet.

He smiled at her, and she returned the smile rather ruefully, pushing open the screen door to come out onto the porch. Her feet were bare, and Jax let his eyes travel up the long lengths of her legs, feeling a still somewhat odd surge of desire. But it shouldn't be odd, he told himself. She wasn't a child anymore. She was a beautiful woman.

He could still remember the first moment he'd realized his feelings for Kevin's little sister weren't brotherly any longer. It hadn't taken him much time to shake off the feelings of oddness *that* night.

She sat down on the top step, hugging her knees in to her chest and looking up at him. ''Now, why am I not surprised to see you?''

''You were expecting me?'' he said with a quirk of one eyebrow. ''I'm honored that you dressed for the occasion.''

''Tell me you don't wish you had shorts on,'' Kelly said.

''You win.'' He smiled, just looking at her. Her dark hair was so long. He wanted to touch it, run his fingers through its silkiness, but instead he gripped the railing. ''How many years did it take you to grow your hair that long?''

She swept her hair off her neck, twisting it and pulling it in front of her and frowned down at the ends. ''I'm going to get it cut. I haven't done more than trim it in almost four years. I'm thinking of going radically short for the summer.''

''Radically?'' he asked. ''You mean, like Vin Diesel?''

Kelly laughed, and Jax was momentarily transported back in time seven years, to the night of her junior prom, to the night he'd danced with her in his arms, holding her for the very first time. It seemed as if they'd spent the entire evening laughing. *Almost* the entire evening…

''That's maybe a little *too* radical,'' she said. ''But I am thinking of getting it buzzed in the back.''

She pushed her hair up as if to demonstrate just how short she wanted it cut, and Jax's eyes were drawn to her slender neck. He liked her long hair the way it was, but she would look unbelievably sexy with it short. Her hair would curl slightly around her ears, frame her beautiful face and accentuate her long, graceful neck.

"I think it would look great."

"You do?" She looked up at him, surprise in her voice.

"Yeah."

She stood. "I've got to get back to work," she said, edging toward the door.

Jax was confused. They'd been having a normal conversation, everything was very comfortable and... He was coming on too strong, he realized suddenly. He'd been distracted, thinking about how much he wanted to kiss her neck, and he'd started mentally undressing her. She knew what he was thinking from the look on his face, and now she was running away again.

He looked down at the uneven floorboards of the porch. It was the only way he could hide the desire he knew was in his eyes. "I brought over Chinese food," he said.

She shook her head no. "Thanks, but I already ate," she said. "Good night, T."

"Kelly, don't shut me out."

His quiet words made her slowly turn around to face him. "Jackson, I can't handle seeing you right now. I need some time. I need my life to be simple for a while. And face it, our relationship has never been simple."

"We can make it simple." His voice sounded calm, matter-of-fact, betraying none of his desperation.

He took a step toward her, and Kelly took a step back, panic flaring in her stomach. If he touched her, she wasn't sure she could resist him. It was bad enough seeing him, talking to him. It was frightening the way her memories of the way she used to feel for him could consume her. It was almost as if they weren't memories at all.

But there was no way she could still be in love with him, not after seven years. No way.

"I have to get back to work," she said again. "I'm sorry."

She went into the house, closing the door tightly behind her. She leaned against it for a moment before climbing up the stairs to her apartment.

Dear Kelly,

Still no word from the American consulate.

The thought of serving ten years in this hell-hole scares me to death. It's unbelievable that this farce could have come this far. I've been framed. It's as clear as the daylight that I know is shining outside, despite the fact that it barely penetrates the thick walls of this stinking cell. I'm being punished for failing to cooperate with this country's current government, failing to reveal the location of the rebel forces, failing to reveal the names of the people who led me to my meeting with the rebel leader.

What's really ridiculous is that I don't approve of many of the rebels' methods in their fight for freedom. But if I betrayed them, it would mean the death of many people, most of them women and children.

So I sit here. Wherever the hell "here" is. Somewhere in Central America. I might as well be on the moon, a million miles away from the land of the free and the home of the brave, a million miles away from your sweet smile, writing letters to you in my mind, letters that have no hope of reaching you until I am free to deliver them myself.

With luck, that will be soon. Your eighteenth birthday is coming, and I intend to be there.

I love you.

Love, T.

Kelly sat at her computer, staring at the empty screen.

Well, it wasn't quite empty. It said "Chapter Ten" about a quarter of the way down, and there were two carriage return symbols after that, along with a tab symbol. The cursor flashed five spaces in, ready to start the first paragraph.

But all she could think about was T. Jackson Winchester the Second, and the best and worst night she'd ever had in her life. It was the best because it had been an amazing Cinderella-like fantasy, with T. Jackson playing the part of Prince Charming. And it was the worst, because after it was over, after all the dust had settled, he had walked out of her life for good, and her world turned into a pumpkin.

Until now.

Seven years later.

Kelly closed her eyes, remembering that May night. Prom night. It had been a night like this one, hot and humid, more like summer than spring.

That afternoon, she'd modeled her prom dress for Kevin and T. Jackson. Kevin had just finished his first year of law school, and T. had finally graduated from college, having had a year off between his sophomore and junior years. T. was hanging out with the O'Briens, kicking back for a few weeks, taking a vacation before facing the realities of the working world....

"Tonight I'm going to wear my hair up," she'd said to them, twirling around the living room to show off the sweeping skirt of her long gown.

"Sweet Lord," Kevin said, staring at her. "When did *you* turn into a girl?"

She made a face at him. "Try opening your eyes sometimes, dweeb. I've been a girl for sixteen years."

She risked a glance at T. He was looking at her, a small, funny smile on his face. She smiled back at him, her heart doing a fast somersault. *He* knew that she was a girl.

"Sure could've fooled me." Kevin grinned. "I thought when you said you were going to get dressed up for the prom, you meant you'd wear your jeans without the holes in the knees and a new pair of cowboy boots."

"Ha ha," Kelly said.

"Just please don't tell me Mom bought that dress with the grocery money." Kevin made a face. "You look great, Kel, but I don't think a prom dress is worth having to eat hot dogs for the rest of the summer."

"This dress used to be Grandma's. It didn't cost a cent. Your stomach is safe."

The gown was outrageously retro, right out of the late 1930s, and it fit Kelly as if it had been made for her from some kind of shimmery, slippery cornflower-blue fabric that matched her eyes.

Kelly turned to find T. still watching her long after Kevin had gone into the kitchen to forage for a snack.

It hadn't been too much later when the telephone rang. Kevin answered it, and bellowed up the stairs for Kelly. She came clattering into the kitchen where

T. and her brother were looking at the newspaper, trying to decide which movie to take Kevin's girlfriend, Beth, and one of her friends to that night.

"It's your boyfriend," Kevin said in a purposely obnoxious high voice, and Kelly snatched the phone away, glaring dangerously at him.

She covered the mouthpiece. "Frank's not my boyfriend. He's a *friend* who happens to be a *boy,* and we're going to the prom together. So don't be a jerk."

On the phone, Frank sounded terrible. He had some kind of stomach virus, he told her. There was no way on earth he was going to make it to the prom.

Kelly slowly hung up the phone.

"What did Frankie want?" Kevin asked. "Can't decide between the sky-blue or the chartreuse tux?"

She wheeled, turning on him angrily. "When are you going to grow up? You're in graduate school, you're supposed to be an adult now, so why don't you act like one? Frank's sick, so I'm not going to the prom, all right? Does that satisfy your juvenile curiosity? Or is there something else you want to know?"

"I'm sorry." Kevin was instantly contrite. "I didn't mean to be—"

"I'll take you," T. said.

"What?" Kevin and Kelly turned to him at the same time.

He was looking at Kelly, and he smiled his easy smile when their eyes met. "I mean, I'd *like* to take you."

Kevin stared at his friend in exasperation. "We're double-dating tonight. What, are you just going to blow off this friend of Beth's?"

"No." T. crossed his arms in front of him, and

leaned casually back in his chair. "I'll call her and tell her I can't make it."

"Because you want to take my little sister to some stupid high school dance?" Kevin laughed. "She's going to love that—"

"It's *not* a stupid dance," Kelly protested.

"Kev, it's her *prom*...."

Kevin sighed, looking from Kelly to Jax and back again. "Then I suppose *I* should take her."

"Gee, thanks," Kelly said. "A night out with Mr. Enthusiasm. I'd rather stay home."

But T. laughed, shaking his head. "No, Kev, you don't get it, do you? *I* want to take her. I *want* to take her. I would *love* to take her...."

Kelly swallowed. What was T. Jackson saying? She heard the words, but the implications were too intense.

T. turned and looked at her, his green eyes lit with an odd fire. "Kelly, will you let me take you to your prom?"

"Whoa, wait a minute," Kevin said before she could answer. He stared at his friend with growing realization, his voice tinged with disbelief. "Winchester, do you have, like, the *hots* for my little sister?"

But it was as if T. hadn't heard Kevin. He was just sitting there, his chair tipped back against the wall, smiling up at Kelly, waiting for her to answer him.

"Yeah." She'd smiled into his eyes as she'd nodded. "T., I'd really like that..."

Looking back now, Kelly knew that was the very moment she'd admitted to herself that she was in love with Tyrone Jackson Winchester the Second. And once she'd admitted it, she realized that she'd been in love with him for years. It wasn't puppy love. It wasn't a crush or an infatuation. It was solid, total, powerful love.

As she sat staring at her blank computer screen nearly seven years later, Kelly had to wonder.

What if T. had really been in love with her, too? What if they'd stayed together the way he'd promised, if he'd been the man she'd married when she was nineteen years old instead of Brad? Would her feelings have lasted?

Jax woke up drenched in sweat.

It was the nightmare again. The same old nightmare. He was back at that joke they'd called a trial.

He'd taken a flight from London a week earlier because the magazine he worked for had secured him a rare personal interview with the leader of the rebel forces in the tiny Central American country. The interview had gone smoothly and he had returned to his hotel room to type up his notes on his laptop computer.

Later that night he was roughly awakened by government soldiers and dragged to an official building where he was questioned about the location of the rebel forces. He'd been scared to death, but he refused to reveal even what little he knew about where he had been and who his contacts were.

Finally, after more than twenty-four hours of relentless questioning, he'd been released.

Back at the hotel, he'd considered calling the American consulate, telling them what had just happened, but there was a flight to Miami leaving almost immediately, and he barely had time to get to the airport, let alone make a phone call.

And he wanted to get out of there. Fast. He would have taken the next flight to Hades if he'd had to.

It was then, on his way to the plane, that the government's military police stopped his taxi. A quick search of his overnight bag led to the discovery of several large sacks of cocaine tucked neatly next to his underwear.

It was such an obvious frame-up that Jackson had laughed.

But as he sat in the ridiculous excuse for a courtroom the next day, listening to the announcement of the guilty verdict and the resulting ten-year jail sentence, he stopped laughing.

He'd managed to get in touch with the American consulate, but they could do nothing for him. Drug charges were out of their jurisdiction.

He was furious. It was so obvious. He was a reporter, he had information the government wanted. It was such a blatant setup. The drugs had been planted in his bag. What about his rights? He was an American—

But Jax had no rights, the consulate finally told him. He wasn't a hostage. He wasn't a political prisoner. He'd been convicted of possession of drugs, and there was nothing anyone could do to help him.

So he went to jail. He did not pass go, and he sure as hell didn't collect two hundred dollars.

Be good, the warden told him, and maybe you'll get out in five or six years.

It had been hell.

Jax had been put, alone, in a dark, damp cell with only a tiny slit of a window. He was let out only for an occasional meal or a walk around the compound. He might've gone crazy, and maybe he even did a little bit, because he started imagining Kelly. He started seeing her there with him, keeping him company, giving him strength. He had no paper, no pencil, but he still wrote hundreds of letters to Kelly. He wrote letters in his mind, letters that would never be sent, words he vowed he'd one day put onto paper.

And somehow he'd survived for twenty horrific months.

For years after, he'd had terrible nightmares, but finally they'd stopped.

So why was he dreaming about it again?

# Chapter 3

After tipping the room-service waiter, Jax brought the breakfast tray to the table and set it down next to his computer. He poured himself a cup of steaming coffee and took a sip of the dark, pungent brew as he pulled his current story up on the computer screen.

Yesterday, when he'd finished writing, he'd left Jared in his horrible little room at the boardinghouse, fuming about the way Jax had spirited Carrie away from him.

Now. To get Jared on that boat for Europe.

Thinking hard, Jax took another sip of his coffee. He hadn't realized shipping Jared off to Europe was going to be this difficult. Jared was right—there was no way he would voluntarily leave Carrie, the way Jax had left Kelly all those years ago.

The two situations weren't exactly parallel, Jax reminded himself. Although Carrie and Kelly were both sixteen, back in Carrie's day, women frequently married at that age. And Jared wasn't Jax. Jared was a hero, while Jax was...only Jax.

He flipped through his notebook. In Jax's original outline, Jared had left Boston and gone to Europe, vowing to make his fortune and return a rich man, rich enough to wed the beautiful Carrie. But Jax had written that outline before he'd fleshed out the characters, before he knew just how bold and dauntless and damned self-confident Jared was going to be.

So now he was stuck with Carrie hidden away with some distant relatives, and Jared crossing his arms and refusing to leave until he found her.

How do you make a man do something he doesn't want to do?

Love.

No, it was because of love that Jared wanted to stick around.

Blackmail.

"Don't start with that dark family secret thing again," Jared said warningly.

"Cooperate, and I won't have to," muttered Jax.

That left money.

No, Jared had already said that he didn't need money to keep Carrie's heart.

What else?

Patriotism?

If Jared had the opportunity to make a fortune *and* at the same time help the Northern war effort...

England had provided weapons to the South during the Civil War. Despite the Northern blockades, English ships continued to smuggle guns to the Confederacy.

Enter Captain Reilly, the same old friend of Jared's father's who had appeared in chapters two and six, thought Jax with triumph. Reilly would offer Jared a chance to sail on his ship, to pirate the British vessels, seize their cargos and deliver the weaponry to the North—at a fair enough price to make a small fortune, of course.

Jax reached for his computer keyboard.

A sharp knock sounded on the door, rousing Jared from his sleep.

He sat up, his heart pounding as he stared into the darkness of his tiny room. Carrie, he thought. Carrie!

But even as he lit a candle, the knock sounded again, along with a familiar rusty voice. ''Jared Dexter, you in there, boy? Open the damned door.''

It was Captain Magnus Reilly, the owner of the ship called the *Graceful Lady Fair*.

Jax wrote quickly, bringing Captain Reilly into the room and letting the grizzled old man describe his plan to Jared.

''What do you say, Jared?'' the captain asked. ''Are you in? We've a chance to make a fortune.''

Jared looked at Reilly in the flickering candlelight. Slowly he shook his head. ''Sorry, old man,'' he said. ''Not this time.''

''No,'' Jax nearly shouted. ''You're supposed to go with him, you fool. Don't you get it? It's your chance to serve your country *and* make some bucks. You'll come back rich, and then there's no way Carrie's family can refuse you.''

Jared crossed his arms obstinately. ''I'm not going anywhere until I find Carrie.''

We'll see about that. Jax gritted his teeth as he deleted the last few sentences that he'd written.

Jared looked at Reilly in the flickering candlelight.

The boy's normally handsome, exuberant face looked pale and tired, thought the captain. And from the looks of things, he'd recently been in a fight.

''Magnus,'' Jared said slowly, ''can you wait a few weeks? I can't leave the country right now.''

What was wrong with him today? Jax pressed the palms of his hands against the headache that was starting to throb behind his eyes.

In his mind, Jared smiled nastily at Jax. ''*I* know what's wrong with you,'' he said, then uttered the words writers hate most to hear. ''You've got writer's block.''

''I do not have writer's block,'' Jax said very calmly. ''I simply have an obstinate, pigheaded, stubborn fool of a character who is refusing to cooperate.''

Jared sat back on his bed, lacing his fingers together behind his head. ''Don't worry, the writer's block is only temporary,'' he returned with equal calm. ''Work this thing out with Kelly and you'll be able to write again in no time, whether I cooperate or not.''

''Just tell Reilly you'll go with him.'' Jax ran his fingers tiredly through his hair. ''Please?''

"Write me a love scene with Carrie and you've got a deal."

"Look, you're gonna have a happy ending," Jax promised. "I can guarantee that—"

"*That's* what's bothering you." Jared sat forward. "There's no guarantee that things are going to work out between you and Kelly. Bummer."

"Don't say 'bummer.' People in the nineteenth-century didn't say 'bummer.'" Jax took a deep breath. "Will you *please* go with Reilly?"

"My offer holds," Jared told him. "Write me that love scene and your wish is my command."

This was ridiculous. Jax readjusted the keyboard and began typing, refusing to be held hostage by his own character.

Without warning, Reilly pulled a revolver from under his jacket, pressing the cold metal of the barrel to Jared's head.

"You're coming with me, boy," he growled. "And you're coming now!"

Jared burst out laughing. "Wow, Jax," he said, between gasps for breath. "That's *really* stupid. There's absolutely *no* one who's going to believe that."

"Oh, shut up," Jax muttered. Cursing under his breath, he saved the job, turned off the laptop computer and went searching for some aspirin.

Dear Kelly,
You appear in my cell again today, and again, even though I know you can't possibly be real, I am thankful for your presence.

You are twelve years old this time, and as you

look around at the rough stone walls, at the damp dirt floor and at the wooden bench and dirty straw that I use for a bed, I can see anger in your dark blue eyes.

You look me over just as carefully, taking in my beard and my long, dirty hair.

You speak!

I can hear your husky voice clearly in the quiet of the cell. Last time you visited, you didn't talk. You only watched me.

"You smell," you tell me sternly, as if it were my fault, and I apologize.

"Sometimes," I say, "when it rains, the guards let us out with some scraps of soap and we can wash—"

You are looking at me oddly, and I realize I am speaking to you in Spanish. It's been so long since I've heard an American voice. I translate, and you nod.

"I guess it's been a while since it's rained," you say, sitting next to me on the straw.

"Soon it will do nothing but rain," I tell you, "and there will be five inches of brackish water on the floor of my cell."

You reach over and take my hand, holding it tightly with your slender fingers.

I notice the scabs on your knees and elbows, and you tell me about falling off of your bike.

I sympathize. I am careful to hide my own healing wounds—three deep cuts from an irate guard's whip that I earned by helping a fellow prisoner to his feet when he stumbled on his way to the courtyard for another endless roll-call session.

But I can tell from looking into your eyes that you know. You also know about the broken rib I received from an earlier beating.

"I didn't cry," I tell you. "They can beat me, spit on me, treat me like less than an animal, but I will not cry. I hold my head up when I walk. I look them in the eye. I am the Americano, and they both hate me and respect me for that."

You look at me as if I am your hero, and for a few short hours, I am.

"Hey," you say, looking more closely at the walls, "igneous rocks."

We spend some time identifying and arguing about the rocks that were used in building this prison.

I almost forget where I am as I chip at the wall to get you a sample for your rock collection.

You leave when the sun hits the correct angle. For forty-seven minutes it will stream into my little window. A narrow strip of sunlight will travel across the wall, and I will stand in it, letting it shine on my dirty face. It gives me hope to know that only a few thousand miles away, that same powerful sun is shining on you.

I love you.

Love, T.

Jax leaned against the corridor wall outside the university classroom, waiting for Kelly.

This was probably a mistake. No, not probably. Definitely. Following Kelly around this way was definitely a mistake. She would definitely be annoyed. But Jax knew only one way to achieve success in life, and it involved a large amount of tenacity and a great deal of perseverance, and all the stubbornness he could muster, which could actually be quite a bit when it came down to it.

He was going to marry Kelly O'Brien. That much was certain.

What wasn't so clear was how he was going to deal with the fact that the bride-to-be didn't even want to have a cup of coffee with him.

After rejecting his offer of Chinese food five days ago, she'd turned him down the next day for lunch. He'd tried brunch the following day, and breakfast the day after that, with similar luck. Yesterday he was reduced to asking her out for coffee, for God's sake, and she'd turned that down, too.

So what was he doing here, waiting for her to come out of class? What was he going to invite her to do now? Go out with him for a glass of water?

Maybe it was time to start over again with dinner.

Sooner or later, she was going to give in.

She had told him once that she loved him. And if she had loved him even only a tenth as much as he loved her, he would bet his entire seven-figure bank account that those feelings hadn't totally disappeared.

The classroom door opened, and students spilled out into the hall. Good grief, they looked so young. Some of them were twelve years younger than he was. Had he really been their age once?

Kelly didn't see him as she came through the door.

She was wearing a denim workshirt with the sleeves rolled up, a worn-out pair of jeans and cowboy boots. Her hair was back in a single braid. Except for the hint of makeup on her face and lips, she looked almost exactly as she had when she was fourteen.

Except almost ten years older, thank God. Her jeans

hugged her body in a way that they never had when she was fourteen.

Jax followed her down the hall, not catching up with her until she stopped to swing open the big double doors that led into the building's main foyer.

Her eyes narrowed dangerously as she stared at him. "You're following me around," she said, not bothering to say hello.

"Yeah," he said, unperturbed.

She went into the foyer, moving out of the way of the steady stream of students who were going in and out of the doors. "Well, stop it," she said sternly. "You can tell Kevin that I'm really okay—"

"This has nothing to do with Kevin," Jax said, shaking his head. "I'm trying to get you to go out to dinner with me, Kel, and if you keep saying no, then you better get used to me following you around."

Kelly gazed at him. "Do you even *own* any socks?"

He looked down at his feet, lifting his pants slightly to get a better view of his bare ankles. "If I go back to my hotel and put on a pair of socks, will you have dinner with me?"

"I can't." She headed toward the doors that led out into the warm spring sunshine. "I have my last exam of the semester tomorrow."

"How about tomorrow night?" Jax followed her.

"How long are you going to be in town?" She stopped on the steps outside the building to fish in her backpack for her sunglasses.

As long as it takes. "At least a few more days." Jax put on his own sunglasses. "I've got some business to take care of on Friday, so..."

They began walking slowly down the sidewalk. The sun was hot on Jax's back, and he slipped off his jacket and rolled up his sleeves. "If you want, I could help you study tonight."

She slid him a sidelong glance. "For an advanced calculus exam?"

"Ouch." He winced. "Are you really taking calculus?"

"*Advanced* calculus."

"Yeah, right. Rub it in." He'd barely made it through trigonometry back in high school. And as an English major in college, he'd purposely stayed far, far away from the math building.

The sunlight glinted off his golden hair. With his dark sunglasses and his million-dollar smile, he looked like some kind of movie star. It was just Kelly's luck that T. Jackson had become better looking as he got older. Now, why couldn't he have thinning hair and a potbelly like some of Kevin's other old college friends?

"Why are you taking it?" he asked. "I mean, I've never known you to be a masochist."

She shot him a quick look, but he didn't realize the irony of his words. He was right, she wasn't a masochist, and that was one of the reasons she didn't want him hanging around.

"I'm taking it because I like science, and calculus is a prerequisite for some of the advanced science courses I want to take next year," she told him. Her cowboy boots made a clicking sound against the concrete sidewalk. "I'm sorry, T.," she added, "but I don't think you'll be any help as a study partner."

"It's been years since you've seen me," he protested. "How do you know I haven't suddenly become a math whiz?"

Kelly burst out laughing.

''How many more semesters do you have before you graduate?'' he asked.

''Three,'' Kelly said. ''I married Brad when I was a sophomore. Appropriate, huh?''

Marrying Brad had been incredibly sophomoric. She'd thought she knew what she was doing, what she wanted, but in reality, she had had absolutely no idea, not one clue. And apparently Brad hadn't known what he'd really wanted, either.

''We moved to California that summer,'' she told T. Jackson, ''and there wasn't enough time for me to transfer to a school out there. So I got a job, and by the time the spring semester started, Brad had been laid off and we really needed the money.''

''Are you going to take this summer off,'' he asked, ''or do you have a job lined up?''

She shrugged. ''Nothing definite. I've interviewed at a couple of places.''

''Spend the summer on the Cape with me.''

Kelly stopped walking. ''What?''

''I live out on Cape Cod,'' T. Jackson said. He took off his sunglasses. She could see from his eyes that he was actually serious. ''I've got a house on the beach, on the bay side, in Dennis. It's this huge modern monster—we've got lots of extra bedrooms, there's plenty of room.'' He stopped, laughed softly, shaking his head. ''Look, I'd love to spend some time with you, and...''

''I won't even go out to dinner with you,'' Kelly told him. ''What on earth makes you think I'd want to spend the entire summer with you on the Cape?''

He put his sunglasses back on. ''I don't know,'' he said. ''You always wanted to. You talked about it all the time, and I just thought...''

"I was *twelve,* T." She wasn't being completely truthful. She'd talked about it when she was older than twelve, too. Dreamed about it. A summer at the Winchester compound on the Cape.

Kelly stared up at him, seeing her face reflected in the lenses of his sunglasses. Truth was, spending the summer on the beach with T. Jackson would fulfill just about every single one of her childhood fantasies. And quite a few of her teenaged fantasies, too.

But as an adult, she knew her fantasies about T. were simply that. Fantasies. She knew what kind of man he was, because she'd been married to a man exactly like him. She no longer had any illusions about living happily ever after with T. Jackson, no matter how charming and handsome and sexy he was.

If she wanted happily ever after—and she did—she was going to have to find a different type of man. She'd gladly trade some of the spark, the sexual chemistry, for a man who would love only her. She wanted a man who gave as much as he took, a man who truly knew how to love, not just *be* loved. A man who kept his promises.

But there was something to be said for spending a few months with T. Jackson Winchester the Second. It would be one *hell* of a summer, that was for sure.

Unless this was just another of his favors to Kevin…

She could just imagine the conversation her brother must've had with T. "Cheer her up," Kevin must've told Jax. "Take her out, show her a good time. She used to have a crush on you, remember? Make her feel important. If anyone can do it, you can."

But it hadn't been a crush. What she had felt for T. Jackson had been so much more than a crush. And did she really want to wreck her romantic memories of her first love by going and having a tawdry affair with the man?

When the answer didn't come as an immediate no, Kelly shook her head in disgust. What was wrong with her?

"I'm going to be busy all summer," she said, starting down the sidewalk again. And she would be. When she finished writing her second novel, she'd start on a third. It was a never-ending process, but one that she loved. And right now her writing was a way to stay safe, insulated from the rest of the world. And from T. Jackson Winchester the Second in particular.

"Think about it," he said.

The annoying thing was, she would. In fact, she'd probably think about nothing else. She'd probably dream about spending the entire summer with T. He'd already appeared in her dreams last night, her imagination clothing him in a hell of a lot less than the bathing suit he'd wear as a standard uniform on the Cape. Her subconscious was giving her a very deliberate message—there was unfinished business between the two of them.

But it was a hormonal thing. It was pure sex, and it had nothing to do with love. Even if she ended up giving in to T.'s persistent demands, even if she ended up sleeping with the man, she'd never let him back into her heart. Never.

"So are we on for dinner tomorrow night?" Jax asked as they stopped outside the school newspaper office door.

"Tomorrow night?" She shook her head. "I don't—"

"Friday night, then."

"No," she said definitely. "I'm going to a meeting in the late afternoon. I don't know how long it'll last."

"I've got something happening Friday afternoon, too," he said. "We can eat later—"

"No."

Jax looked at her, silent for a moment. Then he laughed. "I guess I'm going to have to keep following you around, then."

Kelly took off her sunglasses, sighing with exasperation. "Jackson—"

He kissed her.

It was little more than a light brushing of his lips against hers, but it was a kiss. And it was enough to make her system go haywire. She stared at him in shock.

"See you tomorrow, Kel." He smiled and walked away.

Jared was right. Jax realized it would be much more romantically tragic if Carrie were whisked away to the safety of distant relatives *after* she and Jared had a scene in which they planned to run away together. Jax just wasn't convinced it should be a love scene.

"She's only sixteen," he muttered. "She's too young."

"That's a load of crap, and you know it," Jared countered. "Just because *you* made the mistake of thinking that *Kelly* was too young—"

"She *was* too young."

"You ran because you knew you couldn't deny her anything," Jared said. "You knew if you stayed, you'd make love to her, because she wanted you to. You left because you were scared."

"I left because I loved her!" Jax argued.

"You didn't even have the decency to tell her you were going—"

"Because what Kevin threatened to do was—"

"So what are you saying?" Jared's dark eyes were intense. "Are you saying that you want *me* to make the same stupid mistake you did? I thought one of the reasons you were writing this story was to give yourself a chance to do it over, and do it *right* this time."

"Fine!" Jax threw up his hands. "I'll write that love scene. But I've got to warn you, friend. It's only going to be one night. And things are going to get much worse before you get your happy ending. I've got another 230 pages to fill."

Jax sat in his sports car. From where he was parked, he could see light streaming from the front window of Kelly's apartment.

He'd left his hotel room this evening after writing a passionate scene between Jared and Carrie. Writing sensual scenes made him restless, in need of air. He'd intended to go to a movie, but somehow he'd wound up here.

He'd waited for Kelly this afternoon as she finished up her calculus exam. He'd asked her to go out to dinner again, and again she refused. This time he could barely keep up with her as she nearly ran to the newspaper office. She'd disappeared inside with only a quick goodbye, not giving him enough time to kiss her again.

God, he wanted to kiss her. He wanted to kiss her the way Jared had kissed Carrie in the scene he'd written only a few hours ago. Jax wanted to kiss Kelly the way he had on that night so many years ago—prom night....

At first Kevin had refused to let Jax take Kelly to the school dance. He'd followed Jax all the way downtown, to the tux rental place. A little bell had tinkled as they walked into the air-conditioned interior of the tiny shop.

"I need a tux," Jax told the skinny man behind the counter.

"No, he doesn't," Kevin countered, folding his big arms across his beefy chest. "*I* need a tux." He turned to Jax. "She's too young for you."

The shopkeeper removed a measuring tape from around his neck, and stood looking at them. "You both want tuxes?"

"No." Jax smiled. "Just me."

"No." The fierceness of Kevin's voice was a sharp contrast to Jax's cool control. "Not him. Me. I need it for tonight."

"I'm taking her," Jax said mildly to Kevin. He leaned against a glass-topped counter that held an assortment of bow ties and cummerbunds.

"She's a *kid.*" Kevin's face was pink with anger. "You should be dating women, not little girls."

"Don't you trust me?" Jax asked, his voice level.

"No, not after the way I saw you looking at her this afternoon." Kevin ran his hands through his short red hair in exasperation as he glared up at his friend. "Hell, Winchester, she's only sixteen!"

"I know how old she is."

"You better keep that in mind. She's jailbait, pal." Kevin took a threatening step forward, stabbing Jax's chest with his forefinger. But Jax didn't move a muscle, didn't even blink. "You mess with her," Kevin threatened, "and you'll end up in prison. And I'll personally escort you there."

The two young men locked gazes for several long moments. Then Jax smiled, shaking his head slightly. ''You know I'd never do anything to hurt her, Kev.''

''Mess with Kelly and I'll kill you,'' Kevin repeated, but the anger was gone from his voice.

''I'm crazy about her,'' Jax admitted. ''I'll take good care of her, I promise.''

''You *are* crazy.'' Kevin laughed with disbelief. ''Beth has a gorgeous friend who's dying to get naked with you, but *you* want to go out with a girl who's barely out of diapers. I just don't get it.''

Jax smiled. ''You don't have to get it. Just relax. I want to go out with Kelly tonight, and you want to go out with Beth. We're both doing each other a favor, okay?''

''I still think you're nuts.''

Jax looked at the shopkeeper, who was watching them with unabashed interest. ''I need a tux for tonight,'' he said again.

But the shopkeeper shook his head. ''What're you? Six foot five? I'm sorry, no can do. I only had a few rental tuxes in your size, and they're out. Won't be back in 'til Sunday.''

''Then I'll buy one,'' Jax said.

''You'll what?'' Kevin's eyebrows disappeared under his thick red hair.

Jax smiled at his friend. ''I'll buy one.'' He looked back at the shopkeeper. ''And I'll pay extra if you get the alterations done by this afternoon.''

By five o'clock, Jax had showered, shaved and finished putting on his brand-new tuxedo up in Kevin's room. He didn't remember being this excited about going to his own junior prom.

Kelly's door was still closed, so he headed downstairs to wait for her. Jax stopped in the kitchen first, pulling the flowers he'd bought her out of the refrigerator and carrying them into the living room.

Nolan O'Brien was lying on the couch, reading the newspaper as Jax came in, and he looked over the top of it, smiling. Kevin and Kelly's father was an older, heavier version of Kevin. He had the same red-orange hair, thinning a bit on top, though, the same beefy frame, the same cheerful disposition and millions and millions of the same freckles.

''So you're the sacrificial substitute date for the prom, eh?'' the older man asked, not bothering to move from his relaxed position on the couch.

''It's no sacrifice, Nolan,'' Jax said easily, sitting down in the rocking chair that was across from the couch. He leaned forward to put the flowers on the coffee table.

''A corsage *and* a dozen roses,'' Nolan said, looking at Jax appraisingly with a slow smile. ''I was wondering when you were going to start noticing that Kelly's almost all grown up. Looks like it finally happened.''

Jax smiled.

Nolan folded the newspaper. ''I suppose I don't have to give you the normal 'date speech' that I give the rest of the boys that take Kelly out—you know, the 'no drinking and driving' speech, the 'get her home before midnight' speech…''

''I know your rules,'' Jax said, nodding. ''Although you might want to cut loose with the curfew for tonight. Kelly told me there are after-prom parties scheduled one after the other until sun-up. And then, if it's warm enough, everyone's heading over to the beach.''

Nolan nodded. ''Okay,'' he said agreeably, swinging himself up into a sitting position. "Just don't forget, Kelly comes across as being much older than she really is. Keep in mind that she's only sixteen. There's a big difference between sixteen and twenty-two, Jax."

The older man's eyes were intense. Jax smiled, realizing that Nolan was giving him a polite version of the same message Kevin had delivered at the tuxedo shop: Don't mess with Kelly.

"I know," Jax said quietly.

"Good."

Ten minutes later, Kelly was sitting next to Jax in his little red Spitfire, and they were heading down the road toward town, toward the restaurant where he had made dinner reservations.

Jax glanced over at her, still struck by how beautiful, how elegant and poised she looked.

When she'd appeared in the living room, his heart had nearly stopped.

She was wearing that fabulous blue gown, and her hair was pinned up, swept back loosely, femininely, from her face. She was wearing makeup and her eyes looked more blue than they ever had before, with her long, dark lashes accentuated. Her normally pretty, fresh face looked exotically beautiful with her hair up, giving Jax a good look at the gorgeous woman she was destined to become in the next few years.

Kelly was a child-woman, a curious mixture of innocence and poise, elegance and enthusiasm. She was unconsciously sexy—well, maybe not entirely unconsciously. She wasn't wearing a bra beneath her slinky gown because the back of the dress was open. True, the top wasn't tight fitting, but the smooth material occasionally clung to her lithe body, and the effect was…extremely distracting.

He'd thought he'd have no trouble taking her out like this. He'd thought after four years of being close friends with Kelly that it wouldn't be hard to remember she was still only a kid.

So why was it that he could think of little else but how her lips would feel against his?

Jackson's pulse was running too fast, his heart pounding. Relax, he ordered himself, forcing himself to breathe slowly. Just relax. Stay cool.

"This feels…strange," Kelly said, glancing at T. from beneath her eyelashes. She laughed softly. "You look as tense as I feel."

"I'm not tense," Jax protested, reaching up with one hand to loosen the tight muscles in the back of his neck. "Are you tense?"

"Yeah," she admitted with her usual candor and a brief, charming smile. "I just keep thinking…well… maybe we should go Dutch tonight."

"Dutch?" he said, disbelief in his voice as he looked over at her. "Nope. This is on me, Kel."

"It doesn't seem fair to make you pay for everything—" she turned slightly in the bucket seat to face him "—just because I happen to be female. Especially considering that I shanghaied you."

"Do I look like I'm suffering?" Jax asked, amused.

"You never look like you're suffering. That's why it's so hard to tell whether or not you actually *are*."

"I'll let you know if and when I start," he assured her with a grin as he pulled up to a red light.

She looked up at him, and he returned her gaze. Her face was so familiar. He knew her so well. Or did he? He knew the child, not the woman. And sometime during the past few months, she'd suddenly become part woman. Her skin looked so smooth, so pale compared to the inky darkness of her hair. Yet her cheeks were flushed with a soft glow of good health, her mouth curved up into a small smile, her eyes bright, sparking as they met his own. Jax could imagine himself drowning in the blue depths of her eyes. Imagine? Hell, he *was* drowning.

A short beep from the car behind him told him that the light had changed, and he forced his eyes back to the road. After a moment, he glanced quickly at Kelly, but she was looking down at the small clutch purse she was holding in her lap, a faint tinge of embarrassment on her cheeks.

God, she knew everything he was feeling just from looking into his eyes. He'd learned a long time ago that he couldn't hide things from Kelly, so why should he expect to be able to hide this?

The main problem, was that he wasn't exactly sure what "this" was.

Was he in love with her?

If he wasn't in love with her already, he was definitely teetering. No, not just teetering, he'd already lost his balance. There was nowhere for him to go but over the edge.

Kelly glanced at him again, smiling, and Jax felt a sudden lack of gravity deep in the pit of his stomach.

Free fall. He was in free fall, there was no doubt about it. He'd taken the plunge, and he was falling hard and fast.

Add into the equation all the feelings he was already carrying around for Kelly. It was one hell of an emotional attachment, and one he couldn't deny. Add to *that* this explosively intense physical attraction…

If she were eighteen years old, he would court her ruthlessly. He would use every trick in the book to get her to fall in love with him, too. He would take her out, buy her presents—hell, he'd even seduce her. He would tell her and show her in every way possible that he loved her. He would make love to her endlessly. And then he would get down on his knees and beg her to marry him.

God, he actually wanted to *marry* her, as in 'til death do us part, as in happily ever after. There was just one problem. She wasn't eighteen years old. She was sixteen. Jailbait, as Kevin had so indelicately put it.

For one wild moment Jax wondered if Nolan and Lori O'Brien would give their daughter permission to marry him now. But as quickly as the thought entered his mind, he pushed it away. It wouldn't happen. Kelly's parents would never agree to it. They would say that she wasn't old enough. And they would be right.

There was just no getting around it. Kelly was too young.

That left him only one option. He'd simply have to wait for her to get older.

"This *is* strange," Kelly said. "I think this is the first time I've ever seen you so quiet." She laughed softly. "Usually I can't shut you up."

"Sorry," Jax said. "I was thinking."

"About the job offer you got from that London magazine?"

He looked over to find her watching him, her face serious. "What do you think about that? Should I take it?"

She was quiet for so long, he thought maybe she

wasn't going to answer. But when he glanced back at her, she was still watching him steadily.

"I can't answer that fairly," she finally said. "See, when I think about it, I can find all kinds of reasons why you *should* take that job. I mean, come on, T., you'd be living in *London.* That would be so great. You could spend your vacations in Europe." She looked away from him, out the window, at the spring wildflowers that were growing along the sides of the road. "It's true it's not a lot of money," she continued, "but you'd be paid to write. After a couple of years as a staff writer for the magazine, you'd have name recognition, so if you ever started working on that novel you keep talking about, you'd probably have an easier time selling it."

She was quiet, and he glanced at her again. "But..." he prompted her.

"I'd miss you," Kelly said simply. "That's why I can't answer your question fairly. I don't want you to live on the other side of the Atlantic Ocean."

Happiness exploded inside of Jackson. "Then I won't go. I'll find a job in Boston."

"Tyrone, don't tease."

"I'm serious."

"But—" she started, then stopped, her eyes widening as Jackson pulled his sports car into the parking lot of the Breckenridge Inn, the fanciest restaurant in the area. "Whoa, T., what's this?"

"This is where we're having dinner." Jax pulled into a parking space at the edge of the big lot.

"But this is too expensive—"

"You're worth every penny."

"I would've settled for Bertucci's," she said.

''Why settle?'' Jax pulled up the parking brake and turned off the engine as he smiled at her.

Kelly's eyes danced with delight. ''Why don't you have women falling all over you, T.?'' she asked. ''You're so smooth, you put James Bond to shame.''

''It's the name.'' Jax sighed. ''Winchester,'' he said in his best Sean Connery. ''Tyrone Jackson Winchester the Second... No, see, my name's way too long. By the time I finish saying my name, all the gorgeous women have either fallen asleep or they've gone off with the guy with the shorter name.''

Kelly laughed again and Jax glanced at the dashboard. The digital clock read 5:35. The prom didn't start until eight o'clock. There were two hours and twenty-five minutes before he could dance with Kelly, before he could hold her in his arms. He wasn't sure he would survive until then.

Of course, compared to the four hundred and fifty-nine days he had to wait until she turned eighteen, two hours and twenty-five minutes was a piece of cake.

She was looking at him, her lips moist and parted slightly. God, he wanted to kiss her. God, he wanted to...

''Shall we go inside?'' he asked, opening his door. But Kelly put her hand on his arm. Even through his jacket and shirt, her soft touch made him freeze.

''Jackson—'' she began to say, then stopped, pulling her hand back onto her lap.

''Uh-oh.'' Jax tried to be light, turning toward her. ''You only call me that when you mean business. What'd I do?''

Kelly shook her head. ''There's something I want to ask you, and I'm not really sure how to.''

"You've never had a problem being direct before. Just ask."

She looked down at her hands for a moment, then shook her head again, laughing softly. "This is stupid, but..." She looked up at him. "Is this a real date?"

Kelly was looking directly into his eyes, and again Jax had the sensation of drowning. He was being pulled under again. Sooner or later, he was going to go down, and he wouldn't make it back up. "I think so," he said slowly. "What's the definition of a real date?"

She moistened her lips with the tip of her tongue, and Jackson's eyes were drawn to her mouth. He couldn't look away—he was hypnotized.

"A real date is when you go out with someone that you like enough to kiss good-night when it's over," Kelly said softly.

When, oh when, did the inside of his car get so tiny?

Jax pulled his eyes away from the delicately shaped lips that were only a few scant inches from his own mouth. "Yeah," he managed to say. "This is a real date."

"Could you—" Kelly said haltingly. "Could we—" She laughed self-consciously and started again. "T., this is going to sound really weird, but the thought of kissing you is making me really nervous and—"

"Then I won't kiss you," he said quickly.

"No, that's not what—" She shook her head, laughing again. "See, I was just thinking if you kissed me *now,* I could stop being nervous about it."

"Now," Jackson repeated. He held on tightly to the steering wheel, afraid that if he let go, he'd lose his balance. She wanted him to kiss her. Now.

"I mean, it would take some of the pressure off, don't you think?"

No. No, he did not think that it would take any kind of pressure off at all. Not for him, anyway. Still, when he looked into her eyes, he knew there was no way on earth he could turn her down.

He felt himself lean toward her, closer, closer. He reached out his hand to cup her face. Her skin was so soft underneath his fingers. He ran his thumb across her lips.

Jax could feel his heart pounding in his chest. He was going to be the first twenty-two-year-old to die of a love-induced heart attack. He smiled. There were certainly worse ways to go.

Kelly returned his smile, then closed her eyes, lifting her lips to him. He moved that final fraction of an inch, and then he was kissing her.

Her mouth felt warm and soft as he slowly, gently brushed his own lips across hers. It took every ounce of control he had to keep himself from deepening the kiss, to keep himself from touching her lips with his tongue, from entering her sweet mouth.

Breathing hard, he pulled back to look at her. Her breasts were rising and falling as if she, too, were having trouble pulling air into her lungs.

"T., don't stop," she whispered, and he groaned, knowing he shouldn't kiss her again, knowing he *should* stop right here and right now before this got out of hand.

"Please," she whispered, and everything he knew he should do went right out the window as he bent his head to kiss her again.

This time her arms went up around his neck. He felt her fingers in his hair as their lips met. He felt her mouth open underneath his, her tongue lightly touch his lips.

He swept his arms around her, pulling her against his chest as he gently met her tongue with his own. He wanted to pull her over the parking brake onto his lap, to reach under her light spring shawl to cup her breasts in the palms of his hands. He wanted to kiss her long and hard and deep, and he wanted to keep kissing her until she turned eighteen. And then he wanted to make love to her. He wanted to be her first lover, and her last.

''Kelly,'' he said between kisses, his voice raspy and thick. ''Kelly—''

He had to do it. He had to kiss her just once the way he was dying to. Just one real kiss.

He swept his tongue into her mouth, fiercely, wildly, claiming her, possessing her. He could feel her fingers tighten in his hair as she pulled him even closer to her, as she met his kiss with a passion that equaled his own.

One kiss became two, then three, then more, and suddenly nothing else mattered or even existed. There was only Kelly. Kelly, who knew him better than anyone in the world. Kelly, with whom he shared all of his secrets. All of his secrets, including this one—he loved her, the way a man loves a woman.

But faintly he was aware that time was passing, and somehow, somewhere, he found strength to pull away from her sweet lips.

''Oh, T.,'' she breathed, ''I've never been kissed like that before.''

He closed his eyes, still holding her in his arms, her head against his shoulder as waves of emotion flooded him. It was an odd combination of relief and guilt and love, happiness and great sorrow, all mixed together, blended in a confusing blur.

He held her for what seemed like hours, until his pulse slowed. When it reached as close as he thought it would get to normal for that evening, he released her.

His hands shook as he tried to get the keys out of the ignition, and he dropped them on the floor. He took a deep breath and combed his hair back with his fingers, then turned to look at Kelly.

She smiled as he met her eyes. "Well, I guess you're not gay."

Jax stared at her, momentarily floored. "What did you just say?" he asked in a burst of air, even though he knew he'd heard her correctly.

"A few days ago, Christa asked me if you were gay."

"You're kidding." Christa was Kelly's aunt who had lived with the O'Briens that same summer that Jax had.

"She's been wondering for a while why you don't have a girlfriend. I told her I didn't know what your sexual preference was," Kelly said with a nonchalant shrug.

"*Kel*ly!" Jax's voice reached up an octave in outrage before he saw the amusement sparkling in her eyes, before the smile she was trying to hide crept out.

"Relax, Jackson. I told her that you were straight...but I don't think she believed me. She's very big on proof, and frankly, I didn't have any."

This conversation was getting *way* out of hand. And the clock on the dashboard now read 6:03. Man, had he really sat here in his car for the past half hour making out with Kevin's little sister? Someone was surely saving a place for him in hell, because that was right where he was going to go after Kevin broke his neck.

And Kelly was looking at him as though she didn't want to get out of the car for at least another half an hour.

"Kelly, let's have dinner," he said desperately, his usual cool demeanor slipping. "Please?"

With a smile, she adjusted the rearview mirror and carefully reapplied her lipstick. Jax couldn't bear to watch, afraid he wouldn't be able to keep himself from kissing it off her lips, too.

He forced himself out of the car, picked his keys up off the floor, then went around to open Kelly's door. He offered her his hand to help her out, and she put her slim, cool fingers into his as she smiled up at him. He caught a quick, breathtaking glimpse of her shapely legs through the slit in her skirt and then she was out of the car. He closed the door behind her, reminding himself to keep breathing.

As they crossed the gravel driveway to the front entrance, Kelly slipped her hand into the crook of Jax's arm. He covered her hand with his, unable to keep himself from lightly stroking the tops of her fingers.

"T.," she said quietly as they approached the door to the restaurant. He looked down into her steady blue gaze. "It didn't really help, did it?"

She was talking about those practice good-night kisses. With a laugh, Jax shook his head. "No, Kel, it sure didn't."

"Well, at least I'm not nervous anymore," she said with a small smile.

Yeah, but Jax still was. In fact, now he was *twice* as nervous.

# *Chapter 4*

Dear Kelly,
Another day dawns and I am still here in this damned miserable cell.

One of the guards takes pity on me and slips me some American paperback books that were left behind in the hotel where his wife works as a maid.

There are three of them—all romances. One is a long historical, the other two are shorter and set in the present day. I read them eagerly, voraciously, in the dim light from my little window. I read them over and over again, taking great joy in the happy endings, the tender embraces of the lovers reunited at last.

You come after sunset, when it's too dark to read any longer, and I proudly show the books to you. They are my prize possessions, and I keep them carefully out of sight of the other guards.

Tonight you are sixteen, and you leaf through the books casually in the darkness, far more interested in the paper they are printed on than the words themselves.

"If you write really small," you tell me, "you can use this paper and write between the lines."

I stare at you stupidly.

You laugh. "T., you always said that you'd write a novel if you could only find the time," you say. You lift one eyebrow humorously. "Well, suddenly you've got plenty of time."

I am elated, but only briefly. "I have nothing to write with."

"Ask the guard who gave you these books. Ask him for a pencil or a pen."

"I will."

You smile, and I suddenly realize you are wearing your prom dress. You are so beautiful, my heart nearly stops beating.

You lean forward to kiss me, and I can feel your soft lips, smell your perfume. You take me with you, back in time, and for a while, I am out of my cell. I sit with you in my sports car, clean-shaven and smelling sweet, wearing my tuxedo, and we kiss.

You are still so young, and I'm even older now, and I still don't know better. I still can't stop myself.

I love you.

Love, T.

It was well past 2:00 a.m. by the time Kelly shut down her computer and turned off the lights in her apartment. She moved to the living room window, remembering that she hadn't closed and locked it the way she did every night. As she pulled the window down, the sound of a car's engine starting out on the street caught her attention. As she watched, a sleek sports car pulled away from the curb, dimly lit by the streetlight on the corner. She looked closer, sure that she could see the glint of golden hair through the driver's side window.

The first thing she felt was anger. What the *hell* was T. doing, spying on her until all hours of the night?

But it didn't take long for rational thought to intercede. He couldn't have been spying on her. The only way he could have seen into her windows was if he'd somehow gained access to the apartment across the street. And it was hardly likely that he had gone to such lengths. If he had wanted to know what she was doing, he would've no doubt simply knocked on her door.

So then, what *was* he doing? Sitting out in his car in front of her house for God only knows how many hours?

Why?

The only answer she could come up with was more than a bit alarming. It had to be the physical attraction, the same old irresistible pull that they had nearly given in to on her prom night, so many years ago. *She* still felt it tugging at her every time he was near. No doubt he did, too.

Kelly lay back in her bed and threw her arm across her eyes. She was exhausted, but sleep didn't come. Finally, too tired to fight, she closed her eyes and let her memories carry her back in time to that wonderful, terrible Saturday night of the prom.

She couldn't begin to remember what she ate for dinner at the Breckenridge Inn. She wasn't sure that she even knew at the time. Her attention had been so totally captured by T. Jackson Winchester the Second....

He'd reached across the table between courses, holding her hand lightly, playing with her fingers, making her think about the way he had kissed her in the car. He'd kept up a steady stream of conversation about books, movies, music, anything and everything, but there had been an odd fire in his eyes that had let her know he, too, had been thinking about kissing her again.

When the waiter brought their dinners, he also brought them each a complimentary glass of white wine. T. looked at Kelly, one eyebrow slightly raised, but he said nothing until the waiter left.

''People always think I'm older than I am,'' she said. ''It was a drag back when I was eleven. I used to get into arguments with the ticket lady at the movie theater. I finally had to bring her my birth certificate to prove that I really was under thirteen.'' She smiled. ''But now I'd say it's paying off.'' She toyed with the long stem of her wineglass. ''I wish, at least, that I was eighteen.''

T. was leaning back lazily in his chair, his handsome face lit by flickering candlelight. ''I wish you were, too.''

''I feel like I'm spending all of my time waiting.'' Kelly gazed into the stormy gray-green of his eyes. ''I know exactly what I want to do, I know exactly what I want from life, but it's going to be another few years before I'm allowed to start living.''

''Four hundred and fifty-nine days.''

She looked at him in surprise.

He smiled. "I'm counting." He leaned forward suddenly. "What *do* you want from life?" His eyes were electric green now, and they seemed to shine in the dim light, intense, piercing.

You.

She almost said it aloud. Instead she said, "I want what I've always wanted, the same thing you want—to be a writer."

"So do it," T. told her. "Be a writer. Just because you're living at home, just because you're still in high school, doesn't mean you can't start sending your stories out to magazines. It doesn't mean you can't get published. If you really want something, if you've really figured out what you want, then go for it, work for it, do it. Don't hold back. No matter what else you do, just keep writing."

His face was so serious. A lock of hair had fallen across his forehead, but he didn't bother to push it back. Kelly gazed at his perfect features—perfect except for the tiny scar below his left eye, close to his temple, on his cheekbone. He'd been in a fight in high school, he'd once told her, being purposely vague.

That scar had always been a reminder to Kelly that there was more to T. Jackson than he'd let the world believe from his cool and collected outward appearance. There was a fire inside of him, ready to spark into flames if he was pressed hard enough.

She'd tasted that fire when he'd kissed her. But even when he kissed her so passionately, she'd felt his control, felt him holding back. She'd never seen him when he wasn't in control, and had only rarely seen him rattled. She smiled again, remembering his reaction when she'd mentioned that Christa doubted his masculinity. But still, even then, he'd really only been slightly fazed.

That scar, though, was proof that there was a side to T. that she'd hadn't yet seen. And although the scar interrupted the lines of his face, it added a mysteriousness and an unpredictability to him, and Kelly found that wonderfully, dangerously attractive.

As he gazed across the table at her, his eyes held the same fiery fierceness that Kelly had seen right before he had kissed her in the car—those amazing, industrial-strength kisses. As she watched, he forced his eyes away from her, down to his plate, and stared at the food in front of him as if he hadn't realized it was there.

*If you really want something,* he had said, *if you've really figured out what you want...*

She wanted T., there was no doubt about it. And she wanted him forever. It couldn't be much clearer to her, it couldn't be more obvious.

*Then go for it...don't hold back.*

''There's more,'' she said quietly, and he looked up at her. There was uncertainty in his eyes, and she realized he wasn't following. ''There's more that I want,'' she explained.

As she watched, understanding replaced the confusion. As she gazed at him, she saw his sudden comprehension, along with a renewed flare of the fire that was burning inside of him.

*I want you.*

She didn't have to say the words. He knew.

He smiled at her, but it was tinged with sadness. ''Oh, Kel,'' he whispered. ''What am I going to do about this?''

She picked up her fork and toyed with the food on

her plate for a moment before she answered. "You could start by asking me out on another date."

He reached across the table, lacing her fingers with his. "What are you doing tomorrow night?"

Kelly felt her heart flip-flop. He was taking her seriously. "I've got nothing planned."

"Will you go to a movie with me?" he asked. "We could get something to eat before or after, depending on what time the movie starts."

Kelly looked down at her barely touched dinner and laughed. "Maybe we should skip the meal. Neither of us seems to care much about food these days."

"Is that a yes?" His hand tightened slightly on hers.

"Yes."

"Will you go out with me Monday night, too?"

"Yes."

"Tuesday?"

Kelly laughed. "Yes."

"How about Wednesday?"

"I'm supposed to baby-sit for the Wilkinses. You know, they live down the street."

"I remember," Jax said. "Kevin and I filled in over there for you last year when you got that virus. Do you think they would mind if I came along?"

"No," Kelly told him.

"Good." Jax smiled. "Then that just leaves Thursday and Friday...and every other night for the next one year and ninety-four days. Will you go out with me those nights, too?"

As Kelly gazed into his warm green eyes, she was incredibly, deliriously happy. "Yes," she whispered.

He brought her hand up to his lips, gently kissing the tips of her fingers. "Good."

"Why only a year and ninety-four days?" she wondered aloud.

He lifted her hand to his mouth again, this time kissing her palm. Kelly inhaled sharply at the sensation, and heat raced through her body. She could see the same heat in T.'s eyes as the warm green turned hot. "Because in one year and ninety-four days, you'll be eighteen."

"What happens then?" She watched, mesmerized as he kissed the soft inside of her wrist, pressing her throbbing pulse with his lips.

"Lots of things," he replied, watching her through half-closed eyelids. His thumb now traced slow circles on the palm of her hand, and Kelly felt nearly overpowered by her feelings. She wanted to kiss him again. She wanted…

She knew about sex, even though she had no experience. She'd read plenty of books, seen movies, heard talk, but she'd never really quite understood what the big deal was all about. Until now.

"When you're eighteen, you'll start college," Jackson was saying lazily, still smiling at her. "You'll leave home. You'll marry me."

Kelly pulled her hand free. "Tyrone, don't tease about something like that."

"I'm not teasing."

She looked up at him. His smile was gone. Kelly felt a rush of dizziness, and she started to laugh. "I thought, according to convention, that a man is supposed to *ask* a woman to marry him, not simply *tell* her that she will."

"Oh, I'll ask," Jax had said. "The minute you turn eighteen, Kelly, I'm going to ask…."

But he hadn't. Even though he had disappeared a

few days after the prom, even though he had broken all of the other promises he had made to her that night, Kelly had spent her entire eighteenth birthday waiting for him to show up, to call, to come for her.

But he never had.

Tears still stung her eyes as she remembered the bitter disappointment, the hurt. It was on that day she convinced herself that she had truly stopped loving T. Jackson Winchester the Second. It was on that day that she started moving ahead with her life. It was the day she finally agreed to go out with Brad Foster.

It was better it had happened this way. Better that she'd married Brad instead of T. Because although finding Brad with another woman had hurt her, it wasn't the end of the world. It was simply the end of their relationship.

But if it had been T. Jackson she had found in bed with someone else…that would have destroyed her. Her heart would never have recovered.

Now that Jared was cooperating, Jax's writing should have been going much more smoothly. But it wasn't.

Oh, he managed to write, but it was like pulling teeth, rather than the effortless, almost stream-of-consciousness outpouring of words he was used to.

He sent Jared off to sea for close to two long, dangerous years. But as his hero was triumphantly returning to Boston a wealthy man, the *Graceful Lady Fair* was taken for a British ship and attacked by the Union fleet. Instead of reclaiming Carrie, Jared was wounded and mistakenly sent to a prison camp for Confederate soldiers. It took him another year and a half, and about

100 pages, to recover from his injuries and successfully escape the prison.

But then, finally, *finally* Jared was in Boston.

With a spring in his step, Jared walked down the street that led to the Sinclairs' town house. He hadn't felt this good, this *whole,* in years. It wouldn't be long now before he held Carrie in his arms....

Jax stopped typing, his fingers poised on the keyboard.

Jared tapped his foot impatiently. "What's the matter? What are you waiting for?"

"You're not going to like this," Jax muttered.

Jared froze. "Don't tell me she's not here."

"She's here, all right." Jax started to write again.

And then Jared saw her, her dark hair gleaming in the summer sunshine as she stepped out of the carriage. Her shoulders were back, her head held high—she was exactly as he remembered her.

He wasn't close enough to see the smile that he knew must be on her beautiful face, and he began to run, shouting her name as he dodged the heavy traffic that cluttered the street.

Carrie's head turned, and Jared knew the exact instant that she saw him. Her eyes opened wide, her face went pale and her delicate lips moved as she soundlessly spoke his name.

As he skidded to a stop in front of her, it was all he could do to keep from pulling her into his arms and covering her mouth with his own.

''Oh, come on,'' Jared fumed. ''After all this time, you're not going to let me kiss her?''

''Chill out,'' Jax muttered as he continued to write. ''You're not alone.''

But Jared was aware of the gentleman and two elderly ladies standing near her, so he reined in his desire and simply smiled at her.

She was more beautiful than ever. Dressed as she was, she looked every inch the proper lady, but Jared saw she still had a spark of fire in her deep blue eyes. It was that spark that had become a flame on the day they had met, the day he had found her riding her father's nearly uncontrollable stallion, dressed in her brother's clothes, in the field above the manor house. She had seemed as wild and untamable as the horse, and he had fallen in love with her instantly.

Jared could feel Carrie's eyes studying him, taking in the expensive cut of his clothes, the leanness of his body, the drawn, thin lines of his face.

''I thought you were dead,'' she whispered, her low voice husky with emotion.

''You know this man?'' the gentleman standing beside her asked. He was several years older than Jared, with a round face and a pair of spectacles that magnified his brown eyes.

Carrie turned to look at him, as if she was startled that he was there. For the briefest of instants, Jared saw what might have been fear in her eyes.

''Yes,'' she answered slowly, as if she was choosing her words carefully. ''Harlan, this is Jared Dexter, an old friend of my family's.'' She looked back at Jared, and he saw that her eyes were nearly brimming over with unshed tears. "Jared, I'd like you to meet Harlan Kent. My husband."

It was easy to write Jared's reaction to the news that Carrie had married another man. Jax knew firsthand about the waves of disbelief, anger and pure heart-breaking sorrow that swept over Jared. He knew about the misery and could describe the sensations in absolute vivid detail.

With a few quick sentences, he brought Jared back to the privacy of his fancy hotel room, where his hero put his head down and cried.

Just the way Jax had done when he realized that Kelly would not be his, that he had come home too late.

# *Chapter 5*

Dear Kelly,

August 24. Your eighteenth birthday.

I spend the day thinking about you. I remember how you invited me to spend your thirteenth birthday with you. We went downtown to the aquarium and looked in the top of the big fish tank. We stared at the skeletons of sharks hanging from the ceiling, sharks big enough to eat us both for breakfast and still go hungry.

For the first time in the three months I have been here, I cry.

Worse than the black eyes and the bruises and cuts and broken ribs, worse than the fear that today may be the day they drag me out of my cell and kill me, worse than the insults and the degradation, the filth and the stench, worse than all that, they have made me break my promise to you. That fills me with pain so great that I can't stop the tears.

I try to imagine your day, where you go, what you do.

Do you wonder where I am? Do you expect me at least to call?

Right now I'd sell my soul to the devil for a telephone.

I wonder if anyone even knows where I am.

The warden laughs and hits me when I ask, then tells me the government has told my London magazine that I died in a cholera epidemic.

But, Kelly, I am not dead.

You come to me tonight, eighteen years old and so lovely. Your eyes are so sad. We hold each other tightly, and I fall asleep with you in my arms.

But when I wake up, you are gone.

I love you.

Love, T.

Friday morning dawned gray and rainy. Kelly worked on her novel straight through until the early afternoon, grabbing a peanut butter and jelly sandwich on her way to get dressed to go to the university lecture series.

Normally the dismal weather would have kept her inside, but today's guest speaker was none other than Jayne Tyler, one of the hottest names in women's fiction. Tyler had rocketed onto the *New York Times* bestseller list with her first novel three years ago, and since then she had written five books, each one better than the last. She created hot, spicy characters that seemed to leap off the pages, and stories full of intrigue and passion. She could have her reader laughing on one page and reaching for a tissue to dry her tears on the next. And Tyler really knew what romance was. She knew exactly the right amount of gentle tenderness to throw in to cut straight through to the reader's heart.

Today she was going to speak in front of a roomful of hopeful authors and fans, spilling her secrets. And Kelly was going to be there, paying close attention.

She dressed carefully in her favorite dress, a beige-and-tan-checked shirtdress with a flared, nearly floor-length skirt, and long sleeves that she rolled up casually to her elbows.

The rawness of the rainy day penetrated her apartment, and there was a decided draft up the full skirt. So Kelly pulled a pair of slim black leggings on underneath the skirt. Still feeling cold, she unbuttoned the dress down to her waist and slipped a tank-style undershirt on, then put her arms back into the sleeves. She adjusted the small shoulder pads and rebuttoned the dress. With her black cowboy boots on her feet, a wide leather belt around her waist, her hair back in a casual ponytail, and silver earrings with shiny black stones dangling from her ears, she was ready to go.

Amazingly, the trolley was running ahead of schedule, and as she disembarked, she put up her umbrella against the drizzle and glanced at her watch. She was nearly two hours early. She rolled her eyes. Just a tad overeager. Still, if she had timed it perfectly, the trolley would have broken down and she would have ended up being two hours late.

She eyed the row of shops across from the campus lecture hall as she pulled her denim jacket more tightly around her. Somewhere over there was a shop called Quick Cuts, and Marcy had recommended it soundly the last time Kelly had made noise about getting her hair cut.

She hesitated only a few seconds, then made her way across the street, dodging the puddles as she went.

Jax glanced at the clock on the dashboard of his sports car. They were running late because of this damned rain. Bostonians were notorious for their wild driving skills, and add a little rain to the equation—the end result was sheer chaos.

His sister, Stefanie, was sitting next to him, calmly filing her fingernails.

"There's no way I'm going to find a parking spot," he told her. "I'm going to have to drop you."

"Oh, no, you're not." She put her emery board into her purse and looked up at him. "I'm *not* going in there alone, Jax. We'll both be late together."

"Stef—"

"Relax, darling, they can't start this party without us." Stefanie pulled down the mirror that was part of her sun visor and checked her perfectly styled blond curls. "I'm the guest of honor, remember?"

"I'm not worried about that. I just want to be able to leave on time."

Stefanie's gray eyes were filled with speculation as she looked up from putting on another coat of lipstick. "It's a woman, isn't it?"

Jax kept his face expressionless. He didn't even glance in her direction.

"I *knew* it," she said triumphantly, reattaching the top to the lipstick and tossing it into her purse. "It is, isn't it? You're finally over that girl—what was her name? Kevin's sister. Kelly. The one you wrote that collection of letters to. The one who was so young."

Again Jackson didn't say a word. He just drove the car. They were close enough now to start looking for a parking space.

"You know, your entire affair with her was too dreadfully romantic." Stefanie wouldn't let up. "She was just a teenager, a child really, while you were a grown man. I know forbidden fruit has a rep for being sweeter and all that, but carrying a torch for her all these years borders on the absurd. Not that I don't appreciate the absurd, of course. And it *is* rather disgustingly romantic of you." She watched him carefully. "I was thinking it might be a good story idea for the next contemporary novel—"

Jax turned and glared at her. "No."

"Made you look." She grinned toothily, then laughed at his exasperation. "You're *not* over her, are you? Well, maybe this new woman can sufficiently distract you for a while anyway. Tell me all about her, darling. What's her name? Where'd you meet her—Look, that car's leaving!"

And so it was. Jax braked to a stop behind a small blue Honda that was pulling out of a miniature parking spot. As he wrestled his car into the space that was barely twelve inches bigger than the length of his car, a young woman standing at the crosswalk waiting for the light to change caught his eye. Something about the way she was standing looked familiar. He caught a glimpse of short, sleek, dark hair underneath her umbrella as she turned away.

As he pulled up the parking brake and cut the engine, Jax watched a transit bus speed past. It sent a sheet of muddy water into the air. The young woman jumped back, but not quickly enough, and her skirt was drenched.

"Oh, yuck." Stefanie was watching, too. "The poor thing."

Jackson checked his watch. "Stef, we've got to hurry."

But his sister's eyes had widened as she watched the movements of the young woman on the sidewalk. The woman had stepped back, away from the street, and had set down her backpack and umbrella under the awning of an ice cream parlor.

Jax followed Stefanie's gaze, and watched, too, as the woman calmly took off her denim jacket and placed it on the top of her backpack. She took off a wide brown belt, set that on top of her jacket, then began to unbutton her dress.

She pushed off the top of the muddy dress, revealing a black sleeveless tank top and long, slender arms. Feeling rather like a voyeur, Jax made himself look away. But there was something so familiar about her. He looked back to see her pushing the dress down around her thighs. She wore a pair of skintight black leggings on her long legs. She had very, *very* long legs.

"Do try to keep your tongue inside your mouth, Jax darling," Stefanie said dryly.

As Jackson watched, the woman stepped out of her dress, shaking it slightly to get her cowboy boots free—

Cowboy boots!

"She got her hair cut," Jax breathed, and Stefanie looked at him in surprise.

"You know her?"

But Jax was already out of the car.

Kelly folded her muddy dress small enough to fit into her backpack. She wished she could rinse it out, but the lecture was going to start in just a few minutes. She hoped the mud wouldn't stain before she had a chance to go home and wash it clean.

"God," she heard a voice say. "It *is* you."

Startled, she looked up from where she was crouching to see T. Jackson towering above her.

"I love it," he said simply as she slowly stood and faced him. "Your hair—it's great."

She was gorgeous. Dressed all in black, her leggings and tank top hugging every inch of her lithe body, and with her dark hair cut very short—shorter even than his—she looked like a chic New York City model. Her hair capped her head, cut so short in the front that she could barely be described as having bangs. Pointed sideburns of hair hung down in front of each ear, curving in to accentuate the prettiness of her face, framing her big blue eyes. Her hair was buzzed short around her ears and in the back, but the effect was remarkably feminine. Her neck looked long and graceful and very, very vulnerable.

She looked as if she were twelve again. His gaze dropped down to her body. Well, maybe not exactly...

Kelly pulled her jacket on, more as protection from his eyes than from the cold. "You're following me again." It wasn't even a question. "Do us both a favor, Jackson. Give up."

"You know I'm not going to do that," he said softly. "And actually, this time I'm not following you." He looked at his watch again. "I've got to go—"

"Aren't you going to introduce me?"

Kelly turned to see a tall woman standing next to Jax, her hand possessively on his arm. She was strikingly beautiful, tall and slim, with hair like spun gold that shimmered and curled around her face. Her perfect mouth was curved upward in a friendly smile, but her cool gray eyes were inquisitive, curious.

Surprise rushed through her. This had to be Jackson's wife. Funny how he hadn't mentioned he was married…

"Kelly, this is Stefanie Winchester," Jax said. "Stef, meet Kelly O'Brien."

Stefanie *Winchester.* Oh, Lord, she *was* his wife. The wave of jealousy that shot through Kelly shocked her. No, it couldn't be jealousy she was feeling. Maybe it was indigestion—something she ate. As she shook the cool, slim hand that Stefanie extended, Kelly missed the pointed look of surprise and interest that the blond woman sent Jax.

"My brother's told me so much about you," Stefanie said, her voice cool and cultured.

Brother?

Stefanie was T. Jackson's *sister,* not his wife. Of course. Stefanie. *Stef.* Jax had told her about his older sister, Stef.

Kelly looked up to find Jax's eyes on her. He was watching her steadily, and he smiled very slightly, as if he knew what she was thinking. But he glanced at his watch again and turned to his sister.

"We're late." He looked back at Kelly. "I'll see you later."

She shook her head and opened her mouth to protest, but he stopped her by cupping her face with one hand and pressing his thumb lightly against her lips.

"I *will* see you later," he said, his voice soft and so dangerously positive. "You *are* going to have dinner with me and we *are* going to talk. Tonight."

Kelly couldn't move as she gazed into his eyes. He

was looking at her with an intensity that was hypnotizing. As she watched, his gaze dropped to her mouth, and she knew with a flash of heat that he was going to kiss her.

But he didn't.

Instead he brushed his thumb lightly against her lips, letting his fingers linger before he turned to leave. He walked backward all the way to the curb, a smile spreading across his handsome face.

"You *do* look..." He shook his head, as if unable to find the words. "Wonderfully," he finally said, "amazingly, fabulously, unbelievably, deliciously—"

"You could probably stand to insert an adjective right about now," Stefanie said dryly.

"Sexy," he whispered, but his voice carried quite clearly to Kelly.

"I'll be over about eight," he said.

"No." Kelly finally found her voice, but it was too late. He'd already turned and was halfway across the street.

With a sigh of frustration, she picked up her backpack and her umbrella and went back to the curb, where the Don't Walk sign was flashing. She waited far from the puddles for the light to change.

"Kelly, huh?" Stefanie said, giving Jax a sidelong glance as they went into the university building. "So it's still little Kelly O'Brien that you've got it bad for, even after all these years. Although she's not so little anymore, is she?"

"No, she's not," Jax agreed.

"I thought she got married."

"She did. It didn't work out."

"Lucky you," Stefanie said. "So naturally you've

got your catcher's mitt on, ready to grab her on the rebound.''

''You're mixing your sports metaphors,'' Jackson countered, not commenting on the truth of what she'd just said.

''And *you're* going for the big, happy Hollywood ending,'' Stefanie decided. ''You *are* a hopeless romantic, aren't you, darling?''

''Everything I've ever written has a happy ending,'' Jax told his sister. ''It shouldn't be *too* hard to orchestrate a real one for my life.''

''I hope so.'' In an unusual display of affection, Stefanie reached out and squeezed Jax's hand. ''But you know, real people aren't as easy to manipulate as fictional characters.''

Jackson's smile turned rueful. ''You're telling me. And lately my fictional characters haven't been easy to manipulate, either.''

Dear Kelly,

I have finished.

True, it's only a rough draft, but what more do you want for a first novel written in pencil between the printed lines of a paperback called *Passion's Destiny?*

It's a romance. Why? I needed to write a book with a happy ending, and since I've read nothing but these three romance novels in the past eleven months, I figured it was a good place to start.

And I promise in the next draft I'll change my heroine's first name from Kelly. She is you, though—beautiful and strong and proud.

I read my book over and over. Reading between the lines suddenly has a real meaning for me.

It has been nearly a year.

I pray that someday, somehow I will see you again. I live for that day.

I love you.

Love, T.

# *Chapter 6*

Kelly went into the crowded lecture hall, scanning the auditorium for an empty seat. As usual, there were chairs free in the front, so she went down the sloped aisle and sat down in the second row on the end.

It wasn't too long before the representative from the college lecture series came out onto the stage and, after testing the microphone, introduced bestselling author Jayne Tyler.

Kelly joined the enthusiastic applause, but then stopped suddenly, staring in disbelief at the woman who had walked out and now stood behind the podium.

It was Stefanie Winchester.

T. Jackson's sister was Jayne Tyler?

Why not? thought Kelly, laughing to herself at the irony. She knew Tyler was a pen name.

She spotted T. leaning lazily against the wall in the front of the lecture hall, his arms casually crossed. He was looking out over the audience, occasionally glancing up at the stage, at his sister.

But then his eyes met hers. He straightened up, staring at her, frowning slightly as if he couldn't figure out what Kelly was doing here.

She heard Stefanie introduce herself and her brother and agent, Jackson.

Brother and…

Agent?

Kelly looked back at T. Jackson. His gaze was fixed on her, and he smiled slightly.

Jackson wondered what Kelly was doing here, as she gave her full attention to his sister. He glanced at his watch. Stef's speech would take another forty minutes, then there'd be a question-and-answer period, during which he'd make an attempt to take control. Stef didn't like answering questions, and he couldn't blame her. People tended to ask the damnedest things.

He glanced up at his sister. She looked calm and collected, and her speech had been well rehearsed. She was doing fine. He stopped paying attention to Stef's words. He'd heard this speech too many times; hell, he'd written the damned thing.

He let his eyes drift back to Kelly. She hadn't put up a fight today when he'd told her he was taking her to dinner.

He wanted to hold her in his arms tonight. Quickly he ran down a mental list of posh Boston restaurants, trying to remember which places had a band and a dance floor. The last time he'd danced with Kelly, she had felt so good in his arms, and they'd both been so optimistic about the future….

The junior prom had been held in the high school

gym. The lights had been down low, and the room had been decorated with crepe streamers and helium balloons. It had looked about as romantic as a badly decorated gymnasium could be, but Jax hadn't cared. Just holding Kelly in his arms had been nearly an overload of romance.

From the number of curious stares he and Kelly were getting, Jackson knew he was the object of much discussion among both the other students and the teachers. It was obvious that he was much older than Kelly.

He wanted to pull her close, closer than he was holding her, but he was afraid to. He was afraid of attracting even more attention. But most of all, he was afraid of what people would think. Not about him—he didn't care about himself. But he *did* care about Kelly, and he was afraid people would assume that since he was dating her, she must be sleeping with him.

She still had another year to go in this school, with these kids. It wouldn't be easy for her if she were labeled, tagged with that kind of reputation.

Jax looked down to see her smiling up at him. He smiled back, but concern instantly darkened her eyes.

"What's wrong?" she asked.

He laughed, shaking his head. "I can't hide anything from you, can I?"

Her fingers were twisted in the hair that went down over the back of his collar. She shifted her weight so that her body brushed against his. He could feel her long, firm thighs against his, the softness of her breasts against his chest. It felt like heaven, but he had to make her stop.

"Kel," he said, unsure how to explain. "Have you noticed the amount of attention we're getting?"

She glanced around the room, then smiled back at Jax. "I think it's because you're the most handsome man here."

"The key word is *man.*" Jax took a deep breath. He had to just say it. "Kelly, I'm afraid if we dance too close, people are going to think we're…involved."

"We *are* involved." She watched him steadily. "Aren't we?"

He gazed into her lovely face for several long moments. She was so beautiful, so mature in so many ways, yet still such an innocent. "I meant… *intimately* involved."

A tinge of pink crept across her cheeks, but she didn't look away from him. "I don't care what other people think about me."

"But I do," he said softly. "I care very much. Once people give someone a label, it's almost impossible to change it. Trust me, I'm speaking from experience."

Kelly didn't say anything. She simply gazed up at him, waiting for him to go on.

"You know that I graduated from public high school out on Cape Cod," he told her. "Out in Dennis."

She nodded.

"I only went to that school for the end of my junior year and my senior year," he explained. "Before that, I went to prep school. Lots of different prep schools."

"I didn't know that."

Jax moved with her across the dance floor to the slow rock ballad. Every few minutes he had to remind himself to loosen his hold on her, because every few minutes he forgot his resolve and his arm tightened around her waist, drawing her closer to him. "Yeah." He had to clear his throat. "By the end of my junior year, I'd been kicked out of so many prep schools, there weren't any left that would accept me."

"Kicked out?" Kelly was surprised. "You?"

He released her to point to the tiny scar on his left cheekbone. "Remember that fight I was in?" He put his arm back around her. "Well, I won the fight, but I got booted out of school. And *that* didn't win me any points with the folks," he added with a grin.

"You never told me what you fought about."

"Freshman hazing. The seniors were merciless. I watched one kid after another get hurt by their supposedly harmless pranks, and when they went too far, I...um, went a little crazy."

"What did they do?"

Jackson grimaced. "They put something in the food and made the entire freshman class really sick. I was late to lunch that day, and when I walked into the mess hall and saw all the seniors standing around laughing at all the freshmen—and some of them were *violently* sick—I got upset. When I found out who had masterminded the scheme, I broke his nose." He shrugged. "Apparently making fifty kids blow groceries is good clean fun, whereas breaking a senior's nose is not."

The band segued directly into another slow, pulsating song. Jax could feel perspiration forming on his forehead as Kelly rested her head on his shoulder. He wanted to kiss her, he wanted to hold her tightly, feel the length of her slim, soft body against his. But she was only sixteen. It was good that they were here, with all these people watching. If there ever were a time he needed a chaperone, it was right now.

But even after tonight, he'd have to endure a year

and a half of wanting something he couldn't have. He looked down into Kelly's eyes and he was overcome by a rush of emotions. He loved her, and he wanted to be near her all the time. Sex only played a very small part in the way he felt about her—

Who was he kidding? He would come damn close to selling his soul for a chance to make love to her. It wouldn't be easy to live through the next few years. In fact, if Kelly managed to remain a virgin until she was eighteen, they would both deserve sainthood.

"That was the first prep school," Kelly said, breaking into his thoughts. "Why were you kicked out of the others?"

"I kept getting kicked out because I went in with a bad reputation," Jax told her. "At the second school, I was in the wrong place at the wrong time. Someone set fire to the athletic supply shed, and because I came in pegged as a troublemaker, I ended up taking the blame. By the time I was a junior, I was at my fifth boarding school. I went in on probation, and managed to get asked to leave simply because I dropped my tray in the dining hall one morning."

"That's awful."

"It happens. Once you're labeled, it's all over." He shook his head. "I don't want that to happen to you, Kel."

"T., somehow I don't think my connection to you is going to hurt my reputation." Kelly laughed. "It just might help it, if you want to know the truth."

Jax looked down into her sparkling eyes, feeling his heart expanding in his chest. He loved her. Good God, he'd loved her for years, but he'd refused to admit it, even to himself, because she had been only a child. All that time, he'd wondered what was wrong with him, why he never dated any of the women at school for more than a week or two. He'd led himself to believe that he was simply not cut out for long-term relationships, that one woman simply didn't have the ability to hold his attention for very long. He'd come to the conclusion that marriage and a family were simply not in his future.

But the real truth was, he was more monogamous than most men his age. Kelly owned his heart and soul, had owned it for years. Jax knew without a shadow of a doubt that he was going to love her until the day he died.

She reached up and touched the side of his face, catching a bead of perspiration that threatened to drip down past his ear. "It's warm in here," she said, her low voice husky.

"Yes," Jackson agreed, his eyes never leaving her face. "It is."

In silent agreement, he led Kelly off the dance floor and out of the gym. The air in the lobby was much cooler, and they moved toward the refreshment table.

"Want a soda?" Jax asked and Kelly nodded.

"Thanks. I've got to go, um… What's the correct euphemism?" She smiled. "Powder my nose? That's as obsolete as dialing a phone, isn't it? I'll meet you out here."

She pulled away from him, but Jax didn't let go of her fingers until the last possible moment. He watched her walk down the hallway. She was elegant and poised, full of the self-confidence that made her so unique among her peers. The heels she wore on her feet made her hips sway slightly as she went, and he didn't look away until the girls' room door closed behind her.

But then he turned and came face-to-face with an older man who had silently moved to stand at his side.

"Kelly looks lovely tonight," the man, obviously one of the teachers, said. He was smiling at Jax, but that smile didn't reach his eyes. "I didn't realize she was dating a college…boy."

It was obvious to Jax that this teacher didn't consider him a boy at all.

But he returned the smile, holding out his hand. "I'm Jackson Winchester," he said easily. "I've been a friend of Kelly's for some time now."

"Ted Henderson. What school are you going to?"

"I went to Boston College," Jax replied.

"Went?" Henderson's cold brown eyes probed for more information.

"I've graduated," Jax explained.

"You're *out* of college." Henderson made sure he got it straight. "Isn't Kelly a little bit young for you?"

"I don't see how that's any business of yours, Ted." Jax spoke pleasantly, but the older man's eyes darkened with disapproval anyway.

"I care about Kelly." Henderson crossed his arms in front of him, all pretense at pleasantness dropped. "I'm a friend of her father's—"

"Nolan approves of my relationship with his daughter." Jax didn't know if that was *exactly* the truth, but Nolan O'Brien wouldn't have let him take Kelly to the prom in the first place if he didn't want them to date, would he have?

"If that's the case," Henderson countered, "then I truly doubt that he's seen the way you look at that girl." He shook his head. "You're a grown man, Winchester. She's only a child. You have no right to take the rest of her childhood away from her."

Jax kept his face carefully neutral, taking out his wallet as he turned past the teacher and headed toward the refreshment table. But Henderson followed.

"Kelly should be involved with boys her own age," he persisted. "She should be having lighthearted romances, she should be having fun. I'm sure she's flattered by the attention you give her—what young girl wouldn't be? I'm sure you don't need to be reminded about your good looks."

Jackson paid for two cans of soda, then turned back to Henderson. "Have you finished?"

"Just about." Henderson blocked Jax's way with his bulk, pinning the younger man against the refreshment table. "I just want to make sure you're aware of the laws in Massachusetts regarding statutory rape—"

"I don't need any lectures, Ted." Jax forced himself to speak slowly, without any trace of his anger evident in his voice. "Like you said, I'm a grown man. I'm well aware of any consequences my actions might bring. But I love Kelly, and I believe that she loves me. Now, if you'll excuse me?"

"I don't doubt that you love her, son," Henderson said, his voice surprisingly gentle. "But she's only sixteen. You don't really expect whatever she feels for you will last, do you?"

Jax saw Kelly come out of the bathroom and start down the hall toward him. "Yes," he said shortly to Henderson, nearly pushing past him. "I do. Excuse me."

He walked toward Kelly, watching her face break into a beautiful smile as she saw him. He watched her eyes dance with pleasure, watched her dress cling to her body as she moved. But Ted Henderson's quiet voice trailed after him. "High school should be a carefree, happy time. Your relationship with Kelly can only be a burden, Winchester. If you really love the girl, you won't do that to her."

Jax opened one of the cans of soda and handed it to Kelly when they met farther down the hallway. "They didn't have any cups," he apologized. "I wiped off the top for you."

"Thanks," she murmured, taking a sip of the soda.

He led her back into the dimness of the gym, where they found an empty table off to the side of the dance floor and sat down. He could feel Kelly watching him as he opened his own can of soda and took a long drink.

"You're not having much fun, are you?" she asked softly.

"I'm having a great time—"

"Someone in the girls' room told me that Mr. Henderson was giving you the third degree, telling you how wrong it was for us to be here together." She leaned toward him. "That doesn't sound like a great time to me. We can leave, T. I won't mind if you want to go—"

"Are you kidding? I want to dance with you some more."

Kelly covered his hand with hers, gently lacing their fingers together. "We could go somewhere else and…dance."

Jax felt a hot flare of desire shoot through him as he met her steady gaze. She wasn't talking about dancing. She was talking about… He swallowed.

Sixteen, he reminded himself. She was only sixteen.

"I think we'd better stay here," he said quietly.

"Are you sure?"

Jax laughed desperately. "Kelly, come on. I need

you to help me out, not make things harder than they already are.'' As soon as the words were out of his mouth, he realized just how full of sexual innuendo they were. To his relief, Kelly didn't seem to notice.

''While I was in the girls' room, I heard a little of the gossip that's going around about you and me,'' Kelly said. ''And you were right. I *have* been relabeled.''

''Oh, no.'' Jax frowned with concern. ''Not already—''

But Kelly was smiling, her blue eyes shining with delight. ''They're calling me…a studcatcher.'' She laughed. ''You, of course, being the stud in question. It's a big step up for me from my last label.''

''Which was…?''

''Math nerd.'' Kelly made a face. ''Hardly flattering and particularly galling since I'm planning to major in language arts when I go to college. I like studcatcher much better.'' She grinned. ''Wanna dance with me, stud?''

Jax feigned indignation as he followed her onto the dance floor and took her into his arms. ''Is that all I am to you? Just a stud?''

Her smile softened and her eyes grew warm as she tipped her head back to look up at him. ''Tyrone, I fell in love with you before I knew what a stud was.''

*I fell in love with you….*

Her words echoed over and over in Jax's head. She loved him. She loved him!

''Oh, Kel,'' he breathed.

Both of her arms had been around his neck, and she'd pulled his head down to her waiting lips.

He'd kissed her. Right there in the middle of the dance floor. A slow, soft, lingering kiss…

The sound of three hundred pairs of hands clapping startled Jax out of his reverie. The crowd of people in the university auditorium was applauding. Stefanie's speech was over.

Momentarily off balance, he looked for Kelly. It had grown warm in the room, and she had taken off her denim jacket. God, in that outfit she looked good enough to eat.

As if she could feel his eyes on her, she glanced in his direction.

T. Jackson was staring at her with that same hungry look in his eyes. He *wasn't* going to give up, Kelly realized with a flare of despair. He wasn't going to quit until they gave in to the desire that still burned between them, until they finally made love.

But maybe that was the answer. Kelly watched as he climbed the stairs to the stage and crossed to stand next to his sister. His blond hair glistened in the stage lights, and his teeth flashed as he smiled. He took over the podium from Stefanie, introducing the question-and-answer portion of the program. He spoke easily, confidently, his wonderful charisma set to full power as he fielded questions from the floor.

Making love to T. would probably be pretty damn good.

Kelly gazed at the wide expanse of his shoulders. His muscular arms were covered by the sleeves of his well-tailored tweed jacket, arms that led down to a pair of strong, long-fingered hands that now gripped the sides of the podium. What would it feel like to have those hands touch her body?

It was a rhetorical question, but Kelly's imagination took over, producing a vivid picture of T., naked in her bed, with fire in his eyes as he touched her, kissed her, made love to her— She shook her head, forcing herself to pay attention to the questions that were being asked.

''What's your writing schedule like?'' a woman in the back of the lecture hall asked.

''Jayne usually gets up pretty early in the morning,'' T. answered, ''and crawls straight from her bed to her personal computer, stopping on the way for a cup of coffee. She starts the day by reviewing and revising her previous day's work, then writes until a little before noon. She eats lunch in front of the computer, then about an hour later, takes about a two-hour break—runs on the beach, goes for a swim. After that, she writes until dinner, and usually again after dinner.''

''It's pretty intense,'' Stefanie interjected. ''But this way a book can be completed quickly. After it's all over, I take some time off, head for Club Med.''

As people raised their hands, hoping to ask another question, Kelly lifted her own hand into the air.

Jax focused on her immediately. ''Yeah, Kelly.''

She cleared her throat, raising her voice so her question could be heard throughout the huge room. ''What do you do when you've got a manuscript that doesn't work, but you can't figure out how to make it better?''

He stared at her, a curious look on his face. ''Have you written a book?''

She nodded.

''You never told me that,'' he said, his voice sounding soft and intimate, even over the PA system.

''You never asked,'' she countered. She could feel the curious eyes of the audience studying her as she had what was essentially a private conversation in front of them all.

As if he realized this, Jax shifted his weight, looking out at the sea of faces. ''Well, there are a couple of solutions,'' he said. ''The first is to put that manuscript on a shelf and start something new. After you finish your next project, you can go back to the problem manuscript and look at it with a new perspective.'' His eyes found Kelly's face again. ''The other solution is to find a critique partner. Work with another person, get another opinion. What may seem an insurmountable problem to you might be a quick fix for someone else.'' His eyes seemed to sparkle as he shot her his infectious grin. ''Next question?''

Jax spent another twenty minutes answering questions, and then the program was over. He waited impatiently as the head of the lecture series shook his hand and long-windedly thanked him and Stefanie for being able to do the program for only a small honorarium.

He could see Kelly walking slowly toward the back doors of the lecture hall, talking to another young woman—Marcy something from the newspaper office. Marcy touched Kelly's hair and walked in a full circle around her. Kelly said something, and the two women broke up. Kelly's musical laugh cut through the ambient noise of the big room like a knife to his heart.

He turned to the lecture series head and skillfully interrupted her. ''I'm so sorry,'' he apologized, ''but we've really got to go. Jayne's got another appointment and—''

''Oh, yes, of course,'' the woman said. ''So nice to have met you, and thanks again.''

Grabbing Stefanie's arm with one hand and snatching up her coat and purse with his other, he dragged her down toward the main entrance of the hall.

Marcy was gone, but Kelly stood in the lobby, putting on her backpack. The light drizzle had turned into a heavy rain that fell like a sheet of water outside the open door. About to put her umbrella up, Kelly was ready to plunge into the downpour.

"Kel, wait!"

Kelly turned back to see T. striding toward her.

"Let me give you a ride home," he said. "You don't really want to stand in this, waiting for a trolley, do you?"

He wasn't really standing that close, but it seemed as if she could feel the heat from his body. Again, unbidden, the image of their naked bodies, intertwined as they made love, appeared in her head. Only, this time, the sound of rain on the roof and the duskiness of gray, late-afternoon light coming in through her bedroom windows completed the vision.

Oh, how she wanted him.

It was nothing but animal attraction. Lust. It was the remnants of years of fantasy. If only she could wipe those feelings from her memory, wash him out of her system.

Maybe she could....

Making love to T. Jackson couldn't possibly be as good as she imagined. But there was only one way to prove that, and that was to make love to him. By making love to him, she would satisfy both her curiosity and her desire, and prove that he was nothing special to her, not anymore.

He, too, would get what he wanted, and then maybe he would leave her alone.

"All right," she heard herself say, and saw the surprise in his eyes. He'd been expecting a fight.

"I'll pull the car around," he said, as if he were afraid that if he didn't act fast, she'd change her mind. "Wait here with Stef, okay?" With a quick smile, he was gone.

Kelly turned to find his sister watching her.

"I had no idea you were Jayne Tyler," Kelly said. "I've really enjoyed your books."

Stephanie shrugged almost nonchalantly. "Thanks."

"Is Jackson doing any writing these days?" Kelly asked. "That was always his dream."

"You *do* care about him." The older woman watched Kelly closely. "Don't you?"

It was Kelly's turn to shrug as she looked out the door at the street, watching for Jax's car. "Well, yeah. He was my best friend for years. I'll always care about him."

"Why did you marry that other man?"

Kelly looked up, surprised at the personal nature of the question, surprised that Stefanie even knew she'd been married.

Jax's car pulled up to the curb, saving Kelly from having to answer. "Come on, you can share my umbrella," she said instead, and the two women dashed out into the rain.

Stefanie got into the tiny back seat, so Kelly took the front, shaking her umbrella rather futilely as she closed it and pulled it into the car behind her.

The shoulders of T.'s jacket were soaked, and drops of water dripped from his wet hair onto his face. "I'm going to take Stefanie to the hotel," he said. "And if you don't mind, I'd like to change before we go out to dinner. We *are* going out to dinner, remember?"

"I'm not exactly dressed for anything fancy, T.," Kelly protested. "I don't want to—"

"I didn't mean fancy," he interrupted. "I meant *dry*. I stepped into a puddle, and my sock is wet." He grinned. "I *knew* there was a reason I don't wear socks."

Kelly had to smile. "And here, all this time, I thought you just didn't like to do the extra laundry."

He put the car into gear, signaling to move out into the steady stream of traffic. "If you want, we can get something to eat right at the hotel."

As T. Jackson headed toward downtown Boston on Commonwealth Avenue, Kelly settled back into the comfortable leather seat of his car. She looked out the window, through the drops of rain, and let her mind wander to the last time she'd been in a car with this man….

# *Chapter 7*

It was nearly 5:00 a.m., and T. Jackson and Kelly were parked at the beach. After the lights and glare of three different after-prom parties, the intimate quiet of the predawn was wonderful.

They'd left the last party several hours early, and now they sat quietly talking and holding hands.

T. told her about his dream of becoming a writer. He wanted to write everything—novels, short stories, screenplays. He wanted to write comedies most of all, stories with happy endings.

He talked about growing up, about his family, his parents. They loved him, he'd told her, but they just didn't know how to show it. When T. had been kicked out of the last prep school that would accept him, his mother had been in Milan, and his father had been on a three-month cruise in the South Pacific. He'd talked to each of them on the telephone, and they both said the same thing—military school.

"So I told my mother that Dad was going to take care of everything, and I told my dad that my mother was making all of the arrangements, and I packed up my things and drove out to the summer house we had on the Cape." His voice was smooth and soft in the darkness. "I took a couple days off, did errands, re-stocked the house with food." He laughed softly. "Thank God for credit cards. Then I forged a letter from my parents and went over to the high school and registered. I had a copy of my school records, and I weeded out all the mention of disciplinary action. I left out anything that said I'd been expelled. I entered the school almost anonymously, and I kept a low profile and did okay."

"You lived by yourself?" She couldn't see his expression in the darkness, not until he smiled.

"Yeah. It was tough getting around those parent-teacher conferences, though."

"But your parents must've known—"

"Not until Christmas break during my senior year," he said. "By that time, I was almost eighteen, and they figured I had things under control."

"Weren't you lonely?" she asked softly.

T. was very quiet. "I didn't know what I was missing," he admitted. "Not until I met your family. Not until I met you."

Kelly could see that he was watching her, and she felt his hand touch the side of her face, felt his lips brush hers. She heard him make a low sound, a groan, as he pulled away.

"Kel, we should go home." His voice was raspy.

Her heart was pounding in her chest, making her feel as if she were about to explode. "Please, T., let's not go yet. Let's take a walk on the beach."

Even as she spoke, she slipped off her shoes and rolled down her stockings.

Outside the car, the night air was cold. In the east, the sky was starting to lighten. It wouldn't be long before the sun came up. Kelly turned to see T. standing almost uncertainly by the car. She took his hand and pulled, leading him out onto the soft sand.

"Wait a sec," he said, reaching down to pull off his own shoes and socks. He left them in a pile next to his car.

As they walked along the edge of the water, T. Jackson draped his jacket around her shoulders and held her close to him for added warmth. The water was icy as it occasionally splashed up onto their bare feet, but Kelly didn't care.

She was in heaven.

"I don't want tonight to end," she whispered.

T. stopped walking, turning her to face him, pulling her in even closer to him. "I don't want it to, either."

He kissed her then, and she could feel his restraint. He was holding so much back. She pressed herself against the hard muscles of his chest and, feeling shockingly bold, she opened her mouth underneath his and touched his lips with her tongue.

She heard him groan and felt his arms tighten around her as he parted his lips under her gentle pressure. His mouth tasted wonderful, so moist and warm and soft.

She could feel his control slipping as he returned her kisses. Each kiss was longer, deeper, more passionate than the last. His hands moved across her body, and his jacket fell off her shoulders onto the sand.

One of his legs pressed between hers as they both

tried to get closer, even closer, to each other. She could feel his hands in her hair, pulling out the pins, letting it hang down around her shoulders.

He found the slit in the back of her dress, and the sensation of his fingers on her bare skin made Kelly cry out.

He pulled back then, breathing hard. She could feel his heart pumping in his chest, echoing the crazy beat of her own heart.

"God, Kelly—"

She pulled his head down, pulled his lips to her and kissed him again. He resisted for all of half a second, then nearly crushed her mouth with his as his careful control slipped even further. Kelly felt an additional flash of pleasure, an even stronger flash of heat that seemed to spread throughout her entire body as she realized the power she had over him.

"Jackson, make love to me."

Her words made him freeze, until she began kissing his chin, his neck, instinctively pressing the soft place between her legs against the solid muscles of his thigh. That seemed to drive him crazy, and he kissed her, a savage kiss that made all of his other kisses seem tame in comparison. Together they lost their balance, falling backward onto the soft sand.

And still he kissed her.

She wrapped her arms around T.'s neck, feeling his weight on top of her. His hands swept her body, touching her in ways that left her breathless and wanting more. She felt his hand move up the long, smooth length of her thigh, pushing her skirt up, freeing her legs so that he could lie between them—

That was when Kevin showed up at the beach, looking for them.

That was when her wonderful night with Jackson turned into a nightmare.

Kevin was incensed, pulling Jax off of her. "You promised me!" he shouted. "You gave me your word, you son of a bitch—"

The sky was light in the east, and the first rays of the sun shot up, over the edge of the horizon.

Kelly could see T.'s face in the pale light, and his eyes looked frantic, shocked, as he scrambled to his feet.

"Oh, God, what was I doing?" he gasped. "Kevin, man, I didn't mean to—"

Kevin charged him, but T. didn't make a move to defend himself. "No!" Kelly cried out as her brother's big fist slammed into T. Jackson's face.

T. reeled backward as Kevin hit him again and again.

"You bastard," Kevin kept saying. "You *bastard*—"

"Stop it!" Kelly sobbed, throwing herself onto Kevin's back, trying to hold his arms, trying to keep him from hitting T. again.

Jackson hit the ground, blood dripping from his nose and split lip. He pushed himself up onto his hands and knees until a well-aimed kick from Kevin sent him back down onto the sand.

Kelly threw herself down next to Jax. His face was bleeding, and he held his side as if one of his ribs had been cracked. "Oh, T., I'm sorry," she cried.

"Kelly, are you all right?" he asked, his green eyes trying to focus on her face. "I didn't hurt you, did I? I'm so sorry, what was I *do*ing?"

She shrieked, startled, as her brother roughly hauled

her to her feet. "You stay away from him," he ordered her. "I oughta knock some sense into *you,* too."

He pulled his arm back, as if he was going to slap her the way he had so many times when they were both children. Instinctively Kelly flinched, but then was nearly knocked over as T. suddenly lunged at Kevin.

Almost effortlessly, he took Kevin down. Before she could blink, her brother lay with his face in the sand, Jackson straddling him. T. had Kevin's arm tightly, savagely twisted behind his back, and he pushed it up until her brother cried out with pain.

"You *ever* hit her, it'll be the last thing you do," T. hissed. "Do you understand?"

"Yes," Kevin yelped. "Yes!"

Abruptly T. released Kevin, and they both sat in the sand, catching their breath.

Kevin looked up at Kelly. "Go wait in my car."

"No," she said, wiping the tears from her face. "No, Kevin, I'm going home with Jackson."

There was still a flash of anger in her brother's eyes as he looked up at her. "Jax isn't welcome in our house anymore." He turned to T. "I'll ship your things out to the Cape."

Slowly T. nodded.

Kelly couldn't believe it. He was going to give up, just like that?

"You were supposed to be doing me a favor," Kevin continued, accusingly.

Kelly froze.

"You were helping me out, taking Kelly to the prom, so I could go out with Beth," Kevin said, anger still tingeing his voice. "You *promised* me you wouldn't touch her, you dirtwad."

Jackson had only taken her out as a favor to her brother? Kelly felt sick. He had implied that he loved her, practically proposed marriage to her. But he'd never said the words. He never actually told her that he loved her. But she knew that he did. She *knew* it.

"T.," she started.

"Kelly, go get in my car," Kevin said again.

"Go on, Kel," T. said softly. "I'll call you later."

Numbly she'd walked back to the beach parking lot. Numbly she'd waited for ten, fifteen, twenty minutes until Kevin got into his car beside her and silently drove her home. Numbly she'd climbed the stairs up to her bedroom, peeled off her dress and fallen into bed. But she hadn't slept. She'd waited hours and hours for T. Jackson to call her.

But he never had.

He'd never called, he'd never shown up for their movie date or any of the other many dates they'd planned....

As Jackson pulled his sports car up to the valet at the hotel, Kelly still stared out the window. She'd only seen T. once between prom night and the afternoon last week when he'd shown up at the newspaper office—at Kevin's wedding, when she was nineteen.

Kelly looked up in surprise as T. opened the passenger side door, offering her his hand to help her out. She took his warm fingers lightly, afraid to touch him, but more afraid that if she didn't touch him, he'd realize why.

All his promises had been empty. He had done nothing but let her down ever since prom night. So why in God's name was she still so damned attracted to him?

Because attraction had nothing to do with love.

Love hinged on trust, not on broken promises. But hormones—now, that was an entirely different matter. Kelly's hormones didn't care that T. Jackson hadn't proved to be especially honor-bound. Her hormones only saw a tall, blond, handsome man with a killer smile and a body to die for.

"It was nice meeting you, Kelly." Stefanie interrupted her thoughts. "You should come out to the Cape and visit us sometime this summer."

"Gee, what a swell idea." Jax grinned as he helped Kelly into the hotel. "Why didn't *I* think of that?"

"Thanks, Stefanie." Kelly ignored Jackson. "It was nice meeting you, too. And I really *do* enjoy your books."

"Gotta fly," Stef said. "Emilio's waiting for me." She smiled at Jax. "See you when I see you, darling."

With a flash of blond hair and long legs, she disappeared, leaving Jax and Kelly standing in the posh hotel lobby.

"If you don't mind, I *would* like to change," Jax said.

He began walking toward the elevators, past the entrance to a lounge. To his surprise, Kelly went with him, rather than offering to wait for him in the bar.

"This is a nice place," she said, looking around at the elegantly decorated, airy lobby. The colors were muted shades of pink and rose, with a green-leaf print thrown in for good measure. It was all very soothing and quiet, with thick carpeting and overstuffed furniture to help absorb any excess noise. "I've never been in here."

Jax pushed the up button, and as they stood waiting for the elevator, he watched Kelly. Had she really relaxed enough around him to be comfortable waiting in his suite while he changed his clothes? But she didn't seem relaxed. She seemed quiet, thoughtful almost to the point of distraction.

"What are you thinking about?" he asked.

Her eyes focused on his face. "I was thinking that it's a shame you don't write anymore."

Jax smiled. "Well, I do a little bit here and there."

"But it's not what you do for a living," she said.

The bell rang for the elevator, and Jax held the door open so that she could step inside. As the door slid shut behind him, he pushed the button that said Penthouse. "I'm a Winchester," he said easily. "I open dividend checks for a living, remember?"

"I thought you wanted to write screenplays." Her tone was faintly accusing. "Or novels. Whatever happened to that?"

"Actually, I started a screenplay," he said.

"But you didn't finish it?"

"Other obligations got in the way. I haven't stopped thinking about it, though. The same way I never stopped thinking about you."

"Smooth line, T." Kelly glanced over at him. "But somehow, I have trouble believing it."

"I guess you don't have to believe it," Jax said. "But it *is* true."

He was leaning casually, nonchalantly against the wall of the elevator, feet crossed in front of him, hands in his pants pockets. His hair was mussed and still wet from the rain. He smiled at her perusal, his eyes warm and very green.

Was this elevator shrinking? Kelly looked up at the numbers that were changing above the door. Eight more floors 'til they reached the penthouse level. What was that old saying, out of the elevator and into the penthouse? *Why* did she ever come up here with him?

"What do you want from me?" she asked, point-blank.

He answered with the same laid-bare honesty. "I want to marry you."

Stunned, Kelly heard a ding as the elevator reached the penthouse floor, and the doors glided open. She stared at T. in shock. He held the doors back with one hand and gestured with the other. "After you," he said calmly, as if he hadn't just told her that he wanted to...marry her.

He wanted to marry her.

The initial shock was starting to wear off, and as Kelly walked down the long hotel corridor, she began to laugh. He said he wanted to marry her. What a hoot.

Unperturbed, Jax used a plastic key card to unlock the door and opened it wide, stepping back to let her go in first.

His hotel suite was enormous. It had a spacious living room tastefully done in the same subdued colors that had decorated the lobby. But the best part of the room was the wall of glass that overlooked downtown Boston. The view was breathtaking.

As Kelly walked toward the windows, she saw a set of French doors that led into a huge bedroom. The bed itself was almost the size of her entire apartment. She pulled her eyes away, not wanting to be caught staring.

T. Jackson hung his wet sport jacket on the back of a chair, and as Kelly turned to look at him, she saw that his shirt was wet. He had been soaked by the rain clear through his jacket.

Slowly, she put her backpack down on the floor.

He smiled at her as he pulled off his tie and kicked

off his shoes. ''I'll be right back,'' he said, unbuttoning his shirt. ''Help yourself to the bar.''

There was a wet bar on the wall next to the TV, and Kelly tried to focus her attention on the various bottles of alcohol and soda, rather than the glimpse of hard, tan muscles she'd seen before T. had left the room.

She poured herself a tall glass of seltzer, added a few ice cubes and turned to look around.

There were a number of books scattered about the room. Two of them were Jayne Tyler's most recent releases. A third was a galley copy of what Kelly assumed was to be Jayne's next book, entitled *Love's Sweet Captive.* Seven titles that she recognized from the *New York Times* bestseller list, both fiction and nonfiction, sat on an end table. A week's worth of the *Boston Globe* lay in a pile on the floor. *Premiere* magazine and *Writer's Digest* were open and out on the coffee table, along with several news magazines.

''Grab me a cola from the fridge, will ya, Kel?'' Jax called out from the bedroom.

She pulled a can of soda free from a six-pack that was in the refrigerator as Jackson appeared in the bedroom door. He was wearing a pair of faded jeans and a smile, turning a T-shirt rightside out.

Kelly tried not to stare. It wasn't as if she hadn't ever seen him without a shirt on before. But, Lord, he looked good. His body was well-toned and his skin was smooth and lightly tanned.

His muscles rippled as he pulled his shirt over his head and down across his broad chest.

''What do you really want from me?'' Kelly heard herself ask. Her voice sounded faint and breathless.

His fingers brushed hers as he took the can of soda

from her hand. "I told you," he said easily, his teeth flashing as he shot her a brief smile. "I want to marry you. I wanted to marry you seven years ago, Kelly, and I *still* want to marry you."

Kelly felt a prick of anger and she clung to it, unable to deal with the other emotions that were assailing her. "After all this time, *you're* finally ready—"

"No." He shook his head, his green eyes unyielding, pinning her in place. "*You're* finally ready."

"The hell I am," she said with an exasperated laugh. "I've just gotten out of one foolish marriage. Do you really think I'd be so eager to get into another right now?"

"Do you really think marriage to me would be foolish?" he countered.

"Absolutely."

T. took a step toward her, setting his can of soda on the coffee table. "Why?"

He moved another step forward. His eyes were green crystal, his face unsmiling and serious.

Kelly crossed her arms defensively, determined to stand her ground. "Oh, come on, T.," she said. "Why do you think?"

"I don't know," he said softly, shaking his head. "Seven years ago, you seemed to think marrying me was a good idea."

T. Jackson had that burning light in his eyes as he took yet another step toward her. He was getting too close, close enough to be able to reach out and touch her.

Kelly stepped around him, bending down to pick up her backpack and jacket. "I took you seriously then because I was too young to know better." She put more space between them. "But I know better now."

She had to leave before the horrible memories of the hurt she had felt when he left brought the pain back. But he was standing between her and the door, blocking her way out of the suite.

"I know I disappointed you," Jackson said softly.

Kelly laughed. "Yeah, I'd say I was disappointed," she agreed. "For God's sake, T., you left the country without even saying goodbye to me!" She pushed past him toward the door. "I've got to go—"

Jax caught her arm. "Please, Kel..." He suddenly wished desperately that real life could be as simple as fiction. He wished he could go back and rewrite some of the scenes in his life. But he'd made so many mistakes with Kelly, it was hard to know where to start. He wished at least he'd had a chance to make love to her, to show her how much he loved her. Suddenly he was glad that he had added that love scene between Jared and Carrie to his book. Their one night of love was what bound them together, and it would keep them bound together even as they faced the trials and tribulations he was going to send their way.

But he and Kelly had had no such night. He had never even said the words *I love you* to her.

She pulled her arm away and stared at him, anger and hurt in her eyes. "I loved you so much, T. But it was just a game to you—"

"No!" He raked his hair back out of his face with his fingers. "That's not true—"

"The truth is, you were doing Kevin a favor by taking me to the prom," she said hotly. "But you went kind of overboard, took it a step too far." She reached for the doorknob, pulling the door open. "Well, not this time, Jackson."

But he pushed the door closed with the palm of one

hand, and brought his other hand up against the door on the other side of her, effectively pinning her between his arms. ''No,'' he said very definitely. ''I won't let you run away. You've got to give me a chance to explain.''

T. was standing so close, Kelly could feel heat radiating from his body. She could smell his sweet scent, a mixture of after-shave, shampoo and his own, individual familiar aroma.

''God, you even smell the same,'' she said, looking up into the swirling colors of his eyes. *I give up,* she suddenly wanted to say. *Take me to dinner. Take me anywhere. Take me.*

She knew all she had to do was ask. There was no mistaking the desire she could see in his eyes.

He leaned toward her, as somehow she knew he would, and he kissed her, also as she knew he would. What she didn't expect was the total meltdown she experienced as his lips touched hers.

Her bones became liquid, her muscles useless and her arms, the evil betrayers, wrapped themselves around T. Jackson's neck, pulling him even closer to her. She heard him groan as his tongue pushed past her lips, tasting her, possessing her.

Nothing had changed. Seven years had passed, during which time Kelly had been married and divorced, yet all it took was one kiss from this man and all the old feelings came flooding back. As her fingers became tangled in his soft, blond hair, she tried to stop herself, but she couldn't.

He kissed her, harder, pulling her body in more tightly to him, his hands cupping the softness of her derriere, pressing her hips against him.

He lifted his head then, and Kelly stared into the

turbulence of his eyes. "You know what I want," he said, his voice thick, raspy.

There was no mistaking the hardness of his arousal as it pressed against her stomach. Even though he hadn't asked a question, Kelly nodded, unable to speak.

"I wanted to make love to you the morning after the prom, too." He kissed her neck, her throat, running his hands lightly up her body, touching the sides of her breasts.

She closed her eyes, wanting him to touch her, wanting…

"I wanted you so badly," he whispered. "But you were only sixteen. And I—I didn't even care. I was so crazy in love with you, I couldn't see straight. If Kevin hadn't found us, if he hadn't stopped me, I would've done it. I would have made love to you right there on that beach. You were just a kid, and I didn't even have any protection, and I *still* would have done it, and, Kel, that scared the hell out of me." He shook his head, still amazed that he could have felt so out of control. "So I lost it, I totally lost it. Kevin was beating the crap out of me, and I didn't fight back because I knew I deserved it. And those things he said… I didn't deny it because I couldn't speak, I couldn't even *think.* But I didn't take you to that prom as a favor to your brother. After I saw you in that dress, I begged him to let me take you. I promised him I'd take care of you, and instead I nearly took your virginity—"

Kelly pressed her fingers to his lips. "You weren't the only one there that morning," she said steadily. "I was there, too. And I wanted you as much as you wanted me."

"Kel, you were a kid—"

"So what, T.? I knew what I wanted."

"How could you have known?" he asked. "You were only *sixteen*—"

"I'm not sixteen anymore," she said.

And then she kissed him.

It was a kiss of passion and need, filled with fire and heat and the promise that all they'd started seven years ago would not remain unfinished business. Not for long.

Kelly's backpack dropped to the floor as Jackson pushed her jacket off her shoulders. He heard her inhale sharply as his hands caressed her arms, and he was overcome by the need to touch more of her, all of her. He tugged at her shirt, yanking it free from the waistband of her pants, and groaned as his fingers found the soft, warm skin of her back and her belly. He was lost, lost in the depth of her kisses, consumed by wanting her. Even after all those years, his control was still shot to hell when he held her in his arms. He was possessed, utterly, totally possessed by his burning need.

She moved away from him slightly to pull her shirt over her head. As if in a dream, Jax watched his hands unfasten the front clasp of her bra, releasing the soft fullness of her breasts. He wanted to take his time, to look at her, to touch her slowly, but he was on fire, and he couldn't hold back. He touched her almost roughly, driven nearly mad by the heavy weight of her breasts in his palms. Greedily he lowered his head and drew one taut nipple into his mouth, hungrily tugging, sucking until she cried out with pleasure.

Kelly pulled at his shirt then, and he quickly yanked it off. She reached out to touch him lightly, and the sensation was too exquisite, too intense. He crushed her to him, exalting in the feeling of her skin against his as he kissed her frantically. He was unable to think coherently, unable to think at all.

Jax felt her fingers at the waistband of his jeans, unfastening the button, tugging at the zipper.

"Kel," he groaned, knowing that if she touched him there, he'd never be able to turn back. "Kel, what are we doing?"

Her laughter was low and sexy. "Don't you know?"

He kissed her neck, her throat, letting his hands explore her body. Her hair felt like silk, her skin like satin. His fingers swept lower, and he realized with an electric jolt of pleasure that her leggings were gone. She'd somehow kicked off her cowboy boots and her pants, and now stood before him, naked.

She was beautiful—incredibly, perfectly beautiful.

He felt her tugging at his jeans, pushing them down.

"Oh, Jackson," he heard her whisper as she freed him from the confines of his shorts. And then she touched him. He nearly lost it right then and there, simply from the touch of her hand.

Seven years. For seven years he'd been waiting for this moment.

He touched the softness between her legs, feeling the heat and wetness that proclaimed her desire. Kelly opened herself to him, pressing against his exploring fingers. "Please, T.," she breathed, "I need you *now*..."

She had a condom. She must've had it in her backpack. She handed it to him and, as quickly as he could with shaking hands, he covered himself.

And then the waiting was over.

He lifted her up, and with one fierce thrust, he was inside of her. She cried out with pleasure as he plunged into her again and again.

Kelly's back was still to the door, her arms and legs wrapped tightly around T. as she moved with him. She'd never made love like this before. She'd never felt so desperately wanted, so fiercely desired. T.'s eyes were lit with a wild passion that both excited her and frightened her—frightened her because she suddenly doubted that making love to him once would be enough.

He pulled her down with him then, down onto the floor. He covered her body with his own, increasing the tempo of his movements. She met each thrust by lifting her hips, pushing him even more deeply into her. His hands and mouth were everywhere, adding to the sensations, driving her closer and closer to release.

And suddenly she was flying, hurtling through space as waves and waves of pleasure rocketed through her.

"Yes," she heard T. say through the storm that possessed her. "Come on, Kelly." And somehow, some way, she went even higher.

Jax had only imagined how good this would be, but his imagination hadn't even come close to the reality. As the last tremors passed through her, she gazed up at him. "Oh, T., we should have done this seven years ago," she breathed, still moving with him.

She smiled up at him then, and it was the love he was so sure he saw in her eyes that pushed him over the edge.

He exploded. It was amazing, incredible, impossibly wonderful. He wanted to laugh and cry and...

And she held him tightly, her arms around him, until his breathing slowed. He rolled off of her then, pulling her into his arms. He could feel Kelly watching him staring at the ceiling for several long moments before he glanced at her out of the corners of his eyes. He laughed, not without a certain amount of embarrassment.

"I have such amazing finesse," he said, more to himself than her. "I had seven years to plan the perfect way to make love to you for the first time, and what do I do? I don't even take you into the bedroom. I end up nailing you to the wall."

She laughed. "Is that what that's called? I liked it a lot."

Jackson moved his left arm out from underneath her so he could use it to support his head as he looked down into her eyes. "I'm glad," he murmured.

She reached up to push his hair back from his face.

Jax's smile was sheepish and utterly charming. "I really wasn't planning for this to happen, you know, for us to make love. I was totally unprepared. I'm glad you had a condom." He leaned down and kissed her, a long, lazy, unhurried kiss.

Kelly closed her eyes, feeling her heart begin to beat faster. Could she really want him again? Already?

When Jackson swung her up into his arms and carried her through the bedroom into the huge bathroom, she didn't protest. He set her down in the big shower stall and gently washed them both clean, and still she didn't protest. By the time he had wrapped her in the thick, white hotel towel, she was on fire again. And from the looks of things, he was, too.

He pulled her to his bed and sat down, holding her on his lap. He kissed her, another slow, leisurely kiss that made her tremble. As he held her close, she could feel his heart pounding and knew that he hadn't gotten her out of his system any more than she had removed him from hers.

Once had definitely not been enough.

"Kelly, why did you give in?" Jax murmured into her neck as his hands caressed the smooth, clean length of her body. "Don't get me wrong—I love it that you're here, but I'm just...kind of surprised."

She pulled back slightly to look at him. "I guess I figured that it's time to move on with my life," she said. "We've both had this attraction for each other for such a long time, and..." *Neither one of us would ever really have been free until we proved that sex between us wasn't the magnificent event we'd imagined,* she wanted to say, but couldn't. Because in reality, making love to T. Jackson had been far, far more magnificent than any fantasy she'd dreamed. Instead of being freed by finally making love to this man, she had simply made the chains that bound her to him that much tighter.

But Jax couldn't read her mind, and the words he heard filled him with happiness. She was ready to move on with her life, and it sure seemed as if she'd chosen to move in his direction. "Kelly, I want to make love to you again," he whispered. "If that's okay with you."

She told him just how okay it was with a kiss, and he pulled her back with him onto the bed.

Maybe this time, thought Kelly. Maybe making love to him this time would chase his memory back to where it belonged—securely in the past.

# *Chapter 8*

Kelly awoke as dawn was beginning to edge its way past the hotel room curtains. T. lay in the big bed beside her, his arm possessively draped across her, holding her close, her back against his chest.

She felt the familiar jolt of sexual excitement that always shot through her when she was near this man. It flared into full-blown desire as she felt his most masculine part pressing into her leg.

T. Jackson even wanted her in his sleep.

Being desired so intensely gave her a powerfully strong feeling. It was similar to the way she'd felt as a kid when she'd climbed out onto the roof of the house. She felt daring, bold and adventurous. She felt an adrenaline high, a rush.

But that wasn't the kind of feeling she wanted from a relationship.

She wanted to feel safe and warm. She wanted to

feel secure. She wanted to be cherished, not hungered for.

T. looked so peaceful, so serene, so content as he slept. With his hair disheveled, an unruly jumble of waves falling down across his forehead, with his long, dark lashes lying against his smooth, tanned cheeks, he was, truly, the most beautiful man she'd ever seen. He was funny, smart, bright and fun to be around. But he'd broken her heart once, and there was no reason to believe that he wouldn't do it again. No, she could not let herself love him again.

How could you love T. *again,* when you never stopped loving him? a little voice in her head asked.

But she *had* stopped loving him. She could remember the exact time, the exact hour it had happened.

That was when you *wanted* to stop loving him, the voice said. It doesn't mean you really stopped. People can't just turn their feelings off like a light switch. You still love him.

No, Kelly thought almost desperately. She *didn't* love T., and she could prove it.

Quietly she slipped out of bed and went into the living room. She dressed quickly and grabbed her backpack and jacket, and crept out of the room and out of the hotel.

Standing at the underground trolley stop, she waited for the train that would take her home.

See, she told herself, she didn't love him. If she loved him, she wouldn't have been able to walk away.

Okay, the little voice in her head said. So how come you're crying?

Dear Kelly,

Toilet paper.

They found my book and took it away and now they use the pages for toilet paper.

The warden laughs at the look on my face, at the tears I can't keep from my eyes, knowing he has at last found a way to hurt me.

You come to me then, for the first time appearing when others are around. They can't see you. They don't know it is your strength that keeps me from crumbling.

''Don't cry,'' you order me, your eyes fiery with determination. ''Keep your head up. You've got that book practically memorized anyway. So what if they take the paper that it's written on? They can't take your memory. It's in your head, T., you can write it again.''

You look so beautiful, trembling with your conviction. I smile at you, and I am rewarded by your bright grin.

The warden frowns and sends me back to my cell.

I love you.

Love, T.

Jax woke up with a smile on his face that faded as soon as he rolled over and saw that he was alone in his bed.

''Kel?'' he called out, going first into the bathroom and then out in the living room.

He saw right away that her things were gone. He looked around for a note, thinking maybe she had an appointment and she didn't want to wake him.

But there was no note.

Why would she leave like that, without saying goodbye? Why would she slip out of his room as if last night had been nothing more than a casual one-night stand?

Fear hit him, squeezing all of the air out of his lungs.

No.

No, he wouldn't believe that. Things had gotten pretty intense last night. She must've gotten scared and felt the need for some time alone, to think about what was going on, about what was happening between them.

He crossed the room and picked up the telephone, quickly punching in her number.

She answered on the second ring. "Hello?"

Jackson took a deep breath, determined not to let his paranoia show. "Hey," he said, his voice light. "Good morning."

"Jackson," she said.

Not a very enthusiastic greeting. And was that trepidation he heard in her voice? Or were his insecurities making him imagine things?

"I missed you this morning." He still kept his voice easygoing. "I'm dying to see you again. What do you say I pick you up in about an hour and we have lunch?"

There was a brief moment of silence, during which time Jackson died over and over and over again. *Say yes,* he prayed. *Please say yes.*

"I'd planned to write all day," Kelly finally answered. "I'm not as far along as I'd hoped to be with this story and..."

It sounded like a lame excuse. But Jax understood what it meant to need time to write, so maybe it really wasn't. "How about I pick you up at six? You should be ready for a break by then. We can have dinner."

"I don't think so."

Her words echoed in the great, big, heavy silence that followed. Jax slowly sat down. His heart was in his throat as he finally said, "Kelly, what's going on? I don't—I don't understand."

"T., I already told you that I don't want to become involved with you," she said softly. "I'm not ready to be in a relationship right now."

All that was left of last night's happiness crashed and burned. Jax's knuckles were white as he clutched the telephone. But still he managed to keep his voice calm. "I think you're too late, Kel. I don't know what you'd call last night, but I'd say at this point we've started something that's pretty involved."

"Last night we were finishing something, Jackson," Kelly said quietly. "Not starting it."

"Kelly, please don't say that." Desperation was starting to creep into his voice.

"I'm sorry. I've got to go—"

"Wait, please! Talk to me—"

But she'd already hung up.

Kelly sat in front of her computer, trying to find the right words to finish her latest manuscript's final love scene. This was the hardest part of writing romances. At least it was for her. She kept her thesaurus handy, and had even made a list of words such as *tempestuous* and *untamed* but when she reread the scenes, there always seemed to be something missing.

The telephone rang again and she closed her eyes, trying not to listen as her answering machine intercepted yet another of T. Jackson's telephone calls.

"Kelly, I know you're home." His normally easygoing voice sounded tight, his words clipped. "So answer the damn phone. If you don't, I'm coming over."

She swore softly under her breath, then shut down the power to her computer.

The spring day had dawned warm and sunny after yesterday's dismal rain. It was a perfect day to go running. And now seemed like an especially perfect time.

She changed quickly into a pair of running shorts and her sneakers, pulling a T-shirt on over an athletic bra. Automatically she reached up to pull her hair back into a ponytail, then smiled as she realized that with her new short hairstyle, that was no longer possible. She tied her house key onto her shoelace, trying not to think about T. Jackson.

She'd spent the entire day trying not to think about him. She hadn't thought once about the way his green eyes seemed to glow as he made love to her. She hadn't thought about his rich laugh or the sexy catch that she heard in his voice when he wanted her. And she certainly hadn't thought once about his hard, lean, muscular body, or about that golden tan that intriguingly covered every inch of him.

No, she hadn't thought about him once. She'd thought about him too many times to count.

But she was more than a walking hormone. And there was more to life than good sex.

She wanted a man who would stick around for the rest of his life, not just for a few years until he got tired of her.

But what would it hurt, that pesky little voice popped into her head and said, if you spent the summer with T.? Spend one last summer with a man who drives you wild, *then* start dating only safe, down-to-earth types.

No, she couldn't do that. The emotional risk was too great.

What emotional risk? the voice argued. You say you don't still love the guy. You say you're not going to fall in love with him again, no way—

Damn right. And the best way to not fall in love with T. was to avoid him. There was no doubt about that.

She closed her apartment door, checking to see that it was locked, then quickly went down the stairs. She pushed open the screen door at a run, went out on the porch, down the steps—

And skidded to a stop to keep from slamming into T.

How the hell did he get over here so quickly? Cell phone, she realized instantly. Of course. He must've called her on his cell phone. So much for making an easy escape. So much for avoiding him.

His face looked hard. There was definitely a determined set to his jaw, but his eyes held more than a glimmer of hurt as he stared at her.

"Going somewhere?" he asked.

Kelly sighed. "Yeah, I was going to go running."

"Running away, you mean," he said tightly.

"You're really angry at me." Her heart sank further. She had hoped he'd see that this was for the best.

He laughed, a quick burst of exasperated air. "Did you actually think I wouldn't be angry? Or hurt?" He shook his head. "God, Kelly, what are you trying to prove?"

"T., I didn't mean to hurt you." Her eyes filled with

tears and she fought to blink them back. "I thought..."

"What?" T. pulled her chin up so that Kelly was forced to look him in the eye. "What did you think? That I wouldn't care? That I'd just walk away, disappear, stop bothering you? Say, 'thanks, it was a lot of fun?'"

"Yes," she said honestly, then backed away from the sudden flare of anger in his stormy eyes. "I thought that if we made—if we *had* sex, we'd both realize that the attraction between us wasn't real, that it was based on fantasy, on the past."

He turned away from her, screwing his eyes shut as if in sudden pain. "*That's* what you meant when you said you wanted to move ahead with your life. I thought you were talking about having a future with me, but damn it, you were exorcising me, weren't you?"

When she didn't answer, he turned back to face her. "Weren't you?"

Kelly stared into his accusing eyes, and felt a tear escape and roll down her cheek. "Yes," she whispered.

"Well, did it work?" T.'s voice was raspy. "Did you get me out of your system, Kel? 'Cause it sure as hell didn't work for me."

"I don't know," Kelly said, another tear joining the first.

Jax stared at her. Her eyes were so big in her pale face. She looked little more than a child. But she was no child. Not anymore. They'd both proved that last night.

"Did you really think that all I wanted was to make love to you?" He felt tears burning his own eyelids.

"No, not make love, you called it sex. Is that really all it was to you, Kelly? Sex? Just a one-goddamned-night stand? God, I made *love* to you last night."

His voice shook with emotion, and he turned away, wiping the tears from his eyes. "Goddamn it, Kelly," he whispered. "*Goddamn* you."

"I'm sorry," she said.

"Are you?" He turned back to her. "Then have dinner with me. Spend time with me. Let this thing between us have a chance—"

"No." She realized how brusque she sounded, and tried to soften it. "T., I can't, I—"

"Come to the Cape with me." He took a step toward her, reached for her. "Please, Kelly. God, I'm begging you—"

She moved away. "No!"

He shook his head, defeated, and turned away, heading for his car. But he'd only gone a few steps before he came back. As Kelly watched, he took a business card out of his wallet and held it out to her.

"Take it," he ordered her, and Kelly reluctantly reached for it. "It's my phone number on Cape Cod. In case you need me for anything. In case..." His voice shook again, and he took a deep breath. "This is not over," he said, gazing directly into her eyes. "I'm under your skin—you just don't know it yet. But I'm under there and you're not going to be able to forget me. Especially now, after last night. If that really was just sex for you, Kelly, imagine how good making love to me could be."

Kelly stood staring, long after his car had disappeared.

# *Chapter 9*

Dear Kelly,
For the first time in months I have hope.

A piece of paper has appeared, slipped by unknown hands through the crack under the heavy wooden door to my cell. It lies on the damp dirt floor, white and shining in the dim morning light.

I pick it up slowly, carefully.

It is a card. The paper is a thick linen blend and I run my fingers lightly over the texture of the fibers. It has the feel of a wedding invitation.

I turn it over. There's a picture on the front. A drawing.

A white dove flies up to the sky, escaping the bars of a prison cell. Inside the darkness of the cell, a single candle burns. It is wrapped in barbed wire.

My hands tremble as I open the card. There is writing inside—plain block letters. In English.

"Jackson Winchester, we know you are there," I read. "We are working and praying for your immediate and unconditional release."

There is no signature, but I know who it is from.

Amnesty International.

One month later I am free.

"Oh, please, don't tell me *that's* your breakfast." Stefanie looked with pointed distaste at the cold slice of pizza Jax held in one hand as he opened the refrigerator with the other.

"All right, I won't tell you," he said, pulling out a bottle of beer and opening it.

"When was the last time you shaved?" She followed him up the stairs and into his office.

The spacious room had big windows that looked out over the bay, and an entire wall of bookshelves filled with books of all shapes and sizes, covering a vast plethora of subjects. Jax's computer was set up so that he could look out over the water with a simple turn of his head, but directly above the monitor was a huge corkboard to which he'd pinned information on his current characters and a brief list of the major plot points of his story.

There was a large oak table in the room, with several comfortable chairs placed around it. A couch ran along another wall. The floors were hardwood and the ceiling was high, angling up dramatically.

Jax stood in front of the windows, eating the cold pizza and staring at the sunlight on the water. There was a boat way out, almost beyond the edge of the horizon, and he could see only the tiny speck of its red sail against the brilliant blue sky.

He scratched the back of the hand that held the bottle of beer with the rough stubble on his chin. When *had* he last shaved? But who cared, really? ''Why? Are guests coming today?''

''Just Emilio,'' Stefanie said.

Jax turned to look at her, smiling grimly after he took a long swig of beer. ''Thank God. For a minute I thought we were going to get a royal visit from the King or Queen of Winchester.''

Stefanie laughed. ''Someday you're going to have children of your own, and you better hope they treat *you* with a little more respect than you treat our parents.''

His eyes clouded, and he looked back out the window. ''I'm never going to have children.''

''Ooh, ready to do some wallowing, are we? Poor baby—''

''Don't start,'' Jackson said sharply.

There was a long silence. The red sail had disappeared down behind the curve of the earth. What would it be like to be on that little boat right now? Out of sight of the land, nothing but the ocean and the sky…

''When was the last time you slept?''

Jax shrugged. ''Probably shortly before the last time I shaved.''

''Was that two days ago?'' she asked. ''Or three?''

He turned to look at her. His sister was a picture of health, dressed in her shiny Lycra workout clothes. Her sneakers were so new that Jax almost had to shield his eyes from the glare. Her hair was pulled back off her elegant face, and she wore a light coat of makeup. She was on her way to the fitness club.

''Who knows?'' he answered. ''I'm in the midst of

a creative spurt. I'm not keeping track of pedestrian things like sleeping and eating.''

''A creative spurt.'' She crossed her arms skeptically. ''How many pages have you written?''

''Creativity and output aren't necessarily connected,'' he said, somewhat loftily.

''That many?''

He was silent, staring once again out the window.

''You still want me to screen your calls?''

''Yeah,'' he said. ''I don't want to talk to anyone, except...''

''Kelly,'' she finished for him.

He didn't bother to say anything. Kelly wasn't going to call. He'd waited for two weeks, and he knew with a certainty that, as each day passed, it was less and less likely she would.

''Jax, maybe it's time to move on,'' Stefanie said quietly. ''If you're going to give up, then do it. Give up. But don't sit here feeling sorry for yourself—''

''If I wanted therapy, I would've called my shrink.'' He saw a flash of hurt in her eyes, and he felt like a jerk. ''I'm sorry.''

Stef used the toe of her brilliant new sneaker to rub at an imaginary spot in the carpet. Dressed as she was, with her perfectly coiffed hair and her flawlessly applied makeup, it didn't seem possible that she was the one who'd refused to believe he was dead. She was the one who'd marched into that hellhole of a Central American country with the help of Amnesty International's London office and demanded to see either Jax's remains or the location where he was being held.

Stefanie, who had always seemed more concerned with getting her nails done and shopping at Saks, had almost single-handedly set up the letter-writing campaign that had secured his release.

He owed her his freedom, maybe even his life. Definitely his life.

''The publisher called again about that book you started,'' Stefanie said. ''You know, the collection of letters? They're waiting for the final few chapters. Why don't you send it, Jax? I know you've finished it.''

''I'm waiting to find out if that book's going to have a happy ending.''

She shook her head. ''How long do you intend to wait?''

''I don't want to talk about it.''

''If you don't want to talk to me,'' Stef said, ''maybe you *should* think about calling that psychologist...what was his name? Dr. Burnham.''

Jax stood silently, just watching her.

''Call him,'' she urged. ''Or call Kelly. Do *something*, darling. I'll see you later.''

His sister turned and left the room, closing the door softly behind her.

With a sigh, Jax turned back to his computer.

His main characters had run into each other downtown on the Boston Common. They had exchanged pleasantries. It was all so polite and proper, yet they both couldn't help but think about the night they'd made love.

With breathtaking clarity, Jax had a sudden memory of Kelly lying naked on his hotel room bed, smiling up at him, her blue eyes half closed.

''God *damn* it...'' Waves of anger and self-pity flooded him until he felt as if he might drown.

''Why the hell are *you* feeling sorry for yourself?''

Jared's mocking voice cut through Jax's misery. "*I'm* the one who's in a real bitch of a situation. I'm starting to really wonder what you've got in mind here. Carrie's obviously mad as hell at me, and I don't have a clue why. I mean, for crying out loud, *she's* the one who married some other dude."

"Don't use words like *bitch* and *dude,*" Jax reminded him tiredly. "You live in the 1860's, or have you forgotten?"

"Look at you." Jared ignored Jax's question. "You look like total crap—"

"*Crap.* Another fine word for a historical romance hero."

"—you haven't showered or shaved in days, and you're drinking beer at nine o'clock in the morning—"

"Morning, night, what's the difference anyway?" muttered Jax. "One's got the sun, the other doesn't. Big deal."

"So that's it then?" Jared asked, one eyebrow raised in surprise. "You're giving up on Kelly, just like that?"

Jax didn't answer right away. He just turned to stare out the window as he drank the last few drops of his beer. "I don't know what else to do," he finally said.

"Well, okay, but giving up is really stupid," Jared said. "You automatically lose when you give up. Think about all the heroes in your books. Think about Hank in *Night of the Raven.* He didn't give up when Anna told him she'd fill his hide with buckshot if he as much as set one foot on her ranch. And how about Daniel in *Too Late To Run?* Maggie swore on a stack of Bibles that she'd never fall in love with him, but he won her in the end. Think of all the books you've written—how many *have* you written anyway?"

''One too many, apparently,'' Jax said dryly.

''Kelly's not going to call,'' Jared told him.

''Thanks a lot. Rub it in, why don't you?''

''You've got to call her.''

Jax looked down at the silent telephone that was sitting within arm's reach of his computer. If he called Kelly, she'd refuse to see him. He knew her well enough to know that. No, he was going to have to make her an offer that she couldn't refuse.

And in a sudden flash of inspiration, he knew just what to offer her. ''No.'' He smiled. ''*I'm* not going to call her.''

The telephone was ringing as Kelly unlocked the door to her apartment. She was still breathing hard from her three-mile run. Her skin was slick with perspiration, and her clothes were soaked. But she unlocked the door quickly and bolted for the phone. Maybe it was T.

But you don't *want* him to call, she scolded herself as she picked up the kitchen phone. ''Hello?'' she said breathlessly.

''May I speak to Kelly O'Brien please?'' an unfamiliar female voice asked.

Disappointment. She tried to ignore it as she opened the refrigerator door and pulled out a bottle of seltzer.

''Yeah, this is Kelly.'' The seltzer exploded slightly as she twisted off the cap, spraying her with cool water. She took a large swallow of the bubbling soda right from the bottle.

''Kelly, this is Stefanie Winchester. I don't know if you remember me. We met at that university lecture a few weeks ago?''

T. Jackson's sister. ''Of course I remember you.

How are you?'' Kelly asked. *How is T.?* she wanted to ask. *And why hasn't he called me?*

*Because you told him not to,* she answered her own question.

''Fine, thanks,'' Stefanie said. ''I'm actually calling to ask you for a favor. I'm doing some research for, um, a book, and I need some information on how small-press newspapers are made—everything from planning to layout to printing, and I thought I remembered that Jax had told me you work at the university newspaper...?''

''Yes, that's right.''

''I'm going to be in town tomorrow,'' Stefanie said. ''Would you mind joining me for lunch?''

Lunch. With Jayne Tyler. It smelled very fishy, kind of like *bait.* Now, why did that make her so happy? But if it *was* some kind of lure, she wanted to know about it.

''Lunch isn't necessary,'' Kelly said, testing her theory. ''We can talk right now, on the phone.''

''Well, uh...'' Stefanie hesitated. ''Now's not a really convenient time for me, and I, uh, really would like to get together with you, and, well... How about twelve-thirty at the Bookseller Café?''

''Stefanie, did Jackson put you up to this?'' Kelly asked with her usual bluntness. She took another long drink of seltzer.

Stefanie laughed. ''Yes,'' she admitted. ''He did. He told me if you refused to come to lunch, I should offer to read your latest manuscript, you know, as a bribe.''

Now Kelly laughed, pressing the cold bottle against her forehead. She watched as droplets of sweat dripped onto the tiled floor. ''He's shameless.''

"May I be candid?"

"Of course."

"I don't know what happened between you two," Stefanie said, "but he's been an absolute mess ever since he came back from Boston."

Kelly felt a flash of pain as she remembered the hurt she'd last seen in T.'s eyes. She really hadn't meant to hurt him. She'd been carrying around guilt and remorse for two weeks now, wishing she'd somehow handled the entire affair differently.

She thought about T. Jackson all the time, because of the guilt. Every time she saw a tall, blond man, her heart leapt into overdrive, no doubt because she wanted another chance to apologize to T.

If she could turn back time, she would probably agree to go to Cape Cod with him for the summer. Not because she particularly wanted to go, she reassured herself, although as the mercury climbed higher and higher in the thermometer, it was difficult *not* to think about the cool, blue ocean and the fresh breezes sweeping across the beaches. Never mind how often she thought about a certain pair of eyes that changed color like the sea.

The truth was, she didn't want to feel responsible for that wounded look T. had had on his face the morning after they'd made love. She'd seen that same look in her own mirror the first few months after he'd left for London without telling her. The look was there again when he didn't show up for her eighteenth birthday.

"Will you come?" Stefanie asked.

"My manuscripts aren't perfect," Kelly said. "In fact, I'm having a real tough time finishing my second one. And I can't figure out what's wrong with the first one.''

''Jayne Tyler to the rescue, darling,'' Stefanie said. ''If anyone can help you, it is she. Can I expect to see you tomorrow?''

''Yes,'' Kelly said decidedly. ''Will Jackson be there?''

''Do you want him there?''

Kelly was silent, finishing off the last of the seltzer. ''Yeah,'' she finally said. ''I guess I do.'' That way she'd get her chance to apologize again.

''I'm not sure what his schedule's like,'' Stefanie said breezily. ''I've got to run. Bring whichever manuscript you want. See you tomorrow, Kelly.''

Kelly hung up the phone and headed for the shower, feeling lighter than she had in weeks.

Jax settled himself in the beach chair next to Stefanie as she opened one eye and glanced over at him. She took in his freshly shaved face and clean hair, and, most obviously, his smile.

''Well, well, if the smelly little frog hasn't turned back into the handsome prince,'' she murmured, closing her eyes and turning her face to a better angle to catch the sun.

''What do you think I should wear tomorrow?'' Jax asked, pulling off his T-shirt and dropping the chair back into a full reclining position.

''Since when do you ask me for fashion advice, darling?'' Stefanie opened both eyes to look at him this time.

''If I were writing this,'' Jax mused, ''I'd have the hero show up in an impeccably tailored suit, looking like a million bucks, never mind that the weatherman's predicting another hundred-degree day for tomorrow."

"Fictional characters are so nice," Stefanie said with a sigh, "because they never sweat unless you want them to."

The sun felt warm on Jax's face, and a wave of fatigue hit him. "If I fall asleep, wake me up in a couple of hours. I don't want to fry."

"A bathing suit," Stefanie said. "You should wear a bathing suit and one of those disgustingly sexy undershirt things that reveal more than they cover. As long as it's going to be hotter than hell, you might as well look good while you sweat. Have you ever noticed that when an athlete sweats, it's sexy? But a soggy businessman, now, that's an entirely different story."

Stefanie's watch alarm went off and she put on her hat, careful now to keep her face out of the sun. She only exposed her face to the sun for ten minutes each day. While crow's-feet looked good on men when they aged, women had to be careful.

She glanced back at her brother, but he was already fast asleep.

Dear Kelly,

I am writing this on a real piece of paper with a real pen as I sit on this 727 heading north to Miami.

I am free.

I am flying first-class, and the stewardess offers me champagne, but Stefanie, my sister, shakes her head no. She seems to think I've picked up some nasty bugs during my stay in the tropical wilds of Central America. Her doctors have advised her to let me eat or drink nothing besides bottled water and fresh vegetables until they have checked me out.

There's a hospital bed and a bevy of doctors waiting for me at Mass. General Hospital. Stef tells me she's arranged for a private room, and I laugh. She doesn't get the joke, and I explain—I've spent the last twenty months in solitary. I don't want a private room.

I'll be in the hospital for three or four weeks undergoing medical tests. They'll also be fattening me up. I guess I'm a little malnourished right now.

The warden let me shower and gave me clean clothes before I was released. I have lost so much weight and my beard and hair are so long, I didn't recognize myself in the mirror.

I want to see you, but I don't want you to see me like this. So I'll wait until I'm out of the hospital to call you.

Tonight I will sleep on a bed with real sheets, but I will still dream about you.

I love you.

Love, T.

When Kelly walked into the café, Stefanie was already there, sitting on the outside porch, waiting for her. The older woman waved from the table where she was sitting.

She was alone. No T. Jackson.

Kelly was surprised. What was the point of using Jayne Tyler for bait if T. wasn't even going to bother to show up? Unless he had something else in mind...

The two women greeted each other as Kelly started

to sit down across from Stefanie, placing her briefcase on the floor.

''Oh, sit over here.'' Stef patted the chair next to hers. ''It's so nice to be able to look out on the street.''

With a shrug and a smile, Kelly changed seats.

''Did you bring your manuscript?'' Stefanie asked.

''Are you kidding?'' Kelly was amused. ''No one in their right mind would pass up an opportunity to get a critique from Jayne Tyler.''

''Let me have it now, so I don't forget to get it from you.''

Kelly pulled the heavy manila envelope out of her briefcase and handed it to Stefanie, who set it on the table next to her.

She sat still, returning Stefanie's gaze steadily as the older woman looked at her closely. She was pale, she knew, because she hadn't had much of a chance to get out in the sun. She still ran, but in the very early mornings, just as the sun was starting to rise. The rest of the day she spent inside, in the infernal heat of her apartment, slaving at her computer.

As Stefanie looked at her, Kelly fought the urge to put on her sunglasses, to cover up the dark smudges she knew were under her eyes, the shadows that betrayed the fact that she hadn't been sleeping well for quite some time.

But Stefanie didn't comment. She just smiled and picked up her menu. ''What do you say we order before we talk? I'm starving.''

''But...'' It came out involuntarily.

Stefanie looked at her, eyebrows delicately raised, waiting for her to continue.

What the hell, Kelly thought, and asked, "Isn't Jackson going to join us?" She only wanted a chance to apologize, to clear the air between them.

"He wasn't sure when he could get over here," Stefanie glanced down at her menu, "if at all. I hear the crab salad is wonderful."

Bemused, Kelly opened her menu. If T. Jackson was playing some kind of game with her, he just won a point. She was confused. If he was going to go to all this trouble to get her together with his sister, it seemed kind of silly for him not to show up.

After the waiter came up to their table and took their order, they began to talk. Stefanie was easygoing and self-confident, like her brother, and socially quite adept. She gracefully steered their conversation from one light topic to another. Although the two women came from entirely different backgrounds, they had a lot in common.

Before Kelly knew it, their lunches had arrived.

Stefanie somehow managed to eat and converse at the same time, and without ever talking with her mouth full.

"So I went into the fitness center—" the elegant blonde took a sip of her water "—expecting my personal trainer to be some kind of Nazi drill sergeant, or, even worse, a muscle-bound Amazon commando bitch, and Lord help me, but I must have done *something* worthwhile at *some* time in my life. I look up into *the* most soulful pair of brown eyes that I've ever seen in my life. And those eyes just happened to be attached to this incredible Roman god of a man. His name was Emilio Dicarrio, he told me in this wonderful Italian accent.'' She gestured at Kelly with her fork. ''I'm telling you, it was love at first sight, for both of us.'' Another sip of water. ''At first I thought, God, how tacky. Falling in love with your personal trainer—that's almost as gauche as having a thing for your shrink. Then I thought, he's a gold digger, just after my money. That's what Jax thought, too. But Emilio is one of the few people that I've ever met who's totally happy with his life. He's living in the United States, working in a job he likes. I tell you, the man's *content.* I offered him a chance to do some modeling for some of Jayne's book covers. He did a few photo shoots, but then turned down all the other offers because he thought the work was dull.''

''He sounds perfect,'' Kelly said. ''What's the catch?''

The blond woman's gray eyes were suddenly subdued. ''He wants me to marry him.''

''That's a problem?'' Kelly asked.

''Emilio is only twenty-two years old. He's a baby. He's ten years younger than I am.''

''So?''

''So when he's forty, I'll be fifty.'' She shuddered. ''Darling, it's too terrible to consider.''

''But that's eighteen years away,'' Kelly protested.

Stefanie shrugged, taking a sip of her iced tea. ''So tell me.'' Her gray eyes were suddenly sharp and slightly accusing. ''Why did you come to lunch today? Was it purely mercenary, only to drop off your manuscript, or were you hoping to see my brother?''

Kelly returned her gaze steadily. ''I wanted to apologize to Jackson. I'm afraid I treated him badly.''

"You know, when he came back from Central America—" Stefanie stopped, looking at the puzzled expression on Kelly's face. "Don't tell me. He never told you what happened in Central America?"

"Was that before or after he went to London?"

"Oh, God." Stefanie sat back in her chair, staring sightlessly down at her plate. Why hadn't Jax told Kelly? He had a nearly completed 250-page manuscript of letters to her. Letters that he'd obviously never even told her about…

"Why? What happened in Central America?" Kelly asked curiously.

"No." Stefanie looked up at her again. "Jax will tell you if he wants you to know."

The waiter approached the table. "Ms. Winchester," he murmured. "Phone call."

Stefanie stood. "Excuse me. Maybe that's Jax."

Kelly put her chin in her hand and watched the traffic, both in the street and on the sidewalk. The café looked out on quirky Newbury Street in downtown Boston, so there was a wide variety of people passing by. Overheated men in business suits, delivery men without their shirts on, modern hippies in long, flowing skirts, teenagers with more earrings and nose rings than Kelly could count, tourists in Bermuda shorts and T-shirts with cameras around their perspiring necks….

From out of this teeming mass of humanity, Kelly suddenly saw him. T. Jackson Winchester the Second. His golden hair reflected the sunshine. His eyes were covered by his sunglasses, but the rest of his face looked calm and relaxed. He was wearing…

Kelly swallowed. He was wearing a colorful bathing

suit and a tank top that was nearly nonexistent. The only thing missing was his surfboard.

As he walked down the street, his muscles rippled. As Kelly watched, he turned in to the entrance of the café and opened the door. He hadn't spotted her yet, but it wouldn't be long.

She took a cooling sip of her water, and then there he was. Standing in front of her.

"Hey," he said with a quick smile. "Mind if I sit down?"

Silently she shook her head, trying not to stare at him.

Up close, she could see the light sheen of sweat on his muscles. His shirt was white, matching his teeth, contrasting with his tanned skin. A sudden vivid picture of T. Jackson wearing nothing at all popped into her mind.

She took another sip of water, wishing she could be hosed down. It was much too hot today.

T. sat down across from her, but he kept his sunglasses on. It was unnerving not to be able to see his eyes.

"How are you?" He leaned forward and casually rested his elbows on the table. "How's the writing coming?"

She had missed him.

She hadn't realized it until just now, but somehow she'd let herself get used to him hanging around, following her everywhere. And then when he was gone, something had been missing.

She'd missed his *friendship,* she told herself firmly. Because, face it, that was what their relationship had always been based on. Out of all those years of being close, they had only spent one day as lovers. Well, two, counting the night she'd spent in his hotel room.

Kelly leaned forward, too. "T., I'm really sorry about the way I treated you," she told him. "I don't want you to think that I slept with you as some kind of revenge thing or something like that, because I didn't. I honestly thought it would do us *both* good if we could be free from the past. I didn't mean to hurt you, and I'm sorry if I did."

His smile had faded, but she still couldn't see behind his sunglasses. "Kel, you're apologizing for the best night of my life," he said softly. "Don't do that."

He looked up suddenly, and Kelly turned to see Stefanie returning to their table.

"Well, well, look what the cat dragged in." Stef smiled, stopping to drop a kiss on the top of her brother's head. She turned to Kelly as she sat down. "Sorry about that. The publisher needs some revisions by yesterday. I'm afraid Jayne hasn't been on the ball lately."

"That's the second time you've done that," Kelly said. "You referred to Jayne in the third person, like she's somebody else."

"It's a funny thing about pseudonyms," Jax said easily. "They seem to take on a life of their own." He glanced at his watch. "If you're ready, Stef, I'll get the car and pull it around front." He stood, looking down at Kelly from behind his shades. "Nice seeing you."

He picked Kelly's manuscript up off the table, and left.

She turned to Stefanie, who was signaling the waiter for the check. ''But we didn't talk about small-press newspapers.''

Stefanie smiled. ''Darling, we didn't need to in the first place.''

''But...'' Kelly laughed. ''What just happened here? Did I miss something? Jackson set up this elaborate plan for me to have lunch with you simply to show up, say three sentences and leave? I don't get it.''

Stefanie just smiled.

# Chapter 10

Outside the windows of the office, the beach was dark. Jax sat leaning back, his feet up on the conference table, as he read the last few pages of Kelly's manuscript.

It was good. It wasn't perfect, but it was pretty damn good. The heroine was a tough, feisty Katharine Hepburn type. In fact, the whole story read like a 1940s romantic comedy, with crackling, fast-paced dialogue.

In his opinion, the story had two major weaknesses. One was that the hero's motivation seemed unclear and some of his actions were contrived. The second weakness was in the love scenes.

Kelly wasn't comfortable writing those scenes, and it showed. Instead of being sensual explosions of emotion and feelings, they were sketchy and vague. And over much too soon.

Jax glanced at his watch. It was nearly midnight. Too late to call Kelly tonight.

With a sigh, he stood, stretching his muscles, heading toward the kitchen and the cold beer in the refrigerator.

Damn, but Kelly had looked good today. He was glad that he had been wearing his sunglasses, glad that she hadn't seen his eyes. If she had, she would've seen how badly he had missed her, and how much he wanted to be with her. She would have seen how badly he still wanted her.

He opened his beer with a swoosh and took a long sip.

It had nearly killed him to get up from that table after only sitting there with her for a few minutes. But his goal wasn't to have lunch with her. He was aiming for bigger things.

Such as forever.

He'd noticed her trying not to look at his body today. She hadn't been able to hide the flashes of desire that he'd seen in her eyes. Despite what she'd said about getting him out of her system, he knew that the magnetic pull of attraction he felt whenever he was near her was stronger than ever. And he knew she felt it, too.

She said he belonged only in her past, but she was wrong. He knew that he was her future. And she was his.

He would do whatever it took to prove that to her.

Well, almost anything.

He winced, remembering the way Stefanie had damn near chewed his head off in the car this afternoon. She didn't understand why he hadn't told Kelly about Central America.

When exactly was he supposed to have told her?

At Kevin's wedding maybe? Right after she'd dropped her own nuptial bomb?

He'd tried calling her when she was living in California, but Brad had answered the phone. Kelly's husband had told Jax in no uncertain terms that he didn't want him calling his wife. With a husband as jealous as Brad obviously was, there was no way Jax could resume his role in Kelly's life as friend of the family. He wasn't even sure he wanted to resume that role anyway. Instead, he'd stayed away from her for all those years.

So how could he have told her about Central America?

Maybe he was supposed to have told her in between her classes in Boston, as he chased her down the sidewalk. Yeah, he'd had *tons* of time then.

The night that they had made love, he had thought there would be plenty of opportunities to talk to her in the future, to tell her what had happened, what he had been through. But he'd been wrong.

And Jackson didn't want to tell her now. He didn't want her to pity him. He wanted her to love him.

Kelly couldn't sleep.

It was much too hot in her apartment, even with all of the windows open wide and the fans blowing directly at her.

Without the shades pulled down, light from the street lamp on the corner made bright patterns on the walls as it shone through the trees. She stared at them for a while, unwilling to shut her eyes.

Because when she shut her eyes, she saw T. Jackson.

T. Jackson. Looking better than a man had a right to.

T. Jackson. Giving in to his desire, unable even to walk the short distance to the hotel bedroom before he made love to her.

T. Jackson. Dancing with her all those years ago at her junior prom, smiling down into her eyes.

With sudden clarity, Kelly could see T., dressed again in a tuxedo, standing in the church where Kevin had married Beth.

Kelly was one of the bridesmaids. She and Brad flew down to Beth's hometown of Atlanta to take part in the ceremony....

As the organist had begun to play the wedding march, she had followed the other bridesmaids down the aisle. The crowd in the church had all risen to their feet to watch. Kelly had smiled back into the sea of friendly, happy faces until suddenly she'd seen him.

T. Jackson Winchester the Second.

Kevin hadn't mentioned that T. was coming to the wedding.

But he was standing on the groom's side of the church, at the end of the pew closest to the center aisle. His blond hair was cut short, and his face looked pale and gaunt, as if he'd recently been very ill. But he was smiling at her, his eyes warm and so very green.

As she stared at him in shock, his lips moved as he silently spoke her name.

The ceremony passed in a blur, with Kelly standing up and sitting down with Beth's sisters, who were beside her at the front of the church.

Her mind was a whirlwind of thoughts. She'd never expected to see T. again. His estrangement with Kevin had seemed so permanent, so unmendable. The last time she asked Kevin about him, her brother had been vague, saying he thought Jax was still in London, but he wasn't sure.

Yet here he was. In Atlanta, of all places, for Kevin's wedding.

Kelly felt T.'s gaze on her throughout the entire ceremony. When she looked up to meet his eyes, he smiled at her. God, his smile could still take her breath away.

Her gaze flickered nervously toward Brad, who was sitting on the other side of the church. He hadn't wanted to come to this wedding. He hated flying, and he was already worrying about tomorrow morning's flight home. He was staring sightlessly down at the ground, the muscles in his jaw working.

As if he felt her eyes on him, Brad looked up at Kelly. But he didn't smile. He looked at her closely, the way he did a lot lately, as if he weren't sure exactly who she was. As if he couldn't figure out how he'd suddenly wound up married to her.

The events leading up to their marriage *had* happened fast. Kelly would be the first to admit it. She'd met Brad her senior year of high school, during an orientation session at Boston University. He was an upperclassman, and he had, as he later told her, fallen in love with her instantly.

He was tall, like T., and blond, like T., with the same zest for life evident in his winning smile. He was a senior when she was a college freshman, and almost before she knew it, he had taken her virginity and, she thought, her heart.

Carried along on the waves of romance, Kelly had married him in the fall of her sophomore year of college. Four months had passed since then, and now, looking into Brad's shuttered, expressionless blue eyes, she was starting to wonder just what they'd gotten themselves into.

The ceremony finally ended, and then the wedding party posed for pictures. When that was over, Kelly was whisked into a waiting limo with the other bridesmaids. As the big, white car pulled away from the church, she could see T. Jackson standing there, watching her. He lifted his hand in a wave.

It wasn't until the reception that T. caught up with her. Kelly and Brad were standing near the bar, talking to Beth's older sister as the band played an old, slow song. Couples were on the dance floor, swaying to the music.

Kelly spotted T. on the other side of the room, and knew that he was heading in her direction. She felt the urge to run or hide or—

"Kelly."

She looked up into the swirling colors of T. Jackson's eyes. He looked so thin as to be unhealthy, but his eyes were still the same marvelous mix of colors. Had it really been three years since she'd seen him last? Three long years since the night of her junior prom…

"You look beautiful," he said.

His lips curved into a small smile, and as he stepped even closer to her, he reached out and his warm fingers touched her arm, sliding gently down to her hand. As he pulled her toward him, his gaze dropped to her mouth.

He was going to kiss her, right there, right in front of *Brad*—

And he did.

T. Jackson gently brushed her lips with his.

''I need to talk to you.'' He smiled down at her. ''Dance with me, will you—''

''I don't believe we've met,'' Brad's voice cut in.

T. looked up, surprised, and Kelly took the opportunity to step back, out of his embrace. Beth's older sister was watching with unabashed interest as the two tall, blond men sized each other up.

''No, you're right,'' T. said. ''We haven't met. I'm sorry, Kelly tends to...distract me.''

''Oh, really?'' Brad crossed his arms in front of him.

T. looked slightly surprised at the hostility in Brad's voice, and he glanced at Kelly as if looking for an explanation.

That's when it hit her.

T. Jackson didn't know that she and Brad were married. Kevin hadn't bothered to tell him.

''Are you gonna introduce us?'' Brad asked her, a touch impatiently.

''Brad, this is Jackson Winchester,'' she said. ''He was my brother's college roommate.''

She looked up at T., who had held out a friendly hand toward Brad. The two men shook.

''T., I'd like you to meet Brad Foster,'' Kelly said. ''My husband.'' For some mysterious reason, her eyes had suddenly filled with tears.

T. stared at her, an expression of shock clearly written across his usually unflappable face.

''Oh, God,'' he breathed. ''You're married?''

She tried to smile. ''Yeah.''

''How could you be married?'' he asked, disbelief in his voice. ''You're only nineteen.''

He reached out, pulling her chin up so he could look

into her eyes, as if he were hoping that something he saw there would prove her words wrong.

Brad stepped forward. ''I'd appreciate it if you kept your hands off my wife.''

T. Jackson let go of Kelly as if he'd been burned.

As she watched, tears formed in his eyes. He tried to blink them back. ''I guess I missed your eighteenth birthday,'' he said softly.

Kelly nodded. ''I guess you did.''

''Oh, Kelly,'' he said.

She glanced back up into his eyes, and for one brief moment, he held her gaze, and she saw the white heat of his pain, the depth of his misery.

''Excuse me,'' T. whispered, and nearly ran from the room.

Brad stared after him. ''People always have too much to drink at these things.''

Kelly had spent the rest of the afternoon trying to convince herself that seeing T. hadn't really been that big a deal. Naturally she'd felt rattled; having him there had been a surprise. And as for the nearly overpowering urge to throw herself down on the floor and cry, well, that had had more to do with Brad's news that he'd found a job in California, than with anything else. Hadn't it...?

But as Kelly lay in the heat of the summer night nearly four years later, it all clicked into place.

She'd married Brad not because she loved him, but because he was so much like T. Jackson—or at least she thought he was—with his imposing height and blond hair. And even though she denied it, when she saw T. again at Kevin's wedding, deep down she realized the magnitude of her mistake.

Kelly stared at the ceiling, seeing T. as he had

looked at lunchtime today, walking down the city street, dressed down for comfort in the afternoon heat. She could see the tanned planes and angles of his handsome face as he sat across from her at the café table. She could see the longing in her own eyes, mirrored in the reflective lenses of his sunglasses.

There was no denying that she missed him.

She missed him following her around campus all day and all night, popping up in the most unexpected places to give her a lift or ask her out. She missed hearing his voice and talking to him. She missed the way he listened to her as if every word she said was of the utmost importance.

She missed his friendship, that much was clear.

But she couldn't deny that she missed him in other ways, too. When she saw him at lunch, her body had responded with astonishing speed to his nearness, and she walked away feeling utterly frustrated.

God, she still wanted him.

Aha, triumphantly cried the side of her that always played devil's advocate. I've been right all along. You *do* still love him.

Don't get carried away, she chastised herself. Lust and love don't always go hand in hand.

Still, as she lay awake into the late hours of the night, she could see T.'s stormy green eyes and hear an echo of his voice saying, *This is not over. I'm under your skin.*

Around two-thirty, Kelly fell into a restless sleep, only to dream about T. Jackson Winchester.

"So when are you going to call her?" Jared asked.

Jax was sitting in front of his computer, arms folded

across his chest. A glance at his watch told him it was still not even nine o'clock in the morning.

It was going to be another hot one. He could already see heat waves shimmering out on the sandy beach.

Jax had a similar heat cooking inside of him at the thought of calling Kelly and hearing her voice. And if everything went according to plan, he'd be seeing her in only a few hours.

He would be using her ambition as a means to get her out here, though, to put her within his grasp. It felt like cheating, but Jax reminded himself that he had to do whatever it would take to get her to spend time with him.

"All's fair in love and war," Jared supplied helpfully. "So why don't you call her?"

"Why don't you quit trying to distract me?" Jax said. "I'm not going to call Kelly until nine, and I should probably even wait until ten. Right now I *should* be finishing this damned book, and *you* should be helping."

"Hey, *I'm* not the one who left me hanging here on the Boston Common with Carrie for two solid days." Jared was disgruntled. "And on top of all that, she's still mad at me. Why am I here? What's the purpose of this scene? Maybe you just want to torture me. I suppose that could be it. God knows you *love* to torture me—"

"This is where you notice the bruises on Carrie's face," Jax said, starting to write.

Horrified, Jared looked closer.

Carrie had tried to cover it with powder, but he could see the fading bruise beneath her eye and across her delicate cheekbone. She ducked her head, turning away.

"I have to go—"

Jared caught her arm. "Who did this to you?"

"I fell." She couldn't meet his gaze as she pulled away.

He swore sharply, but it was the sudden tears filling his eyes that slowed her feet. "Why do you stay with him, Carrie?" he asked. "Lord—how could you *marry* him—"

But as she wheeled to face him, it was anger, not sorrow that made her voice shake. "How dare you," she said. "How *dare* you come back here, and how *dare* you look at me as if I were the one who betrayed *you?* God *damn* you to hell, Jared Dexter. *You're* the one who deserted *me!* You *promised* you would come for me—"

"Why didn't you wait?" It came out a whisper filled with his anguish and pain. "You should have waited for me."

He held her by her shoulders, and as he stared down into her deep blue eyes he could see…fear?

"Let go of me," she said. "You're making a scene. If someone tells Harlan they saw me here like this with you—"

Jared released her, feeling sick.

Jared looked up at Jax. "I don't like where this is going."

"You're definitely not gonna like where Carrie's going."

"Going? As in *away?* No, don't tell me—"

"She and Harlan are headed out west," Jax said. "Yippee-yi-oh-ki-ay. They're buying a ranch in California."

''California?'' Jared threw up his hands in disgust. ''Are you sure this book is going to have a happy ending?''

''I'm sure of nothing these days,'' Jax replied.

''Lord save me from depressed writers.'' Jared rolled his eyes.

''Relax,'' Jax said. ''It won't be long now 'til Part Three. Part Three is three years later.''

''Three *years!* What have I been doing for three *years?*''

''Getting richer. Your business ventures keep earning you more money. Everything you touch turns to gold.''

''Everything except my love life.'' Jared sulked.

''You go west,'' Jax said, and Jared stopped sulking.

''Okay. Things are starting to look better. Where exactly did you say Harlan Kent's ranch was?''

''I didn't.'' Jax sat back in his chair. ''But it's near Los Angeles.''

''So what's going to happen?'' Jared was still suspicious.

''First you go to L.A.,'' Jax told him, ''where you find out that Harlan's dead.''

The hard planes of Jared's handsome face softened into a smile. ''Now you're talking. You had me worried there for a while.''

Jax pulled himself back to his computer keyboard, but Jared shook his head.

''It's after nine,'' he pointed out. ''You should call Kelly.''

''Just let me get this started,'' Jax said distractedly.

''You're stalling.''

Jared was right. He *was* stalling. No more stalling.

With a click of his mouse, Jax cleared the computer screen.

Taking a deep breath, he turned and looked at the telephone, then glanced at his watch to be sure it really was past nine.

He picked up the phone and dialed Kelly's home number. It rang once. Twice. Three times. Four.

''Hello?'' She was breathless, as if she'd run for the phone.

''Hey, Kel,'' Jackson said. ''It's me. Jax. How are you?''

''Soaking wet, actually,'' she said in her familiar, husky voice. ''I was just turning off the shower when I heard the phone. Can you hold on a sec while I dry off and grab my robe?''

A sudden vivid image of Kelly, standing with only a towel around her, took Jax's breath away. He almost couldn't answer. ''Yeah, sure,'' he managed to say.

He heard the sound of the phone being put down and then silence for about thirty seconds. Then she was back.

''Sorry about that,'' she said.

''No problem.'' He wiped the sweat off his upper lip with the back of his hand.

''It's funny. I was just thinking about you.''

In the shower? He shook his head. It wasn't going to do him any good to start thinking along those lines.

''What's up?'' she asked.

Funny you should ask… He cleared his throat. ''I read your manuscript. It's good.''

There was silence.

''*You* read it.'' Another pause. ''I thought Stefanie was going to.''

Mentally Jax froze. God, of *course*. Kelly thought

that *Stef* was Jayne Tyler. She had no reason to think anything else. He realized that she was waiting for him to say something, that his silence was stretching longer and longer.

"Yeah," he finally said, hoping his next words would take her attention off the vagueness of his comment. "Look, your story could use some revisions. And that's why I'm calling. I thought you might be interested in letting Jayne Tyler help you with the rewrites."

It was his ace in the hole, his secret weapon, his only shot, and he prayed desperately that it would work.

"You're kidding."

"No."

More silence. He could almost hear the wheels turning in her head.

"Our offices are here at the house in Dennis," he said, mostly to fill the empty space. "I figure you could have the revisions done by the end of the summer."

"Dennis, huh?" She made a sound that might've been a laugh. "It's a hefty commute, considering I don't have a car."

"Um," Jax said. "There's plenty of room for you to stay over."

She laughed. "Now, how did I know you were going to say that?"

"Oh, come on, Kel." Jax closed his eyes and prayed. "Summer on the Cape…?"

"T., will you be honest with me?"

"I'll try."

"Is my writing really any good, or is this just a ploy to get me out to Cape Cod?"

"Yes, and yes," he admitted.

Kelly laughed. "Right," she said. "Okay, answer this one. What does Jayne get from doing this? I mean, I understand *your* motivation, but what's in it for her?"

"Whoa," Jax backpedaled. "Wait a minute. Kelly, this isn't some kind of sexual bribe. I don't want you to think that you owe me anything. I just want you to have a chance to get to know me again. That's all." He took a deep breath. "I'm not trying to buy your love. Or anything else. I'm just trying to get you out here. Once you're here, I'm hoping...you'll fall in love with me again."

"Well." Kelly was slightly breathless. "As long as we're being honest with each other, I have to tell you that I have no intention of falling in love with you *ever* again, Tyrone."

She'd already made that way more than clear. "I know. Will you come anyway?"

"What kind of computer do you have?"

"A PC," he said. "Why?"

"I knew it," she said. "More proof that we're not compatible. I've got a Mac. I better plan on bringing it."

Jax stood, twirled around in a silent dance of victory and then untangled himself from the phone cord. Yes. *Yes.*

"Can you pick me up?" she asked. "Or is that a stupid question?"

"Stupid question," he agreed. "Really stupid. I'll be there before noon. Don't forget to pack your bathing suit."

"Of course," Kelly said dryly. "I always wear my bathing suit when I write."

"Oh, come on. It's summer. This is Cape Cod. You can't *not* bring your bathing suit."

"I won't be packed by noon," Kelly warned him.

"I'll help you pack."

"I must be crazy."

"I promise you, Kelly," Jax said, "you won't regret this."

"I already regret this." But then she laughed. "I *am* crazy. See you later, T."

Jackson hung up the phone and let out a whoop that could be heard clear across the bay.

# *Chapter 11*

''Rule number one,'' Kelly said, sitting in Jax's little sports car as they sped down Route 3 toward Cape Cod. ''No touching.''

''I can live with that.'' Jax smiled as he glanced at her. ''With exceptions, of course—''

''No exceptions,'' she said sternly.

''Well, what if I have to pull you out of a burning building?'' Jax asked. ''Or push you out of the way of a speeding car? Or—''

''I don't intend to spend much time in burning buildings or near speeding cars this summer. Rule number two.''

''All rules have exceptions,'' Jax told her stubbornly. ''And you know it.''

''Rule number two,'' Kelly repeated, crossing her arms. She could be just as stubborn. ''No looking at me like you want to eat me for dinner.''

Jax exhaled a loud burst of air as he laughed. "Like *what?*"

"You know what I mean."

"No, I *don't*—" He was *laughing* at her.

"Yes, you do." She smacked his arm.

"Uh-uh-uh. That was a direct violation of rule number one. No touching."

"You *know* the look I mean," Kelly insisted, choosing to ignore him. "It's like you're taking off my clothes with your eyes."

"Rule number two," Jax repeated. "No taking off your clothes with my eyes. It's gonna make it hard to undress you, considering rule number one. How about taking off your clothes with telekinesis? Is that permitted?"

Kelly couldn't hide her laughter, which was only serving to make him act sillier than ever. "T., you're not taking me seriously."

"On the contrary. I'm taking you extremely seriously." The road was flat and straight and empty, and he took his eyes off of it for a long moment to study her. Despite the car's air-conditioning, she was sticky and hot and—

"*That's* the look," she accused him. "You were giving me that look—"

Startled, Jackson pulled his eyes back to the road. "I was *not*—"

"Yes, you were."

"Well, if I was, I didn't know it. How can I stop doing something I don't do intentionally?"

"Wear your sunglasses."

"Day and *night?*" he said. "Inside the *house?*"

She shrugged. "Whatever works. Rule number three."

"There's more?"

"No sweet talk, no marriage proposals, no constant reminders that you want us to be more than friends, no sexual innuendos."

Jax sighed. "I'm not sure I'll be able to stand the pressure."

"Rule number four—"

"Kelly, you're not giving me an awful lot to work with here."

"No trying to distract me with your body."

"Excuse me? No trying to *what?*"

"No walking around half-naked," she elaborated. "You know."

"Kel, we're going to be living at a beach house," Jax said. "*Every*one walks around half-naked. Including you. I hope."

"Rule number five—No flirting." She looked over at him. "That's going to be a hard one for you. I don't think you're capable of communicating with a woman without flirting."

Jax was silent for a long time. Finally he looked over at her and lifted an eyebrow. "Every single way I could think of responding to that statement could be interpreted as flirting. You're right. I'm completely doomed."

He pulled off the highway and down to the end of the exit ramp. There were no cars behind him, so he put the car in park and turned toward Kelly.

"T. Jackson Winchester the Second's Only Rule." He had a dangerous glint in his eye and Kelly tried to back away, but there was nowhere to go. "Once a day," he told her, "every single day, I intend to break each and every one of your rules. Rules number one and two..." He touched the side of her face, pulling her chin up so that her gaze met his. He looked into her eyes, letting his desire for her simmer. ''Rule number three,'' he whispered. ''Kelly, I want to make love to you for days without stopping. Please, will you stop this nonsense and just marry me?''

''No,'' she breathed, caught in the turbulent green of his eyes. Oh, God, this was a mistake.

He leaned closer and kissed her, but instead of a passionate attack, his mouth was soft, sweet. ''The kiss was a variation on rule four,'' he explained, then he smiled. ''These rules are going to kill me. But frankly, I can't think of a better way to go.''

She could kiss him. She could lean forward right now and kiss him, and, like the man said, stop this nonsense.

Instead, Kelly closed her eyes until she felt the car moving forward. She couldn't give in. She *wouldn't* give in.

Not unless she wanted him to break her heart all over again.

The Winchester house was enormous, and it sat on a craggy hill overlooking the beach. It was modern, with lots of odd angles and high ceilings. No single corner came together absolutely square.

The large living room was a few steps down from the entryway, and it had huge sliding glass doors that led out onto a wide wooden deck. The furniture looked surprisingly comfortable, and the room was decorated all in white and various shades of blue and green—the colors of the beach. There was a fireplace and an expensive sound system and a wall full of books. It was not the cold, imposing room that Kelly had expected from T.'s descriptions of the Winchester estates.

"Nice," she said.

T. laughed at the tone of her voice. "Why so surprised?"

She turned to face him, and caught a glimpse of her own rueful smile in the reflective lenses of his sunglasses. He was making a point to wear them inside the house. "Isn't this your parents' house?"

"Not anymore." He shifted the weight of her suitcase to his left hand. "I bought it from them a few years ago."

"But this *is* the house you lived in when you were in high school," Kelly said.

He smiled, setting the suitcase down. "This is it. Come on, I'll give you the grand tour."

She followed him back up the stairs and then up several more steps into the kitchen. It was huge and gleaming, with two different refrigerators, what seemed like miles of counter space and a center island that contained a second sink. All of the cabinets were made of a light knotted pine, and on the floor was cream-colored ceramic tile. Shining pots hung from a grid on one wall, and fruits and vegetables sat in baskets that dangled from the center beam.

"I keep a grocery list on the refrigerator," Jax told her. "If you want anything special, just add it to the list. I'll pick it up next time I'm at the store."

"I didn't know you could cook."

"I'm a whiz at grilled-cheese sandwiches," he said. "My other specialty is cornflakes. I pour a mean pitcher of milk."

Kelly followed him several steps down the hall. "This is the dining room." He didn't bother to go inside the large room that held a banquet-size table and about sixteen chairs. ''But I don't use it. I eat out on the deck.'' He smiled. ''Or in a restaurant. Usually in a restaurant.''

He led her up a full set of stairs to the second floor. A long hallway stretched both right and left. He turned left. ''This is my wing. It's over the garage.'' He pointed at several doors. ''Guest bedroom, guest bedroom, bathroom. This is my office.''

After peeking into the two very tastefully decorated guest rooms, Kelly followed T. Jackson into his office. It was a big room that, like the living room, overlooked the beach.

''I can move a desk in here for your computer,'' Jax said. ''Or you can set it up in your room, whichever you prefer. Some people don't like writing when someone else is in the room, so...''

Kelly turned to him and smiled. ''T., at school I work in the newsroom. If you don't mind, I'll put my computer in here. Unless you think having Stefanie and me working in here will disturb you?''

''Um...''

''What's in here?'' Kelly curiously pushed open the door that connected his office to another room.

''My bedroom.'' He came to stand behind her, finally taking off his sunglasses.

His room was dark, with the shades still pulled down and the big bed unmade. Clothes were draped over chairs and in piles on the floor. His closet door was open, revealing a row of neatly hung shirts and jackets. The room was cool and dim and smelled good, like Jackson.

It wasn't hard to picture T. asleep in that bed, his hair tousled, his muscles relaxed.

His arms around her.

Kelly took a step back and bumped into him. Her entire back pressed against his entire front, and he put his arms around her to steady her. But he moved away almost immediately, giving her space.

"Sorry," she said.

His mouth twisted into a quick smile that didn't quite reach his eyes. "Hey, it's your rule. If it were up to me..."

Kelly followed his gaze back to his rumpled bed.

It wasn't hard to figure out what he was thinking. It would have been even easier to give in, to throw her arms around his neck and pull him toward that bed.

Kelly was suddenly very grateful that she had set up those rules, because she knew that if T. so much as touched her right now, her willpower would dissolve.

But he barely even glanced at her before putting his sunglasses back on. "I'll get the rest of your stuff in from the car. Why don't you pick which guest room you want to use? There's one more at the end of this hall, and three down on Stef's wing."

He disappeared, leaving Kelly still standing in the doorway to his bedroom. She looked back at his bed one more time, then quickly went into the hall. Moving down to the other side of the hall, Stefanie's wing, he had called it, she picked the room that was farthest away from T.'s.

It was decorated all in green. Green wallpaper, green bedspread, green curtains. There was a dresser and a rocking chair and a huge walk-in closet that was empty. The room also had its own bathroom. Maybe all the bedrooms did, Kelly thought suddenly, wondering at the value of a house this size, with all those bathrooms, *on* the beach.

As T. Jackson carried her suitcase in, he didn't comment on the geography of her room choice. He set her luggage on the floor and nodded toward the bed. "Did you know that's a water bed?"

Kelly looked at it in surprise. "No, I didn't." She sat down on the bed, and felt waves rolling back and forth inside the water-filled mattress. It was fun, kind of like an amusement park ride. She lay back on the bed, letting herself float.

She bounced higher as T. jumped onto the bed next to her. "My parents got it in the seventies," he said with a grin. "Needless to say, this is the room I slept in when I was in high school."

Kelly sat up, staring at him. "Forget this room. I can't stay in here. It's probably haunted with the ghosts of high school girlfriends past. I'd never get any sleep."

T. laughed, propping his head up on his hand, his arm bent at the elbow. "I never brought anyone home, because I didn't want to risk people finding out that I lived alone," he said. "Well, no, that's not entirely true. Mary Jo Matthews came over once. Uninvited, though. We went steady for about a month during my senior year. She dumped me for the captain of the football team."

"Ouch."

"I got over it."

Stretched out next to him on the gently rolling bed, she could remember him as an eighteen-year-old. No doubt all the girls in the school had sighed over him, some of them doing more than sighing.

"I'll bet you did," she said.

"If we had gone to high school together, I would've been scared to death of you."

"Why?" she asked.

"You were a math nerd, remember?" He grinned. "I really stank at math."

"I could've tutored you." God, why did she say that?

"I would've invited you over anytime."

"I think I'd rather have a room with a regular bed," Kelly said.

The water shifted as Jax stood, and the force of the internal waves knocked Kelly over. She laughed helplessly, trying to regain her balance.

Jax held out his hand to help her up, and she reached for it automatically. But he let go of her almost immediately, and she bounced back down onto the rolling surface of the water bed.

"Rule number one," he reminded her.

No touching.

Trying not to swear too loudly, Kelly scrambled for the edge of the bed and got herself back onto the steadiness of the floor.

T. had already carried her suitcase out of the room, and she went into the hall and watched him walk back down toward his wing.

"What's wrong with this room?" Kelly asked, stopping in front of the next closest guest room.

He glanced back at her. "That one doesn't have its own bathroom."

"And this room?" She pointed to the door directly across the hall.

"No bay view."

"Figures," she muttered, following him into a guest bedroom that was on the bay side of the house, one door down from his office, two doors down from his bedroom.

It was larger than the green room, with bigger windows and a bigger bathroom. The carpeting was a dusty rose, and the curtains and bedspread were white. Besides the double bed, the room held a dresser and a wicker chair.

T. Jackson put her suitcase down on the bed. "I'll bring your computer up to the office while you unpack."

Kelly followed him out into the hall again. "Hey," she said, and he turned around to look at her. At least she thought he was looking at her. It was hard to tell since he'd put his sunglasses back on.

"I don't want to unpack," she told him. "At least two years have passed since I've been within twenty miles of a beach. I'm going to go for a swim."

"Mind if I come along?"

*Yes. No.* Oh, brother, she didn't know what she wanted.

No, she knew *exactly* what she wanted. And what she wanted and what was good for her were two very different things.

What had she been thinking when she agreed to come and spend more than two months here with T.? Had she really thought she'd be able to come to Cape Cod and *not* wind up in bed with him? She couldn't be in the same room with him without wanting him. Heck, she couldn't be on the same continent, the same *planet* with him without wanting him.

But she had no intention of giving in to her desire. No, thank you. There was just no way she was going to risk letting him back into her heart. And if she let him get close to her in any way, he was bound to be able to break through her protection. And then she'd wind up hurt.

If T. cooperated and followed the rules she'd set down, that would be only half the battle. The other half was her own feelings, her own wants. Please, God, don't let me start sleepwalking, because my subconscious will surely lead me directly to T.'s bed.

Maybe it would be easier when Stefanie was here. After all, it was Stefanie she'd be working with day after day, not T.

Meanwhile, he was standing at the top of the stairs, watching her, waiting for her to answer his question.

"I'll meet you out on the deck," she finally said, and was rewarded by a quiet smile.

It was the quiet smiles that were the most dangerous.

She went into her room and tightly closed the door.

Kelly stood out on the restaurant patio, leaning on the rail, watching the sunset and drinking a beer. Despite all the sunblock she'd put on today, she'd gotten a slight sunburn, just enough to give her skin a tingling, sensitive feeling. In order to avoid the discomfort that a bra would cause, she had put on a sundress with a halter top.

At first she had hesitated, not wanting to give T. the wrong idea. In fact, for precisely that reason, she had intended to wear either jeans or shorts and T-shirts during her entire stay, but she had a particularly bright red stripe of sunburn at the edge of her bathing suit on her back, and the thought of pulling jeans or even shorts on over that was just too dreadful.

On the other hand, if she'd intended to only wear androgynous, casual clothes while she was here on the

Cape, then why had she even packed this sundress in the first place? Or the three other skirts and dresses she'd brought?

"Am I allowed to tell you how beautiful you look?"

She turned to see T. standing next to her.

"Or is that against the rules?" He leaned next to her against the railing, taking a sip from his own glass of beer.

"I think you already managed to tell me." She stared out at the water. "And, yes, it's against the rules. But thank you, anyway."

"Oh, now, wait. If I'm going to break a rule, I'm going to do it right." He looked at her, letting his eyes caress her face. "You're incredibly lovely," he told her. "Your beauty rivals the sunset and—"

Kelly laughed. "Oh, ack."

"Ack?" he repeated, eyebrows elevated. "I'm waxing poetic, and all you can say is ack?"

"Rule six—No waxing poetic. Especially not on an empty stomach. Speaking of empty stomachs, are we going to eat sometime this century by any chance?"

"It shouldn't take more than another ten minutes." Jax sighed melodramatically. "I remember a time when food didn't matter to you, when my kisses were sufficient nourishment."

"Yeah, well, I'm on a diet, remember?" Kelly countered.

"Just let me know when you're ready for a little bingeing," Jax said.

"Tyrone," she said, all kidding pushed aside. "You promised. I'm not going to stick around if I have to fight you off for the rest of the summer."

"So stop fighting," Jackson's eyes were equally

grave. ''Surrender, Kel. I guarantee you won't regret it.''

The breeze ruffled his blond hair and he carelessly pushed it out of his face as he watched her.

*Surrender.* She could imagine how good it would feel right now to lean back against his chest and watch the sunset with his arms wrapped around her. She could imagine the way his breath would feel against her neck as he leaned close to whisper soft, seductive words to her—

''Winchester. Table for two,'' a voice announced.

Saved.

Not that she had any intention of actually surrendering, Kelly told herself as she followed the hostess through the restaurant to the small, lantern-lit table at the railing of a covered open deck. She slid into her seat, watching as T. Jackson somehow managed to squeeze his long legs into the small space opposite her.

''Please, will you ask the waitress to bring us a couple of bowls of clam chowder right away?'' T. asked the hostess as she handed them their menus. He smiled across the table at Kelly. ''My friend here is starving. I don't want her to start eating the tablecloth.''

Kelly could see the bold interest in the woman's eyes as she smiled down at T. Well, sure, why not? T. had to be the best-looking man in the place. Kelly was getting quite a number of envious glances from other women. But if he noticed, he was hiding it well. To look at him, anyone would think he was oblivious to everyone in the restaurant besides Kelly.

Another woman might've been flattered, or made to feel special by his undivided attention. But not her, no way. In fact, she'd prefer it if he found someone else to look at that way.

He was being careful to keep that hot, hungry, gobble-her-up look from his eyes, but this soft, faintly amused adoration was unbearable in its own way.

The soup came out almost right away, and T. soon gave some of his attention to eating. As they ate, and throughout the rest of dinner, he kept the conversation light and almost pointedly not flirtatious.

Kelly felt herself relax.

Jax felt himself start to sweat. He wasn't sure how long he could keep up the big-brother act.

Somehow he'd managed to spend three and a half hours on the beach with Kelly without breaking any of her damned rules. Despite the fact that her bathing suit was a chlorine-faded one-piece, she *did* look good enough to eat. And watching her rub sunblock onto her long, slender legs…

God, he was in trouble here.

Jax couldn't wait until tomorrow, until he could break her rules again. What was that expression? Go big or stay home. Maybe tomorrow he'd break those rules in a big way. Like by crawling into bed with her in the morning.

Inwardly he laughed, imagining the expression on her face.

On the other hand, he didn't want to push so far that she'd go running back to Boston.

How was he going to live through the rest of tonight? How could he continue to sit here and pretend that Kelly didn't own his heart?

Worst of all, how was he going to tell her the truth about Jayne Tyler? He had to tell her. Tonight.

As the busboys cleared the table, as the waitress brought out mugs of coffee, Jax was silent, staring out at the darkness that had fallen over the water. How was Kelly going to react to his news?

She was probably going to be angry, upset maybe, annoyed at the very least. She might think that he had purposely tricked her, purposely lied to her.

Jax considered waiting until they got home to tell her, but figured maybe if he told her in public, here at the restaurant, she might not yell at him quite as loudly.

She met his eyes as she took a sip of her coffee.

"You're so quiet," she said. "What are you thinking about?"

This was it. The perfect opportunity. "I have a secret I've got to tell you."

Kelly stopped drinking and slowly put her mug down. He could tell that she was thinking carefully, trying to decide what her response should be. He didn't give her time to say anything.

"I haven't told anyone," he said. "Ever. Not in the three years since—well, it's been four, really."

Kelly watched him as the light from the lantern on the table flickered across his face and reflected the shiny gold of his hair. What kind of secret could it possibly be? She was curious and a little worried. He looked so serious, so solemn.

"Well, Stefanie knows," T. said, then smiled. "She'd have to know. I mean, of course she knows."

Kelly hadn't said a word. She just sat there, watching him, thc soft light playing across her beautiful face. Her eyes were dark and almost colorless in the dimness, and her hair curled slightly in the damp ocean air.

"I'm not sure I really want to know what this secret is," she said finally. "But I'm dying of curiosity. What'd ya do, T.? Kill somebody? Rob a bank? Run for office? Have an illegitimate child? What?"

T. Jackson laughed. He was fooling with the container that held little packs of sugar for coffee, and the salt and pepper shakers that were in the center of the table. His large, strong fingers toyed with them nervously.

Nervously. If T. was so nervous that it showed, if he was *that* nervous about telling her whatever this secret was, then it must be serious. Kelly swallowed. Was it his health? Was he sick? She remembered how terrible he'd looked at Kevin's wedding. That was just about four years ago, wasn't it?

Even though she knew she shouldn't touch him, Kelly reached across the table and took T.'s hand, lacing her fingers with his. He looked up at her, his eyes momentarily opened wide in surprise. For that one instant, he was stripped of all his pretense of ease and his self-assuredness. His face looked younger, more vulnerable.

This was the same T. Jackson she'd had a glimpse of the night she'd gone to his hotel room with him. She'd seen that same look in his eyes the second time he'd made love to her that night. She hadn't thought they'd be able to surpass their first explosive joining, but T. had made love to her again so slowly, so unhurriedly, so sensually, the memory could still leave her feeling weak. And as she had gazed up into his eyes, as he had touched her, caressed her, filled her, it had been as if he let her see into his soul.

Now he looked down at her hand intertwined with his and smiled.

"Tell me," she said, squeezing his hand gently.

Jax looked into the depths of Kelly's eyes, carefully hiding the surge of triumph that he felt. She cared about him enough to take his hand. She cared about him enough to worry that this secret was something serious. She cared—

Great. Inwardly he shook his head with disgust as the triumphant feeling vanished as quickly as it came. She had cared enough to break one of her rules—no touching—and that was a step forward, that was real progress in his fight to win her back, but as soon as he told her the truth, she was going to take about twenty-five giant steps back. Toward Boston, no doubt.

"Kel." He wondered if there was some easier way to tell her this. "I'm really..."

She was waiting.

Crap. "No, it's nothing."

"T.!" She let go of his hand, her eyes lit with exasperation.

Now that she wasn't touching him, it was easier. He didn't have to be afraid she would release his hand when he told her, because she already had.

"You're really *what?*" she asked, her steady gaze giving him no quarter.

"Whom." He smiled weakly. "It's not a what, it's a whom."

She blinked. Then laughed. Then pinned him to the seat with a look of disbelief. "Don't tell me. Don't you dare say this is some kind of secret identity or alter ego thing."

"Yes," T. said, and Kelly knew that he wasn't kidding by the amount of guilt she could see in his eyes. "That's it exactly."

Kelly pushed her coffee away, reaching instead for the half-full glass of white wine that she hadn't finished with her dinner. She took a calming sip and slowly put the long-stemmed glass back down. For several long moments she studied the light from the lantern as it shone through the wine, before she looked back at T.

"Are you trying to tell me that you're, like... *Bat*man?" she said, one eyebrow raised.

Jax laughed. "Close." He braced himself. "I'm Jayne Tyler."

She stared at him in shock. Gee, maybe a superhero would've gone over better, Jax thought.

"You're... *what?*"

"Whom," he said gently. "Jayne. Tyler. She may have my sister's face on the book covers, but the words are all mine."

He looked down at his mug of coffee, resisting the urge to shut his eyes tightly against the accusations he was so sure were going to follow.

But Kelly didn't make any accusations. She laughed.

Jax looked up at her.

"You're not kidding, are you?" She was smiling at him.

Wordlessly he shook his head no.

"I can't believe it." She laughed again. "I mean, I *do* believe it, and *wow!* I'm so proud of you, T. You're a writer, a *real* writer, an author. My God, Jayne Tyler is so good. I mean, *you're* so good! Where did you learn to write like that?"

She was still smiling at him, her eyes sparkling with enthusiasm. She wasn't angry. She was...*proud* of him? Jax fought the urge to lean across the table and kiss her.

"You're not mad at me?" he asked.

Kelly shook her head. "No," she said. "Well, maybe a little disappointed that you didn't trust me enough to tell me before this."

"I haven't seen an awful lot of you since I started writing," Jax pointed out. "This is the first time we've really had a chance to talk."

"Uh-oh." Sudden realization dawned. "This means I'm going to be working with *you* all summer, huh?"

*Surrender.* The word came immediately to mind as Kelly looked into the stormy gray-green of T.'s eyes. She'd only spent half a day with him, and already she was considering giving in. She could picture them working together during the day, taking breaks out in the sun on the beach, sharing a quiet, candlelit dinner like this every night and then going home to share T.'s bed. She could picture him kissing her. On the beach, in his office, in the car on the way home from dinner... With very little effort, she could picture them making love.

Kelly swallowed. There was a time not so very long ago when a summer like that would've been a dream come true. She had loved T. so much back then. She would have given herself to him for the summer, believing that the summer would last forever. But if there was one thing the past had taught her, it was that nothing lasted forever.

"Is the thought of working with me so terrible?" T. asked softly.

"No," she said, meeting his eyes. It wasn't. And that's what alarmed her. God help her. If she was with him all the time, she might actually start to believe him when he said that he loved her, that he wanted to marry her. And if she started to believe him, God knows she'd only end up hurt.

Kelly said good-night to T. out in the hall, leaving him standing there as she went into her room and carefully locked the door behind her.

*Surrender.*

Instead, she kicked off her shoes, went into her bathroom and brushed her teeth. She pulled down the shades and stepped out of her dress, gently rubbing lotion onto her sunburned skin. The big T-shirt she slept in was still in her suitcase, so she rummaged for it, then put it on, wincing as it hit her shoulders.

When they got home from dinner, T. had found a note from Stefanie on the kitchen table. She had left on a cruise to Alaska with Emilio. She wouldn't be back until the first week of August.

Kelly and T. Jackson were alone in this big house. It smelled like a setup, but Jackson swore he knew nothing about Stef's plans.

Right.

As she went to pull the white spread off the big bed, she saw an envelope resting on one of the pillows. Curious, she picked it up. The flap wasn't sealed, and she pulled out a single sheet of heavy bond paper and unfolded it.

It was a letter. From T. From his computer's laser printer.

Dear Kelly,

If it were up to me, I'd be in there with you right now. Instead I'm sitting in my office, staring out the window at the night, burning for your touch.

I want you.

I want to feel your lips on mine, your body against me. I want to entangle myself with you, bury myself, lose myself in you.

It is such heaven and such hell having you close enough to touch—

But we're playing by your rules.

So I'm not going to speak the words that are always on the tip of my tongue and constantly tell you how much I love you. I'm not going to show you how much by holding you in my arms and making love to you, the way I want to.

But I am going to write down the words I long to say, hoping that you'll read them, giving me at least a fighting chance to win back your heart.

He had signed it with his bold handwriting. *''I love you. Love, T.''*

Kelly carefully folded the letter and put it back into the envelope. She turned off the light but lay awake for a long time before finally falling asleep.

# *Chapter 12*

When Kelly got back from her morning run on the beach, T. Jackson wasn't in the house. On her way into the kitchen, she glanced out the window and saw that his sports car was gone from the driveway.

There was an envelope with her name on it on the kitchen table and, drinking directly from a half full bottle of seltzer that she'd pulled from the refrigerator, she opened it.

Another of T.'s letters. Love letters, she guessed she could call them. Since she'd arrived over a week ago, he'd left at least a dozen of them around for her to read. She hadn't even acknowledged them, and *he* certainly didn't bring up the subject.

It was as if he were two very different people. One was the good old friend who was helping her rewrite her novel, helping her straighten out the problems with her hero's motivation. The other was this ardent lover who had no shame when it came to writing his desires and passions, all of which involved her.

In this latest note, he described in extremely specific detail just how he wanted to kiss her when he returned home from the errands he was on.

Kelly felt her pulse increase as she read his words. It was scary to know that he was going to kiss her sometime today or tonight. Part of her was really looking forward to that kiss, and knowing *that* scared her even more.

As T. had promised that very first day, he broke all of her rules once a day, and only once a day. He would kiss her, tell her he loved her, ask her to marry him. She was never sure just when during the day that romantic attack was going to come. Several times it had happened first thing in the morning, but other days he had waited until afternoon or even after dinner. As a result, she was kept on edge almost all the time. And even after he kissed her, she found herself anticipating the next day's onslaught.

She also looked forward to his letters. And as much as she realized he was using them to break down her resolve not to get involved with him, she couldn't stop herself from reading them, sometimes over and over again.

Kelly took this latest letter back onto the deck with her and sat down on the steps as she finished the seltzer. Wow, it was going to be another megahot day. She wasn't even going to bother to shower. At least not before she put on her bathing suit and went into the bay for a swim.

She leaned her head back against the banister, feeling the hot sun on her face. She needed to put more sunblock on, or her fair skin was going to burn again.

She'd probably already sweated off the stuff she'd applied earlier this morning.

"Hey."

Kelly jumped, opening her eyes and turning to see T. Jackson standing by the sliding glass doors into the living room.

"Morning," he said. He already had on his neon-green bathing suit with an Amnesty International T-shirt on top. Don't Discount The Power Of The Written Word his shirt proclaimed in large block print. Write A Letter, Save A Life. Kelly glanced down at the letter she still held in her hands. The power of the written word, indeed.

"I picked up some groceries." T. looked at her over the top of his sunglasses. "Wanna help me unload the car?"

Kelly hauled herself to her feet. "Sure."

He stepped back to let her go through the door first, and she glanced up nervously as she passed within inches of him. But his face was relaxed, he was smiling. She couldn't see his eyes through the dark lenses of his sunglasses.

"How far did you run?" he asked.

"About three miles." She took a detour to put the empty seltzer bottle and the letter down on the kitchen counter. God, she wished he would just kiss her and get it over with. "I've got to start getting up earlier," she added. "It's getting too hot, even first thing in the morning. As soon as we're done here, I'm going for a swim."

Jackson pushed open the screen door and went out onto the driveway, where his car was parked.

The trunk was open wide and filled with cloth grocery bags. T. was environmentally correct. Somehow the realization didn't surprise her.

"I got you a present," he said.

"Fudge ripple ice cream?" Kelly lifted two of the bags out of the car and lugged them back toward the kitchen.

"I thought you outgrew that when you were fifteen." Jax carried two bags in each hand.

"Yeah, well, I've regressed." She tried to ignore the way the muscles in his arms and shoulders flexed as he almost effortlessly lifted the weight of all four bags up onto the kitchen table.

With an easy underhanded throw, he tossed her a small bag that bore the label of a local fashion boutique. "I bought you a new bathing suit."

Kelly looked from the bag she had caught to Jackson and back to the bag. "If it fits in this little bag, something tells me I'm not going to be eating much fudge ripple ice cream in the near future."

When she looked up again, T. was standing directly in front of her, and she knew from the look in his eyes that he was going to kiss her.

"Oh, T., yuck, I'm all sweaty." She tried to sidle away from him along the edge of the kitchen counter.

But he put his hands against the countertop, one on either side of her, penning her in. "I want to marry you, remember? For richer or poorer, for better or for worse... I don't think there's an exception for sweaty." With one finger, he caught a bead of perspiration that was dripping down past her ear. "Actually, it's kind of a turn-on."

Leaning forward, he smiled into her eyes and then he kissed her.

The bag with the bathing suit dropped to the floor

as Kelly was surrounded by T. Jackson. His fingers left trails of fire where he touched her, his mouth met hers with a blaze of heat.

"Marry me, Kelly." His breath was hot as he whispered into her ear.

But she pulled free of his arms, and this time he let her get away. "No. I'm sorry." It was the same answer she'd given him every day since she'd arrived.

And just like every day, it didn't faze him. Cheerfully he bent down and picked up the bag she'd dropped and handed it to her. With a smile, he went back to the car for another load of shopping bags.

How could he do it? Every day she wondered how he could kiss her like that one minute, then act as if everything were completely platonic the next. Kelly always felt as if she needed a few hours to recover.

She waited for her pulse to return to near normal, then slowly opened the bag. A bikini. Black and very tiny, although allegedly it *was* her size. She held it up, looking at it skeptically.

T. came back into the kitchen carrying the last of the groceries. "I figured you needed a new bathing suit," he said as he started to unload the groceries. He looked at her and smiled. "That one-piece you have is on the verge of becoming transparent when it's wet. Do you know they actually make bathing suits these days designed to do that?"

Kelly stuffed the bikini back into the bag. "You don't *really* expect me to believe you, do you?"

"Scout's honor. They were totally see-through. I saw 'em in a catalog. It was this amazing catalog with—"

"I meant about my bathing suit," she interrupted. "It's not *that* old."

He looked up from loading liter bottles of seltzer into the refrigerator. ''Hey, *I'm* not going to complain if you want to wear a see-through bathing suit, Kel. I just thought you might want to be warned. If you don't believe me, try it on and step into the shower. You'll see.''

Jax found Kelly in the office, hard at work. The windows were open wide and all the fans in the room were on and it was still hot.

''I thought you were going for a swim,'' he said.

She didn't look up from her computer. ''I changed my mind and took a shower instead.''

He grinned. ''You tried on your old bathing suit, and you found out that I was right.''

''All right. Fine.'' Kelly turned around and sighed. ''Go ahead and say it.''

''Say what?''

''I told you so.''

But he didn't say anything. He just looked at her. Kelly quickly turned around. Damn. She knew she shouldn't wear this halter top, but even the thought of putting on a T-shirt on a day this hot was too unbearable.

''I'm almost done with these revisions,'' she announced, making her voice as businesslike as possible. ''Actually, I *am* done, I'm just inputting the changes. It shouldn't take more than an hour or two.''

''Good,'' Jax said. ''I haven't worked on my novel all week. That'll give me some time to touch base with my characters. After lunch we can work on fixing up your love scenes.''

Kelly cringed. ''Do we have to?''

"Well, no. We don't *have* to. But you'll never sell your book if we don't."

"I guess when you put it that way..."

Jax sat at his computer, waiting the few seconds it took his word processing program to boot up. He popped in his Jared disk and quickly read through the last chapter that he'd written.

Jared was out in California, in Los Angeles. He'd bought himself a horse, a big black stallion, and he was riding out toward the ranch Carrie and her husband, Harlan, had bought nearly three years ago. He'd just found out that Harlan had died some months ago from a fever.

Jax started to write.

> As Jared rode the trail, it was clear the entire area was having one hell of a drought. Dust rose up from the ground, covering his dark suit, making him cough. He tied his handkerchief around his mouth and nose, and pushed the wide brim of his hat down a little lower.

"Yo, so that's Kelly, huh?" Jared said. "Lord, will you look at those *legs!* Oh, baby!"

"Shut up," Jax muttered.

"I didn't say anything," Kelly said.

Jared laughed, his dark eyes sparkling with amusement. "This is great. Finally I can get the last word in. If you talk to me, Kelly's gonna think you're bonkers. And she'll be right. Man, she's beautiful. No wonder you've been so distracted. She's *hot.* I bet you're dying to kiss those shoulders—"

Jax scowled and started writing again.

He saw the dust kicked up by the running horses before he heard the familiar sound of their hooves on the hard-packed ground. Taking his rifle from the back of his saddle, he stuck the heels of his boots into his stallion's sides. The beast reared up on his hind legs, then launched like a Chinese rocket.

Jared saw sunlight reflecting off the barrels of at least four guns as he glanced over his shoulder. Four horses, four riders, four guns. Damned if he knew what they wanted. Damned if he was going to find out.

They fired their first shot at him when he was within eyesight of the gate of the Double K ranch. Carrie's ranch. The bullet zinged just over his head.

Jared took the turn in to the Double K at a dangerous speed, the big horse scrambling for a foothold in the loose dirt.

"There better be a good reason for this," Jared shouted. "If this is just some kind of stupid punishment, I'm going to be very, very annoyed."

"There's a good reason for everything I do," Jax muttered.

"Did you say something?" Kelly asked.

Jax looked up, meeting her inquisitive gaze. "Just arguing with my main character."

"Ah." She turned back to her own computer.

"I can't *believe* you actually told her," Jared said.

"She took that rather well," Jax murmured.

Kelly laughed. "T., do you do this all the time?"

"Do what?"

"Talk to yourself?"

"Hah! See, now she thinks you're nuts," Jared said.

"Do you think I'm nuts?" Jax asked Kelly.

"Are you really having a conversation with your main character?" she countered.

"I'm afraid so," he admitted. "Right now he's on the back of a galloping horse, with four men chasing and shooting at him. He's not very happy with me."

"I don't blame him. If you put me in that situation, I'd argue with you, too." Kelly laughed. "Why don't you stop arguing and just write the end of the scene, get him out of there?"

"Did you hear that?" Jax said to Jared. "Stop arguing."

The stallion was still running like a demon out of hell as he approached the ranch house and the barn. With his rifle in his hand, Jared tried to rein in the big horse, even as he turned to double-check that the four gunmen hadn't followed him this far.

A shot rang out, and Jared felt a tug of pain in his right arm. The rifle clattered onto the dry ground. Damn, he was bleeding and his arm hurt like the devil. He turned, trying to figure out where that gun had been fired from when a clear voice said, "Keep your hands up where I can see them."

Jared nudged his horse, who obligingly turned to face the owner of both the voice and the gun. With his left hand, he swept his hat off of his head.

"Hello, Carrie," he said.

Jax saved the job, cleared the screen, stood and stretched.

"I'm going to get a cup of coffee," he said. "You want something?"

"Are you talking to me or your imaginary friend?" Kelly asked.

"Very funny," Jax said.

"How'd you end that scene?" she asked.

"It was an obvious solution. I had the heroine shoot the hero."

Kelly laughed. "Did it shut him up?"

"Not a chance."

Kelly sat out on the deck, eating a salad for lunch. She heard the screen on the sliding door open and close, heard Jackson's bare feet as he approached. The heavy wooden deck chair groaned slightly under his weight as he sat down, and there was a soft hiss of escaping carbonation as he opened a can of soda.

She glanced at him, and he smiled at her from behind his sunglasses. He'd taken off his T-shirt, and as she tried not to watch, he rubbed sunscreen onto his broad shoulders.

"You know, we can work out here this afternoon," he said. "You're not really ready to start rewriting. We have to talk about the scene first, and we can just as easily do that out here as inside."

Kelly closed her eyes. She was going to sit here and talk about rewriting the love scenes in her book with this man who clearly wanted to have a physical relationship with her. Add into the confusion the fact that she and T. *had* made love not so many weeks ago, and it had been the best sex she'd ever had in her life. To top it all off, her hormones wanted more, particularly when T. sat around half-naked the way he was, like some bronzed, blond sun god.

Kelly sighed. ''All right. Start by telling me what I did wrong.''

''For one thing,'' Jax said, ''the scene's too short. It's over too soon. Essentially you've been building up to this scene, you've been building up to your characters making love since page one. Your readers are going to feel disappointed if you don't give 'em their money's worth.''

Kelly put her salad bowl down on the deck and picked up T.'s soda can. Caffeine-free cola. Good, she didn't think she could stand a jolt of caffeine right now. ''Can I have a sip?''

He nodded, still watching her.

She took a long drink of the sweet liquid. It wasn't as cool as she'd expected. The hot sun had already warmed the aluminum can.

''So, okay.'' She felt a trickle of perspiration drip between her breasts as she handed the soda can back to T. ''How many more pages am I going to have to write?''

''It's not a matter of pages,'' T. said. ''I've read great love scenes that were only one page long. I've also read at least one that was twenty-two pages—''

Kelly stared at him. ''Twenty-*two?* Pages? Of sex?'' She laughed. ''I don't think my thesaurus has that many synonyms for the word *passionately.*''

''Relax. I'm not telling you to write twenty-two pages. Five or six should be fine—''

''Five or *six?* I ran out of things to describe after two paragraphs.'' The sun was beating down on her. She could feel herself starting to burn. ''Can I use some of your lotion?''

T. sat up, his muscles rippling. "Feelings, Kel."

She looked at him. "What?"

He dragged his chair closer to hers, sitting on the edge of it, his elbows resting on his knees. "It's not enough simply to describe who's on top, and who's kissing whom and where."

Kelly felt her cheeks getting warm.

"You should use the actual physical descriptions of the sex to reveal more about your characters," T. Jackson continued. "Do they take it slowly, take their time, or do they tear each other's clothes off? How they do it, particularly the first time, can say a lot about them."

Kelly looked up at T., remembering how they had made love that first time in his hotel room. Oh, boy, that had been explosive.

He looked at her for a moment over the top of his sunglasses, and she could tell from his eyes that he was thinking about that night, too. What did that night reveal about her own character? Kelly wondered. What did it say about the intensity of her feelings for him, that she was willing to make love to him so wildly, abandoning all conventions, ignoring all proprieties?

Not feelings, she corrected herself quickly. What she had with T. had nothing to do with feelings. It was all attraction. All good old-fashioned lust.

Are you sure? that voice in her head asked.

"But that physical description shouldn't be your main focus," T. said as he handed her the bottle of suntan lotion. He took off his sunglasses and gently set them down on the deck next to his can of soda.

Kelly put some lotion into her hand and carefully applied it to her face as he stood.

"You've got to get inside your characters' heads," he said as he walked behind her deck chair.

She turned, surprised, to look back at him as he pushed the big wooden chairback up slightly, releasing the frame from the bar that held it in place.

He smiled at her as he lowered her chair into a more reclined position. "You've got to tell the reader exactly what the characters are feeling."

He leaned over the back of the chair and gently took the bottle of suntan lotion from Kelly's hand. He squeezed some out onto his palm. "And I'm not just talking about physical sensations," he added, looking down at her with a small smile, "although they're good, too."

She pulled her gaze away from him and sat up with her arms tightly hugging her knees. She felt him sit down on the edge of her chair, slightly behind her, and she looked back at him, startled.

He began rubbing the suntan lotion onto the top of her shoulders and her bare back, and she inhaled sharply. The lotion was cool against her hot skin, but it was the touch of his hands that sent chills down her spine.

"It's how your character feels about the person who's touching her that's important," T. continued softly. She could feel his warm breath against her ear as he rubbed a generous amount of lotion down her arm. "Think about it. Your character could get touched exactly the same way by a friend and then by a lover. It could be a handshake, or an embrace, or maybe...maybe someone—a friend, or a lover—is putting suntan lotion on her back."

T. stopped to squeeze more lotion out onto his hand. Kelly turned toward him. "T.—"

"Relax," he said. "And pay attention. Maybe you'll learn something."

He reached behind her and began rubbing the lotion onto her other shoulder. Right, thought Kelly. If she was going to learn anything from this, it was that she liked T. Jackson's touch way too much. And she already knew that.

"So what's the difference?" T. said as if he hadn't been interrupted, as cool and collected as if he were giving a lecture from behind a podium instead of working the lotion down her other arm. "It's in the way your character feels for the person she's being touched by. It's her emotion that can make a simple, innocent caress—" he ran his fingers lightly back up her arm "—outrageously erotic."

Kelly closed her eyes, feeling her insides turn to jelly. No, she did *not* love this man, she told herself. It was just the sun, the heat, making her light-headed.

"The same theory applies in a love scene when the hero, the man your character loves, undresses her." With one deft pull, T. untied the top knot of her halter.

"T.!" Kelly caught the fabric before it fell forward, modestly holding it up against her breasts.

"I didn't want to get any lotion on your top," he explained as she felt his hands on the back of her neck. Wow, that felt good. She closed her eyes again, swallowing her words of protest.

"Your character would have a very different reaction if a stranger walked up and started undressing her," T. continued. "But there's no embarrassment with a lover, only—" his voice lowered slightly "—anticipation." His hand slipped around to her neck, her throat, as he rubbed lotion into her hot skin. He spread the cool, sweet-smelling cream down, lower, covering her collarbone and the tops of her breasts.

Jackson could feel Kelly's heartbeat underneath his hand. He could feel the rapid rise and fall of her chest. Even beneath the loose folds of the fabric that covered her full breasts, he could see the hard buds of her nipples. He was dying to touch all of her, to kiss her, suckle her. This was torture. He smiled wryly. But it was the best kind of torture he'd ever experienced.

He stood, and her eyes opened as he gently pressed her shoulders back against the lounge chair. Nudging her hips over slightly, he now sat facing her. She watched, wide-eyed, as he spread suntan lotion onto her stomach, onto the wide strip of soft skin that was between her halter and the waistband of her shorts.

Kelly stared up into T. Jackson's eyes. How could he be so cool and calm when she was about to have a heart attack? She'd been long reduced to a puddle of desire, and he was sitting there smiling at her as if they were discussing the weather.

She saw it then. One lone bead of perspiration traveling down the side of T.'s face, next to his ear. He *was* rattled. He was just very, very good at hiding it.

But it was as if somehow he knew he'd given himself away. His eyes flooded with heat as he slid the tips of his fingers down below the loose waistband of her shorts. Kelly stopped breathing as his gaze locked with hers. He leaned forward, as if he was going to kiss her, closer, closer, until his mouth was just a whisper away from her lips.

''Foreplay,'' he whispered, his breath warm and sweet against her face. ''When you write a good love scene, you've got to have plenty of foreplay. It's all part of the anticipation.''

He straightened up without kissing her, but his eyes held hers as he said, ''And if you do it right, most of the love scene can take place while your characters still have their clothes on.''

He turned slightly then and squeezed a long, white line of suntan lotion first on one of her legs and then the other, from the tops of her thighs all the way down to her instep. Starting at her feet, he used both hands to rub the lotion into her skin.

His hands moved up her leg at a leisurely, deliberate pace. It was shockingly sensuous, and unbelievably delicious. Kelly opened her mouth but couldn't find the words to stop him. Truth was, she didn't *want* to stop him.

''If you do it right—'' T.'s voice was low now, like a caress ''—one look, or a simple touch between lovers, can be as intimate as making love. But you've got to reveal what your characters are feeling.''

His eyes were smoky gray-green as he looked at her, and now there was no hiding the sheen of perspiration on his forehead and upper lip. Kelly could see his pulse beating hard in his neck. His face held undisguised hunger as his fingers lingered on the soft skin on the inside of her thigh. The lotion had been long since rubbed in, but still he didn't pull his hands away.

''Imagine,'' he said, his voice husky, ''if you loved me.''

This was it. He was going to kiss her. And then they were going to make love, and she wasn't going to protest. She wasn't going to say one word. She couldn't. Not even if her life had depended on it.

But he didn't kiss her.

Instead, he reached for her hand, and taking it, he

brushed her palm lightly with his thumb, drawing circles on the sensitive skin, round and round. ''Imagine how you would feel,'' he whispered. ''Imagine the *emotions* you'd feel just from a simple touch.''

Kelly stared up at Jax. Emotions. Imagine the emotions. She must have one heck of an imagination, because those imaginary emotions were damn near bowling her over.

He put the bottle of suntan lotion into her hand. ''That's what it's really about. Love and emotion. Try rewriting your scene, focusing on what your characters are feeling in their hearts. You'll write a lot more than two paragraphs. I can guarantee it.''

He stood, put his sunglasses on and walked calmly down the steps, heading for the cool water of the bay.

Kelly watched him until he was out of sight.

*Imagine if you loved me.*

She didn't have to imagine. She just had to remember.

And that wasn't very hard to do at all.

# *Chapter 13*

The morning dawned hazy and humid.

After spending the evening writing and rewriting the first love scene in her book, Kelly had had a restless sleep. The setting sun had lowered the record high temperatures by only a few degrees, and the night had been almost impossibly hot.

Never mind the fact that she couldn't stop thinking about the way T. Jackson's hands had felt as he had spread suntan lotion on her legs.

She'd skip her run this morning, take a nice, cool swim instead.

It was a good plan, until she got onto the beach and found T. already sitting there.

"Good morning," he greeted her.

"What are you doing up so early?" she asked suspiciously.

T. shrugged. "Too hot to sleep." He was wearing the same neon-green bathing suit he'd had on yesterday. His hair was wet, and water beaded on his muscular body. He'd already been in for a swim.

It was a new day, Kelly realized, looking down at him. It was a new day, and sometime today he was going to kiss her. Her stomach knotted in anticipation.

As Jax watched, Kelly put her towel down on the sand chair next to his and kicked off her sandals. With one big yank, she pulled her T-shirt over her head.

She was wearing the black bikini. God, she looked fabulous. He grinned his appreciation, but she ignored him.

Jax followed her down to the edge of the ocean, watching as she walked directly into the water until it covered all but her shoulders. He crash-dived in, surfacing near her. Shaking his wet hair out of his face, he moved closer.

"Couldn't you at least have picked out a bathing suit that had more *suit* to it?" she asked, backing away.

"But you look so good in black," T. said as innocently as possible as he moved toward her.

"Where's the black?" Kelly asked. She kept backing away, heading for the beach, exposing more and more of the bathing suit in question to the open air. "When I looked in the mirror, all I could see was skin."

"You look good naked, too. The combination is...very nice."

The water was only up to her waist now, and his eyes swept over her body. Here it comes. Kelly braced herself. He was surely going to kiss her now. But T. just smiled and dove back out into the deeper water.

She had been so positive he was going to kiss her, *so* sure. She had actually started feeling relieved that today's waiting was over. But then he went and didn't do it, damn him. He was driving her crazy, and she couldn't stand the uncertainty another minute longer. "Tyrone Jackson, get your butt back here."

"Uh-oh," he said as he swam back toward her. "What'd I do now?"

"Kiss me. Will you just kiss me, damn it, and get it over with?"

He stood up then, and water fell off his body in a sheet. Two big steps brought him right to her side, close enough to put his arms around her, close enough for her to see that the swirl of color in his eyes matched the sunlit ocean almost exactly. She swallowed and looked away, unable to hold the intensity of his gaze.

"Do you want me to?" he asked softly.

"No!" T. started to turn away. If he didn't kiss her now, she'd spend the entire day on edge— "Yes, okay? *Yes!*"

He looked at her and it wasn't the sizzling look of desire she had expected. Instead, he smiled rather wistfully. But he still didn't kiss her.

"Please, T.," she whispered.

He touched her then, one hand lightly brushing her hair back from her face, his eyes soft. "Aw, Kel," he breathed. "I didn't want to use up today's kiss right now, but you know I can't refuse you anything."

He leaned forward and his lips brushed against hers, gently at first, then with increasing pressure.

Kelly felt his arms go around her, his hands on her bare back, pressing her against him. It was as if the sensation of their two wet, nearly naked bodies was too much for Jackson, because he didn't end the kiss when she expected him to. He just kept kissing her, harder, deeper now. Of course, maybe it had something to do with the fact that her arms were up around his neck, and that she was kissing him as hungrily as he was kissing her.

She wanted him. She couldn't deny it any longer. She was ready to surrender, ready to stop pretending that she didn't lie awake all night, wishing that she were in T.'s bed.

"Kelly, I love you so much," T. said, kissing her face. "I need you."

She could feel his heart pounding, hear the raggedness of each breath as his mouth found hers again.

He pulled her out with him, deeper, and under the private cover of the water, he touched her, cupping the softness of her breasts, caressing, stroking. Kissing her hard, harder, he pressed against her. There was no mistaking what he wanted.

And, quite clearly, Kelly knew that making love with T. Jackson was what she wanted, too.

But suddenly he tore himself away, backing off about five feet. He just stood there, breathing hard and looking at her. His eyes seemed luminous, and Kelly realized it was unshed tears that made them shine.

Before she could say a word, he turned and dove into the water. He surfaced far down the beach and kept swimming, hard, away from her.

"T., come back," Kelly whispered, but there was no way on earth he could have heard.

By dinnertime Kelly convinced herself that her moment of surrender when T. had kissed her in the water had been merely that. A moment.

She had been temporarily insane, momentarily crazed. Hadn't she?

Of course, the fact that T. Jackson hadn't returned from the beach until she was in the shower helped her regain her misplaced sanity. By the time she was done, he had vanished, taking his car with him. He hadn't left a note saying where he'd gone and when he'd be back.

It was definitely much easier to convince herself that she didn't want him when he wasn't around.

She worked all day, pretending she wasn't wondering where he was as she rewrote that damned love scene.

It wasn't until six o'clock, when the sun was sinking in the sky, that Jackson appeared.

"How's it going?" He set cartons of Chinese food on the big conference table, along with several plates he'd brought from the kitchen.

He was still wearing his green bathing suit, though it had long since dried. His hair was a mess, but it only made him look even more charming than usual.

As Kelly met his eyes, she knew immediately that everything she'd been trying to tell herself about T. Jackson all afternoon had been a load of hogwash. If he as much as said a word, she'd throw herself into his arms.

"You getting that scene rewritten?" He opened a carton of steaming brown rice.

"I'm trying." Kelly had to clear her throat before the words came out.

"Want me to read what you've got?"

"I don't think so."

"You've got to let me read it sooner or later." T. flashed her a low-watt smile.

She stood and stretched, then sat down across from him at the table. "Later. Much later." She reached to open the third carton. It was unidentifiable, but it smelled great. Wow, she hadn't realized how hungry she was. She'd worked straight through lunch.

T. handed her a pair of paper-wrapped chopsticks, and they ate in silence.

Finally he cleared his throat. "Kel, I want to apologize for this morning."

She glanced at him, and his eyes were a very serious shade of green. But he couldn't hold her gaze, and he looked away.

"I went too far," he said quietly. "I'm sorry and I—"

"T.—"

"Please, let me finish, okay?"

He looked up at her, and she nodded slowly.

"I don't seem to have very much control when it comes to you. I'm afraid—" He cleared his throat again. "I'm afraid I'm not going to hear you or understand you when you tell me to stop, and I can't deal with the thought that I might—" He shook his head and took a deep breath. "Anyway, you don't have to worry, I'm not going to kiss you again."

It was then that Kelly knew with absolute certainty that she wanted him to kiss her again. Wanted? Hell, she *needed* him to kiss her.

She stood. "Let me get this straight. You're not going to kiss me again, because you don't want to make love to me."

Jax shook his head, laughing with frustration. "That's the problem. I *do* want to make love to you." He watched as she walked around the table and sat down in the chair next to his. "Desperately." He pushed his half-eaten dinner away from him. "You've read my letters, Kelly. You know how I feel. I love you. I'm just afraid—''

''That when I say no, you won't be able to stop,'' Kelly finished for him. ''The message won't get through.''

''Yeah.'' Jax rubbed his forehead as if he had a headache. He stood suddenly. ''I need a beer. You want a beer?''

She stood, too. ''T., wait.''

Even with the windows open wide and the salty ocean breeze blowing into the room, Jax could smell Kelly's sweet scent. She was standing much too close. He tried to take a step backward, but bumped into the table. She moved even closer.

''Watch my mouth,'' Kelly said. ''And listen really carefully.''

''Kel—''

''Come on, T.,'' she said. ''Watch and listen.''

Jax couldn't find any answers in her eyes, so he dropped his gaze to her soft lips.

''Are you listening?'' she asked, and he nodded.

Her lips curved upward into an enchanting smile, and then she said, quite clearly, ''No.''

Jax closed his eyes. Torture. She was torturing him.

''You have any trouble understanding that?''

Eyes still closed, he shook his head. ''Of course not. But these are hardly the same conditions that—''

''Okay, then, kiss me,'' Kelly ordered him.

He opened his eyes. ''What?''

She smiled at him again. ''Put your arms around me and kiss me,'' she repeated. ''Gee, I didn't think I'd have to ask you *twice*.''

''Kel—''

‘‘Come on, Tyrone. *Kiss* me. I can’t prove my point until you do.’’

‘‘And which point is it that you’re trying to prove?’’

Kelly laughed. ‘‘Kiss me and you’ll find out.’’

Forget torture. She was trying to kill him. ‘‘I’m not sure this is such a good idea.’’ He looked down at her mouth, and it was his undoing. She was moistening her lips with the tip of her tongue, and, God, he *had* to kiss her.

She was standing close, but not close enough, and as his mouth went down to meet hers, he pulled her in toward him. Just as his lips brushed hers, she reached up and, pressing the palms of her hands against his chest, she pushed herself back, away from him.

He let go of her instantly.

Kelly laughed. ‘‘You seemed to understand that, too.’’

Jax closed his eyes and pressed the heel of his hand against the bridge of his nose. This was going to be one *hell* of a headache when it finally arrived. If he lived that long. When he opened his eyes, Kelly was still standing directly in front of him, smiling up at him.

‘‘Understand what?’’ he asked wearily.

She reached out and pushed against his chest with the palm of her hand again. ‘‘That,’’ she said. ‘‘You know what it means when I do that, right?’’

‘‘Yeah. It means stop, don’t, no.’’

‘‘Well, there you have it. Two perfectly understandable ways to say no—one verbal, one not.’’

She looked so pleased with herself. ‘‘I hate to break it to you,’’ he said, ‘‘but if you’ve just made your point, you lost me somewhere.’’

"Well, actually, no," she told him. "I haven't made my point yet. In order for me to do that, you have to kiss me again."

Jax sat down tiredly on top of the table. "Kel—"

They were nearly the same height now, and Kelly stepped in between his legs and draped her arms around his neck. "I suppose *I* could always kiss *you.*" Leaning forward slightly, she did.

Her lips were soft, and tasted so sweet. She pulled back slightly, looking into his eyes and smiling before she kissed him again.

Jax opened his mouth under the gentle pressure from her tongue. She was kissing him. Kelly was kissing *him.* He couldn't decide whether to laugh or cry, so he did neither. Instead, he put his arms around her, crushing her to him, devouring the sweetness of her mouth with his own.

Kelly laughed, arching her head back as he rained kisses down her neck. "The reason you didn't hear me say no this morning was because I didn't say it. And if you listen very closely, you still won't hear me say no."

Jax couldn't breathe. "And how about if I pick you up and carry you into my bedroom?" he asked. "Will you still not say no?"

"Maybe you should give it a try," Kelly answered huskily.

He swung her up into his arms.

T.'s bedroom was lit only by the evening sunset. Red and orange light streamed in through the windows, making the white walls seem warm and pink. He set her gently on his bed, and Kelly reached for him, pulling him down next to her. She kissed him and slid her hands up, underneath his T-shirt, glad she'd finally given in.

"Kelly, wait," he said. He was breathing hard, and she knew by the accelerated beat of his heart that he didn't really want to stop. But he caught her hands. "You know how much I want to make love to you." His face was serious as his eyes searched hers.

She nodded. "I want it, too."

"Do you?" A muscle flickered in his jaw as he clenched and unclenched his teeth. "Do you really want to make love? Or is this just going to be sex?"

Kelly tried to smile. "Can't we figure that out later?"

T. was trying to smile, too, but she could see the hurt in his eyes. "An evasive answer. You still won't admit that you love me, will you?"

"Jackson—" Kelly looked down at the floor "—I'm just not ready—"

"For this," he finished with her. "I know."

He was still holding her hands, and he laced her fingers with his, squeezing them gently. "This might come as a shock to you, and God knows it's one hell of a shock to *me,* but I'm not going to settle for sex. I'm not going to settle, period. When you decide to admit to yourself that you love me, then I'll make love to you. But not until then." He drew her hands to his mouth and kissed them before he released her.

Kelly *was* shocked. She was shocked that he would actually turn her down, but mostly shocked at how disappointed she felt. "Well." Her voice sounded breathless and odd. "Who would've guessed that you'd end up being the one to say no?"

But T. shook his head vehemently. "I'm saying yes," he said. "To the question that really matters, Kel, I'm the one saying yes."

## *Chapter 14*

Three o'clock in the morning, and Jax still sat in front of the computer, staring sightlessly at the screen. God, would this night never end?

He couldn't sleep. He'd tried that already, and all he did was lie in bed and think about the fact that Kelly wasn't there with him.

She should've been, and worst of all, she *could've* been. He'd lost his mind. That had to be the answer. No red-blooded, *hot*-blooded American man in his right mind would've turned down a woman like Kelly the way he had. He had suddenly been possessed by the spirit of these damned romantic heroes he obviously spent too much time writing about.

"So go and tell her you were wrong," a familiar voice cut through his thoughts. Jared was sitting on a bed in one of the guest rooms of the sprawling ranch house. He looked dashing, as usual, his thick, glossy hair disheveled and his shirt off. His arm was still bleeding. The bullet had gone clear through, and Carrie was bandaging both sides of the wound. ''Tell Kelly,'' Jared said, ''that you were temporarily insane and that you'll gladly settle for a pure, uncomplicated sexual relationship— Ouch!''

He looked up at Carrie in surprise as she was none too gentle with his arm. ''He *loves* her,'' Carrie said to Jared. ''Has it occurred to you that he might actually want more than just a sexual relationship? And I don't care what you say, *no* relationship is *ever* uncomplicated.''

''Look, guys,'' Jax broke in. ''We're coming up on the ending to this story here. Could we maybe be a little nicer to each—''

''*I'm* being incredibly nice,'' Jared declared. ''Man, she *shot* me, and I'm still offering to stick around and help her defend her ranch and her water rights against those outlaws—''

''I don't want or need your help,'' Carrie said tightly. ''As soon as I'm done wrapping you up, I will thank you very much to take your oversize horse and your oversize ego off of my land.''

''Hang on!'' Jax said. ''Let me get some of this on disk.'' He started to write.

> ''You need help,'' Jared said bluntly. ''Who're you gonna get it from? That old man you got working in your stables? Or maybe that little boy I saw running across the yard a minute ago?''
>
> ''Well, at least I know they won't desert me.''
>
> ''Whoa now,'' Jared said, catching her arm before she could turn away. ''I never deserted you. I *told* you I would come back for you. You didn't wait for me!''

"I couldn't wait."

"You didn't want to wait," he accused her.

Carrie laughed, but there was no humor on her pretty face. "No, Jared, I *couldn't.* I was carrying your child."

Shock. Complete numbing shock. A...*child?*

"We have a child?" Jared breathed.

"A son."

Outside the window, across the yard, the little boy was helping the old man brush down Jared's stallion. Slowly Jared pulled himself to his feet, crossing to the window, staring out at...his son?

Jared turned to her. "Carrie, God, I didn't know."

It had been purely by accident that he had deserted Carrie more than eight years ago. If he had known she needed him so desperately, he would've walked through hell to get to her.

Now she was in trouble again, and he was damned if he was going to desert her a second time.

Kelly couldn't sleep. She sat on her bed, looking at the pile of letters T. Jackson had written to her in the few weeks she'd been here.

He loved her.

There was proof of that in these letters. As if she'd really need any other proof after tonight... T. never would've refused a chance to go to bed with her if he didn't love her.

She felt tears welling up in her eyes. She couldn't let herself love him back. It would hurt too much when he stopped loving her. And he *would* stop loving her. Or maybe he just wouldn't love her enough to stick around. He'd loved her seven years ago, but not enough to fight for her, not even enough to come back for her when she turned eighteen the way he'd promised.

No, she couldn't risk letting herself love him.

The best thing for both of them was for Kelly to pack her things and go back to Boston.

She wiped her eyes on the sleeve of her T-shirt and took her suitcase out of the closet. It didn't take her long to pack her clothes, but the sun was starting to peek over the edge of the horizon by the time she was done.

One more walk on the beach. She'd take one more walk before she woke up Jackson to ask him to drive her to the bus station.

The dawn air was damp, but the sun was already hot enough to start burning off the mist and ocean fog. The beach was deserted and quiet, with only the sounds of the water and the seagulls breaking the calm.

In just a few hours, she'd be back in Boston, back in the noisy city, away from the beach. Away from T.

She'd be alone again, working in the solitude of her apartment, unable to turn around and ask a stupid grammar question or share a joke, a comment, a smile.

Fact was, she was going to miss T. Jackson.

Kelly's bare toes dug into the wet sand as she walked, and she tried to brush away the tears that had gathered again in her eyes. She was going to miss more than T.'s keen sense of humor and his help editing her manuscript. She was going to miss the way his eyes crinkled up at the corners when he laughed. She was going to miss the fact that he could get dressed up to the nines for dinner in a hand-tailored suit and *still* not wear any socks. She was going to miss his teasing, his jokes, the way he smiled at her when he said "Good morning."

And she was going to miss his kisses.

Her tears were falling faster now, and Kelly just sat down in the sand at the edge of the water and cried.

Who was she trying to kid? She was in love with T. Jackson Winchester the Second. There was no doubt about it.

A romantic hero would stick to his guns and not give in.

But Jax wasn't any kind of romantic hero, and the fact remained that as much as he wanted Kelly to admit that she was in love with him, there was no guarantee that she was going to.

The fact also remained that after a long, sleepless night, Jax realized as much as it would hurt him in the long run, he was willing to take whatever Kelly was willing to give. And if that meant having a no-strings, no-commitment relationship based on a sexual attraction…well, at least there would be some pleasure with his pain.

When it came to Kelly, he was weak. He would be the first to admit that.

He stood outside Kelly's bedroom door. There was no sound from inside. Of course there wasn't. It wasn't even 6:00 a.m.

Jax knocked softly on the door, but there was no answer. He tried the knob, and it turned. The door was unlocked, so he pushed it open.

The room was empty; the bed hadn't even been slept in. And Kelly's suitcase was packed and standing in the middle of the floor.

She was going to leave.

Pain hit him hard and square in the middle of his chest, and he struggled to breathe. Kelly was going to leave.

He heard a sound, and turned to see her standing in the doorway. She looked so beautiful. Her hair was tousled from the wind and curling from the humidity. Her T-shirt was damp from the ocean's spray and it clung to her soft curves. Her cheeks were flushed, her eyes bright with tears—

Jax swallowed the last of his pride. ''Kel, please don't go.'' His voice cracked slightly. He tried to smile. ''You win. I'll play by your rules. We'll do this your way.''

Kelly watched him rake his fingers through his thick blond hair. He wasn't trying to hide his desperation from her, and she could see it in his eyes, hear it in his voice.

''T.—'' she started.

''You don't have to love me.'' He took a step forward. ''I know that you care about me, and that's good enough for now.''

He was making a sacrifice. He was willing to toss aside the things he wanted in order to keep her near him.

''No, T.—''

''Kelly, please.'' Another step, and he took her hands in his. His eyes were fiercely determined. ''If you leave, I'm just going to follow you. I can't live without you. I don't want to live without you. I *refuse* to live without you—''

He kissed her, a hard, demanding, hungry kiss that sent fire racing through her blood. With his arms around her as he held her tightly to him, she could feel his heart beating as he whispered, "Please, don't go. I was wrong—"

"No, you were right." Kelly reached up to touch the side of his face and realized her hand was shaking. God, what she felt for this man scared her to death. She didn't want to say the words aloud. But she had to, if only to relieve the look of desperation in his eyes. "You've been right all along—"

"Right now there is no wrong or right," Jax said, shaking his head. "All I know is that I'd do damn near anything to make you stay."

She was in his arms, and he was looking down into the bottomless depths of her eyes. His memories of those eyes had been his savior, his connection to sanity, blurring the line between reality and fantasy during a time when reality would have broken him.

Now her eyes were filled with tears, tears that escaped to run down the exquisite softness of her cheeks.

"You don't have to," Kelly told him quietly, "because, God help me, I love you, T."

Did she just say that she loved him? He stared at her. Had her words been fantasy or reality?

"What did you say?" he whispered.

"I love you. God knows I don't want to, but I do."

Reality.

With a sudden blinding flash, Jax could see his future stretching out in front of him, and for the first time in ages, it was lit by sunshine and laughter. She loved him. Kelly had finally admitted that she loved him.

He kissed her, tasting the salt of her tears, the sweetness of her lips. He could see the love in her eyes. It wasn't new—he'd seen it there before—but she wasn't trying to hide or ignore it now.

"T., make love to me," Kelly said.

"Come to my room," he breathed, and she nodded.

Holding her hand, Jax led her down the hall to his bedroom, drawing her inside and locking the door behind her. He closed the door that led to his office, then turned to look at her.

Kelly stood in the center of the room, watching T. He looked exhausted, and she knew that, like her, he hadn't slept at all last night. But he smiled at her, a smile that erased the fatigue from his face and lit his eyes with happiness.

She realized she couldn't let herself think about the future. She couldn't think about the pain and heartache that would surely come from loving him. There would be plenty of time to suffer when he was gone. But right now he was here, and here and now were what mattered. Here and now his heart was hers.

Kelly smiled at him. "Can we take this from where we left it last night?" She crossed to the bed and sat on the edge. "I think I was over here."

T. walked across the room almost impossibly slowly, holding her gaze every step of the way. The fire from his eyes burned into her body, infusing her with a heat that seemed to rise from deep within her. As he sat down next to her on the bed, he picked up her hands, lacing their fingers together.

He kissed her, and Kelly could feel his restraint. He was holding back, as if he were afraid to overwhelm her, as if he were afraid he'd lose control.

"It's not many people who get a second chance to make love for the first time," he said with a crooked smile.

"I'm going to have to disappoint you," Kelly admitted. "That night in your hotel room? That wasn't just sex. We *were* making love. I loved you then—I was just too stupid to admit it.''

''I'm not disappointed.'' He kissed her again, still so carefully.

Kelly reached up, lightly tracing the small scar on his cheekbone as she looked into his eyes. Like the high school boy who had scarred him in that fight, she knew firsthand about the passion that burned inside of T. Jackson.

She loved T. because he was sweet and kind and funny and smart. But the fact that he could manage so successfully to hide his passion behind a cool and collected facade of control made her love him even more. Especially since she knew that she had the power to take that control of his and tear it to shreds.

Which was exactly what she intended to do right now.

She knelt next to him on the bed and kissed him fiercely, pulling him closer to her, running her hands up underneath his T-shirt, against his smooth, muscular back. She could feel his control slipping as his arms tightened around her, as he returned her kisses. Drawing her leg across him, she straddled his lap, and he groaned.

Together they pulled his T-shirt off, then hers, tossing them onto the floor. Her bra soon followed.

Picking Kelly up, Jax turned, pushing her back onto the bed, covering her body with his. ''I love you, Kel,'' he breathed, touching, caressing the smooth softness of her neck, her shoulders, her breasts.

As he kissed her again, his fingers fumbled with the button on her cutoff jeans. Nearly growling with frustration, he pulled away from her. Laughing, she unfastened the button, then, holding his gaze, slowly drew the zipper down.

As she slipped out of her shorts and her panties, Jax could barely breathe. He was frozen in place, spellbound, hypnotized. "Are you real?" he whispered. "Are you really here with me, or am I dreaming?"

For a long time after he'd returned from Central America, he had been struck by feelings of unreality, expecting at any moment he would awaken still locked in his prison cell. He felt that way now.

Kelly sat up, putting her arms around his neck as she kissed him. "If you think you're dreaming, maybe you better hurry up, get your clothes off and make love to me before you wake up."

Jax laughed, then gasped as her hands found the hardness of his arousal pressing against his shorts. She deftly undid the button and his shorts quickly followed the rest of their clothes onto the floor.

He quickly covered himself with a condom, then slipped between her legs. His hands and mouth were everywhere then, touching her, kissing her, drinking in the softness of her skin, the wet heat of her desire.

"Tell me again that you love me," he whispered, looking down into her eyes.

He was poised over her, the muscles in his arms and shoulders flexed as he kept his weight lifted off of her. His golden hair was a jumble of unruly waves, messed from her fingers.

She smiled up at him, and he kissed her again, as if he couldn't bear to be separated from her lips for too long.

"I love you," she said. "I always have."

He filled her then, both her heart and her body, and for the first time in her life, she felt truly whole. She had loved him forever, a love so pure and true, it had triumphed over the passage of time and all of her pain and heartache. She knew in that instant she would love him until the end of time, long after he'd moved on.

She held him close, moving with him, pushing him farther, more deeply inside of her, hoping if she held him tightly enough, he would never go away.

"I love you," she cried, the waves of her pleasure exploding through her.

She felt T.'s body tighten with his own stormy release, heard him call her name, his voice hoarse with passion.

*Don't ever leave me,* she thought.

It wasn't until T. answered her that she realized she had spoken the words aloud. "I won't, Kel," he said, kissing her sweetly. "I promise I won't."

But it was a promise he'd already broken once before.

# Chapter 15

"Do you want to go for a swim or make love?" T. asked, nuzzling Kelly's neck.

The morning sun was streaming through the windows of his bedroom, and Kelly stretched. "What day is it?"

He smiled at her lazily. "I can only give you a rough estimate—I can tell you the month and the year. Well, wait a minute, maybe I can't even do that. Is it July or August? It could be August."

Kelly laughed. "Impossible. August was at least a week away. I mean, all you need is love and all that, but I just can't believe someone as spoiled as you—"

"Spoiled?" T. feigned insult.

"—could go for a whole week without food," Kelly finished teasingly.

But suddenly he wasn't laughing anymore. His eyes were strangely haunted and his smile disappeared. "You'd be surprised at how long I could go without food,'' he said quietly. But just as quickly as that odd mood had fallen over him, it was gone. He smiled with a quick flash of his white teeth and pulled her on top of him, kissing her hard on the mouth.

''I have a deadline coming up,'' he told her, ''and I'm having a bitch of a time finishing this book. Argh! I don't want to think about it. I don't even want to work on it anymore.'' He kissed her again, then looked thoughtful. ''Of course, if it *is* August, then I'm already late with the manuscript, and there're probably twenty-five very irate messages from my editor on my answering machine.''

''And if it's August, Stefanie and Emilio are back from their cruise,'' Kelly pointed out.

''Oh, damn, there goes our privacy.'' T. closed his eyes with pleasure as she ran her fingers through his hair. ''No more running naked through the house.''

''Have you been running naked through the house?'' Kelly teased. ''Without me?''

''Well, no.'' He caught her hands and kissed the tips of her fingers. ''But you know how it is. As soon as you can't do something, you immediately want to do it.''

''If I tell you that you absolutely *can't* work on your manuscript, will that make you want to finish writing it?''

''No. But I just got a sudden wild craving to play miniature golf.''

Kelly laughed.

''And then I want to call your parents and tell them that we're getting married.''

She froze. T. was smiling up at her. He hadn't shaved in days and his hair was wild, but with his eyes lit with love, he was so utterly handsome he took her breath away. But she wasn't going to marry him. She couldn't. ''T., we're not getting married.''

He was unperturbed. ''Yes, we are.''

''No, we're *not.* Besides, that's not the sort of thing you're supposed to just *tell* someone. You're supposed to *ask*— Didn't we have this conversation once before?''

He turned suddenly, flipping Kelly onto her back, pinning her to the bed with his body. ''Marry me,'' he said, all teasing gone from his voice and eyes. ''Kelly, please, will you marry me?''

As she looked up at him, her eyes filled with tears. ''How many years do you want to marry me for, T.?'' she asked. ''Two? Maybe three?'' She pushed him away from her and sat up on the edge of the bed. ''I can't go through that again.''

''I'm not Brad,'' Jax said quietly. ''I want you for forever.''

She turned to face him. ''That's what Brad said, too. But he changed his mind.''

''Maybe he realized that you didn't love him. Maybe he figured out that you were still in love with me.''

Kelly just watched him quietly, and Jax wished he could get inside her head, read her mind and know what she was thinking.

''I love you,'' he said. ''And you love me. We should have been together right from the very start—''

''If you believe that, then why did you go to London?''

It was a direct question, deserving of a point-blank answer. Jax looked straight into Kelly's eyes and fired both barrels.

''Because Kevin gave me a choice between going

to London or being brought up on charges of attempted rape.''

Kelly was shocked. Attempted *rape?* ''That's ridiculous—''

''You were underage.'' His eyes were intense as he tried to make her understand. ''If Kevin had made any noise, there would've been an investigation at the very least. It would've been horrible, Kel, not just for me, but for you. You would've been examined by doctors, questioned by the police and all kinds of social workers and psychologists. And God, if any word at all had slipped out to the papers, it would've been a total media circus. Your reputation would have been shredded.'' He was silent, looking out the windows at the deep, clear blue of the sky. ''I didn't give a damn about myself, but I couldn't do that to you, so I went to London.''

''Kevin was bluffing!''

''I sure as hell didn't think so.''

''Why didn't you at least talk to me about it?''

''It was part of the deal,'' Jax said. ''I couldn't try to see you. I couldn't call. I couldn't even write to you.''

''I thought you didn't love me,'' she said softly.

He shook his head. ''It was because I loved you that I left. And if I had to do it over again, I'm not sure I wouldn't do exactly the same thing.''

Kelly was older now, but he could still see that sweet sixteen-year-old girl when he looked into her eyes. He had let her down all those years ago.

''You broke my heart.'' It wasn't an accusation. It was a fact. And somehow that made it even worse.

''That part I'd do differently,'' Jax told her.

* * *

Jax sat at his computer, looking out his office windows. If he craned his neck, he could see down to the deck where Kelly was sitting, reading the unfinished draft of his manuscript. She was wearing the black bathing suit he'd bought her. Black bathing suit, black sunglasses, all that lightly tanned, smooth skin…

"Aren't you supposed to be writing?" Jared's familiar voice broke into his thoughts. "Look, Kelly's a real babe, but can't you take your eyes off of her for even a few minutes?"

Jax dragged his eyes back to the computer screen. He had left Jared out in the barn, brushing down his stallion. A light rain was falling outside of the open barn door.

"Kelly's finally mine." Jax laughed. "I am *so* lucky—"

"Yeah, well, she hasn't agreed to marry you, so don't send the tux out to the dry cleaners yet." Jared wiped the sweat from his brow with the sleeve of his cotton shirt. "You may have the 'happily' part down, but the 'ever after' needs some work."

"You're just jealous—" Jax crossed his arms and leaned back in his chair "—because Carrie still won't have anything to do with you."

"Yeah, well, she doesn't trust me," Jared admitted. "But hey, you know what they say about art imitating life."

Jax frowned, leaning forward. "Are you intimating that Kelly doesn't trust me?"

"That's exactly what I'm 'intimating.'" Jared grinned. "Man, where do you come up with these words?"

"I'm a writer," Jax said absently.

"Coulda fooled me," Jared said dryly. "I've been

hanging out, waiting for you to write me out of this barn for days.''

Jax was deep in thought. Kelly didn't trust him? Yeah, it made sense. ''Is it men in general that she doesn't trust?'' he wondered out loud. ''Or is it me?''

''Mostly you,'' Jared guessed. ''You hurt her badly once already. She's waiting for you to do it again.''

''So what am I supposed to do?'' Jax asked, adding, ''God, I must be desperate if I'm reduced to asking *you* for advice.''

Jared leaned against the doorframe, crossing his arms in front of him. Thinking hard, he looked down at the toes of his dusty boots as he scuffed them in the dirt. When he looked back at Jax, there was a twinkle in his dark eyes.

''Maybe you should let life imitate art for a change,'' he said with a smile. ''How do you plan to get Carrie to agree to marry *me?* Just do the same thing with Kelly.''

Jax ran his fingers through his hair and laughed, a short, humorless burst of air. ''It's hardly the same situation—''

''It's *exactly* the same—''

''If you must know, you're going to take a bullet that was meant for Carrie,'' Jax told his character. ''When you nearly die, she's going to realize how much you mean to her.''

''You're going to have me get shot *again?*'' Jared straightened up. ''That's one gunshot wound for every...what? Every hundred and ten pages? Thank the Lord this book's only four hundred and fifty pages long. I'm beginning to feel like I'm walking around with a sign around my neck saying 'Shoot me, I'm a romantic hero.' ''

''Stop complaining,'' Jax said, tipping his chair back on two legs. ''It's going to get you what you want, *and* you're going to save Carrie's life.''

''Just watch your aim, okay?'' Jared began to pace. His big horse snorted and glanced back over his shoulder at him. ''Well, obviously you can't use that same solution for your problem.''

''Obviously.''

''Ahem.''

Jax lost his balance and his chair went over backward with a crash. ''Hi.'' He smiled weakly up at Kelly from the floor.

In the barn, Jared was laughing.

''You really do talk to yourself, don't you?'' She put the notebook that held his manuscript down on the table.

She'd put a big, filmy gauze blouse on over her bathing suit. The tails came down to her knees, but she'd left the front unbuttoned. The flashes of smooth, tanned skin that Jax could see beneath the white gauze made his mouth go dry.

She held out her hand to help him up, but instead of getting to his feet, he pulled her down onto the floor with him.

''I wasn't talking to myself,'' he said, kissing her. ''I was talking to Jared.''

''Jared.'' She nodded. ''You outdid yourself with him. He's a real hunk, and I mean to-die-for in a major way. I think he's your best hero yet.''

''Oh, yeah!'' Jared strutted across the barn. ''She likes me. Watch out, Winchester, you're history.''

''Yeah, well, you're fictional,'' Jax countered. Kelly was looking at him, one eyebrow raised, and he kissed her quickly. ''Sorry. Just…you know…'' He cleared his throat. "So you liked Jared, huh? And how about Kelly— *Carrie,*" he corrected himself, then rolled his eyes.

Kelly laughed. "Ah, the truth comes out with the old Freudian slip. I *thought* she looked suspiciously like me. Well, a glorified, perfect me, anyway. And Jared's obviously you, only not blond and a little bit more stupid."

"Hey!" Jared was insulted.

"More stupid!" Jax repeated happily. "That's a great way to describe him. I like it. More stupid. I can picture the blurb on the back cover now. 'Jared Dexter, stronger and braver than most, more stupid than some—'"

"Oh, shut up." Jared turned his back pointedly, picking up the brush and starting in on his horse's coat again.

Laughing, Jax kissed Kelly. "He's pouting now."

"If you told me you planned to shoot me, I'd pout, too," Kelly said, pulling herself to her feet.

"How long were you listening to me—"

"Talk to yourself?" Kelly finished for him with a grin. "Long enough to know that you're planning to get Carrie and Jared together with the old hero-almost-dies ploy. It's been used before, but that's okay."

She was standing with her back to the windows, and the sunlight streamed in behind her, making her cover-up seem to disappear. "There's just one thing I need to ask you."

Jax held up one hand. "Wait. Let me get rid of some distractions." He cleared the computer screen, then walking toward her, he took her gently by the arm and switched their positions, so that he had his back to the window. From where he stood now, the sunlight streaming in made her shirt opaque again. "Okay, now I'm listening."

"Why hasn't Jared told Carrie where he was all those years?" Kelly asked. "I mean, my God, he went through hell, and Carrie doesn't have a clue. As far as she's concerned, he *did* desert her. Why doesn't he say something?"

Jax frowned down at the floor. This was it. He had to tell her. As much as he didn't want to, he knew he had to. It was definitely time.

Kelly leaned back against the table, waiting for his reply. As she watched, T. moistened his lips and cleared his throat. When he finally looked up at her, he had the strangest expression on his face.

"What's he gonna say?" he asked her quietly. "How's he going to bring it up? It's not easy for him to talk about, you know, what he went through. And it's sure as hell not a topic of conversation to have over dinner. He can't just say, 'Oh, by the way, I spent twenty godforsaken months of my life in a rat-infested prison in Central America.'"

Kelly frowned. What? Wait a minute, Jared hadn't been anywhere near Central America and...

"How *do* you tell someone something like that?" T.'s voice sounded oddly tight. "Do you just walk up and say, 'Sorry I missed your eighteenth birthday, but I was a political prisoner in a country where the phrase "human rights" isn't in the dictionary?' How do you tell someone you love that you were locked in a four-by-eight room, given barely enough food and water to stay alive for nearly two years?"

"Oh my God," she breathed. He wasn't talking about Jared. He was talking about...*himself!*

With a sudden flash of memory, she saw T. as he

was at Kevin's wedding, thin to the point of gauntness, as if he'd been ill or...nearly starved to death. She heard an echo of Stefanie's shocked voice, from the day they'd had lunch together. *He never told you what happened in Central America?*

Kelly felt sick.

"What's he going to say to her?" T. said again. He turned away and looked out the window at the sunlight dancing across the water.

Heart pounding, Kelly crossed toward him. As she put her arms around his waist, he looked down at her and forced a smile. "It's just not easy to talk about."

"What if she asks?" she said softly. "Will he tell her then?"

"Yeah."

"T., tell me about...Central America?"

He closed his eyes and drew a deep breath, then slowly let it out before turning and looking out at the water again.

"I went there for an interview with an opposition leader," T. said. He was trying to sound normal, as if they were talking about last night's Red Sox game instead of his...incarceration. Oh, God. Kelly could see tears in his eyes, but he staunchly ignored them, managing to look only slightly less cool and collected than he usually did. "After I talked to him, the government thought I might have information on the whereabouts of the rebel forces. They failed to, um, persuade me to part with any of my information—of which I had very little—and on my way to the airport, I was arrested. Someone had planted a small fortune in cocaine in my overnight bag. I was sentenced to ten years in prison. I was really a political prisoner, but the American consulate couldn't do anything to help me, because of the drug charges."

Tears escaped from his eyes, and he brushed them brusquely away. "I'm sorry," he said quickly.

Kelly punched him, and he looked at her in surprise.

"Don't you *dare* apologize," she said hotly. "My God, I can't even imagine how terrible it must have been. Jackson, how can you stand there like that and give me the impersonal Journalism 101 synopsis?"

"I'm sorry—"

"*Stop* apologizing!" she shouted. "You should be furious, angry, *outraged* that this happened to you. God, T., did they hurt you? Did you cry? Were you alone? What did you do? Did they make you work? Tell me what it smelled like. Tell me how you found the strength to survive! Tell me how you *felt!*"

Kelly paced back and forth, nearly shaking her fist in the air. She whirled to face him. "*Show* me how you felt, damn it. Get pissed! Throw something! Break some furniture—"

"I love you," Jax said. "And you love me. That's all I need to feel now, Kelly." He pulled her into his arms. "I can show you that, and I will—every day for the rest of our lives, if you'll let me."

She was crying, hot, angry tears, and Jax gently caught one with his finger. "Besides—" he smiled slightly and kissed her "—I don't break furniture. I write."

He pulled away from her and crossed to his big bookshelf. Reaching up, he took a heavy blue three-ring binder down from among all the other notebooks and handed it to her. "This will tell you how I felt."

Kelly looked down at the manuscript as she wiped the tears from her face. "A story?"

''Nonfiction,'' T. told her. ''Although, when I publish it, I should probably give cowriting credit to my psychologist. I'd meant to get this all down on paper when I first came back, but it was my shrink who finally forced me to sit down and write it.''

He kissed her again. ''I'll be on the beach,'' he said, but she'd already sat down at the table, opening up the thick manuscript to the first page. She didn't even hear him as he slipped out the door.

It was called *Letters to Kelly,* she realized with shock. Leafing quickly through, she saw that the entire manuscript was a series of letters—all addressed to her. Heart pounding, she began to read.

After the first few pages, she was in tears again.

Dear Kelly,

I regain consciousness in my cell, and I am surprised—surprised that I am still alive. I'm lucky. I saw the bodies of less fortunate men being dumped into the back of a pickup truck the last time I was in the courtyard.

But then I move, and my entire body screams with pain. And I wonder. Maybe *they* were the lucky ones....

Dear Kelly,

Four days since I've last been fed. You come and keep me company, and we talk about Thanksgiving dinner. You take my hand and pull me back with you, back in time, and I'm at your house. Your dining room table has been extended, and your parents and your grandmother, your aunt Christa and your cousins, Kevin, you and I all sit, bowing our heads as your father says grace.

I stare at the feast on the table, realizing that the leftovers from this meal could keep me alive for months....

Outside the office window, the sun moved across the sky, but Kelly was aware of nothing but the words on the paper. T.'s words. Letters he'd written her, from hell.

T. Jackson was sitting on the beach, arms wrapped loosely around his knees, watching the sunset. The wind ruffled his golden blond hair, and the sunlight flashed as it hit the reflective lenses of his sunglasses. He had a bottle of beer in his hand—he was a living advertisement for the good life.

He looked at Kelly as she sat down next to him. She knew what she looked like—her eyes were puffy and the tip of her nose was red. He put his arms around her and kissed the top of her head. "You all right?" he asked quietly.

"Shouldn't I be asking *you* that question?" Kelly reached up and took off his sunglasses so that she could see his eyes. They were beautiful, greenish-blue in the late-afternoon light, and so warm and loving.

"I'm extremely all right." He touched her hair and kissed her mouth. "In fact, I keep wondering if maybe I haven't actually died and gone to heaven. We're finally together, and you love me, too—"

Kelly started to cry, pressing her face into the warmth of his neck, holding him as tightly as she could.

"Hey," he said. "Hey, come on—"

"I'm sorry." Sobs shook her body. "Oh, T., I'm

so sorry. You came back from that…that…*place,* and I wasn't there for you."

"Kel—"

"All this time I thought you had deserted me, but *I* was the one who deserted you. All that time you were in that horrible prison and I didn't even try to find you—"

"It's okay, Kel." His voice was gentle, soothing. "You didn't know."

"T., I wasn't there for you."

"You're here for me now."

Kelly looked up at him, tears running down her face. "Yes, I am," she said, and she kissed him.

"You know, I meant it when I said that I won't ever leave you," he told her.

He had never stopped loving her. He would never stop loving her. Kelly believed that now. "I know."

T. smiled at her then, and wiping her eyes on the sleeve of her shirt, she managed to smile back at him. It was shaky, but it was definitely a smile.

"So," she said. "You want to go play a few rounds of miniature golf?" She laughed weakly at the surprised look on his face. "Or do you want to skip the golf and just call my parents and tell them that we're getting married?"

T. stared at her, his eyes opened wide, for several long seconds. Then he started to laugh. He kissed Kelly hard on the mouth, then jumped up and started dancing down the beach, whooping and shouting.

Kelly stared at him in shock, her mouth open. T. was acting so utterly uncool. She started to laugh. She loved it.

He froze suddenly, looking back at her.

"Are we really getting married?" he asked, as if he were making a quick reality check.

Kelly nodded. "I take it you still want to?"

He grabbed her hands and pulled her to her feet. "Oh, yeah." He kissed her, a deep, fiery kiss that left her dizzy. He swung her effortlessly up into his arms. His long legs covered the ground quickly as he carried her back toward the house. "This is definitely the best day of my life," he said, taking the stairs to the deck two at a time.

Jax opened the screen door into the living room and carried Kelly inside. He set her gently down, but her arms stayed around his neck and she kissed him. He groaned, opening his mouth under the pressure from her lips, sliding his hands underneath her big gauze shirt. Her skin was so soft and warm. He kissed her harder, deeper, shifting his hips so that she could feel his desire against her. She slid one smooth leg up, twisting it around his own leg, and breathing hard, he reached for the string that would untie the top of her bathing suit—

"Well, well, you two have certainly been busy since I've been gone," Stefanie's well-polished voice cut through.

Startled, Kelly sprang away from Jax, blushing and clutching her overshirt together.

"Stef," Jax said. "On your way in or out? Hopefully out."

She was in the entryway, a small suitcase in her hand. She laughed, amusement in her gray eyes. "Gee, what a welcome home. But no, lucky you, I'm going away for another month or so. Emilio's waiting in the car. We're flying to Italy to meet his parents." She rolled her eyes. ''I've totally lost my mind. I've agreed to marry the man.''

''Congratulations,'' Kelly said.

''Maybe we can make it a double wedding.'' Jax pulled Kelly in close to him, kissing the side of her face.

Stefanie's eyes softened. ''Oh, darling, I'm so happy for you.''

She looked at Kelly. ''Thank God you finally came to your senses. I was ready to wring your little neck.''

Kelly laughed. ''I'm glad you didn't have to.''

''Our flight leaves Boston in just a few hours.'' Stef's hand was on the doorknob. ''I've got to run, but I *am* very glad.'' She waved to them. ''See you when I see you, darlings.''

The door closed with a bang behind her, leaving T. Jackson and Kelly staring at each other in the sudden stillness.

T. smiled, a slow, sexy smile that made Kelly's heart race. ''Where were we before we were so rudely interrupted?'' he asked.

She smiled. ''I think we were about to run naked through the house.''

''No, we've got a whole extra month to do that,'' he murmured, kissing the delicate skin under Kelly's ear. ''We don't need to do that right now.''

She closed her eyes, humming her approval of the placement of his lips and hands. ''Maybe you wanted to go upstairs and finish writing your novel?''

''No, no, not the novel,'' he said. ''But there was definitely something I wanted to do upstairs.''

He took her hand and led her up to the second-floor landing.

"Maybe you wanted to write me another love letter."

At the top of the stairs he stopped and kissed her again and she melted against him.

"Haven't you read enough for today?" He lifted her up and carried her the last few steps into his bedroom.

"There's no such thing as too many love letters," Kelly pointed out.

He placed her gently on his bed, softly kissing her lips.

"Dear Kelly," he said, gazing into the depths of her eyes. "Let's skip the miniature golf, and call your parents much, *much* later—"

"Tomorrow," Kelly suggested, pulling his lips toward hers.

*Tomorrow.* Jax liked the sound of the word. Tomorrow, and the next day, and the next tomorrow after that, sliding way out into the infinite future, he'd have Kelly by his side. It was the only future he'd ever wanted, and it was finally his.

"Tomorrow sounds perfect," he breathed. "I love you. Love, T."

* * * * *

0908/26/MB166

# From the Number One *New York Times* bestselling author NORA ROBERTS

## *Stars*

**Containing the classic novels**
***Hidden Star* and *Captive Star***
Available 5th September 2008

## *Treasures*

**Containing *Secret Star*, the exciting final part in *The Stars of Mirtha* trilogy, plus a special bonus novel, *Treasures Lost, Treasures Found***
Available 7th November 2008

***Don't miss these two sparkling treasures!***